the dragon's skin

the dragon's skin

ross gray

[Lacuna]
2016

Published in 2016 by Lacuna
http://www.lacunapublishing.com

Lacuna is an imprint of Golden Orb Creative
PO Box 185, Westgate NSW 2048, Australia
http://www.goldenorbcreative.com

Cover design by Golden Orb Creative
Dragon eye photo © Anekoho | Dreamstime.com
Silhouetted man © Ross Gray

Text design by Golden Orb Creative. Typeset in 11/13.2 pt Adobe Caslon Pro
Author photograph © Gemma Gray

National Library of Australia Cataloguing-in-Publication entry

Gray, Ross Charles, author.

The dragon's skin / Ross Gray.

ISBN: 9781922198228 (paperback)
ISBN: 9781922198235 (ebook)

Subjects: Detective and mystery stories. Melbourne (Vic.) — Fiction.

Dewey Number: A823.4

Drunk, he slew no hearth-companions.
Beowulf, trans E Talbot Donaldson

As I was walking up the stair
I met a man who wasn't there.
He wasn't there again today,
I wish, I wish he'd stay away.
Antigonish, Hughes Mearns

Every contact leaves a trace.
Edmond Locard: his exchange principle.

Prologue

He is not the hero of the story, the man these words describe. He is not the villain. Although, if you think him so, you may be forgiven. The part he plays in the tale is a minor one, but no less, nor more, important than any other. He is a killer, and if in this story he kills, and you find such things distasteful, don't be concerned, you may avert your eyes. He is not a man who kills from anger or fear or jealousy or envy or any of the petty meannesses of the human spirit. Admittedly, there is a profit motive. He kills people on behalf of other people. But don't judge him too harshly, many people kill. They kill good people and bad people, heroes and villains: they kill people for other people. Executioners kill people. Soldiers kill people, don't they? And we don't judge them harshly. Especially when they kill people for us.

So please, don't be judgemental, keep an open mind as this man and his trade are described.

Trade? He prefers the word 'trade'. Or he would if he ever talked about it. He's a plain man. He's a man who didn't aspire to tertiary education – although he is intelligent and could have done well. He considers it 'a bit of a wank' to call his line of work a profession. James Bond is in a similar type of employment. James Bond is a professional, isn't he? He's a professional who kills people for the people and the State – and HRH of course. And we think that's cool.

Bond, James Bond, and this man share the same trade – or profession if you must. It's a very old one. Not as old as the oldest of course, or the human race would have been a one-horse race. He – and Bond – is what you might call an assassin or hitman or hired gun or – one particular favourite, coined by Raymond Chandler in his eponymous short story – a pencil. That's neat. Eradicating a problem just like drawing a red line through a name on a page. A flick of the wrist. A slash of the pencil. A blood-red cancellation.

However, this is a modest man. He would be the last to place himself in the same league as James Bond. James drives an Aston Martin (or a BMW), wears expensive wristwatches and leads an exciting cosmopolitan lifestyle. Although he frequently works interstate, the furthest this man has travelled on a job is Cooktown. He doesn't have a licence to kill. In fact he neglected to apply for a learner's permit. No, let Jimmy have the limelight, this man is content to remain backstage cloaked in shadows, sharpening his pencil. He's a retiring man.

Some may take umbrage at the elevation of the enterprise of killing people to the level of trade or profession (military excepted). If so, this should be considered: it is not easy to kill a person. Except accidentally of course – then it is much too easy. To select and stalk and kill a human prey – let's not mince words, to do murder – that takes skill and talent and practice, and the kind of mental qualities often attributed to athletes. To arrange an accident, that takes imagination, broad practical knowledge and finesse. By any measure, a vocation requiring such virtues qualifies as a trade, or, if you insist, a profession. And this man is an excellent tradesman.

He bears little resemblance to James Bond – any of them. His appearance is unremarkable, which is an advantage in his chosen field. His hair is a mousy brown, not too straight, not too wavy. It is abundant enough to hide the few strands of encroaching grey, but beginning to show signs of depletion around the crown. This is not evident at the moment because he wears a woollen beanie pulled down to his ears. He has a face as oval as those recommended in 'How To' books on drawing. He has regular features. His ears may be longish and his nose a tad too short, but there is little in this to be made of by a caricaturist – or an identikit. He is wearing sunglasses because, although it is midwinter and very cold, the sun is shining brightly, but his eyes, if you could see them, are that greenish greyish brownish colour called 'hazel'. An odd colour, hazel. It doesn't appear in the spectrum or on the colour swatches of interior designers. It seems to be reserved for eyes when we can't be precise about their colour. He has a scar beneath his left eyebrow that can only be detected at a distance of ten centimetres, and a small brown mole under his chin that nobody notices. Except his children.

As well as the beanie, he is wearing a long, woollen scarf wrapped several times around his neck, a short Drizabone with a quilted lining and many deep pockets, thick corduroy trousers and the kind of rugged boots sold in outdoor adventure stores. The ones with firm ankle support and treads so deep they could remove the topsoil on a quarter-acre block. He is sitting in a park, beneath a tree, on a contoured metal bench near a playing field. He has a large red sports bag beside him that contains a thermos of coffee, two bottles of a popular sports drink, some fruit, a towel, a battered paperback novel, a box of Band-aids and the street clothing of one of his two sons.

A man approaches carrying a plastic bag emblazoned with the logo of a well-known city store, nods to him and sits on the bench. He places his plastic bag next to the sports bag. This man is dressed just as warmly as the other, but his clothes appear to have been liberated from a rack in Toorak Road or Chapel Street rather than Bridge Road, Richmond. He wears soft leather gloves. He has fine blond hair of a shade that will disguise the spread of silver for some time. The baldness on his crown is far more advanced than that of the other man, but it is hidden beneath one of those fur hats favoured by Eastern Europeans (and often seen in James Bond movies). His face is round, and ruddy with the sting of the chill southwesterly. He is beefily handsome and, in age, somewhere about the mid-forties. He too is wearing sunglasses, but if you are interested, his eyes are blue – a colour favoured by corn-silk blonds – a sort of faded-denim blue. He watches the run of the ball on the playing field for a few minutes then speaks.

'Got a kid out there?'

Not-Bond treats the question as rhetorical.

'A soccer dad? Picked you for Aussie Rules,' the blond man says.

'Wife's idea. Reckons it's not as rough.'

'I played when I was young. It can get pretty rough,' the blond man reassures soccer dad.

'With you playing, I'll bet it was,' comes the laconic reply.

'Which one's yours?'

'I thought you'd retired,' says soccer dad.

'There's still some accounts outstanding,' says the blond man. He looks over his shoulder then down the sports ground to where most of the parents huddle against the elements. He places the plastic bag and its contents in the sports bag. 'I hope that's as it should be. Maurie used to handle this stuff.'

'Shame about Maurie. I liked him.'

'Maurie got what he deserved,' says the blond man bluntly. Then he adds, 'I was a bit surprised at the price. Double the usual is a big ask.'

'It's a sliding scale. This isn't a workaday knock, there'll be a lot of sizzle,' says soccer dad. 'I'll have to take the family away for a long holiday till things cool.' He glances around about him. 'And if you want an accident as well. That's expensive. More risk, lots of overheads.'

'If there's any doubt that it is an accident we'll both burn,' says the blond man and stands.

'Don't worry. Even you'll think it's an accident,' says soccer dad.

'When?'

'If it's to be done properly it may take a while to organise. Opportunity is the key.' He is momentarily distracted by some action on the field then he looks back at the blond man. 'But don't worry, you'll be the first to know.' The blond man nods, satisfied.

He watches the blond man walk through the park to his car. It's a Porsche. A red Porsche. He watches him drive away. Then he stands and we can see he is average in height. He hefts the sports bag and saunters around the soccer field, stopping occasionally to shout encouragement to his son's team. Eventually he takes a seat on a bench directly opposite the one he vacated on the other side of the field. No tree. He watches the game.

At the end of the first half his son runs over and drops heavily, muddily, on the bench with an exhausted but satisfied sigh. 'We're winning,' the boy breathes happily.

'So I see,' says proud but reticent dad.

'D'ja see me get that ball across?' the boy asks through vigorous dabs of the towel.

'Sure did. Bloody beaudy. Here.' He hands his son a bottle and an orange. 'Don't guzzle.' He drapes a jacket over his shoulders. 'And don't get cold.'

They bask, silent except for gurgles, belches and juicy sucks, in the bonding of shared glory, and then the boy races off to join his mates. The second half begins.

Down the field a figure detaches from the cacophonous clump of parents and supporters and moves in this direction. It is a blunt brick of a man, rounded on the corners and edges. He is wearing a thick straight woollen overcoat that reaches to his knees. It is buttoned to the chin and the collar is turned up to his ears. His hands are stuffed deep in its pockets. He is hatless and the sunlight glistens on a head that has been shaved to a shadow. At a distance he could be mistaken for something designed by Lego. A scarf, similar to soccer dad's, is draped loosely – and insincerely – around his thick shoulders. Soccer dad's eyes drift from the play long enough to note his progress.

The man from Legoland reaches the bench and, without removing his hands from his pockets, bends like a butted cigarette and sits. His eyes are agate marbles and he watches the game, unblinking. Soccer dad twists around and fossicks through the plastic bag in the sports bag. He extracts a crisp hundred-dollar bill and hands it to Lego man.

'You win,' he says. 'I didn't think he'd have the nerve. How'd you know?'

'Didn't,' says Lego man. 'Just playin' safe.' His voice is deep, but flat, like a bag of wet sand striking a concrete floor. It begins and ends with his words.

'But you knew he'd come to me?'

'Boss knew.'

'Coughed up double, hardly a squeak, just like you said.'

'What'd he want?'

'He wants an accident. No doubts.'

Lego man nods solemnly as if this was expected. 'Give 'im what he wants,' he says. 'It's 'is funeral, an' he's payin'.'

'Poetic justice,' soccer dad says glibly.

Lego man turns his face towards him and he sees the lengthening of the short hard line of the small mouth, which in this man passes for a smile. 'Didn't want 'is own back,' he says. 'Shouldna pissed into the wind.'

'It would be simpler and safer just to press delete,' says soccer dad.

The smile closes down like a computer screen in a blackout. Obsidian eyes swallow soccer dad's gaze, like a thin stream of water poured in a well. 'An accident,' he states. 'An' it better look sweet. The cops are the least of y' worries.'

Soccer dad stares at Lego man, something dawning in his eyes. 'Shit,' he says. 'He hasn't sanctioned this.'

'I've sanctioned it,' says Lego man. 'There a problem?'

'Nah, nah. Just a bit disappointed. Thought he'd owe me a favour.' He sighs. 'Should've known. Weeds his own garden, doesn't he?'

'I owe y' a favour,' says Lego man. ''S almost as good.'

Soccer dad seems to agree. 'But he knew about the contract?'

'Didn't need to. Soon as 'e came to you, Bernie took out a contract on 'imself, didn't 'e?' Lego man has been following the play during the latter part of this exchange. 'Y' son just got a goal,' he says.

Soccer dad's eyes flick to the running and jumping and hugging melee down near the goal then back to the man beside him on the seat. 'You know which one is my boy?'

'Yeah,' says Lego man. His head rotates, owl like, in his upturned collar. His mouth's grim line tweaks to a grin line. 'Research.'

Soccer dad regards him closely. 'You've learnt a lot from him, haven't you?'

'The Boss? Yeah.' There is an odd softness in the last syllable. And for a moment he ceases to look like something that would anchor the bowlines of a battleship. Then, abruptly, he stands and the moment is gone. He pats soccer dad heavily on the shoulder. 'Don't worry, you're not Whitey Poynter.' Thin grin. 'I'll be watchin' the news,' he says as he walks away.

Soccer dad watches the game to its end, distracted from time to time by small inspirations related to his plans for the demise of the blond man. His son's team wins. After the game, to celebrate, he takes his son to a McDonalds. Just like in the ads on telly.

A little over two years from now his son, this same boy, hero of the day, will die. An accident – a real one. No human intention or intervention, just stupid fate or the flap of a butterfly's wing somewhere on the planet. With this event the man described will gain an appreciation of death that had formerly, somehow, eluded him. He will break his pencil in small pieces and never strike out another name. He will let James Bond have backstage as well as front and centre. He will live to a very old age. And not a day of his life will pass that is not tinged with regret and abraded by a question that clots like sand in the perpetually damp Speedos of his immortal soul.

1

'What's he on?'

'Nothing.'

'I find that hard to believe – a gutless wonder like Benny Bovell. He'd have to be revved on something to pull a stunt like this.'

'Ben isn't gutless, just raised in menageries that kept sharks in the bath water. Made him a little tentative about … things. If he's high, he's high on desperation.'

'Jesus, spare me the pop psychology. From you, it's as palatable as a shit foccacia.'

'You invited me to contribute.' The gaze was steady, the slight smile self-effacing, the only movement was his shoulders in an almost imperceptible shrug.

'I *didn't* invite you. Let's make that clear. The invitation came from Benny. You're the only bastard that dumb-arse will talk to.' He tried to skewer him with his cold, hard, don't-fuck-with-me stare. 'Shit!' he said, and looked around at the Critical Incident Unit brains trust: the leader of tactical response, the negotiator from the Behavioural Analysis Unit, the explosives expert, the emergency coordinator, technical support, the silver tongue from police media, lads in uniform and lads not. As the situation dragged on unresolved the numbers in the room had crept up like a mortgage. They all looked right back. The silent consensus seemed to be that this bastard was still their best hope of pulling the faggot out of the fire. He turned to him again. 'Alright. Did the little shit tell you what he wanted?'

'He wants something I can't give him.'

'Oh? Something *you* can't give him? Well maybe amongst all the people Benny has gathered here today,' he swung his arm in a wild arc that took in the room, 'we might find someone who *can* give him what he wants. What the fuck does he want?'

'He wants me to "take care of" someone.'

'So?'

'He also used "get rid of".'

'As in eliminate?'

'I believe so.'

You could hear the dust mites thrashing through the carpet pile.

'If he meant "kill" why not bloody say it?'

'That's not the kind of word Ben likes to use. A bit too … concrete.'

They were in the centre of field operations, which, in this instance, was a front room of a double-fronted federation weatherboard in a quiet suburban street. It was a large room, a dining room intended for entertaining, but it didn't look as if it had done much of late. It had the faint, musty aura of a tired museum showcase. The sunniest room in the house they had been assured, repeatedly, by the older Mrs Aldaker, who occupied the premises with the younger Mrs Aldaker, widows whose husbands, father and son, had been taken from them in the same misadventure some ten years before. Her assurances were redundant on a day like today. It was mid-July in Melbourne. If the sun's rays penetrated the soggy, matted shag that slumped over the city, they would still drown in the grey, persistent drizzle. What's more, the neat bungalow across the road was pregnant with a hazard that might remove the roof at anytime. The two Mrs Aldakers had been relocated to a safe distance protesting that they would be far more valuable making sandwiches and tea for 'our brave young men'. And they had baked only the day before – Lamingtons and date scones!

The team was assembled around a large dining table, its area expanded to maximum by extension leaves. It had been stripped of lace cloth and flower vases and knick-knacks, and was now covered with maps and plans and laptop computers and binoculars and various kinds of communication device. Senior Sergeant Donald Collison stared at the man across the table. He was standing a little apart from the rest of the group, weight on one leg, hands in his trouser pockets, relaxed, just a pleasant afternoon with the boys. He'd removed the damp, police-issue waterproof and the armoured vest. He was wearing a *cardigan* for Christ's sake. There was something vaguely distasteful about someone like him wearing a cardigan.

'Let me get this straight,' Collison said. 'He said if you bring him someone's head on a platter he'll down tools and come out?'

'He wants a promise.'

'He wants you to *promise* to murder someone and he'll come out?'

The man in the obscurely offensive cardigan nodded. 'He was a tad circumlocutory, but that's the gist.'

'Believe him?'

'Yes.'

'And you said?'

'I'd think it over.'

Collison hooted quizzically. 'Well shit, that's big of you ...' he began.

Gareth Nile from the Behavioural Analysis Unit, the official police negotiator, interrupted. 'I think he did the right thing, Don.'

Collison blistered him with a warning glare. Affable over a pot or two – at the pub later with the team he'd buy the first and last rounds – the sergeant was brusque and abrasive when he was at the business end of these situations. His subordinates suffered any collateral humiliation without grudge because he was organised, efficient and experienced and, perhaps more importantly, he didn't take cover behind his desk every time the shit and the fan might intersect. But today he wasn't just brusque: he was bristly. It was the presence of the man in the cardigan – simply because he was an outsider, or was there a history?

Gareth brushed back the thick, long tuft of black hair that sprouted from atop his forehead and nowhere else on the smooth crest of his cranium. Useless as a comb-over, but his kids liked to plait it into a unicorn's horn. And he liked them to plait it. 'Bovell,' he ploughed on, 'would be suspicious if anyone agreed too readily to what – no matter his present mental state – he must be aware is an outrageous request. His reluctance to speak plainly is a ...'

He was ambushed by the sergeant's reaction.

Collison's eyes narrowed as if to conceal some illicit knowledge. His smile was brittle and biting. 'Jesus, Gareth,' he breathed, words dripping with condescension. 'Why do you think Bovell will talk *only* to bugalugs here? Him and no one else?' He turned to the subject of the discussion. 'As Gypsy Rose Lee's mum said, promise him everythin' and give him nothin', and let's get the silly prick out of there.'

'It's not that simple,' said the other. His pose didn't change but his head moved in a leisurely arc as his eyes glided calmly over every face at the table and back to Collison's. Their gazes tangoed for a few beats then Collison scanned the table in a swift mirror movement.

'C'mon in here,' he snapped, spun on his heel and strode to a door directly behind him. The other man smiled in brief apology to the room and followed.

In the electric hush of their wake a whisper was clearly audible. 'Who the hell *is* this guy?' breathed a young uniform. An older uniform craned towards his ear, one hand cupped to his mouth.

Collison, in the act of opening it, spun on them from the door. 'The Senior Constable doesn't know who he is, Constable. And if he ever did, he's forgotten.' His eyes flashed around the room. 'What's more, this man,' hooking his chin at the passing cardigan, 'is *not* here today. In fact his very existence is a matter for conjecture. Am I clear?' He stared balefully at the targets of his tirade until he heard a chastened, 'Yes, boss.' Then he stalked through the doorway and closed the door, firmly, behind him.

They were in a bedroom. It was much darker than the room they'd left, its only window shadowed by the verandah. The dry musk of pot pourri struggled in the gloom with the cloying sweetness of perfume. They almost masked the faint, metallic sourness of urine. The older Mrs Aldaker's room – arguably.

'A bit hissy these days, Don. Gargling soap or just watching it?'

All Collison could see was the dark shape of the other man silhouetted against the muted light from the window. 'I find it ludicrous that you, of all people, have scruples about this,' he said. 'Can't bear to tell a fib? Or hate to break a promise? Cross your bloody fingers if it'll make you feel better.' He jammed his fists on his hips and breathed deeply. 'What's so bloody complex?'

'If I promise to kill this person I'll have to do it.' It came flatly, matter of fact, out of the shadow. Collison was momentarily at a loss for words.

'Why the fuck ...?' he spluttered eventually.

'You said it yourself, Don. Why will Ben talk only to me? One: he believes I will do what I say I'll do. Two: he believes I'm capable of doing what he wants me to do.'

'So? Poor, old, disillusioned Benny can cry himself to sleep in his cell at night.'

'Exactly. If I promise Ben and don't keep to it, the entire prison population will know ...'

'Who's gonna take any notice of a no-hoper like Benny ...' Collison began before the absurdity of their dialogue's tangent struck him. 'You arrogant prick,' he spat. 'This is about your precious integrity. Jesus Christ! What the fuck have you become?'

'You're snug in the citadel, Don. I'm out here where the wild things are.'

'Buy a bumboy and move to Bali.'

'My word's my *Kevlar*: that's all I've got. Bad faith's bad for business.'

'Business?' Collison's voice kangarooed in pitch. 'Business ...? There's a four-year-old girl over there that ...'

'That's the point, isn't it?'

'*What?*'

'Did you hear anything that was said?'

Collison shook his head. 'Wire was lousy, we lost every second word.' Now he suspected that wasn't an accident.

The shadow turned toward the window and moved the lacy curtains with a fingertip; the planes of his face were marbled by cold, liquid light. 'Ben's not the most coherent communicator at the best of times, but, when you sort out the dross, I think what he really wants is to protect Briette.'

'Blowing her to smithereens is a funny way of doing it.'

'We'd have a crater over there if that was his plan. But, whatever fate he wants her saved from, he obviously thinks it's worse than death. He's screaming for help.'

To an old campaigner like Collison, that was axiomatic. The trouble is, if you can't convince the poor bastards that help is on its way, they may resort to the final solution – or dissolution. 'Is that who he wants you to bump, someone who's a threat to his daughter?'

'I think so. He won't give details until I agree to do it.' He turned his face from the window and his features were darkened, but Collison could see the small shadow-etched curl in his left cheek that betrayed a smile. 'He assures me it's someone who deserves to die.'

'Oh good,' said Collison. He appraised the dark form embroidered in the lace of the curtain. 'Is there anything else I need to know but they,' thumb over shoulder, 'don't?'

'You know Ben. All over the place like aunts at an Italian wedding.' He moved the curtains aside once more and stared thoughtfully through the window. 'Today he's as focused as the mother of the bride, no doubts how this day will end – for him.'

They stood in the false gloaming of a dimly lit room on a wet afternoon in silent contemplation, of each other, of their own doubts and fears, of the consequences of the next utterance. A buzz of voices and activity reached them from the other room. The man by the window suddenly spoke.

'You know the ring-a-rosy: Ben loses job, Ben steals, gets caught, goes to gaol, Sharon shacks up with someone till Ben gets out – anything to protect the kids. She didn't go back to him last time. That was about four months ago.'

'Shit. It's not Sharon …?'

Cardigan man shook his head. 'No. Then Sharon's dead, Ben's in gaol, what happens to the kids? Ben is terrified his kids will end up like him, in institutions and foster homes. Dysfunctional parents they may seem, but they love those kids. The day Sharon realised she was pregnant they stopped using hard drugs – *both* of them – just like that.' He chuckled softly. 'Found larceny a lot harder to kick; but, they had mouths to feed. Anyhow, Ben says he has open access to them, so that's not the issue. And he worships Sharon the lover, but she was a gift he always expected the gods to snatch back. No, he's lost faith in Sharon the mother. Ben thinks she's into something that puts the kids in jeopardy. That's my guess.'

Collison accepted the point with a grunt. 'Why not do the job himself?'

'C'mon, Don – Ben? Carry out a killing? He's an echidna not a boxing kangaroo. He'd have to steal the price of a hitman, and his larceny's strictly small change. He's violence phobic – if he was going to commit *suicide* he'd use a Freudian slip.' He smiled sadly.

'Blowing up a day-care centre is passive protest, is it?'

'Ben and Briette are the only two at risk.' He turned and gazed thoughtfully through the window towards the centre across the road. When he turned back to the room he seemed to have resolved something.

'Why not just *ask* you? For old time's sake,' said Collison.

'I don't know,' the man said. 'Maybe he's more perceptive than I thought,' he added, as if to himself. 'I can get them out, Don, no dents, no scratches. If I can't persuade Ben or find an opportunity to take him cleanly, I'll make the promise.'

Collison lofted his chin and scratched his neck as he considered the words. 'Let's give the caucus a little background, so they don't sulk. And then do it,' he said. 'Lay the warm and fuzzy stuff thick. You know boys: take the toys out of the box and they want to play with 'em before they put 'em back.' He swung abruptly towards the door, then hesitated and glanced back. 'If you have to make a promise will it be one you intend to keep?' he asked.

'I think it's in the best interests of us both if I don't answer that. Don't you?'

Collison snorted.

'Oh, and Don? No wire.'

'Just bugger this one the same way you did the last.' He jabbed a blunt finger at the other man. 'But leave the fucking phone over there on speaker!'

'And no body armour.' He hooked his thumbs in the soft wool of the cardigan. 'It gives me a ... cuddly look.'

Collison held the man's gaze, trying to penetrate its languid blue surface. 'Your funeral,' he said, shrugging. 'Tell me something. You've gotta be shittin' yourself, but you act like you're going to tea with a maiden aunt. What's the gimmick? Or don't you give a stuff?'

'I die before I cross the road.'

Collison's eyes dug at him to unearth any irony, then, 'How very Zen of you,' he snarled. 'Anything else I can do to protect and serve?' he added and yanked wide the door.

'May I borrow an umbrella?' asked the man in the cardigan as he passed by.

2

When Ben Bovell got out of bed early that morning he was surprised how refreshed he felt. He must have slept soundly last night. If he had, it was the first time in years.

The irony didn't escape him.

Then he noticed how calm he felt. He was eating his breakfast – Coco Pops and cold milk – when he noticed. He noticed that he hadn't had at least two fags before breakfast, one before and one after he got out of bed. And he noticed that he didn't really want one. He was glad about this because Brie didn't like the stench on his breath. Today of all days he wanted to do nothing that drove a smile from his daughter's face.

He smiled at the tattered movie poster on the back of the door: a horse and his buckskin-clad rider, both of them pissed, leaning against a wall. He noticed he felt good. He took his feelings and laid them on the scratched and stained Formica table top beside the cereal bowl. And he reflected upon them. Perhaps reflection is too sophisticated an act to attribute to Ben. He looked at them. And he was pleased with what he saw. The mere fact of their existence seemed to validate his plans for the rest of the day. Ben didn't recognise euphoria. Such a state was alien to him when he was stone cold sober.

Once, when he was in prison, he'd seen that Mel Gibson movie about Hamlet. It was shown in one of the classes that he took which earned brownie points for parole. He hadn't understood a word of it. But the bloke who taught the class explained that Mel was nuts because he couldn't make up his bloody mind to do something. That whole 'to be or not to be' bit. But Ben wasn't nuts.

And Ben Bovell wasn't 'Benny' today. Ben was most definitely 'Ben'. And Ben was going to take arms against Benny's sea of sorrows. Ben was going to end them. To be, to be, to be. To be Ben.

And then not to be.

He looked at his watch. It was a good one. He needed a good one for today. He'd nicked it. Plenty of time. Today had more than enough hours. He felt pride in his cool calm. He felt he was behaving just like his hero. He'd see him today too. There was plenty of time.

He decided to have another helping of cereal. There was some left in the box and he may as well finish it. He emptied the contents of the inner bag into his chipped bowl then folded it neatly. He flattened the box and pushed them both to the far side of the table. He poured the milk and then reached across and switched on the electric jug. It was bought for a couple of dollars at a Brotherhood shop and the automatic cutoff didn't work. He noticed the Heinz Baked Beans tin in the corner near the fridge was full, so he swapped it for the SPC Two Fruits tin. As he settled back into his chair and scooped up his cereal he listened to the slow, metallic tock of the roof leak in the tin and the warm throaty groan of the jug. For some reason the sounds were like music.

Ben was living in a two-room fibro bungalow in Sunshine. It was raining in Sunshine. Well it was dripping. It was a small bungalow: he could reach almost anything in the kitchen without getting up from the table. There was only one leak. It wasn't over his bed. It was comfortable enough. It was cheap. It was in the backyard of an elderly aunt of a girlfriend of a mate of a bloke he'd shared a cell with. The aunt was alone and lonely and didn't want much rent, just the imagined security of a male presence on the property. A few dollars to cover power, water, heating and sundries, a few evenings on the sofa watching telly with the landlady and effusive praise of her very ordinary cooking, was all it cost.

When he finished his cereal he made a cup of instant coffee and drank it as he washed his bowl and spoon and cleaned up some dishes from the night before. He made his bed then took his towel and meagre toiletries, grabbed the Coco Pops packaging and, holding it above his head, he ran across the backyard to the old weatherboard laundry attached to the back of the house. The plumbing had been moved indoors decades ago, but he had use of the old toilet and shower that still functioned in the laundry. He stuffed the packaging in the recycling bin near the laundry door, had a bog, a shower, brushed his teeth and was scampering back across the muddy lawn in his tattered terry-towelling within fifteen minutes.

He dressed carefully. He put on his best clothes. They weren't much: jocks, jeans, polyester shirt, jumper. But they were all clean, freshly washed, and the jumper was a genuine wool blend and it had no darns. He'd had to pinch a pair of sneakers because his others had a hole near the little toe. They were a bit tight, but he wouldn't be wearing them long. His socks didn't have any holes.

The bed-sitting room had a bunk bed against one wall, a small veneered particleboard chest of drawers, an armchair upholstered in brown vinyl and a veneered plywood wardrobe, circa 1950. He opened the wardrobe, took out a large cardboard box and placed it on the chest of drawers. He checked the grey world visible through the grubby window and decided there was little chance of being observed. He opened the box and removed the – he liked to call it – device. He held it up and admired it. It was all his own work. It was the only thing he had ever made. The only thing he had ever completed. He had tried to make stuff in prison, but it didn't get finished – or fell apart. This was finished and it would work. All the parts were stitched and glued and taped into an old canvas vest, one of those that fishermen and hunters wore with lots of pockets and pouches. He'd found it at a Salvo's op shop.

Double-checking through the window he carefully donned the device, shrugging it on with small movements of his shoulders and zipping it gingerly so as not to dislodge the wires. He looked at his reflection in the age-freckled wardrobe mirror. He smiled, satisfied. From the wardrobe he took a bulky green parka – St Vinnies; the colour may have been that of grass once, time had tinted it horse-shit. But it was clean. He put it on with similar care and inspected his reflection again. He nodded, very satisfied. He wrapped a long scarf with Collingwood colours around his neck and carefully zipped the jacket. Another mirror inspection. Then he pulled a black and white beanie over his dark mop of hair.

Ben Bovell was a little below average height. He had a slight build and the kind of stooping posture that Woody Allen's movie persona affected. On any other day he had the anxious hand gestures and compulsive speech mannerisms as well. Sharon had been the first to point this out. She liked Woody Allen movies. Or she did until that business with Mia Farrow's adopted daughter. But that's where the similarities ended. Ben had a face the shape of a plump strawberry, and black hair so thick and curly his head looked too big for his body. He wasn't handsome, but he wasn't ugly. His face was saved from plainness by large, dark, eyes: liquid, nocturnal, of an endangered species. And lashes most women would kill for. He was a sort of sable Noddy. The combined bulk of his 'device' and parka did not appear odd below the head above the collar.

After rotating before the mirror until he was satisfied, he took some money from the top drawer of the chest. He put a few notes in his pocket and folded the rest and placed it on the kitchen table under the boy-trying-to-kiss-a-girl salt and pepper shakers. It was this week's rent. He gently patted his pockets, gazing absently around, then he returned to the bedroom and found a doll in the second drawer, a black plastic Barbie clone. It was naked. He pocketed it as he left the bungalow and locked the door. He walked down the crumbling concrete driveway beside the house and turned left onto the footpath. He slipped the bungalow key in the letterbox as he passed the front gate. He walked to the Sunshine station and caught a train to Flinders Street. From there it was a twenty-five minute tram ride, and he legged the last two blocks to the day-care centre.

The centre had a high fence of vertical steel rods. It was saved from penal severity by a top trimmed in long scallops between the main posts. There was a lot of glass. The renovated brick veneer house had been refitted with big double-glazed windows. The children would never be out of sight anywhere in the grounds. There was colourful play equipment in both the front and back yards and lots of trees. You had to give it to Sharon: she could pick 'em.

He was very polite. One of the women saw him open the childproof gate and approach the sliding glass doors. She slid the door open and smiled. She blocked his entry with her body and asked if he was a father of one of the children. Ben told her he was Briette Kitchen's father. Brie saw him at that moment and yelled out happily. He waved to Brie, the woman turned and he slipped past her over the threshold. He faced the woman with his back to the room. The woman was about to launch her spiel on the security protocol of unheralded visits by parents, but Ben hushed her with a finger to his lips. He opened his coat and revealed the device and said, 'It's cold outside. An' rainin' a bit. Get all the kids – not Brie. Get 'em in their coats an' ats. It's orright. I won't 'urt ya. Jist be calm. Smile an tell 'em it's a 'scursion or sumpin'. It's orright, missus, I don't wanna hurt yas. Okay?'

'Is that …?' said the stunned woman whose eyes had not wavered from the device.

'Yeah. It is,' said Ben. Brie had run to him and grabbed his hand. She was trying to pull him over to her table to show him something. He looked at the woman. The initial shock was wearing off. She seemed to be taking his measure. He wasn't a big man, but she was a big woman. 'Don't be silly, luv,' he said. He was so cool. He was proud of himself.

He let Brie drag him to her table but kept an eye on the woman. She watched him like a bird watching a lazy cat, looked out the door, looked at the children and made up her mind. She strode across to the other woman and spoke quietly and urgently to her. The face of the other woman popped up over her shoulder, saucer-eyed. Then after a furious discussion they both nodded approval of some course of action they had hammered out and they turned to the room. They both cut smiles in the fragile crusts of their faces, clapped their hands loudly and the first woman announced: 'Alright children. Quiet now! We have a very special visitor here today. Mr Kitchen is here to see how well we do our fire drill. Let's show him we're the best in Melbourne.'

It all went smoothly from then. The only problem he had was that Brie wanted to do the drill. She was a bit dark on him for a while. That's when he produced the doll.

In all his planning he had forgotten about food. He hadn't thought it would take so long. Fortunately the kids didn't think to rescue their lunches from the fire, and there was some good stuff: muesli bars, Cheezels, peanut butter and Vegemite sandwiches, and the negotiator bloke, Gareth, he brought over some coffee while they were waiting.

The hardest bit was keeping Brie entertained without her playmates. She was watching TV at the moment, *Bananas in Pyjamas*. Other channels were interrupting their usual programs for updates on the 'day-care centre hostage situation'; fortunately the ABC was exhibiting more sensitivity. He was pacing the perimeter, his ear tuned to a radio he had found, turned low, and he felt his first small shock of panic when a journalist reporting from the scene speculated about a 'third negotiator' approaching the centre. He spun around and peered through the curtains. A tall figure, face hidden by an umbrella, was opening the gate. He wasn't wearing the blue police jacket but Ben knew it was him, not a third party. He breathed a sigh of relief. Then he tensed again. He was just wearing a bloody cardigan. No protection of any kind. Ben had seen him in action; he was most dangerous when he looked most harmless.

Ben scurried back across the room and sat next to Brie in front of the television. This was the Grand Final. He wished that he felt like one of his beloved Magpies, but he didn't, he felt like a bloody sparrow. And he was taking the field against a hawk.

3

The man shook the umbrella, leaned it against the outside glass, stepped through the open door and slid it closed. His eyes took measure of the space: bright colours, wash and wear, no fragile objects, tiny town furniture, solid and soft, no sharp edges, a safe and secure environment. He rubbed his hands together vigorously, slipped them into his pockets and said, 'Damp and nippy out there.'

'Did the experts look't the pitches y'took?' Ben asked from the couch, the only big person seat in the room. A nod in reply. 'An' yeah?'

'They think it looks like a bomb.'

Ben knew the difference between 'looks like' and 'is'. 'Well, they'll hafta take me word, won't they?'

'They will.'

Ben knew the difference between 'they' and 'we' too. 'You don't think I'm capable uv buildin' a bomb.' It was an expression of hurt, accusation and question.

'Today, Ben, I think you're capable of anything.'

Ben studied him, looking for the sarcasm, the irony, the hidden barb. Then he relaxed and smiled. This bloke had never done that to him, he was sure – as far as he could be sure. He wouldn't do it today. 'Why d'you call me "Ben"?' he asked abruptly.

'That's your name.'

'I mean, y'know, everyone calls me Benny. 'Cept you. And Sharon.'

'You told me once, remember? Ben, not Benjamin, not Benny, Ben's what your mum called you. It's on your birth certificate.'

Ben smiled sadly. 'You always make everythin' sound simple.'

'It can be, Ben,' he said. 'I'm going to sit there,' he added, indicating with his eyes and a slight movement of his head. He moved forward to the centre of the room and sat on the thick woven rug, legs crossed. He rested his elbows on his knees and his chin on his interlaced fingers. Through-out the manoeuvre Ben's hand hovered over a switch attached to the vest near his solar plexus, the trigger of his device. The lips of the man on the floor twitched upward, acknowledging the precaution. 'I can't do anything tricky from this position.' Ben wasn't so sure.

Briette suddenly giggled. She had her father's dark curls and big brown eyes. 'Daddy, Uncle Dave, lookit B1's doing.' Both men laughed dutifully and watched the flicker of bright primary colours on the screen until B1 ceased his antics.

'It is simple. F'you,' said Ben. 'Say "yes" an' we all walk out. Say "no" an' you walk out. Real simple.'

'C'n we see the end before we go?' Brie asked with innocent alarm.

'Sure, sweetie,' Ben reassured her hastily. But her words were like a splash in a puddle and his eyes locked with the other as ripples of their meaning spread through the room.

'It's not simple,' said Uncle Dave. 'We have a dilemma …'

'What?'

'… I'm not leaving.'

'Waddaya mean?' Ben could feel panic pushing at his gullet.

'I'm staying here until the end.' This didn't match the picture Ben had in his mind of its unfolding. 'Is it Sharon?' Uncle Dave added sharply before Ben could adjust to the ramifications.

Ben was off balance, reeling. 'What?' His voice was spiralling in pitch. Brie turned a wide brown gaze on him, a small frown creasing her perfect cream coffee brow. He fought to choke it down, regain control of its timbre.

'Do you want Sharon … removed?'

'What?' He was aghast. 'How … how could … No! No!' It was said with force but in a hoarse whisper. Brie was right next to him, why the fuck was he whispering? He stared into the blue eyes as they scanned him with a calculation that was almost a caress. Surely he didn't believe it was Sharon? He couldn't! He was trying to throw him off balance. Calm down, Ben, keep your shirt on. The day is yours.

He stared back at the eyes, hard, something he could never remember doing before. He smiled slyly. 'You know it's not Sharon,' he said firmly.

The man on the rug smiled and gave a small toss of his head conceding that gambit. 'Who?' he asked guilelessly. And Ben, ambushed by a reflex, almost answered him. Cheeky bastard.

'Y'know the deal,' he said.

They held each other's gaze for some time. Then Uncle Dave, with something like admiration in his voice, said, 'Why couldn't you live every other day of your life like you're living this one, Ben?'

And Ben answered, with something like wonder in his voice because he knew the answer, ' 'Cause I was afraid.'

The man on the rug looked at Ben, looked at Briette, then his eyes slid over the television set to the bench in a large servery separating the room from a kitchen. There was a phone on the bench, a speakerphone, and it was engaged; the police had asked for it to be left that way. They'd be listening to B1 and B2 if they could hear anything on the line at the moment. His gaze came back to Ben.

'I want to tell you a story, Ben,' he said. At his words, Brie, who was obviously tuned into the real world and the electronic simultaneously, turned expectantly towards him. He chuckled. 'That's a nice doll, Brie.'

She rubbed her cheek against Ben's arm. 'Daddy gave it to me. Look, it's black.'

'So it is, sweetheart. Very pretty.' He patted his left thigh. 'Want to come and sit on Uncle Dave's knee?' Ben's arm shot out across Brie's chest. 'Don't worry, Ben. You can flick that switch quicker than I can get to my feet.'

Brie looked up, puzzled. 'Can I sit on Uncle Dave's knee?' Ben hesitated then slowly drew his arm back. He didn't want Brie getting upset. The girl bounced from the couch, trotted over and plumped herself down in the nest made by the crossed legs of the man on the rug. She tapped his chin with the doll and he smiled and moved its arms about. Then her attention went back to the *Bananas*.

Uncle Dave's eyes moved to Ben's face. 'Once upon a time, long ago, there was a policeman,' he said. Brie's face turned up to his. He responded to the body language. 'Back in those days policemen were called "knights". Do you know what a knight is?' Brie nodded. 'They wore bright shining armour. And there were dragons. It was the policemen's – the knights' – job to catch dragons if they were bad – devouring beautiful maidens and things like that – and put out their fire. Are you with me, Ben?' Ben nodded. 'But it wasn't easy to capture a bad dragon. A poli … knight had to have the King's permission. And he couldn't get the King's permission unless he could bring the King proof that the dragon was being a bad dragon. And he couldn't do it alone. He needed the help of other knights and the King's men, so that no one was hurt – not even the dragon.

'Now the knight knew that a bad dragon had eaten three maidens already, but he couldn't find any proof for the King. So the knight made a dragon suit and he put it on and he went and lived with the dragons.'

'Where did the dragons live?' Brie piped without taking her eyes from the TV screen.

'In caves, big dark caves, deep underground. Then one day the bad dragon saw a new dragon he hadn't met before. It was the knight in his dragon suit, but he thought he was really a dragon. The bad dragon wanted to show the new dragon that he was the smartest and baddest dragon of all. So he came up to the knight and boasted that he had eaten three maidens. And he said that he was going to eat more and more, whenever he felt hungry, and the King and all his knights would never catch him. In fact he said, he was going to eat a maiden that very night.'

Brie slung her head back and he felt her breath on his chin. 'What's a maiden?'

'A young girl,' he smiled.

'Like me?'

'Like you. When you're a bit older.'

The baby browns swung down to the screen again. 'A bad dragon.'

'A bad dragon,' he concurred. 'Now the dragon's cave was a long way from the King's castle. The knight knew that even if he could get the King's permission and the King's men, he would never be able to get back in time to catch the dragon before he devou … ate the maiden …'

'Did he cook 'em with his fire breath?'

'Ah … yes, sweetheart, he did. But he liked 'em rare,' he added dryly, his eyes on Ben. 'The knight decided that it was better to save the maiden than to obey the King's rules. So he took out his sharp, shiny sword and, after a mighty battle, he chopped off the dragon's head and put out his fire for good.'

'No more cookin' maidens.'

'No more cookin' maidens. But because the knight broke the King's rules he had to take off his shining armour and never be a knight again.'

'He could wear his dragon suit!' Brie chirped brightly. This amused Uncle Dave no end. But she couldn't see what was funny.

'At least he still had his dragon suit,' he agreed through his chuckles.

'I like that story.'

'I'm rather fond of that version, myself.' His eyes were holding Ben in thrall. 'Do you know the moral of the story, Ben?' Brie gave her father a casual, curious glance. Ben knew he had been privileged by the telling of this tale. He was well aware of the arch references. He had just heard the closest thing to a confession the teller was ever likely to utter. Though its bearing would be brief, the burden of trust thrilled and scared him shitless. But what fucking moral?

'I, I … I …' He shrugged helplessly.

'Can't guess, Ben?' Now the eyes were cold fires. Ben was transfixed. 'The knight did this for a maiden he had never met. Never laid eyes on. Didn't know her name. Didn't even know which, of all the maidens in the kingdom, she was. Imagine, Ben, imagine, if he did this for a complete stranger, imagine what he would do for someone he knew and, and … cared about.' He dipped his head and kissed Brie's crown. She glanced up quickly and rubbed her curls vigorously. 'Let's get out of here, Ben.' His eyes snapped down and up. 'Soon as *Bananas in Pyjamas* finishes.'

Then Ben had a waking vision, burned with the hard-edged clarity of the television image. He saw himself thumb the toggle switch on his chest, but before the world dissolved in brilliant nullity, he saw the man on the rug simply roll and his daughter roll with him, a marsupial child, and the blast never touch her.

He had his hands tucked under his thighs. His fingers were cold, but they were there to stop their shaking. What he sought had been sensed not seen, unclear to him until now. A figment of faith, he had shambled toward its vague trace and stumbled on it. He'd got what he wanted. The bond was forged. The realisation was burning through the channels of his being like overproof liquor. The day was almost done. He knew he couldn't wring it for any more. Only one more chore. It was anticipation of this that had his hands shaking.

'Okay,' he said.

'Brie darlin', Uncle Dave has to make a phone call.' He lifted her and rose to his feet, unfolding in one smooth movement. As Ben noted the athletic ease of the action, he wondered if he had ever been in control. 'Need any help getting out of that paraphernalia?' he asked Ben as he lowered Brie to the couch.

'She'll be right,' said Ben. He watched him cross to the speakerphone. He listened to one side of the conversation as he stood, tugged down the zip and began to shrug off the vest.

'Don? You there?' A voice crackled and hissed. 'We're coming out.' Crackle, crackle. Something like a footy crowd barracking on the radio. 'About ten minutes. Plenty of time to stand down the troops, get fingers off triggers.' More crackle and hiss. 'We'll leave the, ah … device in here.' Crackle, crackle. 'He hasn't got a gun.' Crackle, crackle, crackle. 'The woman was frightened. Her imagination played tricks.' Hiss, crackle.

'No. All three at once. We'll come out holding hands, one on either side of the little girl.' Crackle, crackle, crackle. 'Sorry, Don, you have a lot of adrenalin-jacked personnel running around out there. Always the chance of an overachiever in a crowd. I'll bring them across the street to you. Spread the word.'

'What's that, Daddy?' Ben looked down. Brie was pointing at the vest hanging in his hands.

'Just somethin' Daddy made, luv.'

Brie reached out and tripped the switch.

4

'If you're going to look out that window put a bloody face shield on, Gareth.'

The window was in the gabled wall of the house that thrust forward into the small garden. Phil Severs thought they were far enough from ground zero of any explosion that the likes of Benny could concoct, but flying glass was a distinct possibility. It was difficult enough seeing clearly through layers of wet glass and drizzle without imposing another. He noticed movement on the roof of the house to the right of the day-care centre. The angle looked wrong. He doubted it would provide a vantage for surveillance or sharpshooting. The residents of the street and its neighbourhood had been evacuated for the duration. The police roamed over their homes at will.

'Okay, Don,' Gareth Nile said and turned from the window. The room was less crowded now. Various personnel had dispersed on their tasks. Everyone left seemed to be in thrall to the sounds emitted by the receiver on the dining table.

'Why don't they turn off the bloody television?' someone complained.

'Keeping the kid busy,' said Don Collison. He stood at the end of the table, his head bowed, chin on his chest, concentrating.

'There! There it was again. Dragon. I said someone said "dragon".'

'TV. It's a kid's show.'

'It sounded like our phantom negotiator.'

'We're taping this. The audio-heads'll unscramble it.'

'Whassat? Laughing. Someone's laughing.'

Don looked at Gareth, up from under his brows, a forehead of quizzical furrows like rills pushed in wet sand by wind and tide.

'Laughter is good,' said Gareth. 'Whose is it?'

No one seemed to know. Everyone moved closer, craning to pick out meaningful sounds from what, to Gareth's ear, was mostly white noise. But some of these people were experts in electronic eavesdropping; they could pick a raspberry from a fart at a boarding-school band practice. When a clear loud voice suddenly bleated from the plastic box Gareth had to stifle a snort of mirth. There wasn't one around the table who didn't pull back abruptly trying to disguise a red-handed expression caught on his or her face.

'Don? You there?'

Don jerked forward and leaned his weight on the table. 'Here! What's happening?'

'We're coming out.'

The celebration around the table was driven by the release of tension. Collison opened his mouth to give instructions but the disembodied voice overrode him; it flatly stated what was going to happen next. At different points he interjected to protest the plans that unrolled from the speaker, but to no avail. He was clearly annoyed that he wasn't calling the shots but ultimately he acquiesced.

'Who the fuck does he think he is?' growled constable Hoarse Whisperer.

'He thinks he's the man on the spot,' Collison snapped. 'Okay, you heard, ten minutes,' he bellowed at the room. 'Constable …?' he said to the woman monitoring communications.

'Baxter, sir.'

'… Baxter. Gimme a mike.' He was scooping his fingers back toward his body in an urgent gesture. The constable passed him a headset. 'I want this broadcast to every unit.' Baxter pressed buttons on her console and nodded to him. His mouth began to shape the words as the voice squawked from the speakerphone again.

'Don?'

'Yeah? What?'

'Brie just triggered the bomb. Get a bang out of it?'

Don stared at the phone, his face a study in granite. Then he said with crisp, measured articulation, 'Tell Benny that one of my techs is going to fix that bomb. And when it is in perfect working order, I am going to kick it so far up his arse he'll be able to sell his turds to *Al Qaeda*.'

Any fear left in the room was dissipating quickly, transmuting to anger, amusement or disappointment. Collison cut a swath with his glare and everyone felt vaguely guilty for succumbing to Benny's deception.

'The mother's here,' said Baxter.

Collison's authority returned with the decisiveness of his response and everyone seemed to snap back behind him in professional rearguard formation. 'Where?'

'Down at the Wattle Street cordon,' said Baxter. 'Carrying on a treat.'

'Right. It's safe now, but we don't want any soap opera in the middle of the street. Have them bring her here around through the back lane.' Collison turned to Nile. 'Get your gear on, Gareth. You and I are going over there to drag Benny out by his ears. A little something for the media. Might still extract some dignity from this bloody pantomime.'

Nile squirmed into his police-issue waterproof. 'You handled it the only way you could, Don. There was no way of knowing if the bomb was the real thing. It might be. Phil still has to check it out.'

Collison tossed off curt instructions to the team. Then he pulled his jacket on. He paused at the door. 'You all did well,' he said gruffly. 'Good experience if nothing else. Constable Baxter put out the word for all personnel to stand down. At ease, but alert until we secure the bastard.' He joined Nile on the front verandah. The two men hunched and squinted at the house opposite. The sky sagged over the street like a sheet of soggy cardboard. The rain was a cold wet film that hung in the road like a dirty shower curtain. Gareth could barely make out the barricades at each end of the block.

'Don't think there's too many photo opportunities out there, Don.'

Collison grunted. 'C'mon.' His foot touched the first step down from the verandah deck, when he stopped and breathed, 'Shit, they're coming.'

Nile looked up. Three figures were emerging from the gateway opposite, huddled under the borrowed umbrella. Nile paused on the verandah, but Collison hooked the hood of his jacket over his head and continued down the garden path to the gate. Let him have his moment, thought Nile, no need for us all to get wet.

Then the afternoon fell apart.

The road was just wide enough to have a narrow median strip. It was newly planted with native grasses and wide-spaced, drought-ravaged saplings that looked like moulting feather dusters. Gareth wasn't that far from the action but the actors looked like smoke in a fog.

As the small cluster of figures crossing the street stepped from the curb, one broke away at an angle and ran to the median, then stopped and turned. The tall figure left behind flung the umbrella away and scooped the small figure into his arms. The man who ran shouted two words back at him, but Gareth didn't catch them. They were drowned out by Collison's cry.

'Benny, you bloody moron, stand still or you'll get yourself fucking shot!'

The front gardens of the neighbouring houses were suddenly bristling with armed and armoured coppers, like malevolent black garden gnomes. Blunt commands punched through the mist. Benny Bovell was blind to their existence. He turned toward the sound of Collison's voice, eyes shadowed under his hood trying to locate its source through the drizzle. Then, spying Collison, he shoved his hand in the pocket of his parka, and moving purposefully towards him, he withdrew it again.

Gareth Nile had a degree in psychology. He was a senior constable in the Behavioural Analysis Unit. He knew all the theories, he had read all the literature, and would still say years from then that no matter what the fact later proved to be, he saw Ben Bovell pull a gun from the pocket of his snot-coloured parka. He knew by the end of that day what he saw was an illusion. But he saw it. He saw its lethal black snout. They all saw it.

All except one man. He was closer. He had special knowledge. He raised his hand and pivoted, clutching the child to him, his torso contorted to shield her from sight and sound and stray projectiles. He called out as he turned, repeating a single phrase that might have been 'It's a toy.' But Gareth never heard the words. Their sense was lost in the rattle of gunfire.

When Benny pointed his ersatz weapon Gareth rammed his back against the wall of the house, the blind end of the verandah. He could see Don Collison at the bottom of the short path squatting behind the solid wooden front gate, cursing and scrabbling in his clothing, trying to pull his weapon free. Gareth wasn't armed. He could see the child drawn swiftly into the hunched form of the man as if pulled into a tent from the storm. He couldn't see Ben Bovell. The burst of gunfire was short. And it didn't really rattle. Dampened by the dead, waterlogged air, it popped dully like corn in a microwave oven.

Then it stopped.

All this: a blur of seconds.

Gareth eased his back along the wall to peer around its corner. But before he reached it he saw the huddled figure on the far side of the road rise with the child in his arms. He saw Collison stand, his gun hanging by his thigh. Without looking left or right, cardigan man strode out towards them. He heard the door open behind him and someone come through talking softly but urgently into his radio. He stepped away from the wall and scanned the road.

At first all he could see were four or five men edging forward, their weapons pointed at something on the other side of the median strip. Then he saw the shapeless mass: the collapsed tent, the fragile membrane that failed to withstand the storm. Gareth turned back to the door. He was about to shout when Collison stole his words. 'Get the fucking ambulance down here fast!'

'It's coming!' the man at the door called as he ran past. It was the boss of the State Emergency Services team. Gareth followed him down the steps. At the curb, cardigan man, holding the girl with her head pressed into the hollow of his neck, was brushing past Collison. He didn't alter his pace or glance at Don as he spoke.

'It was a doll, Don. A black plastic doll. I told you he didn't have a gun.'

Collison, whose intent must have been to intercept him, swivelled like a toreador to avoid a collision and barked at his back. 'Who the hell can believe what you say anymore?' Then he spun on his heel and joined the SES man as he hurried to the scene. The street was filling up with coppers who, bereft of purpose, had abruptly become bystanders. The lights of the approaching ambulance haloed in the mist.

Gareth met the man and child at the gate. 'Is she okay?'

'Let's get her out of the rain.' They sidestepped to let Phil Severs and his bomb crew through.

'Where's Daddy?' said the girl, her voice muffled. She raised her head. Her eyes were large and bright and moist, her bottom lip was quivering. 'Where's my doll?'

'Mummy's on her way,' Gareth said quickly.

'Where's Mummy?' the girl immediately responded, jerking her head around.

The man in the cardigan gave Gareth a glance that he felt like a stab of ice-cream pain, through to the back of his brain. 'She's coming,' Gareth assured her, nodding. 'She should b—' He was cut short by a commotion back in the house.

'Get your bloody hands off me! What was that noise? Where's my daughter? Y'gonna hang there useless as a nun's twat, what the fuck's goin' on?'

They were climbing the steps to the verandah, the child twisted in her protector's arms. 'Mummy?' She turned back and pushed herself to arm's length to look in his eyes. 'Mummy, Uncle Dave!' Her face was trapped between conflicting emotions.

As they walked through the front door the girl called out and a small bottle-blonde woman burst from the living room. 'Jeezus, Briette, you're alright. Y'frightened the shit outta me!' She snatched the child from Uncle Dave's arms. 'Sorry, sorry, luvvy. Soap and water. Mum's usin' bad words again. Jist a bit worried.' She crushed the child to her and planted loud, vigorous kisses over her head and brow. Then she seemed to notice the two men for the first time. Her eyes slid over Gareth and discounted him, but when they fell on Uncle Dave, held fast. She had beautiful eyes, wide and green and slightly tilted, like a cat's. Their lids were large but not heavy, and they were green too. She had the kind of face for which a little makeup is too much, but it looked like someone from Revlon had been practising on it. It was what was in the eyes that interested Gareth.

There was definitely surprise, perhaps fear; suspicion and anger made an appearance; none of these were odd under the circumstances, but he hadn't expected guilt. Finally her eyes were filled with defiance. She held Uncle Dave's gaze and demanded. 'What the fuck – sorry, Brie baby, Mummy's bad – what are you doing here?'

'Ben asked for me.'

'It's none of your fuckin' business!' she snapped defensively. There it was, the fear and guilt were back. She forgot to apologise to her daughter for her vulgarity. 'Where is Ben? Where is the silly bugger? What've you done with 'im?'

'He's been shot, Sharon,' he said softly. Her body and face froze. 'Wait here. I'll go and see what the damage is.' He turned toward the doorway. As he did Collison came through it. He looked at the tableau in the hallway and summed up the situation.

'He's alive,' he said. 'But not in top shape.'

Sharon had a new culprit to release upon. 'You fuckin' bastards, you fuckin', fuckin', fuckin' weak cunts … pigs … you …' Her voice became shrill.

The child's eyes grew wide with fear. She began to whimper. 'Mummy, Mummy …'

'Sharon,' said Uncle Dave quietly, nodding toward the child. 'Briette.'

Sharon stopped immediately, choking on her words. She held the child closer and buried her face in her thick hair. Then her head snapped up, her eyes awash with anger and tears, her cheeks muddied by mascara. 'Where is 'e? I wanna see 'im.'

'Not possible,' said Collison. His voice was bluff but softened by sympathy. 'They've got to move him fast.' The sound of a siren working itself up to melodramatic pitch drew all their eyes to the grey world across the threshold. 'There he goes now,' Collison added redundantly. 'We'll get you to the hospital.'

'Mummy. Where's Daddy? Where's my doll?' the frightened child sobbed. The questions were a way to grapple with her confusion but they offered her mother another vent for her boiling emotion. A reflex grab to retain the dignity of righteous rage.

'Where's her doll?' she demanded of Collison. 'Where's m'daughter's bloody doll?' It was clear to Gareth that she was desperately clutching to a raft of anger for fear of drowning in grief. She wasn't coming apart in front of these bastards, she wasn't going to lose any more than she had today. The female officer who had escorted her hovered uncertainly in the background.

'It's evidence now, Sharon,' said Collison looking at his shoes. 'Sorry.'

'Evidence?' She stared at the three male faces looking down at her. She was a short woman. She appeared stocky in her thick winter clothes. Her face wasn't beautiful but it was striking. Her mouth was small, her bottom lip full, like a small pink pillow. She had high cheekbones and the bridge of her small nose was curved. There was something of a fragile, predatory bird about her. Where it was visible her complexion was pale olive, and Gareth guessed she was really a brunette. 'Evidence!' she repeated with gathering vehemence. 'What the fuck kind of doll is this?'

'It's the kind that makes little girls happy and grown men cry,' said Uncle Dave. 'Come on, Shaz. I'll explain everything.' And he put his arm gently around her shoulder and shepherded her and the quietly sobbing child into the bedroom and closed the door.

'Well, he's useful for something,' said Collison as they walked into the living room.

'What's the damage?' asked the police media spokesperson.

'Only three shots fired – there's a plus,' said Collison. 'All accounted for, another plus. On the debit side: they're in Benny's back.'

'Shit!' said the media man.

'Maybe you can highlight the quality of police marksmanship.'

'They had no choice, Don, he was pointing a gun at you,' said Gareth.

'He was pointing a *doll* at me, Gareth,' said Collison dropping into one of the Mrs Aldaker's over-stuffed chairs and squeezing his forehead between thumb and fingers so that it puckered like a quilt. The rain had plastered his hair to his skull and exposed its sparseness. 'A black plastic fucking doll.'

'Shit, shit, shit!' said the media man.

'When our friend is finished in there,' a roll of the head to the bedroom, 'help him vanish. The press has a long memory. Get a look at his face, and you'll need more spin than Cyclone Tracy. Don't worry, he won't be interested in publicity.'

'We were helped in our negotiations by a friend of the family who wishes his privacy to be respected?' said the media man, drawn, in the way of his tribe, to the silver lining.

Collison shrugged. 'The bullshit is your department.' He stared at his feet and the media man stared at him staring at his feet. 'I'll talk to you when the shooters have been debriefed.' When it was clear no other advice was forthcoming, the media man made a clucking sound with tongue and teeth and left the room.

After a minute or two of retreat into their own thoughts Gareth said, 'Did you see what he did when the bullets started flying?'

'He fell over, Gareth.' There were equal measures of fatigue, exasperation and sarcasm in his tone. 'A fairly normal reaction in those circumstances.' Their minds hadn't been dwelling on the same thing.

'Not Benny,' said Gareth. 'The Fair Unknown.' He gestured with his chin toward the bedroom door.

Collison slowly raised his head. His sardonic gaze slid up Gareth's length from his shoelaces to his face. 'Took Arts at uni did you, Gareth?' he said.

5

You wore your school uniform short in those days. And, out of the orbit of parent and teacher, you hitched it higher. Almost, but not quite, revealing the white scoops of your cottontails. Boys got herniated eyeballs trying to bend light when you sashayed by.

Her bra could carry cantaloupes when it wasn't carrying her.

She was short but she had good legs. And the tops of them were very cheeky. She had an hourglass figure. Her school uniform, slightly flared in cut, flounced over her hips like a fluted lampshade. But few boys had the temerity to grope for the switch no matter how much they lusted for illumination. She chose the ones to turn her on.

She didn't do well at school. Academically. It wasn't lack of grey matter, it was the distractions. She put it down to hormones. She had the brains, she just lacked the common sense to use them. Or maybe she was seduced by power: the raw, visceral, sensual power that wears the mask of lust.

Lust. She remembered it squirming and wriggling in her knickers, insinuating its silken-furred body between her thighs, skittering on the pink pads of its tiny clawed feet across her belly, pricking her breasts with needle teeth. It filled her body with its lithe muscular heat and stared from her eyes with its predatory gaze. And it watched as, caught in the high beam of her bold breasts and her green regard, small boys withered and big men dithered. But, with few exceptions, none approached the light till she come-hithered. She felt this primal creature awaken at a very early age.

The exceptions: the cock-for-brains who imagined she was a cunt-for-brains. The ones that were too dumb to read the signs or too arrogant to heed them. Poor bastards, she felt sorry for them – at first. The ones she couldn't deal with, Russell could.

Russell, the big brother who was so much older than her he was more of a protective uncle. Big, taciturn, lumbering Russell who'd inherited all the tall genes in the family. Russell, who'd beat the shit out of anyone who, by word or deed, showed less than the respect he deemed her due. Russell, on whom the tractor rolled. Russell, who through sheer will and physical labour might have saved the farm if the tractor had kept its equilibrium.

Russell was the firstborn. After him came stillborn and cot death and miscarriage and miscarriage and miscarriage and then nothing. But when hope had shrivelled and it was almost too late, she was born.

While her mother endured stoically the famine of her body, the land mocked her with blight just as barren. Drought, bushfire and flood, the unholy trinity – and of course, banks. The banks were the operative curse as she grew up. Her father had never possessed the green thumb of his forebears. His land had always been kind to him and forgiving. The brutal vehemence of its insurrection unnerved him. He withdrew from the scathing light of the fields and shrank into the shadows of the house. And he took a bottle with him. Russell fought on. Until the tractor rolled.

Her brother's body had not been long in the earth when they raped her – some of the exceptions.

In those days – well, even in these days, out there – you didn't report it. It would be assumed she asked for it. At the time she assumed as much herself. She didn't tell anyone: pride, shame, denial, sheer bloody-mindedness. Instead she raised her chin and strutted around town more bumptious than ever. That was a mistake. It was a challenge, and they thought it was safe to come back for more.

So she found another Russell.

He was big, very big. He was strong. His strength was legend in the district. He was a good-looking boy. Although his eyes were a lovely, soft, azure, the glow of intellect was dim in them. But when their gaze fell on her they lit up and he all but drooled – had done since sixth grade. He was a gentle giant and generally harmless. But he had a short fuse and a short attention span. If he sensed he was being ridiculed only swiftness of foot could save you. If you had the stamina to stay out of his reach long enough he forgot why he was chasing you and was diverted from pursuit by the next thing that drew his eye.

She recruited him the way Delilah recruited Samson, but she didn't trim his locks. The Philistines were her prey. He was her instrument. The strategy was hers and she executed it with the ruthless stealth of a guerrilla leader. Her Samson stalked each one of her rapists and beat them to a pulp. One had his spleen removed and another wore dentures the rest of his life. The last had an injury the name of which could not be spoken. He left the district as soon as he could walk.

No charges were made or laid, no accusations uttered. But, through some social osmosis, the town was steeped in latent knowledge. A conspiracy of silence gathered around the subject. 'Samson' was spirited away. The laughter of old friends became brittle, their conversation brief and their time short. Eyes never quite focused on her after that.

She was already thinking about leaving when she missed her period. Her decision was firming before she missed again. She had to leave. She couldn't look into her parents' bleached, bleak eyes and tell them.

She came to the city.

Of course she had a miscarriage. But by then her hubris had soured to self-loathing, and it was all sex, drugs and rock 'n' roll. And there was no going back.

The exceptions. There were two more exceptions. Exceptions of a different order.

One was Ben Bovell. He didn't wither or dither or drool. And he didn't have a cock for brains. Ben Bovell, who put no value on himself, but saw great worth in her. Who had no belief in a future for himself, but saw a future for them both; who somehow knew they could save each other. She'd never tried to manipulate him – sexually. And, if today was any indication, she still didn't know what made him tick.

And there was this one. What the fuck made him tick? Why would someone like him bother with Ben – or her? What did he want? He must want something. Everyone did.

His agenda was well hidden. Yet he appeared to have no hidden agenda. He was said to be dangerous. Some very hard men feared him. But it was the reputation they feared, and reputations were ninety-percent bullshit – in her experience. Still, somewhere in her gut she knew it wasn't all hype. He was a wee bit dangerous. Like – what was that word in her old school history book – terra incognita. He wasn't terra nullius.

Look at him. Look at her. Look at them both. How many times had they met in Brie's short life? Fingers of both hands? A dozen? Yet there was no awkwardness between them, took up where they left off, took each other for granted. Comfortable. She called him 'uncle'. Where had that come from? Grown men saw the Big Bad Wolf, little girls saw Grandma.

And look at them – him hunkered at her eye level – in deep and meaningful dialogue in a child's tongue. Small conspiratorial smiles, bright baby blues and browns locked in some sort of esoteric communion. She stepped behind her daughter and put her hands on her shoulders.

'What'd Ben want from you?' she demanded.

His wise-child eyes glided up to her face. 'Help.'

'Great help,' she sneered. Then sighed. 'What kinda help?'

'A private day-care centre in a nice middle-class suburb, Sharon?' he asked mildly as he stood.

She placed her hands gently over her child's ears.

'Fuck off,' she said. The words sounded a little strangled.

The benign expression didn't waiver. His eyes drifted lazily down to

Brie and he winked. She felt her daughter's cheek and brow bunch subversively against her palm.

'Fuck off,' she said. 'Please.'

6

'Nobody knew, y'know,' he said. 'Around here I mean. Not until after he died. We knew about the old lady before him. I mean he died first. But we discovered the old girl before we found out he was dead.'

She knew by the change in the timbre of his last words that he had turned to look at her again. She felt his gaze slide down her profile and come to rest at her lips. He kept looking at her lips, directed most of his conversation to her lips. He took an interest in her breasts and legs too – and probably her bum, but she didn't have eyes located to confirm that. He was curious about her body below the chin, but only the barest hint of its outlines was available for scrutiny. It was swaddled like an Eskimo's in January. So he ogled her lips.

It was so bloody cold here. She'd endured nights in the desert which were colder, but it was cold and wet here. It didn't simply feel cold, it looked cold. It was all in the mind and she knew it. And she hadn't had time to acclimatise. Most of her days since touchdown at Tullamarine had been spent in air-conditioned, over-heated boxes – workplace and homebase. Even now she was in an air-conditioned over-heated box. She could open her coat or remove it, but she didn't want to provide him with his eye candy. She looked out the window.

The countryside rippled by with the gentle green undulations of a washed-out quilt. It bled away to where the low grey cloud seeped into it and earth and sky melded in a pearly wash. Dark trees, aqueous smudges and dobs, marked its sodden fabric in dribbled rows or spots and spatters. Every now and then the hard edge of man-made things pressed forward as if against moist tissue. It looked bleak. It looked beautiful. It looked bloody cold.

'No one around here knew what he did. I mean, they still don't know. You know – the public. Well, not even we knew then. The local cops, I mean.'

He said 'I mean' a lot.

Ahead where land approached sea, a darker stain spread from the muddied hem of the damp grey skirt of sky. It was the first pale hint of the low ranges that sat like a mountainous dyke between ocean and plain.

'Otways,' he said, nodding. 'Thin broth down here, it'll be pea soup up there. And probably like a drive through a car wash.'

The topography began to bunch and wrinkle. The road began to dip and weave. Drizzly diaphanous curtains billowed in their path. The abrupt arms of the wipers swept them aside.

'I was wet behind the ears. It was my first station.' He paused and looked at her again. She looked at him this time. She knew what was coming next. She wanted eye contact to field this question. His eyes dropped to her lips. 'You're pretty young,' he said. 'I mean, you look young. How long've you been out – I mean in – the job that is?'

'Four years,' she said. And gave him her emerald-cut gaze. His eyes swivelled back to the road.

'Jeezus. Musta done something to please the boss, eh?' he said. 'To earn this, I mean.' To his credit, his ears burned bright red when he realised the implication in his words. It shut him up for a while.

'Suppose you went to uni?' he asked eventually. He was ferreting for why she was one of the chosen.

'Yes,' she said.

'I just left high school and went straight to the academy. Well, I mean, buggered around for a coupla years in between. Aren'cha hot in that jacket?'

'I'm fine.'

'Met my wife down here. Farmer's daughter. Married. Went back to Melbourne. Didn't like it. Came back here. Didn't like it. Didn't like the marriage, turns out. I mean, we're divorced now.'

I'm available, I mean.

'Used to go huntin' with him. In the shooters' club. Fuck he cou … I mean, shit he could shoot. Moving targets, stationary: didn't matter. Well, I mean, bloody obvious when you think about it – in retrospect I mean. Considering what his *real* job was. Locals used to wonder how he kept the farm viable. I mean, it wasn't real productive. Probably still wonderin'. Locals. I mean, I know how – now.'

I bet most of the locals do too, she thought. Make a great little copper's story to pull the chicks on a Saturday night.

'What was he like?'

'Nice bloke – you know. I mean, quiet. Kept to himself. But – have a pot or two with the boys. Didn't drink much, though. In the CFA. Didn't go to many social functions. Polite to women. Couple of local girls trailed their hooks. But he didn't bite. Didn't seem to have much to do with girls. Not around here, I mean. Used to go up to the city now an' then. Of course, I mean, we know why now. Most people, then I mean, thought he had a skirt up there. There was a bit of speculation he might be gay, of course. None of the women'd have that.' They drove a way in the hum of the heater.

Then he added, 'Well, I mean, what would you think? The way he took care of his mum. Everyone thought he was a nice bloke. Couldn't fault 'im. Women thought the sun shone outta his … I mean, took your life in your hands, say something against him in earshot of some sheilas around here.'

'She was an invalid? His mother?'

'Yeah. Well that was it, wasn't it? I mean, be alive today, if she wasn't. He went off to Melbourne, didn't tell anyone. Expected to be back the next day, prob'ly. Maybe that night. Often didn't bother anyone if he was only gone a day. Course, he didn't come home. Poor old bird starved to death up there before anyone found her.'

'How come it took so long? They'd need a relative to confirm identity.'

'Dunno,' he shrugged. 'He used his father's name – in his … city business, I mean. Known by his mum's name round here. I mean, she went back to hers when his dad shot through. Well, we know now he didn't shoot through. I mean, he didn't get far if he tried. And he sort of insulated her. Silent number here. Mobile phone for Melbourne. Two postal addresses. And probably a whole lot of other stuff, I mean, stuff they wouldn't tell a bush constable.'

'But he was known to Homicide?'

He chuckled. 'Yeah. The Murder Club knew him. They could look but couldn't touch. Never arrested s'far's I know. Interviewed a coupla times apparently. No material evidence. No witnesses. A bit of a legend though – 'mongst career crims, I mean.'

'Do you think the mother had a clue?'

He shrugged. 'Your guess is as good as mine.'

They were winding upward now. Tall eucalypts climbed hillsides showing knobby ankles beneath the petticoats of cloud, and waded knee deep through wet, smoking ferns down into the gullies. He was concentrating on the road. But he still managed to flick a glance her way.

'So, you went to uni and, you're – you know – I mean, I hope you don't mind me saying this, but, you're a bit of a looker.' Here it comes, she thought. 'I mean, why'd you become a cop? You coulda been a model, or on *Neighbours* or something.'

'Too fat, couldn't act. My dream was to be an administrative assistant, but I couldn't type,' she said.

His ears pinked and his eyes slid towards her again. 'Yeah. 'S okay, you don't have to tell me,' he said amiably.

She felt a twinge of guilt. He was a nice enough bloke, just trying to make conversation – and, just incidentally, her. She wondered why she was acting like a cold fish: possibly because she felt like a cold fish. 'It was you that found her?' she asked by way of amends.

'I'm at Colac now. I manned the Forrest station then. Bob, my boss I mean, the senior constable, married, lived at Apollo Bay. I got most of the night shifts. Wally Coutts, a neighbour, 'cross the valley from them, got woken by a dogfight. I mean, one of their dogs had tried to pinch his dogs' tucker. This was a bit odd. He, I mean Des, looked after his dogs real well. Then Wally realised he couldn't recall seeing any lights from the house for a few nights. Myra, Wal's wife I mean, she said she hadn't been asked to look in on the old lady. So Wal went over, couldn't raise anybody, rang me. Could smell her soon's I got the door open.'

'I know she couldn't walk, but was she so feeble she couldn't drag herself to the phone?'

'Phone by the bed. She'd dragged herself to the kitchen. She was lying with her head against the pantry door. I mean, when I found her.'

'Was the door open?'

'Locked.'

'Locked?'

'Yeah. Fridge, freezer, I mean everything edible, in there.'

'Why lock a pantry? Did the old lady have an eating disorder or something?'

'Nah,' he said and there was something sly in the smile he flipped across. 'Guess.'

'That's where he kept his ill-gotten gains.'

The smooth motion of the car gave a little hiccup. 'How the f— I mean, you saw that in the files.'

'No, I haven't read the file on his death. The case I'm reviewing, he's more likely for the villain than the victim.'

He gave her a doubtful glance. 'Then what are you doin' down here?'

'Had a break in classes and I thought I'd kill two birds with one stone. Tourism and research. See the sights, absorb some background colour.'

'See the Apostles?'

'Thought I'd go back along the Ocean Road.'

'And – at Detective Training School I mean – they give you these old cases to, what, study? Like, for assignments?'

'They usually give us classic, text-book case studies as models. But one of our lecturers likes to challenge us with unsolved and unproved cases or stuff-ups in investigation. We're supposed to analyse them and write a critique of procedure and such. We're not expected to solve the crime, just point to where we think the investigation was flawed or evidence was lacking. We can offer a hypothesis if we want.'

'You all get the same one? To study, I mean.'

'No, there's a selection.'

'Why'd you pick this one?'

'They hand them out randomly. I got another case. But some of us were comparing and I recognised a name on this one and was interested. The person who got it originally was happy to swap.' The person who got it originally was Howard, and he was willing to do anything to increase his chances of getting into her knickers.

'What, Des's name?'

'No. One of the detectives.'

'It was a Homicide demon that twigged. About the pantry, I mean. Had us pull the whole bloody thing apart. Weren't real happy – till we saw the loot. I mean took a whole bloody day. But he was so bloody certain. Secret panel an' all. Sharp boy. Young fella. Then, I mean. Not so young now I guess. Tall, fair hair. Can't remember the name. Had a theory about the phone too, if I recall.'

She was still young enough to think she was brighter than Day-Glo at times, and old enough to know she wasn't. But she couldn't help it; she had to strut her stuff. There were only a limited number of positions available for interstate coppers on courses at the prestigious Victoria Police Detective Training School. Her super had recommended her for one of them. She knew she was chosen on merit, she didn't need to prove anything to anyone. But she had to show off.

'She knew.' Swiftly, before he could expound.

'What?' He shot her a look.

'His mother knew what Des was doing. That's why she didn't use the phone. She knew something had gone wrong. Rather die than make things worse for him. No greater love.'

He glanced at her suspiciously. 'You sure you didn't read the file?'

'A bit of speculation like that wouldn't be in it anyway,' she pointed out. He conceded. He huffed an appreciative sound.

'Huh! You're good. I mean, no wonder your boss picked you. That's exactly what the Homicide cop reckoned. The blond bloke.'

'I've no doubt he did,' she said with a small private smile.

He cast her another suspicious glance. 'Smarter than a pop-up toaster, that one.'

And by extension, me too, she thought smugly.

'There's Wally's place,' he said suddenly. Something like an embossed impression of a house slipped by through the silvery slick trees. 'And on a clear day you can see the house over there across the valley. Can't even make out the valley today. But, I mean, there's nothing there to see anymore, really.'

'No worries,' she said. 'I'll just soak up the ambience.'

'Well, I mean, okay,' he grinned. 'If that's what turns you on.'

7

He'd waited as long as he reasonably could, as long as politeness would allow. He always tried to squeeze as much time and as many words as possible between utterance of the two names. Then, hopefully, the inevitable reference would be overlooked.

'Oh, and did I introduce Detective Sergeant Beverley Nunn?' Detective Senior Sergeant Ian Buckley inquired artlessly.

He glanced at the aforesaid sergeant and could discern the pressure of her tongue in her downy cheek. The man in the chair showed no inkling that he had made the connection. Either didn't get it, had a sophisticated sense of humour or didn't give a damn.

Buckley cradled the notion that Beverley Nunn and he had not been tethered in partnership by accident. It was someone's idea of a joke. It annoyed the hell out of him. He had a sense of humour, but this was irresponsible. It undermined their authority as soon as they identified themselves. Bev shrugged and said it was his problem. Call them Nunn and Buckley, she said. But that just appeared as if he was self-consciously avoiding the obvious and made it worse – in his opinion.

The man in the chair nodded and smiled at Beverley Nunn. They all smiled at Beverley Nunn – at first. She made Cate Blanchett look like the Wicked Witch of the West. In the nice cop nasty cop ploy, however, Bev was the nasty cop; but they kept that up their sleeves. It compensated some for the Buckley and Nunn handicap.

'Thank you for coming in,' said Buckley. They were in one of the less intimidating interview rooms in the Victoria Police Complex in St Kilda Road, but it was still severe in design and austere in furnishing. 'We were willing to come to you.'

'No trouble,' their interviewee said amiably.

Most people didn't like cops to be seen calling, but if they were in plain clothes, given a choice most would opt for a home ground advantage. But this one, maybe this was his home ground.

'As I said on the phone,' Buckley began. 'Sergeant Nunn and I are from Ethical Standards. More or less the equivalent of IID in your day.'

'I read the papers,' he smiled.

'We have been assigned to review police practice and procedure in the matter of the siege, and subsequent shooting, of Ben Bovell,' Buckley continued. 'This is routine in these circumstances, it isn't a criminal investigation and you're here as a friendly witness. Now I realise you know all this and may have participated in similar inquiries when you were a member of the police force.' Buckley knew he had. A very big Internal Investigations

Department investigation – shortly before he resigned. 'But, as you know, I need to cover the formalities. It is your right to have legal advice if you wish, but this is an internal investigation of the behaviour of the police not of any civilians incidentally involved.'

There was no sign of anything other than calm patience in the blue eyes.

'Our main concern is to learn as much as we can from the situation so we can improve procedures in the future,' Buckley pressed on. 'You will do no one any harm by being completely honest and candid.'

Completely honest – that was the thing. When Buckley went looking for background from someone who'd known this man back when, they'd shepherded him to Neville Marks in Homicide. Marks was supposed to know him better than most. They had been through the Academy together and were said still to have an association. He'll tell you the truth and nothing but the truth – but if you want the whole truth you'll have to ask all the right questions: that's what Marks had said. Well here we go, thought Buckley.

'Do you have any objection to our recording this interview? It will be used to ensure accuracy in our report.'

A small shake of the head. He flicked the switch and made the usual motherhood statement.

'Would you state your name, please, and present address?'

He did so.

Buckley identified himself and Nunn for the benefit of the recording. 'Mr Edge, David – may I call you David? Good – David, on July fourteenth you were contacted by an officer of the Special Operations Group who informed you of the situation at the day-care centre at one hundred and nine Curtin Street, Hawthorn, is that correct?'

'Yes.'

'The circumstances were clearly and fully explained to you?'

'Yes.'

'In particular, that Ben Bovell was in a hostage siege situation, threatening to take his life and that of his daughter and would not speak to anyone but you?'

'Yes.'

'And you agreed to attend the scene and speak to Ben?'

'Yes.'

'Did you feel that you were coerced or placed under undue moral pressure at any time?'

'No.'

'Were you made fully aware of the threat – the alleged bomb – how dangerous the situation was at the time, David?'

'Yes, but, barring an accident, it wasn't very dangerous for me.'

'Why do you believe that?'

'Ben Bovell is my friend and I believed he meant me no harm.'

'Were you asked to approach the building?'

'I suggested it.'

'In hindsight, do you consider Senior Sergeant Collison behaved recklessly in allowing you to approach the building?'

'Don was reluctant to take that step. But Ben would only talk face to face. I volunteered, and he knew I had the knowledge and experience to handle a situation like that. I would have done the same in Don's position.'

But you're a notorious taker of the left-hand way, thought Buckley. Nevertheless he smiled. Someone from Police Media – who would be pleased with the answer – was watching. An unarmed man who was shot after he surrendered himself and his hostage was not good press. He didn't glance at the video camera. But his interviewee did – with a small smile, not much more than a hook of dimple in cheek. So, everyone in the room knew they were under observation. No tricks now, Ian, only a straight bat will do.

'You agreed to approach the building, find out what Bovell wanted and photograph the explosive device if he let you?' Another affirmative. 'But you entered the building?' Affirmative. 'Why?'

'To photograph the bomb. And it's what Ben would have expected of me.'

'To put him at ease?'

'Yes.'

'Not to avoid exposing him to a sharpshooter?'

'It had that advantage.'

Buckley grunted and cast a wry glance at Nunn. 'So, it was your decision?'

'Yes.'

'Ben Bovell made a demand, but you didn't reply to it at that time. Is that correct?'

'I had agreed with the team that it would be look, listen and learn. The negotiator couldn't get close, so they didn't know exactly what they were dealing with.'

'It's been established that the first listening device you wore was faulty. But when it was to be replaced Don Collison intervened and ruled out wiring you. Is that how you remember it, David?'

'Yes.'

'Was there some agreement between you and Senior Sergeant Collison concerning the listening device?'

'There were some things – of a personal nature – that I may have had to discuss or agree to in order to persuade Ben to give himself up. Don and I felt it was neither wise nor necessary to have them on the record.'

'These things related to Ben Bovell's – ah – odd demand?'

'Yes.'

'Then, David, removal of the wire was a condition of your proceeding with negotiations?'

The blue eyes lazily rose to the camera and the comma curled in the cheek again. 'Yes,' he said. 'Don knew I'd nobble it anyway, if he insisted.' Buckley had no doubt that he gave the watchers what he knew they wanted.

Then his gaze slipped smoothly across to Beverley Nunn where she leaned casually – and with hip-thrusting provocation, Buckley thought – against the wall. He grinned at her with a sort of expectant invitation. Shit, thought Buckley, he's waiting for the fat lady to sing. He knows who's Kath and who's Kim in this duo. If he wanted to draw her out he succeeded.

'That's where we have a problem, Mr Edge,' Nunn said, pushing herself from the wall with her shoulder. 'We only have your word about Bovell's terms. And it was an exceedingly strange demand.' She folded her arms beneath her breasts and paced in a tight circle rocking from heel to toe. 'You're asking us to believe that he hatched and carried out this elaborate plan to extract from you a promise? No action or proof, no guarantees, no unbreakable contract, no immunity from prosecution? What was he going to do, call the ACCC if you reneged on the deal?' Her voice dropped an octave or two. 'What do you want, Ben? I want you to delete someone from the electoral roll, Dave. For you, Ben, anything. You're a good mate, Dave, can I go to gaol now?' She spun on her heel and stood, hip cocked, eyes ablaze. Buckley lived for these moments. It was all the sex he got these days. 'In fact, Mr Edge, held up to the light of logic, the whole scenario has the bone structure of a jellyfish.' At this point, thought Buckley, he should demand what reason had he to lie.

'True,' Edge agreed reasonably.

Beverley Nunn was caught a little wrong-footed by the candour. She was approaching the table, but she stopped, feet as far apart as possible in her tight skirt, hands went to her hips. She gazed up under her brow and pursed her lips. Christ, she looked hot like that, thought Buckley.

'I take it you have an explanation to offer?' She was inviting Edge to dig a hole for himself and they all knew it. If he reached for his lawyer it would indicate something. Just what – Buckley wasn't sure.

Edge said, 'There wasn't much rational logic in his actions. But then, he wasn't acting rationally.'

'That tautology doesn't get us very far, does it, Mr Edge? Are you suggesting there's another kind of logic we can employ?'

Buckley had his floorshow; he interposed: 'Mr Bovell may be willing to shed light on his behaviour when he is able, but we have some points of fact to clear up here.' Nunn retreated. Buckley addressed Edge. 'You said,' he referred to his notes, 'something like, "Ben's really focused today. He knows how this day is going to end." You said this to Collison. Do you recall these words?'

'Yes.'

'What did you mean by them at the time?'

'I thought Ben was resolved to get what he wanted, or die trying.'

'In hindsight, knowing the bomb was a fake, what do you think?'

'I think I was wrong. He was resolved to die *when* he got what he wanted.'

Buckley sat back. He looked at Nunn, and couldn't resist a glance toward the camera. 'You're implying a subtle and sophisticated plan, David.'

'I underestimated Ben. And I second-guessed myself.'

'Would you care to elucidate?' said Nunn.

'I've seen the faces of people who've made final and fatal decisions. Ben had the look. Exhilarated but at peace, wise, sad, but a little smug. But, I couldn't believe he'd hurt Briette. That's what made me doubt the bomb. I didn't think he'd risk an accident with Brie around. On the other hand, I was sure he didn't have a gun, how was he going to top himself? I assumed – if my gut was right – he planned to let Brie go with me, wait until we were clear and then blow himself up. Of course, in those situations, provoking police fire is always a possibility. That's why I insisted we leave together. When he didn't make a fuss I thought I'd let my imagination get the better of me.'

'So,' said Nunn. 'He walks, he suddenly snaps, grabs the doll, runs to get clear of the girl, waving the doll like a gun, and bang, bang?'

'No.'

'No?'

'He brought a black plastic *unclothed* doll with him. Perhaps to keep his daughter happy and distracted during the ordeal. Maybe guilty conscience. Perhaps it was an object with limitless versatility. But I tucked it into the bib of her overalls. Ben buttoned her coat up to the neck. He pulled the doll from his own pocket – not from Brie's jacket. He must have known that in the heat of the moment no one would pick it for anything but a gun.'

'You're suggesting he brought the fire down on himself? It was his intention before he left the building?'

'There were a lot of shiny new toys to distract a four-year-old in there. Why bring a cheap, secondhand, black doll?'

'He was planning it right from the start?' Nunn's scepticism was almost palpable.

'I badly underestimated him. I didn't believe he was capable of lateral thinking.'

Before Beverley Nunn could press her agenda, Buckley said, 'Well, as I said we can ask Ben Bovell about his plans and intentions if and when he's fit for interview. However, from what you witnessed, am I correct in assuming that you have formed the opinion that the police were forced into a position where they had no choice but to open fire?'

'Vision was poor. I knew what it was, and it looked like a gun to me. And Ben appeared intent on shooting Don.'

'Senior Sergeant Collison?'

'Yes.'

'In other words, in circumstances forced upon them, the police used *reasonable* force?'

'Yes.'

'Is there anything you want to add, that our questions haven't covered?'

'No.'

From the corner of his eye Buckley could see Nunn taking a breath to launch a new assault. But they had what they wanted. 'Thank you, David. Interview concluded at …' He gave the time and flipped the switch on the machine.

Beverley Nunn stood over David Edge like Xena the Warrior Princess. 'We have the what, when, where and how, Mr Edge, but they've found more fucking weapons of mass destruction in Iraq than we have reasons why, here.'

'If you get to know Ben, Sergeant Nunn, you might find his motives have an internal logic – emotional, psychological. But you need to take the time to get to know him. Have you got the time?'

Nunn glared down at him. He absorbed the heat without discomfort. They both knew there weren't enough hours in a copper's day.

'Then you'll have to take my word, for now.'

Nunn wasn't going to let go yet. 'He called out something – when he pulled his stunt – to you. Two words. What were they? Nile thought it was a name.'

'There were a lot of people yelling a lot of things.'

'Look …' Nunn bridled.

'Any change in his condition, do you know?' asked Buckley stepping between them verbally.

'I'm not in the loop. The last I heard, he was too weak to risk an operation.' This shut everyone up.

When he was gone Nunn said, 'Fucking cold prick.'

'Seemed to warm to you.'

She gave him the finger. 'Jeezus, Ian, you don't buy this bullshit – an elaborate, convoluted suicide plot? Do me a favour.'

'We've got what we need, Bev. Physical evidence and material witnesses all concur. Textbook. Let's us off the hook.' He shrugged. 'You heard him, have you got the time?'

She looked up under a wintry brow. 'I wonder what he promised the poor little bastard.'

Buckley popped the tape from the machine. 'According to Collison – everything.'

8

Hazel Walker did experience a misgiving. It was when she was pouring the hot water into the teapot. But it was only a momentary misgiving, lasting from when the water splashed into the belly of the brown ceramic pot to when it lapped the bottom of the spout. And it was just a teensy misgiving. Well, if she thought about it, it was two misgivings really, one sort of plopped on top of the other like pancakes – or those drop scones Clarry liked. And, she supposed, if she thought even more about it, one was probably more of a little twinge of guilt than a true misgiving. Perhaps a guilty feeling could be a misgiving? She'd look it up in her Macquarie Dictionary when her visitor left. Anyway, the guilt was the bottom pancake; the misgiving was definitely the one on top.

The misgiving was about her visitor (in an indirect way so was the guilt). Her daughter-in-law and her niece were constantly warning her about the dangers of letting strangers, particularly strange men, into the house. Who'd want to jump her old bones? she'd scoffed, raising eyebrows. Jump her bones: she liked that phrase, she'd heard it on her favourite soap. She had tried, she really had, but old habits die hard. And here she was letting all manner of stranger cross her threshold. Of course some of them had been policemen and she didn't think they would count. And Bron and Trish, they were lovely girls, and had her best interests at heart, but if they visited more often she wouldn't be tempted.

The guilt, though, wasn't about that. The guilt was about having so many visitors (and so much pleasure) because a very bad thing happened to someone else. Someone she liked a lot, who had been very kind to her.

The misgiving was about that. In particular, it concerned her present visitor. But it was as submerged as the bottom of the pot, before she finished pouring. Who'd want to jump her bones? Not a nice-looking young man like that, surely. And what did she have to steal? Her collection of salt and pepper shakers? Everyone said they must be very valuable, but she knew they weren't – just sentimental frippery.

She slipped the crocheted cosy over the teapot – it was a cold day – and placed it on the tray with the cups and saucers, plates, sugar bowl, milk jug, Monte Carlos, Tim Tams and date scones. It made a fearful rattle as she lifted it and carried it down the draughty hall.

'Hold on, I'll give you a hand,' came a voice from the lounge room.

'No, no! You stay there and keep an eye on things,' she cried over the clatter of the tea tray.

She put the tray on the low table between the couch and the widescreen television set, backed to her end of the couch and fell the last few centimetres into its plush cushions. She sighed deeply and smiled at her visitor.

'Ooh, I think I got a little out of breath,' she said. 'Now, what's happening?'

'The one with the jaw …' her visitor said, fingers spanning his lower face and pulling down.

'Ridge.'

'Ridge has been having a very long discussion with someone who might be his brother, his father-in-law or his uncle, perhaps all three.'

'I'm sorry,' Hazel said, reaching for the remote. 'I should have taped it.'

He placed his hand over hers, which she had to admit gave her a little fright (or was it a thrill?). 'No, it's alright, let's watch.'

'You don't mind?'

He just smiled and gave his head a small shake. She pushed her spectacles onto the bridge of her nose with one finger and turned to the TV. They sat on the couch in silence until the ad break.

'That was funny,' said Hazel as she poured the tea. He looked at her and one eyebrow hooked a little higher. 'What you said about Ridge.' He smiled. 'I know they're silly. These serials. But I enjoy them.'

'Many of the girls do too,' he said as he took his cup.

'Girls?'

'Ladies, really, that I work with.'

'They can watch these shows during the day?' Hazel asked, a little intrigued. 'Is it night work?'

'A lot of it. Service industry. All go one minute, time on your hands the next.'

The ads finished and Hazel's attention returned to the telly. The scene was a hospital room. The patient was a woman with strategically placed bruises and wounds decorating her pretty face. A handsome man with a cute child in his arms and another pretty woman were at the bedside. Everyone in the room took turns to say deep and meaningful things very slowly with long pauses between. When the man and child left the pretty patient called the pretty woman closer to the bedside to whisper weakly in her ear. She bit her instead, and accused her of malevolent manipulations designed to turn her husband and child against her. Dramatic theme swells. Fade to black.

There had been another question in Hazel's mind about that job, those girls, but by the time the final program credits rolled she'd forgotten what it was. 'Well,' she said. 'Now we can talk. Have you had a biscuit? Just help yourself. I hope you like what's there. I've had so many visitors over the last week. I haven't had time to stock up my pantry.' She giggled girlishly. 'Too many cups of tea and cakes. I'll be getting fat.'

She followed his gaze as his eyes swept the room taking in the cluttered crystal cabinets, tabletops and shelves.

'You have an interesting collection,' he said. 'And a big one. You must be dedicated.'

Hazel shrugged. 'Not really.' She stared across the darkening room to the fading light in the grey oblong of the window. She reached over the fat arm of the couch and switched on an ornate standard lamp. The matching pairs of shapes and figures crowded toward the light like partners at a masquerade. 'They just – accumulated.' She smiled privately as she smoothed her dress over her knees and picked some crumbs from her lap between thumb and finger and dropped them on her plate. 'Clarry, my husband – late husband – spent a whole fortnight's pay to take me to a posh restaurant the night he proposed, and I – you're not a policeman?' She fluttered a shy, sly smile at him.

'No,' he said.

'I stole the salt and pepper shakers,' she confessed. 'It did seem like the right thing to do at the time. It felt so, so daring. He stole my heart, I stole the shakers.' She laughed gaily, like a girl. 'Then it became a habit. Not the stealing, I didn't do that anymore – well once or twice, at places where they wouldn't sell them. I'd buy them on holidays and special occasions. They were like good-luck charms and mementos. Then people began giving them to me. I can tell you who gave me which, and when.'

'A lot of happy memories and good fortune,' he said.

'Mostly. Not all.' She smiled wistfully. 'But they're all important. Without some sadness how do we know we're happy? It's like music, isn't it? You need high notes and low notes to make your tune.' She sighed softly and gazed around at her collection of odd couples. She could feel his cool gaze upon her. He had eyes like Clarry: blue as a summer sky when pleased, blue as polar ice when not, and like a misty morning when pensive. 'Mr Bovell didn't have any salt and pepper shakers. I gave him one of my favourite sets.'

'That was very good of you.'

She shook her head. 'No, no. He was kind to me. He was a nice man.' She pointed at one of the cabinets. 'He gave me that Mickey and Minnie Mouse. He stole it.' Clarry's bright blue gaze locked on hers. 'He must have done. It's a collector's item. Mr Bovell couldn't afford that.' Her eyes drifted back to the cabinet. 'It's one of the sad memories now. But, happy too.' She knew he was appraising her with increasing approval. 'I knew – well, guessed – about Mr Bovell, Clarry …'

'David.'

'Pardon? Yes, David, of course. I'm sorry, what did I call you? It doesn't matter, just old age. I knew about Mr Bovell because he was a friend of a friend of Trish's Shane. Shane was in gaol before they married. For something he didn't do, Trish says – but well, you know.' He smiled. He knew. 'I guessed Mr Bovell was just out of prison and couldn't get a job. Shane's a nice boy and I'm sure his friends are too. But they have been naughty. Trish says Shane's square now. "Square" – I think that's the same thing as "going straight" in American TV shows.' He smiled as he reached for another Tim Tam. He offered her the plate and she shook her head.

'Are you square, David?' she asked, a little mischief in her eyes.

'Quadrilateral,' he admitted after some consideration. 'A rather irregular one.'

She tut-tutted. 'You like Tim Tams?'

'One of my weaknesses,' he said with a guilty grin.

'See the tape over there?' She pointed to a chair near the door with a neat roll of something blue and white on it. 'Crime scene tape. I've been a crime scene,' she said proudly and giggled. 'Or my bungalow has.'

Hazel sipped her tea and watched her visitor sip his and eat his Tim Tam. Then she said: 'He said you'd come.'

'Ben did?'

'You're Dave, aren't you?'

'Most likely. My name is David Edge.' She realised she hadn't asked his name. It was her vague recollection that he offered it, but she wasn't paying attention. She had invited him in immediately he said he was a friend of Mr Bovell's.

'He left something for you. In an envelope. I didn't look at the front. None of my business. He said "Dave'll come, make sure he gets it". So I suppose it's addressed to you.'

'It probably is. You didn't mention it to the police?'

'It wasn't any of their business either. It's a private package. I'll fetch it when we've had another cuppa.' She studied him, possum-like through her thick lenses. He didn't protest that he was late for an appointment or had to get home to the wife, didn't sneak a quick peek at his watch. He was relaxed, unhurried. He paid his social dues, this one. That was like Clarry too.

'Mr Bovell's – Ben's – tune was rather flat, I think?' she said.

'Not many highs,' he agreed.

'He loved his children dearly. That was a high.' She snuck a quick calculating glance at her visitor. 'He thought highly of you.' The blue eyes became watchful over his teacup rim. 'He said to me once – we were sitting here like this – he said he only had two real friends. One was a woman, Karen—'

'Sharon.'

'—Sharon. The other was Dave. He said with friends like Sharon and Dave you didn't need more.' Hazel had the distinct impression that, although he smiled, her visitor wasn't pleased to hear this. 'They said on the news that Ben has a bullet in his spine.'

'A fragment. Lodged between his fourth and fifth vertebrae.'

'A fragment. Is that better?'

'I don't know.'

'Will he be paralysed?'

'He can't move his arms and legs at present. So I've heard. If they can operate successfully, who knows, he may be good as new, one day.' He placed his cup and saucer on the table and sank back.

Her spectacles seemed to fill like goldfish bowls. She could feel rivulets cooling on her cheeks. A pendulous droplet swelled and swung on the tip of her nose. He stretched across and took the tissue box from the small table next to the Jason Recliner: an arm's reach supply for the soaps. Suddenly, as she dabbed at her face, she was telling him everything she knew about Ben Bovell – which wasn't much. It was as if he interrogated her without asking a question.

'… his favourite actor is Lee Marvin, did you know? He said he was tough, but he could be funny and dumb and kind as well – that's why he likes him. We often sat here and watched old Lee Marvin movies. *Cat Ballou* – quite a lot – *The Professionals* I think another was called … and let me see … *The Emperor of* … something …'

'When was the last time you spoke to him?' he asked when she'd exhausted her memory.

'The night before he, he … He sat where you are now.' Then anticipating his next question, 'I thought someone who was going to do what he did would be sad – depressed or agitated. But he seemed happier than I'd seen him. Just kind of excited. He said things were sorted between Sharon and him – that he knew what he had to do. When he told me he wouldn't need the bungalow anymore I assumed he was moving back with her. He said "this time tomorrow I'll be square".'

They sat in silence for a while, then he said, 'Do you think I could have Shane's address? I'd like to talk to this friend of Ben's.'

She nodded her head and turned away to blow her nose noisily.

'Thank you,' he said.

'He left his salt and pepper shakers in the bungalow,' said Hazel. 'When he's allowed visitors I think I'll take them to him. They've always been good luck for me.' She began to inch her bottom forward in preparation to rise. He got up from the couch and offered his hand. 'Thank you, Clarry,' she said. 'I'll get Ben's package for you now. And then you can tell me what I missed on *The Bold and the Beautiful*.'

9

'Did your *Halifax* put together a profile?' Damn! She knew it was a mistake as soon as she said it. The flip terminology gave him a wedge to drive between their dialogue and its subject.

'Halifax?'

'Forensic psychologist.'

'Ah. Huh, huh, huh. I get it.' He smiled – a zebra crossing with no black stripes. He tilted his head to one side and studied her face through hooded eyes. 'You know you could be Rebecca Gibney.'

'I know. I tried to be once, but Becky threw a hissy fit. Seems to think she has first dibs.' She took a sip of her drink. 'And she's blonde.'

The smile stayed right where it was, just under his nose. She was impressed. 'No, really,' he persisted. 'Have you ever considered peroxide?'

'Often. But only when I'm depressed.' Bloody hell. Stop the twee banter, he thinks you're flirting.

He had to think about that one. Even though his expression said he didn't get it, he was alerted to change tack. He gave a clipped stagey laugh and ploughed ahead. 'And what sort of things could possibly depress a beautiful, intelligent girl like you?'

She shrugged and pouted her plump pink bottom lip. 'Global warming, patronising male colleagues, the paucity of creative pickup lines.'

He got that. The zebra crossing closed to traffic. He disguised it reasonably well though, with a pull on what was left of his beer and a scan around the crowded bar for a tardy friend. She felt a little sorry for him.

'My round,' she said cheerily, even though she didn't want another drink.

He looked at her closely. She immediately regretted her words. Bugger, he's going to make another run.

'I think, my dear constable,' he said with sage pomposity – she was unsure if it was feigned or sincere – 'that you feel ill-treated by the male of the species.' Maybe he didn't get the last bit. 'It's clear that one of the bastards in our brethren has not paid you the respect and adoration that is clearly your due.'

Nope, he wasn't joking; he meant it. You can't verbalise diarrhoea with your tongue in your cheek. She had best nip this in the bud.

'You're very perceptive,' she said, smiling. 'I've made a vow not to become involved with a colleague. Or,' and she tickled his retinas with her green lasers, 'a married man.'

'Well there's one strike against me,' he grinned, dropping the older and wiser act.

'Sergeant!' she said in the tone of a kindergarten teacher admonishing her favourite naughty boy. She looked up under her lashes in a way that usually made men put their hands in their pocket or cross their legs. He crossed his legs and his grin became sheepish.

'Awright. Two strikes.'

'Three, I'm afraid.' May as well nail it down.

Abruptly, he conceded the match. And seemed relieved. Why the hell do men do that? she wondered.

'How did you know?' he asked, after downing half his beer. 'About being married?'

She pointed to his left hand. He had his elbow on the bar and his hand dangled over the edge. His right thumb and forefinger were rubbing his ring finger at its base with a twisting motion, as if tightening a nut.

'You did that every time you handed me a compliment today,' she said. 'Or looked at me in a … certain way.'

'Well, I won't apologise for my compliments,' he said. 'You're – and I mean this, it isn't a come on – you're the prettiest cop I've laid eyes on. Believe me.'

'Unfortunately I do.'

He scoffed a brief low laugh and stared at her sceptically. 'You can't tell me you regret being a looker?'

She offered a deadpan, parchment dry, response. 'I'd trade beauty, brilliance, success and wealth, just to be loved for what I am.'

'Huh – huh – huh,' he chortled uncertainly. 'That doesn't make sense.'

'No. If you really think about it, it doesn't.' She glanced across his shoulder. 'There's a big bloke just come in. Lots of dark curly hair, dressed like a vet from the Yorkshire Moors. He's looking for someone.'

'That's him,' he said without checking. 'Say something nice about his jumper. His wife knitted it.' He turned around and waved his arm, 'Nev, mate, over here.'

Good, she thought. She was finally getting close to what she'd been seeking all afternoon.

Her drinking companion, Detective Sergeant Frank Ricciardelli, was enrolled in one of the units she was taking at the Detective Training School. When he heard she had the 'Jogger Murders' for homework, he had volunteered to take her on a tour of the crime scenes. She thought she'd detected that look in his eye at the start, but his behaviour had been strictly professional, out there on the tracks.

The tracks were shared walking and bicycle paths that spidered the city, mostly following creeks and rivers and connecting green belts and parks.

'This was where the second one was found,' he'd said earlier that day, as they stood in a wide smooth path of packed clay and fine gravel where it swerved away from the creek bank and climbed steeply to the adjacent bushland reserve. 'As you can see this spot is out of sight of the park, unless someone's standing right on the edge of the slope there. And some-one coming along the path beside the creek, or on the footbridge, can't see you.'

She walked back to the bend. The footbridge was a couple of hundred metres away. The rear of commercial premises and blocks of flats over-looked the opposite bank. They were separated from the creek by a long high chain-link fence.

'But he didn't do her here,' he said. Do her: she cringed inwardly. 'There wasn't a scrap of forensic evidence found at any of the scenes that suggested he killed them on site.'

Her eyes swept around and probed between the dense shrubs and trees that bordered the path on the landward side.

'The bush around here was scoured a kilometre both ways,' he said in anticipation of her thoughts. 'You can see it's real thick. You couldn't drag anything in there without leaving signs. There were places near the other sites where he could have done it without trace – if he was lucky. But no evidence was discovered. The conclusion was that he raped and killed them somewhere else and brought their bodies to the places they were found.'

'But this was the track she ran on? She ran past this point?'

'You've read what I've read. Regular as clockwork. Three or four times a week. Never missed Tuesdays and Thursdays. That was one thing they all had in common: a very regular routine.'

'And a tendency to work late and run after nightfall,' she contributed. 'Plus big boobs, long legs and natural blonde hair.'

'They all looked like Barbie,' he agreed. 'Oh, and they were left near water. The psychologist was fond of that point.'

'The coroner's report said they had abrasions and bruises indicating they put up a fight. They died of strangulation immediately after or perhaps during sexual penetration. There was no seminal fluid found.'

'There were traces of the same condom lubricant found in the vaginas of all three. The first victim had been a virgin. The only odd thing about this one was that two different types of lubricant were detected. He either raped her more than once and changed brands, or she had a boyfriend who never came forward.' Ricciardelli was wearing gloves but he worried the root of his ring finger with a nervous winding motion. 'You've just read a copy of the summary report,' he said. 'I was able to look at the files. Believe me, the report's very detailed and thorough. As an investigation it was textbook. That's why it's used as an example. An investigation carried out according to Hoyle – about as close as you can get to procedural perfection. It's meant to teach us that you can do everything right but still get no result.'

'Do you agree with the conclusions?'

'It's hard to imagine any other possibilities.'

'If it was a serial psychopath, how do you explain the sudden cessation after the third murder?'

He shrugged. 'It happens. He got scared. Maybe we got close and didn't know. A bus ran over him. He left the country.'

'There was a dissenting voice,' she said. Her gaze flicked back and forth between the footbridge and the block of flats that bordered the path that connected to it.

'The report acknowledged that. But I'm a fan of Occam's razor,' he said dismissively.

'What about Sherlock's razor?' she grinned. 'Once you've eliminated the possible, whatever's left, no matter how improbable, must be the answer.'

'No facts or evidence were produced to support that hypothesis.'

'Desmond Poynter died and the murders stopped.'

'A lot of crims died or got put behind bars that month. Are they all suspects?'

'This is where Poynter's body was found, isn't it?'

'It's a school assignment, Constable. You're not meant to solve the case,' he said in fluent pedant. She faintly recalled saying something like that herself once. 'Poynter was a professional. Pros keep their kills simple and plain. They use Occam's razor.' He grinned at his own joke. 'Less can go wrong that way.' The addendum suggested he'd been tempted, at least momentarily, by the idea.

'A lot of psychopaths are professionals of one kind or another,' she had said.

Now she watched the approach of the man he'd promised to introduce her to. He weaved towards them around crowded tables, high and low, stools and chairs and boisterous, happy-hour knots of humanity. He was surprisingly agile for such a large, bear-like individual. He deftly hooked a vacant chair from a nearby table as he passed and dropped into it beside Ricciardelli, dwarfing him.

'G'day,' he said. His dark eyes glittered with some private mischief. 'You must be the cute copper from Broome I've heard about.' He thrust a huge paw at her across the table. 'Nev,' he said, grinning. 'Nev Marks.'

'Carol Porter,' she replied with a smile as she was almost lifted from her chair by the ripple effect of his handshake.

'Right,' he said cocking an eye at Ricciardelli. 'Y're draggin' the chain, father.'

'A pot, Nev?' asked Ricciardelli with a wry twist of the lips. He glanced at her. 'Another one, Carol?'

'I'll nurse this,' she said.

He made his way to the bar. Marks slouched back in his chair and regarded her with that hint of amusement still in his eyes. His glossy jowls were thick slabs of gunmetal blue. 'Ricky Ricardo tells me y've met Dave,' he said, with a sideways nod in Ricciardelli's direction.

'Briefly. I arrested him.'

'He escape?' Marks grinned, the muscles in his jaw flexing his face into a pear shape.

'I let him go. He was innocent.'

'Dave's anything but that,' said Marks dryly. 'We have a mutual friend, I reckon.' She arched a quizzical brow. 'Gaylord Kiss. Met 'im a coupla years back.'

'Oh,' she said. It sounded like punctuation: a period.

'Oh-h-h,' he said. Dialogue by inflection. He smiled down at his hands resting on his belly. 'M'wife's a Carol, too,' he said looking up again. 'She was a cop. Worked on the case y're interested in. She's the one y'should talk to. Y'gotta lot in common.'

'What? We're cops and Carols?' She smiled. She was getting to like this bloke.

'Nah,' said Marks. 'Much more than that.'

She stared into the dark eyes. What was flickering in their depths? And what in hell did he mean by that?

'Wanna meet Carol, Carol?'

10

Tommy discovered it was difficult maintaining dignity and engaging in civilised and reasoned argument when your fly was undone, your nose was in a urinal and someone's foot was on the back of your neck. This was hardly a revelation. There was no need to experience the situation to appreciate it. Simple use of imagination would suffice, but why would you imagine such a circumstance? You'd have to be some kind of sick wick-twiddler, like a masochist or a novelist, to bother.

Tommy had ducked down to the Valley at sparrow's fart to catch the canter of a couple of likely gee-gees and grease a strapper he knew who knew things – things about horses. He'd watched a gallop or two, milked the strapper for all he could – which proved to be a half a cup of soy – and was legging it for the car park when nature whistled urgently from his satin polyester boxers. Cold weather and coffee: the bane of the baby boomers.

He thought he might have to piss against the back of the stands but, as luck would have it, the public toilets were open – and deserted. He drained the dragon and was giving its head a damned good shake, wondering if he could get out before he was asphyxiated by the pungent fumes of disinfectant, when something like Phar Lap at full gallop slammed between his shoulderblades, and spread him like Vegemite over the porcelain tiles. Then his legs were either taken from under him or they chose to cut and run without telling him. He found himself flat on his belly, his face wrenched painfully to one side, trying to suck into his lungs air that was not diluted by urine.

Through the pinheads of light that were bobbing before his eyes to the rhythm of his agony he could see his stainless-steel thermos still standing where he'd placed it an aeon ago. Perhaps if he could just reach it he could – what? – impress his assailant with his ability to pour a cup of kindness, yet? His assailant: now there was the rub. It might be helpful to figure out who that might be. Let's see, to whom did he owe money? Well, fuck, everyone. But he wasn't in so deep that anyone would kill him. Was he? Nah, that'd be just bloody silly. How'd they get their money if he was a worm farm? And you wouldn't feed a greyhound a pound of his flesh. Nah, just a friendly warning.

His brain was clearing. He began to run a list in his mind. It was a long one, and he didn't think he'd left anyone off. There wasn't a name on it that would have scratched him – not yet. He couldn't pick a favourite. He decided he wouldn't lay out on this one, he'd just lie here, patiently, until the stewards announced the result of the photo.

It seemed as if he'd been there for hours before he heard the voice, but it was probably only seconds. Time dragged when you weren't having fun.

'Nice coat, Tommy – cashmere, alpaca? Nose hairs of the Afghan Fruit Yak?'

'Oh shit!' said Tommy. Because his left cheek was pressed like a waffle into the stainless-steel grid over the urinal trough it sounded more like 'Ugh thshith'. 'Maeve?' he added, panic pinking his voice. It sounded more like 'Maypth?'.

'G'day, Tommy.'

Oh shit, thought Tommy, becoming really concerned for his wellbeing for the first time since hitting the wall, I'm listening to my own piss dribble by under my left ear and Maeve Maguffin's size ten Doc Marten is jammed under my right. In Tommy's narrow universe this was a revelation, of the apocalyptic kind. And Maeve assumed the proportions of a rider capable of sitting astride all four horses. Oh shit!

'G'day, Tommy,' Maeve repeated with prejudice. The pressure on his face printing the words in bold type.

Oh good, thought Tommy, the cops'll be able to take a plaster cast of my cheek and identify the bitch by the tread of her clodhoppers.

'G'ay, Maypth,' he said. It looked like his luck, a rank outsider at the best of times, might have thrown a shoe. Maeve-fuckin'-Maguffin! Built like a brick shithouse, with a face that kept a thousand ships in dry dock. She hadn't been on his mental list. He didn't owe her money but she'd be representing someone to whom he did owe money – and more; someone his list had also not included. A teensy oversight there, Tommy.

He felt the pressure from Maeve's boot ease. Tentatively, gingerly, he struggled to his elbows. The vapours of his breath and the vapours of his waste entwined like old friends snuggling against the chill.

'Don't bother to get up for me, Tommy. Just make yourself comfortable while we chat.'

'Can't I at least turn around, Maeve? Y'know how I love t'see ya.'

She gave him a not-unfriendly cuff over the ears that buoyed his hopes – a little. 'Don't get frisky, Tommy, this is business.'

Her mouth was closer to his ear when she said this and the sour fumes of alcohol swam to him through sweet waves of mint. Tommy's hopes lost their water wings. Jesus! Maeve was off the wagon. A sober Maeve was fearsome; a drunk Maeve was awesome. She was not a happy inebriate. And a less than sober Maeve on a mission for the sisterhood was – well, there wasn't a word in the dictionary; not that Tommy had looked lately.

He began to adjust his demeanour to one more suited to his new appreciation of the circumstances. Adopting a querulous tone seemed to have a soothing effect on Maeve's savage breast. Not that he was an expert. He hadn't had that much to do with Maeve. She loomed more as a legend in his life than a corporeal presence: a whispered sanction, like the bogeyman.

She was a dyke, so they said. And they said she was a dyke because she was too fucking ugly to get a bloke. And she had a chip on her shoulder the size of a mallee root because she was too fucking ugly to find another dyke who would let her save the Low Countries. That's what they said. She certainly didn't spend anything on appearances or self-improvement. In fact she seemed intent on the reverse. Like a sort of anti-Michael Jackson, time seemed to be colluding with Maeve to carve her into Captain Hook rather than Peter Pan – or maybe the crocodile. Maeve had been a cop back in the good old days before Commissioners of Police marched in parades of gay pride. They said she put the hard word on a superior officer and was on the footpath in civvies before the ink dried on her resignation. That's what they said.

Tommy understood those good old days. These days? Shit!

Maeve was patting him down. She had his wallet. He felt his scrotum, and everything in its proximity, shrivel. Christ, now she had a handful of his belt and had hefted his backside up to grope around his balls. She wouldn't find anything there: he doubted that his ship would ever leave dry dock again. She removed his shoes.

'Jesus, Maeve,' he said, querulously. 'I just paid off on a tip. I'm runnin' on empty.'

'Who's my client, Tommy?' Maeve coaxed.

His voice wound up in pitch. 'How the fuck wo—'

'Tommy!'

'Janet,' he conceded with a sigh.

'And what does Janet want, Tommy love?'

'Three thousand two hundred and seventy-two dollars.'

'And ...?'

'And forty-five cents.'

'Glad you're retaining your sense of humour, Thomas.' She flicked him on the tip of the ear with her finger. 'And ...?' she prompted.

'And the kid's birthday present,' he said grudgingly. And querulously.

'She'd like that delivered,' said Maeve. 'Personally.'

'Aw jeez, Maeve ...'

'And then there's the matter of my fee.'

'Oh jeez, Maeve!' Querulous scratched. Indignant in the mounting-yard.

'Tommy.'

'If the tip I just got doesn't pay off, Maeve, I'm rooted. Honest. I'm down to me uppers.'

'A lotta tread there, Tommy,' she said, tapping him on the head with his Florsheims.

'You know what I mean.'

'Serial monogamy is a lifestyle for the rich and famous, Tommy, not the piss-weak and poor. You're lucky this ain't a class action.'

Tommy looked as if she'd accused him of child molesting. She dropped his shoes under his nose. 'Must be getting cold down there, eh Tommy? Here, get up and park your arse in the bog and we'll discuss terms.'

'Thanks, Maeve,' he said, genuinely grateful. She wasn't a bad old piss-ant after all.

When he was settled in the toilet stall inspecting the damage to his clothing and relocating his jaw she said, 'If the tip pays off Janet gets fifty percent.' He began to protest but she silenced him with a scowl. 'Then fifty percent of your winnings until you've paid back what you owe her – plus costs.'

'Jesus, Maeve, I got other people I owe.'

'No kidding. Tell me their names, I'll have a word.'

'Would you, Maeve?' he asked, eagerly.

'Get y'hand off it, Tommy,' she said, dryly. 'Now. The details. Horse? Race? And remember this: I know the strapper. More important, he knows me.' She put her eyes right on his and rammed them against the back of their sockets with her glare. Tommy felt any chance of getting out of this cheaply evaporate. 'And even more importantly, Tommy, I know where you live.'

Well, there you go, the fix was in. Maeve in the trifecta. He sat staring at the stained, cracked floor tiles. 'Howja know I was here this morning?' he asked.

'How d'you know a gorilla shits in the mist?'

He looked up with heavy-lidded eyes and a doleful grin. 'What'd I do to deserve this?'

'Now you know why mother taught you to be a cunt, Tommy. She meant you for someone 'xactly like me.'

As Maeve Maguffin drove to her little place in Brunswick for break-fast, Etta James's version of 'At Last' was played on the ABC. She knew how it would affect her but she couldn't bring herself to turn it off. She never could. And it always reminded her of the blonde sergeant. Every-fucking-thing reminded her of the blonde sergeant: that most disastrous misreading of the signs in a long and execrable history of misreading signs that began when she was fourteen. Why was she, Maeve Maguffin, who was so fucking good at sussing character and motive in the criminal underclasses, so fucking inept when her heart was involved? Jesus, she couldn't even tell if the object of her desire was gay or not! Christ, that sergeant was beautiful.

The café's façade looked like an abandoned laundrette that even graffiti artists shunned. But the food was so good she salivated every time she passed an abandoned laundrette. She was hunkered down behind her newspaper in her warm corner trying to slip her coffee a wake-up call with a wee dram from her hip flask, when she heard a chair scrape the floor on the other side of her table. She allowed the newspaper to droop as she prepared to snarl across the top of it. At first she didn't recognise the intruder. Sunlight reflecting into the café from the wet road and buildings was causing a glare that threw him into sharp silhouette.

'G'day, Senior Constable Maguffin,' he said.

He always said that. He still thought of her as a cop – or pretended to – even if no one else did. She leaned back, sliding the flask surreptitiously into a pocket below table level.

'Oh, it's kiddie-cop,' she said flatly. She'd been his first partner when he dropped off the Academy assembly line, legs all wobbly and pinfeathers gummed to his body. She'd taught him everything he knew about the streets.

They sat staring at each other for a long time. He was the only one who could hold her baleful stare for any length of time. It was an unacknowledged game they played, to see who blinked first. A waitress came with her breakfast and to take his order so they could both withdraw from the field with honour.

'What do you want?' she said as she cut into her eggs benedict.

'I want you back on the wagon,' he said. If the loaded fork hesitated on the way to her mouth it was virtually undetectable. 'I have a job and you'll need your wits about you.'

'I'm not interested in the scraps from your table.'

'I wouldn't offer them. This is one I can't do. I'm too well known by the subject.'

'Who?'

'Sharon Kitchen.'

'Ben Bovell's squeeze?'

'She know you?'

'Nup. Lately, she's been on the box a bit.'

He nodded, satisfied.

'You're the mysterious "friend who didn't want to be named who helped police with negotiations"?' She semaphored quotation marks with her knife and fork.

He nodded again.

'What do you think she's done?'

'I hope she's as clean as a fresh coat of Teflon.'

She chewed some more egg. 'Should I use harsh abrasives?'

'As much as needed to test the warranty.'

'You're almost sexy when you talk like that,' said Maeve.

'I know what women want,' he said with all the sincerity of a chocolate-coated Ryvita.

11

The Rose Garden was a brothel.

And Rose Garden – christened Rose Garden Smith, truncated for professional reasons – was a madam.

Rose was the madam of The Rose Garden and co-owner of The Rose Garden and its sister establishment The Crimson Grotto. Rose had been a whore for more than two quarters of her life and a madam for about its last quarter. She and her silent partner owned fifty percent each of Rose Bed Enterprises, which consisted of the two brothels, a thriving escort service facilitated through the front desk of The Rose Garden, miscellaneous real estate and a share portfolio. The girls called him Big Boss and her Little Boss. It was a reference to size not power, but it was a sobriquet never uttered within Rose's hearing.

When Rose first became a madam and a partner in The Rose Garden her share was a mere twenty percent. Her first partner in business, who'd retained the lion's share, had needed her for a front otherwise her portion would have been much smaller. Her first partner was a man she feared.

Her present partner was a man she loved. This was recognised – and discreetly acknowledged – by all those who worked at The Rose Garden, save Rose herself and the object of her sublimated affection. Perhaps Rose resisted conscious recognition of her feelings because she was old enough to be her partner's mother.

It was her present partner who was the subject of her present conversation.

Rose was in her office at The Rose Garden talking to Charlotte O'Brien. Charlotte was one of the brothel's receptionists. She had worked here for – what? Rose tried to remember – it must be at least two years. Rose had thought Charlotte wouldn't last two days when she hired her. She'd been very young, naive and wide-eyed then. She was still young and naive, but not so wide-eyed.

Charlotte had a crush on her employer. Not Rose, her partner. She'd held this crush from the moment she laid eyes on him two years before.

Unfortunately, if he was too young for Rose, he was too old for Charlotte, and in more than just years. Although it was clear to everyone else at The Rose Garden that any feelings he returned were paternal in nature, Charlotte remained steadfast and maintained her romantic affection.

And that was the issue at the heart of the present exchange.

Charlotte sniffed loudly and Rose stripped another two or three tissues from the box and handed them to her. She received a soggy wad of paper pulp in exchange.

'Thank you, Charlotte,' Rose said dryly.

''S okay, Rose,' Charlotte said damply.

Rose sat and waited until Charlotte got her moisture under control. She was uncomfortable with this motherly role. Her style was more Dean of Women or dominatrix.

Charlotte breathed a deep sob. 'I thought he was such a kind man,' she said sorrowfully.

'Kind? No he's not a kind man, Charlotte, never that,' said Rose. Charlotte looked at her with mild surprise. She'd expected Rose to defend him. She wanted Rose to defend him. 'The other side of the "kind" coin is "cruel",' Rose continued gently – for Rose. 'He's not cruel.' Charlotte's wet gaze held on Rose and her head moved in agreement. 'He's a ruthless man, Charlotte. The other side of that coin is compassion. That's a currency I prefer to carry in my purse.'

'It wasn't what he did,' snuffled Charlotte. 'It was what he said. When he did it.'

'What was that?'

'Wax on, wax off. When he hit them. That's what scared me. It was the way he said it – like a joke.'

'Wax on, wax off?' Rose was puzzled.

'It's from an old movie,' Charlotte said blowing her nose. '*The Karate Kid*. I've seen it on television.'

Rose was still puzzled. She didn't understand the reference. She didn't watch much television. 'You'd better tell me the whole story, right from the beginning,' she said.

'What, *The Karate Kid*?'

'Charlotte,' Rose groaned.

'Sorry,' Charlotte sniffed.

They had come into The Rose Garden somewhere around eleven the previous evening. There were two of them. They were very young. It was difficult to judge their ages. They were very big boys. Charlotte placed them in their late teens, early twenties at the most. Their clothes were sloppily casual with expensive brands. They swaggered and spoke loudly with the braggadocio of the novice or what the girls called 'the tourist'. The curious kid or Rotarian, wound up by their mates, come to ogle, look but not touch, to exit sniggering, feeling sophisticated and superior. Saturday night fever.

Charlotte was on the phone arranging an escort date for an interstate politician. She smiled her most winning professional smile – in Charlotte's case, indistinguishable from her real one – pushed a copy of the house 'menu' across the desk towards them and raised one finger to indicate she would be with them in a minute. They took the menu and walked away from the desk perusing it with sotto voce whoops and guffaws and making dirty little schoolboy sounds. They quickly became bored with that and one wandered towards a door from which trickled the sound of a piano; the other turned and stared intently at Charlotte. Something about his expression made her feel uneasy, exposed. She turned her back on his gaze as she finalised the details with the pollie's minder. When she looked back the reception area was empty.

Rose liked to call the room where the workers and their clients made first contact 'the parlour'. It was a large dark wood and leather room of soft colours, soft furnishings, low tables and low lighting. There was a bar at one end where the girls could treat their clients to liquor and coffee. The coffee was free, the price of the liquor was added to the price on the menu. There was a large flatscreen TV high on one wall at the bar end, and a glossy black upright piano near a small low stage at its opposite. A man with blond hair sat at the piano playing 'Honeysuckle Rose'. Neither of the two young newcomers could have identified the song: it was just some old shit.

There were two or three fully-clad males in the room and a half dozen or so females in various stages of undress. A redhead in a black baby-doll negligee sat by the piano sipping coffee and watching the pianist's hands move over the keys.

'Shit,' said one of the boys. 'Looks just like one of the old man's business meetings.'

'Bit of a fuckin' disappointment, eh Ray?' said the other.

'Seen one fuckin' whorehouse, you've seen 'em all,' said Ray.

'Seen one fuckin' whore, you've seen 'em all,' said the other.

They spoke loudly intending the room to hear. The male clients turned and stared. The boys mugged goggle-eyed faces at them. Other than a brief glance, the girls paid scant attention. The piano player seemed not to have heard at all. They sniggered at their wit and punched each other lightly in self-congratulation.

Charlotte appeared at the parlour door and sized up the situation. She couldn't smell booze, but suspected they'd been popping something.

'Gentlemen,' she said crisply but sweetly. 'I'm sorry to keep you waiting, if you'll come with me? We like to get the financial side out of the way first. Then you can relax and enjoy the evening. Have you had a good look at the menu? Cash or credit?' She turned her smile on them and tripped it to high beam. Usually the threat of getting down to business and the mention of money was enough to scare the tourists off.

They turned to face her. They were built like ruckmen who'd been ducking training. She felt the unsettling stare of the dark one on her again. He was handsome in a steak and eggs sort of way, and now she noticed the pocks of old acne.

'Gentlemen?' she prompted, the cheery professionalism of her voice masking her growing disquiet. She was distantly aware that 'Honeysuckle Rose' had segued into 'Your Feet's Too Big'.

'Are you on the menu?' the dark one asked and the pink tip of his tongue slipped wetly along his fleshy lips.

She'd heard this question before and learned to deal with it. But the tongue gesture shocked Charlotte because she was sure it was an unconscious one. If he had pantomimed licking his lips it would have been ludicrous, adolescent.

'No!' she said more abruptly than she should have. She heard herself and she sounded alarmed, not in control. 'No, I'm the receptionist I'm not a … a sex worker.'

'Oooh, Chas, I reckon we've got fresh meat.' He reached into his jacket and pulled out a wallet. He fanned it open to show an array of credit cards. 'Fetch the boss. I wanna fuck you, baby, and I can pay whatever he wants.'

Charlotte realised the music had stopped. There was a sudden loud chord. Everyone looked towards the piano. The pianist was sitting facing the room; he had a friendly smile on his lips.

'Gentlemen,' he said. 'I can see you aren't familiar with the rules in an establishment like this.'

'Shit, Ray, it talks,' said Chas.

'One of the rules,' said the piano player, ignoring him, 'is that, ultimately, it's ladies' choice. If a lady doesn't want to take you upstairs she doesn't have to.'

The two men regarded him indulgently with arrogant eyes.

'Does anyone want to entertain these gentlemen?' the pianist asked the room. All the girls flicked their eyes over the two, their expressions deadpan. Charlotte noticed Yasmin had one hand behind the bar. There was a button there. There was a similar one behind the reception desk. 'So you see, gentlemen, there's no point in your lingering.'

Chas's and Ray's smiles were twisting into sneers.

'You want to fuckin' try and throw us out, Elton?' said Ray.

The pianist shook his head and turned back to the keyboard. Ray and Chas looked at each other as if they were trying to work out if this was a sign of cowardice or contempt. Before they could make up their minds there was another voice in the room.

'That's my job, fellas.'

The man in the doorway looked like a huge skittle in a suit. But one that only a wrecking ball could knock over. His skull had been dipped in black shoe polish and buffed to a shine. His smooth brow was pinched in an expression of mild perplexity and his gaze held Ray and Chas as if they were the answer to Life, the Universe and Everything. He wasn't very tall but he seemed to fill the doorway.

'There's two of us, short arse,' Ray said.

Skittle man stepped forward so that they shielded him from the eyes of the others in the room. He opened his coat just enough to give them an exclusive view of what was under his armpit. 'There's two o'me too,' he said and stepped back to let them pass through the door.

Ray looked back at Charlotte. 'I still wanna fuck you,' he said. Skittle man nudged him through the door.

'Are you okay, Charlotte?' the pianist asked gently as he approached.

'I'm fine thanks, Mr E.'

'You handled that well,' said Mr E, the pianist.

The girls gathered around praising and patting her. The redhead hugged her and said, 'Goodonya, Charlie.'

'Would you like to go home early?' asked Mr E, the pianist, Rose's partner and Charlotte's other employer. 'Yasmin can fill in at the desk.'

She shook her head. Then the phone rang. 'I'll get it,' she said and hurried back to reception.

Rose interrupted Charlotte's story. 'Had David just dropped in?'

'No. Mr E had been playing the piano all evening. Mostly Blues and stuff. I think the girls would have liked something livelier. He was in an odd mood.'

Rose couldn't fathom why Charlotte persisted in calling him 'Mr E'. All the girls called him David. 'And he stayed to walk you home?'

'He told me to take a taxi and charge it. Apparently he was very upset when he found out I was walking.' Charlotte had difficulty disguising her pleasure at this. 'Tess said he just grabbed his coat and bolted after me.'

Charlotte had been standing at the entrance to the park. It was reasonably well lit and normally she would cut diagonally across it. But tonight she hesitated. She was trying to convince herself that she was being silly, that the events of the evening had unsettled her and stirred shadows in her imagination, when she heard the running footsteps. At first that sound scared her more than the park, then she saw the blond head bobbing under a street lamp and heard her name. She felt a thrill tingle through various unmentionable parts. He'd run after her!

The mist of his breath haloed around his head as he reached her. 'Disobeying a direct order from the boss, I should ask Rose to dock your pay,' he said, showing scant sign of his exertions.

Charlotte giggled and silently upbraided herself for doing so.

'Where do we go from here?'

He's going to walk me home, Charlotte squealed in her mind. 'I usually go through the park,' she said. 'It's quicker.'

He looked into the darkness under the trees, then turned to her. 'It's cold. Best take that route tonight.'

As they started on the path that curled between the shrubbery he said, 'Why are you working at The Rose Garden, Charlotte?'

She held a long shrug. Her collar brushed her ears. 'I was desperate for a job, but it was an accident really,' she said, wondering if she should tell a story that made her appear stupid. 'I thought I was being interviewed for something else. I was writing down the details for so many jobs – and you know, my eyes.' Charlotte was wearing contacts now, but the lenses of her glasses were thicker than the Antarctic ice shelf. 'I had the wrong phone number.' She could see him smiling in the faint light. 'And then – at first – it was … curiosity I suppose. But I got to like the girls, and it was interesting, and it pays well, and, and I've got good bosses.' The last was almost whispered. She blushed in the shadow of her upturned collar.

'Everything a girl could want,' he said.

About midway through the park there was a large square of lawn bounded on two adjacent sides by a high, dense hedge. Sulphurous light from the goose-necked security lamps reached here, but the shadows were long. The path looped across the grass into the dark elbow of the hedge. It was prudent, despite the wetness of the grass, to cut across the neck of the loop and back onto the path at the far end of the hedge. But her escort followed the path into the shadows. Charlotte's heart fluttered in amorous fear and anticipation. But he strolled beside her with his hands in the pockets of his jacket.

As the path approached the end of the hedge a dark figure stepped onto it, legs spread, blocking their way. Its shadow cut a dark rift between them. Charlotte sucked in a sharp breath, almost choking on the chill air.

'Well, i'n' this a surprise,' said Ray. 'The cock teaser and the ivory tickler out for a bit of nookie.'

Her eyes on Ray, Charlotte instinctively shrunk into the lee of her companion, but he moved away, stranding her like a chicken in the road. She stared at him, shocked. He had removed his hands from his pockets and was pulling on kid-leather gloves. He was turned side-on to Ray and he casually glanced to his left. His breath smoked from his lips and dissolved in the night. Charlotte was certain her eyes, not her most reliable organs, betrayed her again. She thought she saw him smile. She snapped a panicky glance over her shoulder. Chas stood in the path a few metres behind.

'The beds upstairs musta been fully booked, eh, Chas?' Ray took a pace forward and snarled. 'We'll look after the slut's needs, Elton.'

'Fuck off or you won't able to tickle your dick with what's left of your fingers,' Chas chimed in.

Charlotte was staring at Mr E. Her chest was being squeezed like a toothpaste tube in a fist. She could feel her jaw going up and down but no words came. Her erstwhile protector seemed more interested in the smooth fit of his gloves than the drama unfolding around them. His eyes came up and gripped hers. They were calm and cool and, even in the subdued light, blue.

'You go on home,' he said. 'I'll take care of this.' He stepped to the middle of the path, facing Ray.

'Watch her,' Ray growled to Chas and propelled himself swaggeringly at the man before him.

He was as tall as Mr E and much heavier. The punch he launched might have shattered bone had it landed. Ray grunted as the ball of knuckle and flesh at the end of his arm struck air and he was wrenched forward by its force: a shotputter who forgot to let go. His target pirouetted like a weather-cock spinning in the slipstream of the blow. 'Wax on,' he said as his right leg came up, around and rammed out. Charlotte heard a dull crack, and Ray screamed.

She was aware of Chas advancing on her, but she couldn't move. An icy fascination welded her to the spot. 'Jesus fuck,' Chas hissed at her ear and swerved away towards the cry. Then he baulked abruptly, caught in a limbo of anger and fear. He stared helplessly at his friend, who writhed on the ground spitting expletives and groaning in pain. Charlotte watched as Mr E moved with insolent leisure behind Chas. By the time Ray's mate had reasoned that discretion was preferable to valour the path of his retreat was cut. Chas turned and froze when he saw it. He swayed jerkily from side to side like a cobra that knows the mongoose has his measure.

'Kill the cunt!' Ray chewed through his agony.

And Chas uttered a strangled war cry and swung an arm like a mace.

Charlotte clenched her eyes and the sounds of 'Wax off,' the wet snap of bone and Chas's pain filled her ears.

'Are you alright?' she heard and opened her eyes. He stood between two contorted figures that moaned on the grass. His face bore an expression of concern.

'I'm okay,' she lied, hugging her chest, her body now colder than the night.

He turned and bent over Ray, who cringed. He searched through his clothes then moved to Chas who whimpered a feeble, wordless plea. When he straightened he held their wallets. He took a notebook from his pocket and wrote details from each wallet, then tucked them back in the clothes of the cowering men. 'Have you got a mobile?' Ray mumbled something. When he stood he had a phone in his hand; he thumbed the keys as he walked along the path a few paces. He spoke a few words, then asked Charlotte the names of the two streets at the nearest corner.

'Raymond, Charles, I know your names and where you live,' he said tossing the phone to Ray. 'It's a small world, Charles. Is your father still in real estate? Or have they caught on to his scam?' Chas swore weakly. 'Gentlemen, your names and faces will be circulated to every brothel in this city. And if I find myself downwind of you again, I remind you that you have three more limbs and a neck.' He walked over and heaved a bleating Chas to his feet. 'A taxi's on its way. Help your friend up.'

'I gotta fuckin' broken arm,' grizzled Chas.

'You have a spare, Charles. Don't worry, I'll share the burden.'

Tears had overwhelmed Charlotte again.

'You left them on the corner of the park waiting for a taxi?' asked Rose.

Charlotte nodded, holding a tissue to her nose. 'He was worried about me. I'd started to shiver and I couldn't stop. Shock, he said.' Salty runnels glistened on her cheeks. 'I don't know what to do, Rose. I think I'm frightened of him now.'

'Charlotte,' Rose said gently. 'There were two men. He couldn't fight by Marquis of Queensberry rules. It could easily have got out of hand and then what might have happened to you?'

'He broke bones, Rose. It was like … like something in the Bible. He … he *smote* them.'

'Charlotte,' said Rose, and the mother was gone from her voice. 'What do you think the Knight on the White Charger does after he finishes singing love songs beneath your balcony?' She didn't wait for an answer. 'He rides out and smites your enemies. He slays the Dragon and cleaves the Black Knight in twain. And they die in agony in pools of blood.' She patted Charlotte's thigh and her voice softened. 'Our knight expects no favours of us. That's why the girls in this house feel safe.'

The eyes that Charlotte turned on Rose were forlorn pools in the blasted moor of her face. 'Rose … Rose … it was my fault.'

House-mistress Rose was in charge again. 'Tosh! Nothing was your fault, Charlotte!' Each word was a nail driven to the head with a single blow. 'It's their testosterone and they should control it!'

<h1 style="text-align:center">12</h1>

The sky was the barrel of a black, bottomless well dusted with ice crystals. Rose squinted up through the small fogs of her breath. There were chinks of light in the top floor windows. He was at home and awake. The only other lights in the building shone from the first floor and the ground-level shopfront to the refuge for street kids. She hadn't been here before tonight – the sanctum sanctorum. She didn't know anyone who had crossed the threshold. If he entertained visitors, she'd heard, it was in the coffee shop behind her.

An empty W-class tram rattled past with 'Depot' displayed as its destination. She crossed the road. How to gain access was the immediate question. The Vietnamese newsagency, the tattoo and body piercing shop Pics 'n' Pins, and the adult bookshop A Good Hard Read, were all in darkness. It was late Sunday night.

An adolescent girl dressed, dyed and painted in black was slouching in the doorway of the refuge. The visible parts of her body looked like they'd caught all the shrapnel from an exploding hardware store. Wordlessly, she directed Rose around the corner with an abrupt thumb and a lazy roll of her head.

Rose found the doorway on the narrow side street. She felt a rare stab of apprehension as she pressed the button. If he was surprised to hear her voice he didn't show it. He buzzed her up. She climbed the narrow staircase to the top floor. There was a sign stating 'David Edge, Research Consultant' on the door facing the top of the stairs. He stood, hip cocked, backlit in an open doorway at the other end of the landing.

'G'd evening, Rose,' he said, stepping back to draw her through the door. 'To what do I owe?'

'I apologise for the intrusion, David,' she said as her eyes swept the room she'd entered. It was a large room but somehow cosy. Its atmosphere was warm and comfortable. The furnishings were spare but not sparse. There were no sets or suites, just a colourful mix and match. Earth colours, rusts, ochres and greens. One wall was bookshelves from floor to ceiling. The TV, audio equipment and a venerable upright piano lined up along the opposite wall. The end wall was taken up with the windows, heavily draped, that overlooked the street. At the other end of the room was a huge bench that divided the room from the kitchen beyond. Orchestral music was swelling from small speakers high in the corners. 'And for the late hour,' she added. 'I won't keep you long.'

'It's okay. I was relaxing after a class,' he said as he took her long coat and hung it on a tall bentwood stand to the left of the door.

'Class?'

'I run survival skills classes for the kids downstairs. You've got to work to their hours – catch 'em when you can.'

'Survival skills?'

'Self defence and how to manage cops,' he said with a wry twist of the lips.

She walked over and smoothed her palm over the bench top. Tasmanian oak: its grain like dark currents snaking lazily in the tallowed depths of still water. 'Nice,' she said.

'Can I get you something to drink?' He had a half glass of red wine in his hand.

'Nothing alcoholic, thank you. I'm driving.' It occurred to her that she had never seen him drink. She'd only ever observed him pretending at leisure, while actually working, perhaps holding a glass in his hand but never sipping from it. He didn't drink when he worked. And he was the only one who knew exactly what his work was – and its hours.

'Take a seat,' he said as strode into the kitchen. 'Tea, coffee? A tour of the ancestral home?'

'Tea.' She lowered herself into a large greenish leather armchair.

'Indian, Chinese, Australian, green, black, herbal?'

'Do you have any chamomile?'

'Chamomile it is,' he said as he opened a cupboard. 'There's a remote on the table if you want to turn the music down.'

'Mahler?' she asked.

'*The Titan.*'

When he brought her tea he settled himself, reclining, on the long dark red couch, a dusky orange cushion behind his shoulders, his wine glass on the floor beside him. He studied Rose lazily, waiting for her to speak. She took a sip of her tea, and took his measure over the rim of her cup.

'Are you drunk, David?' she asked. Rose had no time for social niceties and the folderol of manners.

The small dimple in his left cheek twitched into a comma. He waved a hand at a bottle of Yarra Valley Pinot on the low, time-pitted and patinaed blackwood table between them. It was still half full. 'No, Rose,' he said. 'I can't afford to get drunk. Lower my inhibitions and God knows what will jump over them and run loose in the world.'

Rose had surprisingly smooth skin for a woman of her years. She had protected it her entire life from the sun and other conspirers with time. When she frowned it was – almost shockingly – obvious.

'It's okay. I'm not depressed. Just having a drink and a think.' He raised the glass to his lips.

'Is it Ben Bovell?' He glanced at her but didn't answer. 'How is he?' she asked.

He took another sip of his wine before he answered. 'Critical. They removed the bullet fragment from his spine but couldn't do much else for him.'

Rose looked into the cup nursed in her lap. 'Paraplegic?'

'It seems he'll be able to breathe without help.'

They sat in silent contemplation of his words for a while, then she said, 'Benny isn't your responsibility.'

'Then whose?'

She had no answer. She noticed his eyes drift to a large manila envelope lying open on the table next to a scatter of books with creaky academic titles. It held something about the size of a bar of soap. A DVD case lay across the flap. She thought the title was *The Killers* – but hoped it was her imagination.

'It's about Charlotte,' she said. His eyes flicked up to engage hers. 'Is that why you punished those boys? Because you couldn't save Benny?'

'You should go back to Mills and Boon, Rose,' he said, grinning. 'Those psychology books will rot your brain.' The nature of their respective reading habits was a running gag. Rose read anything that sandwiched words between two covers.

'I understand the necessity to incapacitate the first one as quickly as possible,' said Rose without smiling. 'But breaking the second boy's arm seems bloody-minded.'

He didn't respond. He swirled the wine slowly in the glass, its sanguine light rippled under his chin. She thought of buttercups and the love of butter.

'And taking her through the park? I won't have one of my girls used as a tethered goat, David.' She waited, still no response. 'How did you know?'

'I didn't know,' he said at last. 'The attention one paid Charlotte worried me. I had a … a foreboding. I didn't *know* until Ray stepped out in front of us. He couldn't have got to that point before us if he'd been following. They must have been watching the Garden for some time and learned the route Charlotte took home. They may have been watching other girls.' He took a sip of his wine. 'I think they wanted to experiment in rape. They thought they could do it to a prostitute and get away with it. They imagined a pro wouldn't go to the police and if she did the cops wouldn't care. I think they also believed they'd be raping something worthless and so their conscience wouldn't bother them.'

A hot, bristling ball had been pushing up into her chest cavity since she spoke to Charlotte; now Rose felt it melting away.

'I crossed the park because – if they were around – it was the only chance to draw them out. Before it was too late.' He gave a small sad grimace. 'I'm sorry about Charlotte.'

'She'll survive. But you may have lost a devotee.'

'Probably for the best.'

'Whose best?' As his lips pressed a sardonic hook, she added, 'A girl like that could be your salvation.'

'No salvation for me, Rose.' He sipped his wine. 'And broken bones? I think they'll find they're severe dislocations.' He ignored her let's-not-split-hairs expression. 'They both had to suffer pain and fear, Rose. It might be enough to give them pause. The alternative was to let them assault Charlotte, then the police could act.' He sipped some wine. 'They had to be … diminished.'

'Wax on, wax off?'

He smiled ruefully. 'I did enjoy it more than I ought. It was about Ben. A bit.'

'You're such a good detective, David.' There was criticism implicit in the flat statement. Rose, like many others, thought he was wasting his talents. 'I don't know how you do it. Those lateral leaps of logic or intuitive insights. Creative anticipation – or whatever the trick is.'

He stared sadly into the red dregs staining his glass. 'The trick is to imagine the worst a human being might do. The trick to *that* is to imagine the worst that *I* might do.'

'You're not a bad man, David.'

'Ah. Yes I am, Rose.' A small smile. 'And I'm a good man too. But then, aren't we all?'

Rose had no ready reply to that. 'Is this really the ancestral home?' she asked eventually.

He nodded. 'My grandmother lived here. Her father owned half the block. She left this building to me.'

'And you gave it away? To street kids?'

'More or less.'

She sank back into her chair and let Mahler flow over her. 'I'll take the tour when I finish my tea,' she said.

13

The house was a single-storey, double-fronted terrace house, with a narrow garden and a picket fence. It was painted in bright colours and looked like something Noddy might contract from Bob the Builder. It didn't look like something the man she met in the pub would inhabit.

Carol pushed open the neat picket gate. It swung without a squeak. She walked up the short brick path and stepped onto the decorative tiles of the verandah. They looked to be the same vintage as the house. So did the ornate brass knocker. When the door opened in swift response to her knock she had the feeling her approach had been observed.

She didn't know what she'd expected. The ebullient but enigmatic Detective Sergeant Marks had left her with the impression she would be confronting her doppelganger when she finally met his wife, the other Carol. Physically at least, nothing was further from the fact.

She, Carol Porter, was average height, maybe shading toward the shorter end of the range. Her hair was auburn, maybe shading toward the redder end of the spectrum. Her eyes were green, shading to deep emerald. And, as had been established on more occasions than she cared to count, she had the face and figure of a soap opera soubrette. Unfortunately.

Carol Marks was tall, close to one hundred and ninety centimetres Carol Porter guessed. She was whippet lean with the taut, stringy gauntness of a long distance runner, or an alcoholic who is narrowly prevailing in an endless war of attrition. Her smooth skin vacuum-sealed the sinew, muscle and bone of her face. It was almost translucent over the strong ridges of her brow and nose and cheeks. A fine intaglio around her eyes rippled into a fan of deep crinkles when she smiled. Her hair was crimped and fine and cut close, a silver skullcap burnished on her head. At first Carol thought she was face to face with the first platinum blonde she'd ever met. Then she discerned the silver threads amongst the gold – far outnumbering the gold. Carol Marks was greying prematurely.

Hers was a face that wouldn't be described as beautiful or pretty when she was Carol Porter's age, but was growing handsome with the years. It was a face that was striking, a subtle aesthetic alchemy of complexion, hair and her eyes. Her eyes were deep violet. Her wide mouth stretched in a smile that disappeared into deep furrows cutting an arc from where the short blade of her nose flared. When the smile faded the lines etching her face dissolved like a stagelight illusion. But at the moment the smile was still there.

'The other Carol I presume,' Carol Marks said to Carol Porter. She wore faded jeans and a huge yellow woollen jumper that might have been one of her husband's. It bunched in thick folds around her wrists and hung off one shoulder revealing a black bra strap. She hitched it up, thrust out a long arm and took her visitor's hand. She had a firm grip. 'Come in, come in,' she added, stepping back and drawing Carol across the threshold. 'The place is a mess,' she said as Carol followed her down the hallway. 'But then it always is.'

It didn't look particularly messy to Carol, just kicking back in a comfortable disorder. It was cosily warm and smelt like fresh bread. The interior was just as colourful as the exterior but the combinations of hue were more subtle and restful. They passed down the dark hall, through a bright skylit open area with a glistening kitchen on one side and a lived-in living room on the other, and emerged into a small glassed-in area with cane furniture, cushions in primary colours, a jungle of flamboyant plants and a stone-flagged floor. It faced north and the rays of the sun turned it into a bio-slab of the Kimberley. Thank God, thought one of the Carols, natural warmth at last.

There was a round glass-topped table laid out for afternoon tea. 'Let me take your coat,' said her hostess. 'Hmm. Bit chilly for you down here?' she added, appraising the coat. 'Coffee? Tea?'

'Love some coffee,' said Carol, as she shrugged off her outer layer.

'I hope you like blueberry muffins,' said the other Carol and she and the coat disappeared back into the house. 'Got some in the oven. Should be ready.'

'Yum!' Carol called after her. She wandered to the glass-paned wall. The garden looked like a bush block that was yet to be cleared for development. There could be a lost tribe living in there.

'Here we are,' she heard from behind. She'd been daydreaming, soaking up the sun, and had lost track of time. Her hostess was unloading a plunger of coffee and a steaming plate of huge muffins from a tray onto the table. She made her way over and sat facing the sun.

'Well,' breathed Carol Marks as she settled in the chair opposite. She had placed her body to take advantage of the sun also, but angled obliquely toward her guest. She turned her face to the woman across the table and placed her violet gaze very deliberately on Carol.

'Thank you very much for giving me your time,' said Carol. 'Neville said you wouldn't mind. I hope that's true.'

The face opposite crinkled again. 'Skid was tickled that I agreed,' she said. 'Have a muffin.'

'Skid?' queried Carol through an eruption of steam, as she cut into the muffin.

'The academy mob from our intake call Nev that.'

'Why was he so pleased about you speaking to me? Have you avoided shop talk since you retired?'

'I didn't retire.' Carol Marks's face was smooth as marble. 'I was invalided out.'

'Oh, I'm sorry.' So the reformed alcoholic observation was spot-on, Carol Porter thought complacently.

'I'm schizophrenic,' her hostess stated, her voice as flat as tarmac. Before her guest could react she added, 'We seem to have it under control at the moment. I haven't had a psychotic episode in over a year. Your visit is a bit of a test. In the past I haven't reacted well to reminders of my former life. That's why Skid was pleased: it meant I felt strong. But,' she leaned over and pushed down the plunger on the coffeepot, 'I'm schizophrenic. That's the context of this information you're getting. It's only fair that you know.' She picked up the pot and began pouring. As she slid the full cup across she smiled. 'It helps me too, if it's out on the table. I'll leave the milk and sugar to you.'

Well, stick that up your prim little ego, clever boots. Carol didn't know what to say in response to the frankness. She decided the woman across the table sought neither comment nor sympathy. 'I don't think there's any reason to doubt the reliability of the witness.' She smiled and took a sip of coffee. 'Hmm, good.'

Then the other Carol took her by surprise again.

'What is it that interests you so much about this sordid affair?' she asked, fixing her with those violet lights. 'Is it the case, the crime, the criminal – or the cop?' She took a large bite out of her muffin, chewed and mumbled between squirrel cheeks. 'Or do you just want to be top of the class?'

'Well,' Carol said, a little too defensively. 'They're all part and parcel aren't they?' But she didn't think the violet eyes were fooled.

Carol Marks's lips tweaked in a thin, wise smile. 'You're going to all this trouble so that in your paper you can argue the contract killer theory as an equally viable solution, dazzle them with your analytical brilliance, and take big fat credits home to WA that will justify their faith in you?'

'Something like that.' When she heard it from her namesake's mouth, as a raison d'etre, it did sound a little reedy.

The other Carol's smile stretched wider and her eyes glittered with a crystalline sharpness. 'You know the murder statistics of course,' she said. 'Most murders are committed by someone who knows the victim. They're the easy ones. We solve almost all of them. Even if we can't get enough material evidence to make a case in court, we usually know who did it. Random, motiveless killing is harder. But it's usually uncontrolled, unplanned, sloppy, and nine times out of ten someone dobs the killer in.

Underworld killings?' She shrugged. 'Well, that's more a case of who we know than what we know.' She paused to sip her coffee.

Carol watched her eyes over the rim of her cup and said nothing. She knew she was rehearsing this as a prologue to something else. And she kept saying 'we'.

'Then there's our serial killer. Apparently random, if we can't detect the pattern. Nothing but a symbolic connection to the victim, and then, only in the fantasies of the killer. The best we can hope for is that he wants to get caught or we get lucky. We have to wait until he's killed so many that he becomes over-confident, someone who knows him smells a rat, or we accumulate enough data to identify or anticipate him.' She took another muffin from the pile and began to pull it gently apart, popping bite-sized pieces in her mouth. 'There are so few serial killings in this country that they hardly register as a statistic.' She popped another piece of muffin. 'Of course, contract killings aren't top of the pops either.'

Carol was doing a detective training course, she felt a sudden urge to show and tell. 'Two percent of total murders,' she said a little hurriedly. 'According to recent research,' she added feebly, as is if in apology for interrupting. The other Carol just smiled at her. 'There's between about seven and ten contracts a year in this country.' There was still no response from across the table. She ploughed on. Much too breathlessly, she noticed. 'Most of those aren't cool professional hits. They're usually crimes of passion. Someone in a broken relationship hires an amateur – occasionally a professional – to knock off a partner or the ex or the third party. Only about five contract killings per year are successfully completed. They're usually professional ones.'

'So,' said her hostess. 'You would argue that the statistics favour a "contract killer" hypothesis over a "serial killer" hypothesis in the Jogger Murders case?' She flipped another bit of muffin, chewed, smiled, and said, 'Interesting.'

Carol began to wonder about her motives. Was the case an itch this woman could no longer reach? And was this tête-à-tête an audition for the role of back scratcher? If it was, Carol Marks's next words implied that she'd won the part.

'They weren't treated as serial killings until the fourth murder. That's when we got involved,' she began. She sounded like an officer launching a briefing.

'Fourth?' Carol interrupted. 'I thought there were only three.'

'Officially, yes. But we – the three of us in Davy's little group – always thought of it as four. Davy postulated that another, earlier, murder was part of the picture. He suggested that it was … practice.' She faltered as if challenged by some memory or association. 'A sort of dry run.' Her smile was narrow and bleak. Her eyes were no longer cut-and-polished amethyst but dull stone. Her head tossed as if to shake cobwebs away then she leaned forward in her chair, renewed.

'To begin at the beginning,' she said. 'Davy – Skid said you've met him?' Carol nodded. 'Davy was the lead on the third – or fourth – murder. Once the similarity to the others was established, and they were officially connected and recognised as serial killings, a taskforce was established. Davy and the detectives investigating the other murders were subsumed into it under Bruce Tolliday, a senior sergeant. Bruce was plodding, but always well organised, very careful, very thorough. You probably gathered that when you read his report. He was far from persuaded by Davy's theory, but he held a high opinion of his ability, and Bruce wasn't one to let a stone remain unturned. He gave Davy the green light to pursue his own line of inquiry and allowed him a couple of uniforms for the legwork. That's where we came in, Jac and me.'

'Jack?'

'Jac, Jacinta McCluskey. Eyes like yours. Curly, red hair, freckles. She and Davy had been a bit of an item at the Academy. Of course, that was before the Counsel for the Defence.' Seeing Carol's mild puzzlement she flipped a hand in dismissal. 'Ask later. Whole other story. Anyhow, we were handpicked because Davy knew we were on his wave-length.'

'What I don't understand,' said Carol. 'There's only a broad outline in the report of your investigation, no details. Was it just a matter of here's another possible explanation that fits the evidence and we should test it? Or was there a specific clue of some kind? What was the catalyst?'

'Apart from statistics?' Her hostess grinned teasingly. Carol grinned back. 'But you're right. The statistics do support the minority report. I'll get some more coffee.' And was out of her chair before Carol could decline.

'The clues,' Carol Marks said, when she strode back into the room with a new brew. 'It was more a matter of different interpretations than different clues. The three significant factors were the lubricant, the keys and the locations.'

'The keys?' said Carol. 'The lubricant and the locations were in the report as important factors connecting the three murders. I can't remember anything about keys.'

'Because Tolliday, and most of his team, didn't see them as important. In fact they were regarded as a bit of a red herring. A minor wrinkle in a nice neat theory. And, to be honest, they could have been just an anomaly: one of those unexplainable little things that keys, for reasons of their own, like to do to irritate us. Even Davy thought he might be reading too much into it.' Her eyes scanned Carol's expression: a storyteller checking to see if her audience is hooked.

'Right,' she said. 'Girl one lived at home with her parents. Girl two lived alone. Girl three had a flatmate. Although all three were carrying very little – why would you when you're running? – keys were found on the bodies of girls one and three. Girl two, the one who had no one at home to open the door, didn't even have a front door key. She was wearing a bum bag that was open but still had her wallet in it. The original investigating detectives reasoned, at the time, that her murderer was someone who knew her, and took her keys to remove something from her flat that might incriminate him. But her flat seemed undisturbed and no one familiar with it could identify anything that was obviously missing. That didn't mean there wasn't something missing.

'When the taskforce took over all three cases the speculation around the keys shifted to the possibility that the killer wanted a souvenir: either the keys themselves or some small personal item in the flat. That fits the broad psychopathology of a serial murderer.'

'But he didn't take the others' keys,' Carol interjected.

'Exactly. But she was the only one who lived alone. And it was reasoned that, if he had chosen his victims as carefully as he seemed to, he would know that. She provided the best opportunity for a souvenir. Of course there was a simpler explanation, and everyone was aware of it: she forgot to zip her bumbag and lost the keys along the track or in the struggle with her killer. No keys had been found anywhere near her body. But of course, by then, it was generally accepted that the victims weren't killed where their bodies were found. The absence of the keys was consistent with this and, in fact, seemed to support the theory. And no keys had been turned in, despite repeated calls through Crime Stoppers. This was disappointing; it may have pinpointed the killing ground.' A sip from her cup punctuated each point.

'That's where Davy came in. Out of the blue, during a brainstorming session, he asked if the creek had been searched for the keys. He was told no, because you would have to throw them from where the body was to reach the water. They couldn't accidentally drop in from the bumbag – even in a violent struggle. He suggested that if they were in the creek it would change the whole way we were looking at the problem, and that we should at least check the water to eliminate that possibility. Everyone else thought it was a waste of time, but Davy's argument about eliminating the possibility of being on the wrong track won over old braces-and-belt-Tolliday, and he brought in divers. They found the keys in under an hour.'

She stopped while she poured herself another cup of coffee. Carol waited. She was beginning to feel tension, expectant excitement. When she was at the site of the second murder she'd felt the same thing, some vague presentiment of its significance. Somewhere in the back rooms of her mind she felt movement, like the sliding of bolts and withdrawing of tongues in a dark, heavy door.

'That's the point where Davy and the rest of the team diverged.'

'Finding the keys didn't change their minds?' asked Carol.

'It provoked a lot of discussion but in the end the consensus was that, on balance, it was insignificant – still just a red herring. But it sent Davy off at a tangent like a pool ball from a good break. Tolliday decided to err on the side of prudence and let him have his head. Until then Davy, like everyone else, had been looking at all the similarities between girl two and girls one and three. Now we started to tease out the differences.'

'Which were?'

'Well, there were a lot of incidental ones of course. One had a boyfriend and was a virgin, one had a boyfriend and wasn't, and one had no boyfriend but wasn't a virgin. Not very significant in itself. However number two, who had no known boyfriend, was the only one who may have had intercourse with someone other than her murderer shortly before her death. Again, so what? But Davy felt that curious little anomalies were accumulating around girl number two. The more we found the less coincidental they appeared in aggregate. He noticed that there was a subtle difference in the location of the second murder scene. All three were recreation tracks. All three were beside water. But number two was by far the most risky site for the murderer. The other two sites were more isolated and shielded from casual view. Only someone on the track itself could expose him. You've been to all the scenes?'

'Yes. I know what you mean. The thought crossed my mind. There's that row of flats and shops across the creek. Why choose that point when there was a bushland reserve only metres away?'

'Davy called us out there one day. Girl two was tall, like me. He had her keys tied to a long piece of twine. He got me to hold them in my right hand – she was right-handed – and run along the track from the direction of the footbridge. He came from the opposite direction and timed it so we passed near the spot she was found. Jac recorded it on a video camera. As he got level with me he thrust out his arm, caught me high across the chest and stopped me dead. I landed on my arse. Started calling him every obscenity I could think of when I could breathe again. He stood there grinning like a Cheshire Cat.'

'The keys landed in the creek,' said Carol.

'A metre, give or take, from where they were found.'

'But that suggests they – or she – was killed on the spot? Or at least attacked at that point.'

'And if she was, the others could have been. Conditions were much more favourable for the killer in their cases.'

'That doesn't seem probable. Or make sense. Too risky.' Carol took another muffin and broke it in half as if the solution might be a blueberry. 'He would have to subdue them – the bodies showed signs of struggle?' Carol Marks nodded. 'Rape them, arrange their bodies with legs spread toward the water, and clean up the scene so well that it looked like it happened somewhere else.'

'That didn't seem to worry Davy. Jac and I were well aware of his knack for seeing the wood and the trees, but we thought he was getting carried away with his theory and trying to make the facts fit it. We didn't realise he had a bit of knowledge that we hadn't.'

'What was that?'

'Ah.' The face across the table broke into a nest of grin lines. She raised a slender white finger. 'First. He got us working on motive. Why?' She smiled as if at a private joke. 'Who? wasn't something Davy cared that much about. Why was girl two killed at that point? And why did she have her keys in her hands? Jac checked the original interview records and found that a girlfriend ran with her sometimes. But never on Tuesdays or Thursdays. She questioned the girl and established that they normally ran out and returned along the same route. The scene of the murder was about halfway between her home and the return point. Because of ETD the assumption we'd worked on was that she was on the return journey when attacked. If she was only halfway home, why did she have her keys in her hand?'

Carol almost thrust her hand up. 'The footbridge and the flats!' She failed to suppress the schoolgirl excitement in her voice.

The other Carol was smiling and nodding. 'I got the key duty. It took me a day, but I found a lock that one of her keys opened. No one was home. I couldn't enter without a warrant, and we were sticking strictly to the book. Jac and I questioned everyone in the apartment block and found someone who eventually admitted recognising her. He knew about the murder but claimed not to have made a connection. His flat was on the ground floor and he could see the stairs from his kitchen. He sometimes saw her go up and come down an hour or so later. He thought she was having it off with one of his neighbours. No one knew who lived in the flat her key fitted. A neighbour who'd seen her at the door a few times assumed she was the occupant. Thought she was "a stuck-up little piece". When we got our warrant we discovered it was furnished like a motel suite: a queen-sized bed, a mini bar and tea and coffee makings. No sign of permanent occupation.

Turned out she owned it. Part of a portfolio of investments left to her by her mother. It hadn't been offered for lease for over a year.'

'So every Tuesday or Thursday she ran by and if she saw a light in the window she found her exercise another way,' Carol said. 'It probably didn't add much to her usual return time and no one noticed.'

'The flats had been canvassed for possible witnesses, but that's all. Under the circumstances why would you think of something like that? Can't blame the original investigators.'

'So you had a suspect?'

'Nup. We wanted to find the boyfriend. But we didn't think he did it. At least not the present one.' Carol's brow curved quizzically. 'Using the crime scene photos. Jac lay down in the pose and position of the body. And, if you sighted along her body between her legs, guess where she was aimed like a huge, kid's shanghai?'

'The flat,' answered Carol. 'What did the rest of the taskforce say to all this?'

'Well it hit the fan. There were professional egos involved. She was the daughter of an MP. There was pressure to keep the sensational aspects under wraps. Most thought it was still a sideshow. It explained the other condom lubricant, the keys, but little else. Some were willing to entertain the idea of a copycat hiding his crime amongst serial murders. But none would come at Davy's idea.'

'Which was?'

Carol Marks stared at her hands in her lap. Her fingers knitted and unravelled. Then she drew herself higher in her chair; her back became ramrod straight. She took a breath and let the air out slowly through lips that were an underscore. 'He showed the taskforce the video Jac had shot of the keys experiment. The bit where he hit me and I hit the deck. Then, using me again, he demonstrated how he could disable me with a single blow, rape me, kill me, and arrange my body with minuscule disturbance to the scene. It was very impressive ...'

'He hit you?'

'No,' she chuckled. 'Too dangerous. He explained how it worked. A blow to the throat that would virtually paralyse the victim and would look like part of the strangulation process to the pathologist. It left the killer plenty of time to provide evidence of rape and a struggle. Then finish her off and arrange her body. We all thought they were pointed at the water, which is what we were meant to think. But girl two was pointed across the water.'

Carol needed to show she could make the team. 'He used some object with a condom on it and roughed them up: broke their nails, skinned their knuckles, bruised them. And then he strangled them. They were probably half dead already. If he was extremely cool and efficient it would only take a minute or two. And if he was that cool and efficient …'

'He'd be a professional,' Carol Marks completed her sentence.

'That was the knowledge David Edge had that you didn't? How to do it.'

The woman on the other side of the table answered with a weak smile that was more of a bleak grimace. 'Apparently, when the solution occurred to him, he did some research of the contract killing fraternity. There are not many true professionals in Australia. He already had a name for the taskforce …'

'Desmond Poynter.'

'Desmond "Whitey" Poynter. In hindsight that was his mistake. He should have kept it to himself until we had Poynter screwed down. He already had a reputation inside the shop as a talented detective. Then he strutted his stuff in front of the entire taskforce and drew the attention of some powerful and dangerous people. It was the beginning of the end for Davy.' Her brow wrinkled into a Gothic arch like a cathedral portal. Her smile was small and sad, a pinched flutter of lips. 'And for me.'

The words were breathed with a timbre of resignation. The afternoon was waning. Snared by memory, she gazed deep into her backyard jungle. The sun had slipped low. The trees were a dark impenetrable mass fringed with red gold against a deep purple sky. In their depths her violet eyes glowed like rooms bathed in black light. And her guest was moved to wonder how many of those last words were tainted with paranoia.

'The moon was his undoing,' she said softly, almost sang. 'They were killed on the full moon. Each one. It was much too … Hollywood.'

Somewhere in the house a key rattled in a door and a voice boomed in the hallway announcing its other owner. 'Home!'

'Skid!' Carol Marks said, suddenly back in the room, her body and the moment. 'You'll stay for dinner.' It wasn't a question.

14

Sharon Kitchen didn't know what the fuck to do. She was caught between the biggest fucking rock and the hardest fucking place she'd ever been caught between during a life spent in a geological fucking sandwich. Wash your mouth out, Shaz.

It was her own stupid fault. It was always her own stupid fault; hers and the men in her life. But then, except for the rape pack (maybe even the rape pack), she brought them into her life. Dragged some of them in kicking.

And it wasn't just the rock and the hard place; there was the fucking quicksand underfoot. Then again, maybe she was caught between a rock and a hard place and an even harder place – or a bigger rock.

These thoughts were rattling around in her brain like a pocketful of pebbles as she stepped into the lift on the ground floor of the Royal Melbourne Hospital. It didn't occur to her to wonder why she was thinking about her problems in clichéd abstractions. If it did, she would have to put names and faces to these flinty objects and face the bleak reality of her situation with all its tragic possibilities.

The kids were in Ruby Fleet's tender loving care; nothing wrong with that in itself. She trusted Ruby. Ruby was a good mum. She was a tough little bugger – a Koori had to be – but when it came to kids, doe-eyed and doughy. Her boys would have had Ruby wrapped around their little fingers and licking the sugar off before Sharon got to the end of the block. But she had to come in. She came in every night. Every night since the, the … accident. She didn't look too closely at her motivations for this compulsion, either. Not yet. She wasn't ready yet. But sooner or later Shaz would have to grab Sharon firmly by the shoulders and take a good, long look at her.

She was alone in the lift. She poked the button for her floor and stared blankly at the illuminated numbers above the doors. They waxed and waned like a procession of stars across the making and unmaking of the universe. She looked up at the trapdoor in the ceiling. She tried to disentangle her reflection from the pale grey shimmer of the stainless-steel walls. But she was glad she was lost in the dull iridescence. Her gut lost mass as the lift slowed and stopped. The door shrunk away making a cul de sac of the cubicle, and left her exposed to the muzzle of the long white corridor. And at its end the very hazard incarnate she didn't want to encounter: one of the rocks. Or the quicksand.

What should she do? Flatten her back against the wall and hope the door closed quickly? They never do when you want them to. Step out smartly and turn sharply right or left, and hope her manoeuvres went unnoticed? Too late, she'd hesitated too long. Matters were taken out of her hand as her space was invaded by a bustling clutch of people. It looked like three generations of the same family and a tussle immediately broke out between the ankle-biters in the hierarchy over who had lift operation rights. She could have used them as camouflage and slipped easily away, but she shouldered through and heard the door shish behind her.

Sharon stood with her feet apart and her arms hanging stiffly by her sides cushioned in the bulk of her coat. In her mind's eye she suddenly saw herself as if in long shot from the opposite end of the corridor: a small blonde Chinese gunfighter in a spaghetti western. Her adversary glanced from a white-coat, to whom he was talking, and looked at her. And a gut-wrenching zoom sucked her into close-up.

Fuck! Her eyes flicked around. Had she said that, or thought it? But she had to face him sooner or later. It may as well be now. And fuck him! She was the one with the right to be here. Not him. He had no rights. What the fuck was he doing here? The heat of her rising anger had vulcanised trepidation into indignation. Her fear became fuel that melted and evaporated in righteous flames. She curled into a spitball of Greek Fire and catapulted down the corridor.

But if she had been rock, he'd have been paper. If she'd been scissors, he'd have been rock. As it was, he was water, tall and cool. Before she altered the temperature by a single degree she was sputtering on his smooth surface.

'What are you doing here?' she hissed, glaring up at the blue eyes. They smiled mildly down on her. Fuck him! She hated that: always looking like he understood.

'Ms Kitchen …?'

Her attention swung violently toward the white-coat. He was one of Ben's doctors. She had been so fixated on *him* that the identity of the other party hadn't registered. But her anger was launched, committed to some target, like a heat-seeking missile.

'What are you talking to him about?' she snarled at the doctor. 'He's not family! You said family only! He's got no right to visit Ben …'

The doctor had taken a few small steps backward. He was calculating a hasty projection of the collateral damage from this little explosion, and could foresee himself as part of it. 'Ms Kitchen, Ms Kitchen,' he crooned. 'Sharon …'

'Don't Sharon me,' she snapped. 'You university ponces stick together like – like …' She made the mistake of looking away from her secondary target to her primary one. He was standing loose-limbed, his weight cocked on one hip, one foot pushed forward. His hands were in his pockets and his dusty blond head tilted gently down. His amused eyes were on her and there was that little dimple hooked in his left cheek that looked like a smile even when his lips didn't. She could feel the flame guttering: almost hear the quenching hiss.

Of all the men she'd known there were only two who could take her by surprise, in answer to whose onslaught she had neither strategy nor arsenal: Ben and this one. Fuck 'em! They didn't play by the rules of engagement: men's, women's, hers, anyone's! Fuck 'em both!

She swung her guns back on the doctor before she lost all her firepower. 'I don't want this p … p … person,' Jesus she couldn't even call him a prick, 'anywhere near Ben!'

'Shar ... Ms Kitchen, perhaps we could talk about this in the family lounge? I don't think it's occupied at the moment.' He put out a hand to shepherd her in the direction of the room reserved for people standing vigil on loved ones in critical condition. His hand hovered near her shoulder blades. She didn't move and he didn't dare touch her.

'Alright,' she capitulated suddenly. 'I'll talk to you later,' she said to the doctor dismissively. He smiled – courteously he believed, but it was in fact – weakly. 'C'mon,' she growled at the tall fair man whose name he had momentarily forgotten, and she steamed off down the corridor, nurses and aides glancing off her bows. And the man ambled in her wake: a tug and a tanker.

There was no one in the room. Its walls were white like all the others, but less harshly lit. The furnishings were simple, practical but comfortable. There was carpet on the floor and a tiny kitchenette with tea- and coffee-making facilities in the far corner. Sharon marched to the centre of four couches arranged in a hollow square, and turned, hands on hips, to face the man closing the door.

'Take off your coat,' he suggested amiably, as he slipped out of his jacket.

'I'll take off my coat when I fuckin' want to,' she said, as she took off her coat and threw it across the room to a chair against the wall. She watched him as he crossed to the chair and laid his jacket and her coat neatly across its back. He wandered towards the other end of the room.

'Cuppa?' he asked.

'No!' she barked.

'Okay.' He came back around the end of the nearest couch, sat down, leaned back and crossed his legs at the ankles. She waited tensely for the cool blue eyes to lock on hers, as they inevitably would. 'What's the problem, Shaz?' he said gently.

'What's the problem?' she almost shrieked. She heard the shrillness in her voice and made much ado about finding a place to sit as far as possible from him. She let her body fuss about its comfort while she wound her pitch back a few notches. 'What's the fuckin' problem.' Her voice was still loaded with intensity but it sounded controlled. 'Ben's a stone's throw away,' she spat, her right hand waving at a wall. 'Fucking machines doin' everything for him 'cept think. If he fuckin' lives, he'll be lucky if he's anything more than broccoli below the neck. And I ... I ...' Shit don't lose it. Not in front of him.

'You what?'

'I gotta find a way to fuckin' look after him, that's what!'

'Why?'

'Wha ... Why?' She was gobsmacked. She was shocked to find that despite the carapace of wrath she'd raised Roman Turtle-like around her, he'd found the gap between the plates and cut to her soft centre. She'd assumed he, of all, understood.

'I thought you and Ben were no longer a couple?'

'We … we're not living together. No.' She could hear herself on the defensive, her verbal feet scrabbling for purchase and power in the battle-field mud. 'It's … we … Shit! We're not fuckin' any more – okay? But Ben's still the kids' father. He's still me best friend. Orright? I just … I … I gotta get on with me life. Ben's … just … like …' She stopped, strangely out of breath. Her chest heaved as her mind grasped about to find words. Ben's like – what? What was the truth of the matter? He waited for it; she could feel him waiting. She wasn't looking at him; she stared blindly at the low table top between them. A blur of magazine cover dissolved into her con-fusion, began to crystallise and slip into focus: *New Idea*, something about Tom and Nicole. Fucking old magazine, fucking old idea. 'Ben's not what I need anymore. I've gotta chance to …' She pushed her fingers into the dark roots of her hair and dragged her palms down her cheeks. Through her fingers, as they slid past her eyes, she saw that electric blue alertness in his. Jesus, Sharon, don't go there. She bit off the thread of her words. 'I love Ben,' she said. 'But I'm not in love with him. I never was. It was always a sort of … of …' Her voice trailed away.

'Companionship?'

'Sumpin' like that.' The impetus of her anger was faltering like fitfully cooling steam. 'Yeah, we're mates,' she added with a touch of wonder. And that was it: the right word.

'How are you going to take care of him?'

'I'll sue the fuckin' police for millions,' she fired up again. 'We'll be orright.'

'Have you got any idea what that'll cost – with no guarantee of success?'

She glared at him defiantly.

'I was there, Shaz. The police didn't stuff up. Ben brought their fire down upon himself. He gave them no choice. I would have shot him if I'd been a cop.'

'He's a stupid fuckwit, but why the fuck would he do a thing like that?' Down, down, very deep, she knew the answer, she knew all the answers. But she wasn't going to ask the questions. She was never going to ask the questions – not now. She held his gaze. It was her last chance. Outstare him and everything will be alright: her will haggled superstitiously with logic.

'Don't come the raw prawn with me, Shaz.' The knowing was in the blue-eyed smile again. 'This is David, Uncle Dave.'

Her simmering anger was about to boil over once more, when he extracted a paper from an envelope that he took from his pocket, and tossed it on the table between them.

'What's that?' she asked in a voice laced with some alarm. He just nodded toward it and gestured for her to pick it up. 'What is it?' she said as she unfolded it with fingers that behaved more like toes. 'Is this …?'

'Enduring power of attorney,' he said.

'What's that mean?' But she knew what it meant. It was just that she couldn't process all the ramifications. A cold void was swelling like a balloon in her bowels, pressing her vital organs up into her throat.

'It means I have all the rights you were referring to earlier. You and Ben never married. You ended the defacto relationship recently. You have no rights. In law.'

He was watching her carefully. Waiting to gauge her reaction. But she had none to offer for assessment. She was undone. For the first time in her life she was speechless. A huge hand had thrust into her chest and snatched her breath away. He waited.

'Wh … where … how did you get this?' she said at last. Her voice sounded faint and distant, like a cry across a rushing river.

'He left it with his landlady.'

'But … we're mates. He knew … musta known I'd look after 'im. Mates look after mates.' Although she hadn't yet given the inner desolation shape, found its form in words, the idea that Ben had lost faith was reaming her out. It was an assault on her integrity that felt like corporeal dismemberment.

'Mates don't dump their garbage on a mate's front lawn and leave town, either.' He smiled as if he was delivering a birthday greeting.

'Wha …?' She was exhausted, punch drunk. What the fuck was he talking about?

'Think it through, Shaz. Believe in Ben. He believes in you.' He beamed like a prophet bringing news of the Messiah. She must have looked like an alien abductee whose brain was siphoned out – because that's what she felt like.

He leaned forward, elbows on knees. 'You see, for the first time in his life Ben thought of everything. Even the possibility the cops wouldn't kill him outright. He knows himself. He knew he would probably stuff up, somewhere. He made sure that you and the kids wouldn't bear the consequences if he did. You wouldn't be left with the burden of him. He took out an insurance policy. Me.' She stared at him, uncomprehending. 'It's an affirmation of his faith in you, Shaz. He knew you'd try to look after him, and so he quarantined you from cost and responsibility. He cut you free.'

She shook her head and flapped her hands, as if the room was choked with cobwebs. 'Are you sayin' this was some sort of stupid suicide attempt?' Her voice pitched high in disbelief.

'What has he said to you?'

'Nothin'. He can hardly breathe. What's he gonna say?' She stared at him. He merely returned her gaze, patient, expectant. Waiting for what – her enlightenment? 'Nah,' she shook her head violently, 'that's ridiculous.'

'Think about it. If Ben was going to top himself, how would he go about it? Can you imagine him putting a gun in his mouth? Blowing himself up? Poison, overdosing?'

'He wouldn't OD. He's clean,' she said in knee jerk and realised how silly it sounded as she spoke.

'Have you seen the TV footage?'

She shook her head. 'Can't.'

'It was attempted suicide, Shaz, and it was very elaborately planned.'

'But he thinks of you as a mate, too.' She could see the fallacy in his reasoning. 'Why would he drop all this shit in your lap and piss off?'

'Ah Shaz. But this is Ben. In his simple Ben way he thinks of me as rich and powerful. Someone who can make bad things and bad people go away, just like that.' He snapped his fingers and Sharon jumped inside her skin. 'He's appointed me your Fairy Godfather.'

The benign blue eyes held her in their beam. Any fire left in her cooled to ash. Fairy – unlikely, even if he didn't fuck the girls at the Garden – but Godfather …? She shivered. Her head drooped below her shoulders and she stared vacantly at the lines on her palms in her lap. The lifeline on one hand was long, and deep as a river valley; on the other it broke into forks and tributaries. Which one did they read? She couldn't remember – left, right, right, left? None of this kept her mind from the vast hollow inside. It couldn't be sustained. It was about to implode. Then there'd be a backwash, wouldn't there? An eruption she couldn't suppress. It would be soon. She mumbled some words, so low even she didn't hear them.

'What?' he said.

'You've gotta go!' They were strangled gargles, not words.

'Okay, Shaz,' he said gently. He stood, walked to the chair behind her. She heard the soft rustle as he collected his jacket. She felt his hand lightly touch her neck. She heard the door close. She lurched to her feet, stumbled to the sink in the corner and emptied herself with shuddering convulsions into the stainless steel bowl.

As the stinking matter flushed away she heard a soft metallic tink-tink-tink. It was like the first drops of an approaching storm on a corrugated iron roof. She realised she was crying. She couldn't recall doing that before.

15

The night was diamond bright and diamond sharp. A diamond-hard cold chilled like the thought of a razor drawn slowly across flesh. Needles of raw air probed the lungs and stung the sinuses, tasting like ice crystals on a chipped tooth. She waved and called her goodbyes to the silhouette in the warm oblong backglow of house and home. The lean shadow puppet waved back.

Before she climbed into the car she tugged her thick, padded coat snugly about her and craned her head back to look up into the bowl of indigo sky. You couldn't see the night sky here through the muddy glow of city lights. Well, not what she thought of as night sky: an engulfing cloud of Milky Way, diver Earth swimming through a vast school of scintillating fish in black ocean depths. But you could see its representatives, like backbenchers scattered through a half-empty chamber.

The car door swung open. 'You'll freeze y'bum off out there,' said the driver, igniting the engine. And she ducked her head and climbed in. She'd arrived by tram but was leaving by car. Her host insisted on taking her back to her digs. He brushed the fog of their breath from the windshield with a parka-clad forearm. The demister hadn't yet kicked in. The wipers cut a fan in a frosting of dew that would be ice by morning. The car swung out from the curb and slid down the barrel of the kaleidoscopic street.

She glanced at her chauffeur. Physically, except that they were both tall, you wouldn't make a match of Carol and Neville Marks. Carol was tight and spare. Her husband was loose and overabundant. There seemed to be unruly bits of him in excess that he needed to pull in or tuck away from time to time. He combed his large bristly hands through his hair and thick curls sprang between his blunt fingers like black wool escaping from a split bale. He never managed to get the entire perimeter of his shirttails under his belt at the same time. Her vocabulary was educated middle-class; his speech was blue-collar vernacular. He seemed to delight in it. His polished bluestone jaw was starting to look like basalt. He probably had to shave twice a day. He hulked over the wheel, his eyes on the road. Bands and bursts of light slithered slickly up the windshield and flickered on his face like an old movie.

They hadn't returned to the subject of the Jogger Murders after Neville Marks arrived home. Any reference to the job was limited to humorous anecdotes and comparisons of crime fighting in the wildernesses of the Kimberley and Melbourne. Mostly they exchanged tourist tips. She and Neville had shared a bottle of Peel Estate Zinfandel between them. She'd consumed the lion's share and there was a glassful left in the bottle. Carol Marks didn't partake.

'D'ja get what y'needed?' Nev asked suddenly. 'F'y'essay or whatever.'

'Carol was a mine of information,' she replied. 'The only detail we didn't touch on was how David Edge reached the conclusion that Desmond Poynter was the killer.'

'Well,' said Nev, grinning across his thickly padded forearm. 'Only one person knows that.'

'Carol said something odd.' Nev shot a sharp glance at her. 'She said that when Edge named Poynter as a suspect it was the beginning of the end for him and for her. What did she mean?'

He didn't answer for some time and seemed to be negotiating the narrow suburban streets with overweening diligence. He didn't look at her when he eventually responded.

'You interested in the crime, the crim or the cop?' His gaze held hers for a few beats. His caterpillar brows inched up his forehead.

Shit! They were joined at the hip. 'Your wife used almost exactly the same words.'

'Yeah?' He seemed pleased. 'Whatcha say?'

'Is that what you think we have in common: an interest in this case? 'Cause frankly, I can see little else,' she said, avoiding his question.

His dark eyes flashed at her. 'Oooh, you've got a lot more'n that, Constable.'

'Why did you bring us together? Was I some sort of tough love therapy?'

'Maybe a little. I thought it'd do 'er good to talk it all through with an objective party. I wanted t'show 'er she was strong enough now.'

She studied his profile. She could feel a tension. He was going to unload – something.

'It was coincidence,' he said abruptly. 'Nothin' more. That's when the first signs of Carol's problem appeared. Course we didn't know that then. Only picked it up lookin' back after she was diagnosed.'

'You're not suggesting …?'

'Cause 'n' effect? Nah. But there was a lotta paranoia in the air – didn't help. Difficult to untangle the real from the imagined. And Dave's a mate.'

'Did she suspect him of some sort of hidden agenda or cover-up?'

'Well, that's it, innit? He *was* involved in a cover-up.' His grin was sad and resigned now. 'She didn't tell y'any o'this?' Carol shook her head muttering a negative and he continued. 'When Dave started t'get interested in Poynter 'e set off an alarm somewhere. Anyhow, 'e was offered money t'lose interest in Poynter. He did the right thing and reported it, but was ordered t'take the money, play along and see where it led. Well it led to a major undercover operation that lasted three years with Dave playin' bent copper f'the duration.' He glanced at her, his mouth a sour twist. 'Course no one knows this at the time. All hush-hush. The girls, Carol 'n' Jac, were bloody confused. Suddenly Dave's back-pedalling on Poynter and doesn't seem to be tryin' real hard to contribute to the taskforce. Then Poynter's body is found in the same place and in the same pose as the second murdered girl. And all sorts of rumours are doin' th'rounds 'bout the sort of people Dave's associatin' with.' He concentrated on his driving for a while, then he said: 'In Carol's mind her fate and Dave's sortuv got tangled together by that case.'

'He's a close friend, isn't he?'

'Y'know Dave's the only one of our friends who Carol never had any paranoid delusions about. She's thought everyone we know has been plotting against her, at one time or another. But not me. And not Dave. Y'know what she said to me once? She and Dave are alike, she said. They both 'ave a chorus of angels and demons in their heads. Hers tell 'er the tune to sing and when to sing it.' They were waiting at a red light. He put his eyes on hers and held them there. 'But Dave, she says, he's not another chorister, he's the choirmaster.'

'That could be her illness talking.'

'Probably. But she believed 'e found a way of livin' with angels and demons – and still be Dave. It gave 'er hope.'

The light changed and they slipped across the deserted intersection.

'Ricciardelli believes David Edge killed Desmond Poynter,' she said. They were on a broad, treed avenue now. She didn't know its name or its geography. She didn't know the city. She had to give herself into the hands of strangers to get from A to B.

'There's a body of opinion ascribin' to that view,' he agreed grudgingly.

'Does Carol share it?'

Nev snorted soft chuckles through his nose. 'Huh. Nuh. In Carol's eyes Dave c'n do no wrong.'

Perhaps in Carol's eyes you can do murder and do no wrong, she thought, but she said: 'Another thing: Carol said *who* did the murders wasn't something Edge cared that much about.'

'I think she meant that as a general observation. Dave's not interested in apportioning blame. Guilt, retribution, justice, punishment – all bullshit to 'im. It's why people do the things they do that puts a caber up 'is kilt.'

'I hear he comes from money?'

'His mum and stepdad don't have as many houses or hotels on Marylebone and Mayfair as Murdoch or Packer, but enough to stay on the board.'

'And his father went straight to gaol and never passed GO again.'

'Done your homework.' Nev laughed dryly. 'Psychobabble time,' he said, then seemed occupied by the driving process for a while. 'He rarely talks about 'imself – or 'is family. On the odd occasion he does y'c'n tell his dad and 'im were close. Still good mates with 'is mum. In 'is early teens when it happened. Musta hurt.' He began braking the car for another red light. 'When 'e was a cop 'e didn't like chargin' people unless 'e was real sure. Okay arrest record. Brilliant conviction rate, but. DPP loved him. Bloody bloodhound, our Dave. If the scent was there 'e'd get 'em. Course 'e didn't 'ave a life.'

'Never married?'

White teeth flashed in the dark crag of his jaw. 'Neck deep in vestal virgins these days. When would 'e find the time or the inclination?' Nev chortled, studying her from under the dark shrubbery of his brows. 'So it is the cop?'

'We only had one conversation, in a holding cell; I was releasing him from custody. He gave me a local name he said was "interesting". It was. I did a bit of overtime that kickstarted an investigation. Got results. The brownie points I earned got me this berth at the Detective Training School.' She shrugged in an attempt to fool herself, if not him. 'He just seemed an interesting character. And a case he worked on might be an interesting case.'

'Yeah,' said Nev, flat and dry as a Salada.

'So, what?' she asked quickly. 'You're saying all his cases were a ... a sort of displaced attempt to understand his father's motives?'

'Buggered if I know. Dave's a sealed volume in a plain brown wrapper.' He seemed about to add something, then checked the flow. They were approaching an amber light. He was wordless for a while, his palms on the steering wheel, his fingers gripping and releasing; his jaw worked in rumination. She suspected he was chewing on her. 'Step on a crack break your mother's back,' he said suddenly. 'Ever play that when y'were a little tacker?'

'In kindergarten. Miss Bennett in preps said it would lead to obsessive compulsive behaviour in later life, so I stopped.'

'Very funny,' he grunted. 'I thought if I ate all m'vegies mum 'n' dad wouldn't fight and never leave me.' He shook his head. 'Where do kids get the idea that they're responsible for the actions of adults?'

'He couldn't save his father, but he can save the rest of the world?'

'Doubt it's that simple,' he said, face turning away as he took a right. 'But I don't think Dave can abide the thought that Humpty Dumpty might fall off the wall while 'e's sitting beside 'im.'

'So, all this adds up to what? You don't think he killed Poynter?'

'When it comes t'people, Carol, Dave's a Greenie. Likes to think everyone's morally recyclable.' Neville Marks sighed, gunning the engine. 'I'm not sure what 'e'd do if 'e found someone who – *categorically* – wasn't.' Then his eyes were on hers and they were hard with meaning. 'But I'll guarantee this: no matter what 'e's done, or does, he won't blame angels or demons. He'll own his actions. That way at least, 'e is the choirmaster.'

And you can't risk doubting him, can you, Nev? Is that the crack that might break Carol's back?

16

He left the building by the front entrance. He walked right by her, looked directly at her. He didn't acknowledge her existence. Strangers in the night. Braces and fucking belt. They were on the job. It didn't matter that the target was nowhere near. He would live the fiction until the job was done. She'd never worked with anyone who could imagine all the scenarios for possible disaster as vividly as he, but what impressed her most was his capacity to maintain a regimen that operated on the assumption that if each and every calamity could come to pass, it would.

Here she was playing shadow to a suburban hausfrau's Peter Pan and he acts as if she was deep cover in a dangerous sting. But then, he'd lived the undercover lie himself for three years, and the habits of relentless vigilance are not easily expunged. She knew – she had lived lies of her own. And perhaps he knew more than he was telling. Don't be a stupid bitch, of course he knew more. He always did. Working for him was an article of faith not a contract. But he'd have her derrière covered. He wasn't often taken by surprise.

But neither, it would seem, was Sharon Kitchen.

He'd probably thought she was taking a risk hanging around the hospital foyer swaddled like a sore thumb, but it was fucking cold out there. Freezing to death in a car with a stuffed heater in a fucking hospital carpark didn't count as humour, even of the ironic kind, in her book. And anyway, you couldn't run an engine just to keep warm on surveillance; too chancy, might give the game away. She was in one of his cars. He had a tiny fleet – cheap, secondhand, popular models, nondescript, invisible. She was rotating a selection – great bloody selection – with her own bomb, while she tailed Sharon.

And Sharon was sharp.

Nevertheless, Maeve was confident. She was confident she could remain here for another hour, because she was confident about her target's movements and whereabouts during this particular slab of any given twenty-four hours. Sharon was upstairs in the intensive care ward. She would stay until the end of evening visiting hours. She always did. From the time Maeve had become the caboose on her train till tonight, she had not missed once.

And Maeve knew what she did while she was there. A duty nurse who assumed Maeve was a journalist had provided the information – human interest, a salve to any conscience. The nurse said Sharon sat at Ben Bovell's bedside and held his hand. The nurse had never heard a word pass between them. But Maeve knew that didn't mean they didn't communicate.

Sharon was smart. Sharon was tough. Edge and Maeve had done some things they weren't proud of to survive on the streets. They had done what was necessary. They had lived the lie. Sharon had lived the life. She had done what was necessary. The fact that she was alive, intact and thriving was proof of that pudding; no need to eat it, if it wasn't palatable. Maeve couldn't afford to underestimate her. Sharon could use this dull routine to lull any watcher into a false sense of security and slip away.

But Maeve didn't think so.

Maeve thought the routine itself was the point: the trips to deliver the kids to school and kindergarten – a new one for Briette; the trips to the gym; the trips to the shops; the trips to visit friends. All the toing and froing of the boring daily round, that was the point. Nothing unusual, nothing out of the ordinary; look, Maeve, nothing up my sleeve, nothing down my trackie daks. All of it the mise en scene of a soapie little drama of a blameless middle-class existence. All for your viewing pleasure, Ms Maguffin.

Day after day as Maeve had watched the sands trickle through the hourglass (and Sharon run barefoot in it), she formed the distinct impression that it was being kicked in her eyes.

Unless the bloke from City Water, the pizza delivery boy and two Mormons got a quick handjob at the door, Shaggin' Sharon, the man magnet, had no current male friends. The only man who managed to get a tool in the kitchen was a geriatric plumber – and he took his footprints away with him.

Odd.

And middle class? That was the nub of it. When did Sharon become lower middle class, as opposed to lower criminal class? And *how* – if the intelligence offered to and gathered by Maeve was correct – did ex-whore, ex-user, ex-social-security-rip-off-queen Sharon become middle class? Middle-classness was bought or borrowed not bequeathed.

Sharon wasn't flaunting conspicuous wealth, but her lifestyle didn't fit the picture that had been painted for Maeve. That picture, Edge warned, was about six months old. Sharon was still living in the old neighbourhood but she'd moved into its frontier of encroaching gentrification. Her wheels weren't in the luxury range, but she had a shiny new hatchback. Briette's new kindergarten was one in a leafy suburb where you paid for the swings and roundabouts. And Maeve had discovered that Sharon's oldest boy was on the waiting list of one of the better private secondary schools. How was this being funded? Maeve doubted that even Centrelink could be screwed to a tune that would finance that gig.

Sharon's only nod to gainful employment was desultory distribution of a brand of 'natural' skin care products. Whence, then, did her resources come? What – or who – was her self-sourcing Magic Pudding?

And where, as Edge asked – the question that framed Maeve's quest – where was Sharon Kitchen during the hours that Ben Bovell held Melbourne's finest at bay with a whimper as big as a bang? Where could you be for a whole day in a contemporary western city that the electronic fingers of the media, longer than the arms of the law, could not reach to beat upon your eardrums? And if not your eardrums, those of someone who knows where to find you.

Edge – and now Maeve – was certain that nothing could have kept Sharon away if she'd known. One thing Maeve was sure of was that Sharon had not seen her, but Sharon knew she was being watched. Perhaps 'assumed' was a better word. Sharon assumed she was being watched because she felt the cool wash of Edge's interest. Consequently, it was now a waiting game. Could Maeve outwait Sharon? How patient was Sharon? How patient was Maeve? And it was a game of diminishing returns for Maeve. The longer the stand-off lasted the more likely was her exposure. Then the game was lost.

Maybe it was time to try a different tack. Just what that tack might be she would have to ponder. Maeve braced herself to venture back into the brittle night.

In the end the solution was simple.

17

Shane Clarke was on the dunny when he turned up. Not the one indoors. The original one in the backyard that the dog-eared corrugated-iron lean-to leaned against. The one that would be standing when the lean-to was a rust pile and the house pulped by dry rot. The one built like a brick shithouse, because that's what it was. The one that'd be standing when the developers eventually moved in, probably with a heritage order slapped on it, a monument to the bowel movements of our ancestors. Shane was on that dunny.

It was Shane's dunny, sort of. A sanctum in which to sit and think. Or sit. It was near the shed. But Trish encouraged him to come out here to crap – even in the middle of winter. She indoors always used it indoors. Girl poo smelt sweeter than boy poo, he didn't know why: secret women's business. Trish was working nights this month.

And it was bloody cold: Brass Monkey and Eskimo Pie weather. A definite pain in the arse. He was anxious to get his King Gees up past his knees again. Then he heard the voices.

'G'day, mate. Lookin' for Shane?'

Bloody Perce. He'd have his nose hooked over the fence like Foo and his eyes would be sliding around like eggs in a frypan giving the visitor the once-over – and over. If Shane wasn't square these days he'd have had to move out or bury Perce in his backyard. He may still have to resort to interment. Despite his knack for shutting out all forms of intrusive noise while he was working, there was a limit to the amount of unsolicited advice from a droning know-all that could be endured.

'Yes,' said the voice Shane had heard on the phone. 'Is he about? He said he'd be in the shed.'

One wall of Perce's house – the wall facing Trish and Shane's kitchen window – was only partially painted. With completion scant hours away the painter had descended his ladder, placed the brush and paint can at Perce's feet, tucked his ladder under his arm and walked off the job. Perce, who had loitered at his shoulder (or the foot of his ladder) since the job began, uttering handy hints and handyman homilies in his nasal monotone, called after him, 'Not gonna pay ya.' 'Money ain't everything,' was the painter's equable reply as he secured his ladder. A year and half later the wall was still unfinished and the paint can and brush still sitting where the painter left them. The paint had dried in the brush.

Perce was silent. There was only one reason for this, Shane knew. He would be rolling his eyes, jerking his head and gesturing with broad sweeps of his nose towards the dunny, while his mangy Groucho Marx eyebrows trampolined on his forehead. Perce was silent on matters of bodily function. Unfortunately, this was an isolated discrimination.

'Ah,' said the voice. 'Thank you.' There was a smile in it.

Perce, who had none of his own, used Shane's visitors – and those of the neighbours to the far side and rear of his property. Shane, trying to go about his immediate business as quietly as possible, was waiting for the usual interrogation to begin. He was surprised when Perce said with proprietorial alarm, 'Aah mate, I don't think Shane'd wancha t'go in there.'

'Oh, I think he'll be comfortable with it at the moment,' said the soft voice. Well, what do you know, a man who appreciates the privacy of the bog. Shane had had some misgivings when he'd agreed to meet the voice in person, but they were beginning to dissipate.

He wriggled his battle-scarred King Gees over his shoulders, opened the door and looked at the sky. It sat on the morning like a thick grey wafer, the icy leftovers of the night sandwiched beneath it. Once upon a time backyard anarchy had been constrained by the weight of a solid concrete desert, but it had decayed into a crazy quilt of sad stony isles in a sea of disreputable life. He island-hopped to the crumbling gully trap. From the corner of his eye, as he bent over a glacial dribble of rusty water, he glimpsed Perce's obsolete Footscray guernsey and superannuated Kmart trackies dancing behind a gap in the fence.

'Shane, mate?' A hoarse stage whisper. 'Yuv got a visita.' They only had a quick splash but his fingers began to ache. He straightened, wiping his hands on his overalls. Perce was performing a manic mime. His head seemed to pivot on his nose as his eyes rolled and the visible half of his face rocked towards Shane's workshed. His eyebrows danced their hip hop. 'Talks posh,' Perce added. 'Dressed swank, but gotta clapped-out Commodore.'

'Thanks, Perce,' he replied, low, slow, flat. Shane habitually spoke as if he was waiting to hear what he had to say, so, if he didn't like it, he could take it back before it reached another ear. He tucked his hands in his pockets for warmth and approached the dark opening of the shed. His gait was too deliberate to be an amble, but its pace was leisurely.

He had to admit to curiosity. He had never laid eyes on his visitor, but he had heard stories. Mostly extravagant tales from Benny Bovell, who seemed to hero-worship him as some sort of benevolent crime lord, or a super-cop who had nothing but the best interests of criminals at heart. Benny didn't seem aware of the contradictions in his characterisations. However, Shane had heard other stories, colourful prison scuttlebutt, that seemed to corroborate some of Benny's folklore – the ambiguities of it, at least. This bloke had put one or two of Shane's fellow inmates inside and they didn't have a bad word to say about him. Others swore he was a ruthless hardman responsible for culling legends like Whitey Poynter and Blackjack Barker. The polite voice on the phone hadn't matched any picture he might have pasted together from these scraps.

As he approached a shadow moved on shadow in the shed, and before the man materialised in the pale daylight Shane heard the mild voice again: 'It's not as clapped-out as it looks.'

And the 'swank' clothes were jeans and a thick woollen jumper. To Perce, haute couture was a tracksuit with stripes.

He was taller than Shane – Shane was a smidgeon above average. Their hair was similar in colour though, a sort of beach-sand blond. His looked like the kind of hair that a barber couldn't muster. It gave the long face beneath the boyish elan of an urchin, but the eyes were as old and as blue as an ocean. He reminded Shane of a painting he'd seen once. It must have been a photo of a painting because Shane had never been inside an art gallery. A Digger or a Light Horseman or someone like that, from the First World War: a young bloke who's seen more than enough, but is not diminished.

He put out a hand. 'David Edge. We spoke on the phone.'

'G'day.' Shane shook his hand. 'Shane.' He wrapped his arms winglike across his chest and swapped his weight awkwardly from foot to foot. 'Um. Want t'come inside?'

'Is your wife home?' When Shane nodded he added, 'How private is this?' He indicated the work shed with a slight tilt of his head. His amused gaze slid over Shane's shoulder. Shane glanced back at the fence. Perce was working on the broken paling that gave him so much trouble when Shane and Trish had company.

'Should be right,' said Shane.

Retreating into the shed they entered an atmosphere of dust and oil, hot metal and ozone. Shane was not conscious of the familiar smell of his workplace. Although he could never articulate this, it registered as a feeling of sanctuary as he crossed the threshold.

The house was pretty ordinary, but rent was cheap. The shed was the main reason for taking the place – well, for Shane. It stretched across the back of the block. The Falcon, which was parked at the foot of the drive, usually occupied one end. At the other end, furthest from Perce, in a patch illuminated through a sheet of Laserlite in the roof, a car chassis was raised on concrete blocks. Above it a motor hung in a sling of chains. Below a small grimy four-paned window in the end wall a rugged wooden bench was cluttered with tools and mechanical bric-a-brac. Gas cylinders and an electric welder colluded in its shadow. In a corner a venerable potbelly stove squatted next to a pile of old timber that prickled with rusty nails. Shane fed some chunks to the stove. He stirred up a small inferno with a blackened metal rod that might once have been part of a car and turned to face the other man.

'Benny's not crash hot, eh?'

'Not crash.'

'What's th' … um pro … pru …'

'Prognosis? Not good.'

Shit! Why did he have to reach for a twenty-dollar bloody word? 'Cause he didn't want this bloke to think he was a fucking dill, that's why. Now he thought he was a fucking dill. 'What? Won't live?' Shane's phlegmatic face registered concern.

'Won't walk.'

'Jesus!' said Shane. It was hard, abrupt, a rare tone for him. David Edge was caught in dramatic relief by the skylight, his mop of hair casting his face in shadow, but Shane could feel his gaze. 'Born at the foot uv shit hill, weren't 'e?'

'And given a straw instead of a shovel,' his visitor agreed.

Shane shook his head. He stared at his boot toe as it worried the grease-soaked dust. 'C'n y'visit?'

'Still in intensive care,' said Edge. 'But I'll let you know when it's okay, if you like.'

'Thanks,' said Shane. 'Can't believe 'e did it. 'E's so … harmless,' He looked up under his brow. 'What do y'want to know?' he asked flatly.

To his left there was an empty packing case that once held something automotive; Edge dragged it nearer to the potbelly and sat on it. 'Something set him off,' he said. 'His domestic situation changed. But that, by itself, isn't enough. I think he was brooding on this for a while. He was released from prison only a few months ago, so, I'm guessing, something happened inside that tipped him over onto the slippery slope.'

'Th'poor little bugger swallowed a lotta shit in there too. But I wasn't inside on his last stint. I been square a while now.' Shane rolled a drum of some kind of fluid across to the stove, tipped it on end and sat on it. 'If 'e couldn't get a job, 'e was gonna steal and end up canned again. 'E knew it.'

'How did you get to know him?'

'He was gettin' … hassled by this cunt: Varney. A poofter basher who kicked a kid to death and put another in a wheelchair …'

'Terrence Varney. We've met.'

'Uh, oh. Yeah well …' That's right, he was Homicide. 'Y'd know then.'

'I'd know.' Edge's eyes seemed grey, hooded and weary, his lips compressed in a cynical smile. 'Model prisoner,' he said. 'Modelled on the worst clichés from Hollywood movies: shaven head, pumped muscles, tats, Anglo-Saxon dialogue.'

'Moron's even got FUCK tattooed on th'knuckles uv one hand and KILL on the other,' Shane added with a sour chuckle. 'We made it known that Benny was one of ours and off limits. There was usually one of us with him when he wasn't in his cell.'

'We?'

'Me, Scrum …'

'Scrum?'

'Scrum Nicholls. From Wagga. Thinks rugby's a football game. And Nigger James.'

'Nigger?'

His shoulders and eyebrows moved up in a 'beats me' gesture. 'Nickname since 'e was a kid. Only blackfella where 'e grew up, 'e reckoned. Sorta proud of it.'

'A rose by any other name.' Edge grinned. 'Or a badge of courage.'

'Varney is a nasty bastard but 'e's a gutless mongrel. An' we're three big lads.' His brow and lips flickered with humour. 'Well, I'm the short-arsed one.'

'Was James or Nicholls inside with Ben anytime during his last stay?'

'Don't know about Nigger. Scrum was. It was 'im told Benny about Auntie Hazel's bungalow. He got out 'bout a month ago.'

'An address?'

'No worries.' Shane wrote the address in a small notebook. 'Moved back in with an old girlfriend.'

Edge looked at the motor suspended above the shell of the car. 'What did you do to earn an all expenses paid holiday? Redistribute spare parts?'

'A bitta cut and paste,' Shane confessed, almost bashfully, as he passed the notebook back. 'I'm square now,' he hastened to add.

'So Hazel said.' The cool blue gaze locked on him thoughtfully. 'What're you doing now?'

'Between engagements.'

'How would Trish feel about you working in a brothel?' When he noted Shane's reaction he added, 'Security.'

'Security?'

'Everyone needs protection these days, Shane.' He stood up and began moving to the door.

'I'm not a scrapper,' said Shane, as he trailed in his wake.

'Oh, the last thing we want is a scrap. Lost the battle if you have to fight.'

'We jist bluffed Varney,' he admitted with a grin.

'It's mostly bluff, Shane. But we'll teach you a few moves to keep you out of trouble.' He turned as they stepped into the dull light. 'Self defence,' he added facing Shane. 'Gives you confidence to keep your hands in your pockets.' He was standing with his hands in his pockets. He removed one. It held a card. He passed it to Shane. 'Talk it over with Trish. If you're interested ring that number and ask for Ernie Duggs. Use my name. Thanks for your help.'

As he walked away Shane said, 'You could've got all that from me over the phone.'

'You get a lot of words over the phone, Shane, but not much information.' He tossed this comment over his shoulder and continued down the broken driveway.

He wasn't sure what was meant, but Shane knew he had felt the scrutiny of those eyes that fluxed and froze between grey and blue even when they looked the other way. He looked down at the card. It was quite classy, you wouldn't guess it advertised brothels. The Rose Garden and The Crimson Grotto – Jesus! Trish'll spit chips.

'Old friend, Shane?' Perce bobbed up a few palings down the fence.

Shane stared at Perce's wall with its patch of blue paint in one corner. It looked like a window envelope with a stamp attached. 'Whadya reckon, Perce?' he said eventually in his measured, laconic way. Perce's caterpillar brows crept up his forehead. 'Me up th' ladder 'n' you on the ground, an' we finish that fuckin' wall.'

'Jeeze, would ya, Shane mate? No kiddin'? That's really white uv ya.'

Shane's lips twitched in a dry, private smile. He took a black and yellow and red striped beanie from his back pocket, pulled it over his sandy curls and went back into his shed.

'A brothel?' Trish said later and pondered the card with artless school-girl eyes. 'Y'reckon you could get me inside for a peek?'

Trish. She never ceased to surprise him.

18

He was still perspiring when he got back. He could feel flat opaque police eyes pressing on his back like gun muzzles. They weren't there of course, but no amount of solid logic would bump the anxiety. He was on probation and walking around with a pocketful of illegal substances. It was just this kind of crap he had wanted to stay clear of when he got out, but what could you do? You can't abandon a friend, someone who has taken you in, who has forgotten or forgiven your past shitfulness, leave her strung out. He'd scored before, countless times, routinely, like picking up a litre of milk and some fags at the corner shop. But now, determined to get out of the life, he had the shivering fits of a virgin. Slicks of sweat glued his shirt to his backbone and his jocks into his bum crack. Its trickle made a water feature of his ribcage and engorged the waistband of his jeans, which chafed like a damp beach towel. He could smell his own funk. He smelt guilty. He looked guilty. He knew it, but he couldn't find his way back into the cool zone. He tried to reconstruct the old street attitude from flesh and gesture but, with feeble detachment, he watched it become a plasticine animation of a thing unrecognisable, uninhabitable.

His hollow footsteps clanged in the stairwell, rattling the graffiti and scattering refuse like small litter critters. He cringed at the sound of his progress, afraid of it attracting larger more predatory life forms. Jeezus-Cha-rist! Two years in limbo and he'd lost his nerve. He'd heard if you hadn't used your legs in a while you had to learn to walk again. Bloody good thing he was moving to square street. He laboured upward through the pall of piss and decay.

When he reached Flick's floor he cracked open the door on the landing and peered along the drab corridor – nothing, of course. He swung the door wide and swaggered unconvincingly down the hall in a fast cooling, greasy baste while one hand fossicked absently for the key. He couldn't resist a furtive glance left and right as he opened the door, which meant that he sidled over the threshold and was only tangentially aware of a presence in the room, a presence he assumed was Flick.

'Daddy's brought 'ome the bacon, Flicksy,' he said as he secured the deadlock with ponderous care. He turned and took several steps into the room before he gave the presence his full attention. His body stopped before he did, causing a spasm, which combined with a loud blurted 'Fuck!' gave him whiplash. It wasn't Flick. He didn't know who the hell it was, but it wasn't Flick.

'Mr Nicholls? Val Nicholls? I'm a friend of Shane Clarke.' The presence stood and extended an open hand in Scrum's direction. Scrum stared at it as if it was attached to a booby-trapped Mason.

'What?' he piped.

'Felicity is in the bathroom.' The presence smiled – with sinister mildness, Scrum, in his discombobulated state, imagined. 'My name is David Edge. I hope I haven't come at an inconvenient time. I would have phoned, but ...' He let the sentence hang. Flick's service had been cut off and both of them knew it.

'I ... you ... ah.' Scrum pushed a hand into the thick black shagpile that carpeted his cranium. His fingers seemed to become ensnarled. 'Ah ... where's y'warrant?' he said, finding the formula. His right hand was knitted to his head, his left stuffed deep in his jacket pocket.

'I'm not a cop,' said Edge. 'No need to worry.'

Scrum should have said well fuck off then, but his wits had taken a smoko; he said: 'You look like a cop.' Well sort of. He acted as if he owned the bloody room, like a cop, but the eyes were different. They looked at you, not at some identikit projection of you. Abruptly Scrum's hand was free. 'Where's Flick?' Edge turned and inclined his head toward a door next to the tiny kitchen that had a splintered depression in it the size of a fist. 'Flick! Flick?' Scrum yelled. 'You orright?'

The door snapped open and a woman emerged. She looked like a rough sketch for a Japanese anime character. Her body was narrow and slight, her head was large and elfin, her eyes liquid orbs too big for her face; her hands looked like mail-order prosthetics, their knuckles and wrist joints knobby, their mechanics barely hidden. Her hair was short and cut like a maize field that a large herd of something had stampeded through. She might have been wearing her big sister's clothes. She was insubstantial, as if she had been rubbed out and re-drawn a number of times but the artist remained dissatisfied. Her face was blurred and smudged.

She halted a few shuffling paces into the room. ' 'M orright,' she mumbled. Her hands were twisting and balling her stained polo-neck jumper with such febrile urgency that the handlebar relief of her collarbone was intermittently exposed. Her eyes, enormous blood blisters in sallow white skin, never left Scrum. There was something fearful and imploring in them, trusting but already betrayed, like a dog that expects to get a beating or a bone, but is never sure which.

Scrum's eyes jiggled back and forth between her and his visitor like dice shaking in a palm. Then he felt them held by a cool gaze. 'I'm not a cop, Scrum,' a soft voice reassured him. 'Give her what she needs or we'll have a medical emergency on our hands.' He moved across the room dragging a crumpled brown paper bag from his jacket pocket. Felicity snatched it to her belly and Scrum wrapped a protective arm around her shoulders as they slunk across the room through the only other door.

When Scrum came out of the bedroom ten minutes later the man whose name he had forgotten already – if he had ever heard it – was in the kitchen pouring hot water over home-brand instant coffee in the only two mugs Flick possessed.

'Your milk's yoghurt, but I found some sweetened condensed that's palatable. Milk and sugar?' asked the man in the kitchen. 'There's plenty of sugar.'

'Three sugars,' Scrum mumbled automatically. His gaze strayed vacantly around the tiny flat. The flaking walls were a colour – if colourless was a colour – somewhere between cold porridge and semen. The doors were pea-soup green: the shade featured in horror movies. The colour of the floor covering was indeterminate: it might be carpet or an application of ear wax and belly button lint. The stovetop was a coagulated pizza with the lot. The bench tops and the counter demarcating the kitchen were littered like a beach cove that collects the jetsam of abject tides. Flotsam was crawling across the floor, perhaps seeking a place to spawn. How did Flick get around inspection?

The man in the kitchen, apparently concerned with nothing but stirring the contents of two mugs, stood, from Scrum's viewpoint, waist deep in a trash pile. Like a glamorous streetwalker he seemed to belong and not belong to his milieu. He didn't look or talk like a cop but acted like he was backed by some sort of authority. Jesus! Maybe *this* was a fucking inspection.

He came around the kitchen counter with a coffee mug in each hand. He smiled as he handed one to Scrum. It was hot, and at its touch the chill now permeating his body shocked Scrum.

There was a pitted chrome chair with no seat padding, a sagging vinyl settee with a wooden frame and broken arms and a bean bag deflated to a giant cow pat. Scrum sat on the settee, his visitor took the chair and said, 'How long has Felicity been on pharmaceutical benefits?'

Scrum stared at him blankly at first, then his mind found the wavelength. 'Are you an inspector?' he retorted defensively.

'I'm not a cop. Was once, but never an inspector.'

'Nah, nah. With the 'ousing mob?' Scrum clutched his coffee close to his chest just under his chin, absorbing its warmth.

'No, not with any mob. My name is David Edge. I spoke with Shane, he thought you might be able to help me.'

Scrum stared dumbly, a single deep furrow splitting his otherwise smooth brow. His head moved ambiguously. It was his affirmative nod, but it was indistinguishable from a vague bobbing motion. Scrum's head and neck were joined in a formation that resembled an inverted bucket sitting on his broad, thick shoulders. His jaw line was distinguishable only as a darker smudge looping from ear to ear in the black pepper of his beard. Ned Kelly's helmet would fit Scrum as snugly as a balaclava. He slurped some coffee. It scalded his soft palate and like a slap on the cheek brought some of the old Scrum back to consciousness.

'Can't even fuckin' 'elp meself,' he said with a glum chuckle. He gazed into the wishing well of his coffee mug. Abruptly, he became aware that the silence had lasted a long time and his head jerked up. David Edge was sipping his coffee and studying him through a thin rope of steam. 'What?' He wasn't sure if an answer was expected to some unheard question.

'How long has she been in the life?' Edge asked.

'In it when I met 'er. 'Bout sixteen then. Five years ago, I reckon.'

'Is she a working girl? How does she pay the bills when you're not around?'

'Dunno,' Scrum half whispered into his coffee, eyes downcast. 'Don't ask.' He shrugged. 'Wouldn't tell me anyway,' he mumbled. 'I'm tryin' to help 'er!' He looked up, defiance sparked in his eyes, then sputtered as he turned with a helpless gesture toward the door that hid Felicity. 'But ... she looks like she's gonna ... die or somethin' if ... I ...'

'She's going to drag you back down, you know that, don't you?' Scrum didn't want to hear this; he could feel his anger rising as an antidote to the truth. Tension in his forearms transferred to the surface of his coffee and it broke in choppy waves. He kept his eyes stubbornly downcast. 'Do you think you can save both of you?' the soft, reasonable voice insinuated.

'You're a physically strong man, Scrum, tough I imagine, and probably have the will, but it's skills and resources you don't have that you need. How long do you think it will be before you're robbing Peter to pay the piper, and back behind bars?'

Scrum shook his head like a bull with entangled horns. David Edge placed his cup on the floor and with a subtle movement shifted his centre of balance. When Scrum's gaze came up like belligerent artillery lifting the camouflage of his brows, his visitor appeared relaxed, leaning slightly forward as if he had asked an opinion of Essendon's chances for the premiership and was hanging on the reply. But there was an alert something in his eyes that gave Scrum pause.

'What th'fuck d'you want?' he demanded eventually.

'Ben Bovell,' said Edge simply.

Scrum's belligerence began to melt away. 'Shit,' he said. It began to dawn on him who he was entertaining: Benny Bovell's make-believe friend. 'You're that Dave?'

'I think so.' Edge smiled, scooping up his coffee and settling back into his chair.

'Jesus,' Scrum said flat as a floor. It was a bit like learning that Cher never had surgery. Benny thought anyone who didn't kick sand in his face was a bosom buddy, so Scrum had scoffed at his guardian angel bullshit. Fucking unbelievable. Here the angel was sitting in this pigsty sipping coffee as if it was in a trendy little place in Rathdowne Street. Bugger me, Scrum thought.

'I'm trying to find out why Ben did what he did. I think something – or things – happened while he was in prison. You might be able to help me find out what.'

Scrum's head was bobbing and he was jabbing at the air between them with a stubby finger. 'You're that bloke on the telly the cops wouldn't name, aren'cha?' he said triumphantly, then frowned. 'Didn't Benny tell ya why?'

'Not in so many words. Did you notice anything odd – well more odd than usual – while he was in the last time? Or did you notice an abrupt change in his behaviour?'

'Poor little cunt,' said Scrum, forgetting his own troubles momentarily. ' 'S'e gonna live?'

Edge nodded. 'Not vertically.'

He absorbed the ramifications of the two words slowly. 'Ah, Jeezuz shit. Fella can't win.'

'Between us we might put a score on the board for him.'

Scrum stared at the man in the chair. He might have been the Cat in the Hat. Fuck, he was actually going to do something. 'What're ya gonna do?'

'Find out why, then … what's necessary.'

A chill that had nothing to do with stuffed heating or cold sweat skittered over his skin. There was fear in it, but also elation. He gulped the remainder of his coffee.

'Shane said Terry Varney liked to needle Ben – in more ways than one. Did Varney say or do anything that …?'

In gaol you mind your own business. You think about and talk about only those things that concern you directly. You don't second guess and speculate on the actions, words or thoughts of others unless those others ask you to – and they rarely do. You keep your nose raised to the wind for danger and do the best imitation of all the wise monkeys that you can muster. You're too busy watching the movements in the grass around you to pay attention to the grass around anyone else. Now, he recalled swish and sway that at the time he took to be the random product of the prison wind. And now, looking back from his fresh vantage, he thought he saw a pattern, and it clustered around Benny.

'Fuck,' he said. 'Maybe it wasn't bullshit.'

Edge leaned forward and Scrum couldn't help thinking of those old African safari movies where the lion suddenly looms on the rock above the hunter's head. 'What bullshit was that?' he asked quietly.

Scrum told him what he remembered, what he knew – which wasn't much – and what he guessed. He told him about those meaningless, unconnected things that might have subterranean conduits. He told how Varney, frustrated in his physical abuse of Benny, had resorted to psychological abuse, taunting him at every opportunity with verbal vitriol. 'Mean shit, like sayin' he knew Sharon was shaggin' a toyboy.' He told Nigger James's tale about springing Varney alone with Benny and, when he butted in, Varney protesting innocence, saying that Benny had sought him out, and Benny backing Varney. About Varney's inexplicable ceasing of hostilities toward Benny, virtually ignoring him. He told of Benny's change of mood, of him becoming thoughtful and withdrawn and associating with 'stir fries' Scrum had never noticed him with before. 'Y'know, I'd forgotten till now. I saw Benny talking to "Essendon" Weill once.'

'The "Don"?'

'He normally gave violent nutters like that a wide berth. Makes sense though. Now.'

Edge listened as if to a confession, occasionally interjecting, and then only to clarify a point or prod his memory. 'You didn't think Varney's attitude strange at the time?' he said when Scrum finished.

'Nuh – well – a bit. But Varney had his own worries. We put it down to the whisper.' Edge raised an eyebrow. 'There was a bitta noise doin' the rounds that someone 'ad turned Varney over for an old job. And there was murder in it.'

'You don't know what old job?' Scrum bobbed his head, negatively this time. 'These things you remember, do they have a time frame?' Edge asked. 'What came first? How far apart? Or did they happen around the same time?'

Scrum's brow crevassed along its geological fault line. 'Aah … Varney started his "toyboy" shit about four, five months before Benny was released. I heard the stuff about Varney being dobbed on coupla months before Benny got out – I think. Benny was pissed off by the Sharon stuff but 'e didn't get real quiet until the last months.'

'Quiet?'

'Yeah.' The fissure in Scrum's brow threatened to split his forehead as he struggled for a way to express it. 'Long time ago, in me teens I reckon, I was at the footy an' saw Ablett kick a goal. Right in fronta me. 'E kicked the ball an' then turned and walked away before it had gone between the sticks. Everyone else's glued t'the ball. I couldn't take me eyes off Ablett. Never forgot the look on 'is face. Jist calm, y'know? He knew he 'ad the goal before the ball left 'is boot. Benny looked like that.' He uttered a low chuckle. 'Nigger made a joke 'bout Benny planning a gaolbreak. Reckoned it'd be just like Benny to escape when 'e only had a month to go.'

'James? Can you recall when he came across Ben and Varney? Before or after Ben became quiet?'

'Nuh. It was just an odd thing that stuck in me mind.'

Edge sat back, pushed his hands into his pockets and gazed thoughtfully towards the bedroom door.

After a long silence he said, 'Are you in work?' Scrum nodded. Edge's gaze pierced him.

'It's legit,' Scrum protested.

'I can get Felicity off the street and into a clean house where she'll be respected and protected …'

'House?'

'Brothel. But no drugs: strict rule at the Garden and the Grotto. What a girl puts in her body is her own business, but when it's her reason for living it's bad for business. I have a friend who runs a rehabilitation program, I think I can get her in. When she's straight she's got a job.'

This time two hands became snared in Scrum's hair. His cheeks ballooned and he exhaled breath in a long, thin stream. 'Is that a condition? Does she 'ave to go into the brothel t'get in the program?'

Edge shrugged and smiled. 'No. Do what she likes. But the job's there if she needs it.' He took a card from a pocket and skimmed it across. Scrum watched it spin and hover to rest on an exhausted settee cushion. 'Talk to her about it. You can contact me through that number.'

Scrum folded his arms and bent forward resting his elbows on his knees; from the corner of his eye he contemplated the card where it lay.

'Learn to swim before you try to save the drowning, Scrum,' said David Edge.

19

In the end the solution was simple.

Maeve ran it past her employer.

It was one of those Melbourne days. Those ones that astonish the jaded winter visitor, but to dyed-in-the-wool Melburnians their eventual advent is a secret certainty. Those ones, the existence of which interstate friends can never be convinced, that, like a tram running on time, take the locals by surprise. Just when you are feeling wretched, sulky, victimised by God and Nature, almost persuaded that Queensland couldn't be that bad, Melbourne produces such a day.

The sky is high and blue. Too high, too blue to be a spring sky or an autumn sky. A faraway sky, like a reflection of itself in a freezing mountain lake. The sun is even more distant but when its rays make a direct hit they sting like summer. Winter huddles in shadows, an indigo understudy in the wings. There is no moisture to hold pearly warmth suspended. No zephyr to nip the cheek. The air is pure and thin and spritzig. It tickles the back of the throat and sparkles on the tips of the ears. Sidewalk tables burst into human blossom. The pale smoke of conversation and laughter is burnt quickly away. These are Lygon Street days.

When Lygon Street leaves Carlton and thrusts northward into Brunswick it carves an arrow-straight viaduct, a broad bitumen canal. And just when you are becoming convinced it will sweep you into an ever-widening delta of space and light it clenches: the sidewalks become chaotic and crowded, bumper sniffs bumper. For a few blocks beyond the shoulder of its bottleneck the café life that flourishes at its base regenerates with renewed vigour. Carlton remains a mostly Western feast, but here an Eastern banquet tumbles from the cramped cornucopias of the plain shops onto the pavements. And the chatter and clatter of the street barely remembers Istanbul was Constantinople.

They were seated at a table outside the Gelobar, like sensitive-new-age workers breaking for brunch between assembly lines of cars and pedestrians. Maeve was eating a confection that was proscribed by Weight

Watchers as a weapon of mass destruction. Her companion's spoon was biting into a large wedge of something rich, dark and containing enough chocolate to ensure the solvency of Belgium.

'Do you come here often?' he asked.

'Only with you, sweet acres,' Maeve answered around a mouthful.

'This could kill you quicker than the grog or fags.'

'If you let me drink on the job, I wouldn't have to subject myself to this.'

Edge savoured another spoonful and licked a sticky dob from his upper lip. 'What makes you so sure she isn't dinky?' he said.

'Mmm not,' said Maeve as she engaged cholesterol and carbohydrates with righteous diligence. 'Just a feeling. She's *too* routine, too brain-dead bloody regular. Doesn't fit the picture you painted of her. It's like she's tickin' all the boxes on the Single Mother of the Year Application Form.' She smacked her lips loudly. 'And you were right about her finances. She's not exactly throwing the cash around, but the car's new, her clothes have labels, kids fitted with all the latest electronic attachments. Income and outlay don't jibe.'

'And you're sure she hasn't found your range?'

'Never be a hundred percent. But if she had us on her radar she'd know how to elude us. She's made no attempt. So she's either got nothing to hide or she's playing it safe.' Maeve broke off to pay due respect to her food. 'What I want to do is give her someone to confirm whatever suspicions she has.'

'So she thinks she knows who's watching her,' he continued her thought. 'Her eyes are on him, and when she finds a way to dodge him you're waiting to get on her tail. Can you control that situation?'

She paused over her sweet long enough to indicate the notebook on the table between them. 'You've seen the log of her movements.'

'You think she'll use her visits to Ben to slip away and return undetected?'

'When she's satisfied that we just sit in the carpark and wait for her to come out, don't check on her, she'll be pork through a goose.' Maeve's lips smacked loudly. 'Mmm delicious. Wanna bite?' She extended a spoonful toward him.

'Hmm, not bad. Who've you got wagging the dog while you sit here sunning yourself?'

'Wagging the bitch strictly speaking.'

'Not nice, Maeve,' he said with mock delicacy.

'You've got a soft spot for Ms Kitchen, haven't you?' He gave a small rock of his head, a hitch of his shoulders. 'Speaking of soft spots – I heard something.'

He raised his eyebrows above levelled eyes. And she felt it rather than saw it – the shift. He'd guessed what she was going to say next and he was closing down all access to his soul. It was like watching the ripples on a lake when the wind suddenly drops and the water is mirror smooth. It's uncanny, not because it's as if something has happened, it's as if something has un-happened. It's a negative, impossible to prove. Cops see it a lot in cops who work undercover and must constantly guard and hide their true thoughts and feelings. It becomes second nature, a pure, self-protective reflex. In the end the best ones, the ones that survive, don't know they're doing it. He'd worked undercover for a long time. But unlike others, who play a variety of roles, he'd played only one – himself: a darker version of himself. The habit would never leave him. For some that knew him well it was a keep-off-the-grass sign.

But Maeve, who knew him well, waltzed across the lawn. 'I heard it on the grapevine ...' she sang – badly – to lighten the moment. 'A rumour.'

'Juicy?'

'I heard the Counsel for the Defence is going to walk down the aisle ...'

'Just a bee's sneeze to apple blossom time.'

'... and the man on her arm ain't you.'

'She never asked me.'

Maeve snorted derisively at his quip, then said, 'I was in court the day you two first laid eyes on each other, remember? Her cross-examination of you verged on the pornographic. I thought the judge would have to call a cold-shower adjournment.'

'Who is Sharon's tail?'

'Christ, you're tragic.' He said nothing and showed nothing, no displeasure, no annoyance, not even disinterest. 'Pixie O'Halloran,' she said giving in at last with an elaborate show of disgust at the swain's failure to fight for the hand of the fair maid.

He grinned. 'Pixie is walking the mean streets?'

'She likes these jobs. Gets a lotta knittin' done.' Maeve placed her spoon in the centre of her empty plate and pushed it away. 'For a decoy I need someone who knows the ropes ...'

'Sharon'll expect a male.'

'... but someone who'll stick in the mind when he's spotted. She's a sharp little piece of business, so we can't afford to be obvious.'

'How about Carl Fokker?'

Maeved smiled. 'Yeah, I forgot about Sneaky.' Carl 'Sneaky' Fokker had a visage designed by an odd collaboration of architects: those who built Stonehenge and those responsible for the termite mounds of the Central Desert. An aimless wanderer along life's littoral edge, he never sought but often found; like a beachcomber, he was constantly surprised, fascinated and satisfied by the endless simple riches the sea tossed at his feet. The picaresque hero of his own modest fantasies, he believed he lived by his wits – but it was just luck: his good and others' bad. If a punter was careless with possessions or negligent of the wealth in his care Carl was amiably willing to provide a life lesson. And profit therefrom. 'He'll do nicely,' said Maeve.

She took up her spoon and reached over to help Edge finish his Death by Chocolate. 'D'you think her big secret is a toyboy?'

'I doubt it. The Sharon I know would be broadcasting in prime time if she'd pulled a young stud.' He put his spoon down and wiped his lips on a paper serviette. 'The fact of a boyfriend isn't what she's coy about: it's not the what, but the who. Varney would have to be plausible to get under Ben's skin.'

'We both know a lot of Varneys, Coco Pops – bloody ratbags. Very nasty and dangerous, but ratbags. Pathological liars, say whatever comes into their heads to get what they want. May be brutal morons, but they have a genius for findin' the soft, pink, tender bits of flesh 'n' spirit.' Maeve scooped up the last crumbs on Edge's plate. 'Thus endeth the lesson.' She scowled into the passing crowd as if it harboured a Varney or two, and said, 'Fucking Varney, if he was outta his depth I'd piss in the pool – his kind should be drowned when they're pups.'

20

'David Edge is a Chinese Whisper.'

Two days before she heard these words, Carol had been asked to stay behind after class. It was the last class of the course unit. The assignments had been returned after assessment – with the inevitable mixed reception. But she'd done well. Very well.

She was wondering what her lecturer wanted. As usual – well, since puberty – in situations like this she was apprehensive. In her student days she had been asked to stay behind more than once to endure specious praise of her intellect while liquid eyes dribbled down her cheeks and dripped off her chin into her cleavage. For a time, back then, she began to lose faith in her intelligence: her mind doubting its value as its sibling rival, her body, stole all the attention. She had become like a mother divided by the guilt of an impossible choice between two children, knowing that she must favour one. Her will was hostage to the dilemma.

Now she watched the momentary rebirth of these twins. And she realised she was watching herself watching parts of herself. Descartes definitely got it wrong with duality. If there was just mind and body who was the third party in here? Soul? And who was the watcher watching the watcher of the watched? An infinity of mirrors. Is this what happened to Carol Marks? Did she chase oblique reflections of herself until, unable to tell watcher from watched, she was lost in the funhouse, just another trick of light? Were her angels and demons fragments and facets of herself, which she nourished or neglected, selected or rejected, each demanding a pound of flesh?

As a teenager, existential angst about her mind and body would send her into this myopic self-audit. She longed to grow up and get over it. (The ride to the yellow brick road, Dorothy, was a tornado; the trip home was a breeze.) She hated situations that recalled that time. (Get over it?) She was impatient to get past the moment and out the door. But she waited while her lecturer dealt with a student who clearly wasn't impressed with his grade, and was doing his aggressive best to establish that a self-assessment of his abilities was more reliable than a disinterested one.

While we're waiting, Carol, riddle me this: who was the Carol that, when set the task of a simple written assignment, travelled three hundred kilometres to rubber-neck a murderer's house? Who was that Carol? Who was the one that visited the scenes of all the crimes; the one that inter-rogated the friends of a man who had nothing to do with her essay, and perhaps nothing (or everything) to do with the mystery of the deaths of three (four?) girls? Who was that Carol?

Was it the same Carol Ann Porter who pursued the puzzle of her lover's betrayal and investigated her rival? Was it the Carol who picked up a name that was casually dropped and turned it over letter by letter like an ana-gram of a crime, until its owner was incarcerated and an illegal network was unravelled like a piece of shoddy crochet? What motivated that Carol? What was she trying to prove? Was a puzzle, any puzzle, purely because it was a puzzle, an affront? Or did the solving of each puzzle justify her choice: that her mind deserved love more than her body? Or did the Carol that watched all the fragments of Carol know that the mind flourished while the body withered and this Carol wanted love and love everlasting?

'I'm sorry about that, Carol.'

Her body hopped in an involuntary reaction, tweaking her mind in its labyrinthine wanderings. She'd lost track of time and space.

'Oh,' he said. 'I didn't mean to give you a fright.' He chuckled. 'You were somewhere else then. I apologise for keeping you. Some students won't take a pass for an answer.'

'That's okay,' she said with a small, embarrassed smile. Her gaze slid to the window and then flicked to the doorway. 'I'm not in a hurry.' False words, considering her recent mental journey.

'I won't keep you long,' he assured her. She could tell that he meant it and she blushed inwardly at her teen-queen hubris. You're only a legend in your own lunchtime, Carol, there were still some men who preferred home-made jelly roll lovingly packed by their wives. 'It's about your essay.'

'Is there a problem?' insecure Carol asked.

'No, no,' he said. 'If anything it's too good.' When her brow creased in concern he raised a hand. 'No, no. Don't read anything into that. I just mean it indicated a diligence in research and analysis that went way beyond the call of academic duty.' He stopped and smiled expectantly. She didn't know what to offer as a response – he was clearly seeking one.

'Um. Thank you. I … I was interested in … intrigued,' that was a better word – should deflect more questions, 'by the case, I suppose.'

'Oh, we could see that. We could. Very thorough. And very percep-tive. I can see how you won your place on the course.' While he spoke he was shuffling papers together on his desk and stuffing them in a scuffed leatherette briefcase. He tucked a couple of books under his arm and indi-cated the door with a flat upturned palm. 'We can walk and talk if you like.' He attempted to glance at the watch on his left wrist and a book slipped and fell as his forearm rolled over. Carol scooped it up. 'Thanks, thanks. As you might have guessed I'm running late. Kids.' He raised long-suffering brows but grinned from ear to ear. 'Can I give you a lift anywhere? Well not anywhere.' He grimaced apologetically as they stepped into the corridor. 'I'm heading north.'

'Thanks,' said Carol. 'I'm fine. Not far to go.'

He nodded rapidly, striding out. She had to trot a little to pick up his pace. 'Good, good. Now what this is about is …' He waved to a colleague and almost dropped the books again. 'As you know all papers are moder-ated by a second assessor who doesn't have contact with the students.' He looked a question at her. She nodded. 'Well the moderator for this assign-ment was a retired police officer who does some teaching at the school … in other course units. He was very impressed by your work and would like to meet you and discuss it. Would you like that?' He peered at her closely. She didn't know what her face betrayed but he added hastily, 'He's some-thing of a local legend on the force. Very fondly regarded. An encyclopedic knowledge,' he swung an arm wide to demonstrate the extent, and almost threw his briefcase down the hall, 'of the recent history of the Victorian Police. We're trying to persuade him to write his memoirs.' The large glass doors opening onto the car park slid silently apart. Carol pulled her coat snugly around her. An icy breeze whipped strands of silky hair into a derv-ish on his pink pate. 'He is genuinely impressed by the perspicacity of your analysis, Constable.'

The glance he gave Carol from the corner of his eye seemed a little sly. She wondered what she had betrayed in the essay. They were weaving through a grid of stationary vehicles. He locked his briefcase between his elbow and ribs and struggled to manoeuvre something from a pocket inside his jacket. She rescued the bag before it fell.

'Thanks,' he breathed heavily. 'This is a contact.' He exchanged his briefcase for a card. 'His name is Harry,' he tapped the card, 'Harry Keyes. You'll like him.' He nodded encouragingly. 'And he really would be pleased if you got in touch.' He placed his burden on the bonnet of a dark blue Camry and began searching his pockets.

'Thanks,' said Carol looking at the card. 'I'll think about it.' He had turned to face the car and pressed his remote lock control, so she wasn't certain she had heard him correctly. 'What?' she asked.

He spun back mildly alarmed. 'Oh I didn't mean anything ... you know? It was meant as a compliment ... I mean ... Harry just assumed ... because of the ... um, coincidence ... I imagine ...'

'I'm sorry,' said Carol. 'I didn't catch what you said.'

'Oh ... oh, I see. I was just repeating what Harry said.' Carol waited. 'He thought you were male.' Carol waited. 'Because he was a man, you see?' Carol waited. 'The ... the person your analysis reminded him of ... he was a man. I don't think Harry was being sexist.'

'Oh, that ... that's fine.' She brushed it away. 'I didn't hear what you said, that's all.' She waggled the card. 'Thank you.'

He lifted his hands to ear level and his head beat a tattoo of short nods. Then he climbed into his car and with a smile and a brief wave drove off. She couldn't help feeling there was something secretive in the smile. Her impulse was to throw the card away – patronising bastards – but even as it welled up in her she knew she wouldn't succumb.

'A Chinese Whisper?'

She'd phoned him yesterday and here they were in a restaurant (his treat) at Docklands (cops didn't come here to eat, he'd said). The restaurant sat over water on New Quay, the only completed pier in the development. They were surrounded by choppy waves, boat moorings, disused warehouses, cranes, excavations, eateries catering to any purse, lifestyle fantasies and high-rise seaview follies.

'You're not familiar with the term?'

'Perhaps it's regional.'

'I'm sure you would have played it at some time. It's that game where someone whispers a phrase in someone's ear and it's passed along the line from ear to ear, and then what the last person hears is compared with what the first person said.'

'Oh, yes. I've never known what it was called.'

'Chinese Whispers,' he said. 'I've no idea why. It might be racist.'

She had first seen him in profile. When she entered the restaurant and gave his name she was directed to a table by a window. Almost all tables were by a window – the building's seaward frontage was a curved glass wall. It was yacht clubbish – or a movie set version thereof. He was seated in silhouette against light reflected from the water reading a menu or wine list. At first she thought a trick of the aqueous light had removed his nose. As she drew closer she could see that his heavy-rimmed glasses were obscuring what little nose he had. They perched on a button of flesh that protruded above his top lip like a small balcony joining his nostrils. The bridge of his nose was little more than a stepping-stone. He sensed her approach, his face turned and his hand came up to steady the precarious spectacles. He had a jellybean head and small jug ears; his hair was a wiry steel-grey thicket. He was the closest thing she'd seen to a living cartoon. She began to smile, she couldn't help it, he was the user-friendliest looking cop she'd ever laid eyes on.

He stood, removing his glasses – or catching them before they fell – and smiled a warm welcome. 'Ah, you must be Constable Porter,' he said shaking her hand. 'Bevan said you could make an old man wish he was a young recruit again.' For some reason the compliment didn't annoy her as usual; the grandfatherly flirting was bundled in woolly good humour.

'You don't seem so old,' she found herself saying. 'Carol.'

'Harry Keyes,' he said, smiling. 'Harry.' He gestured to the opposite chair and waited for her to sit before taking his seat. 'I was sussing the wine list. Would you like something to drink?' He handed the list to her.

'A glass of red would be nice,' she said without looking at the list. 'I'll trust your judgement. Something local?'

'Not Margaret River?'

'I can always get that,' she said with a smile.

Keyes beckoned to a waiter and ordered a Pinot from Mornington Peninsula. The conversation was small talk – was she enjoying Melbourne? had she been before? her opinion of the course – as they made their selections from the menu and the wine was poured.

'I imagine you're wondering why I wanted to meet you,' he said at last.

'Just a tad curious.' She had only taken a small sip from her wine, for form, and nodded her approval. She didn't want the edge taken off her wits.

'A tad,' he said almost to himself with a brief, private smile. He took a long sip while bright eyes between bristly brows and the rim of his glass studied her. 'I'll be blunt,' he said as he placed the glass on the table. 'I'm a blunt man. But lovable with it,' he added with an impish grin. He paused then said, 'How well do you know David Edge?'

The question took her by surprise. 'What makes you think I know him at all?'

'Well, you didn't ask who he is,' he said teasingly, his eyes twinkling up from under his brow. 'But actually, Bevan Humphris told me that when you asked to change the subject of your analysis, one of the reasons you gave for your interest in this case was that you had met one of the detectives on it.'

'There were a lot of detectives on the case. Why assume that I was referring to David Edge?'

He shrugged. 'Your paper favours his viewpoint. There are conclusions drawn that couldn't have been based solely on information you were provided with in the class materials. Your "voice" in the writing sounds like his.'

'Are you suggesting my paper was ghost written?' She could feel anger clawing up her gullet. It must have scraped her vocal cords, because Keyes rapidly raised placating palms.

'No, no, of course not. I wouldn't have given it such a high assessment if I believed that it wasn't all your own research and writing. But ...'

'But?'

'Well to be blunt, again. You haven't allowed yourself to become a – what's the term? – a cat's paw for David?'

She noticed his use of the first name. 'What's your relationship to David Edge?' she demanded.

He noted her use of the name. 'It seems,' he said, 'much closer than yours.'

'I met him two years ago.' Her elbows were on the table and her face was thrust toward Keyes. 'We spoke for a short time – only minutes. He gave me some information. I have no idea why. But it led to me gaining ... um, professional advancement. I got points on the board it may have taken a long time to score otherwise. I hardly know him. But ... I suppose ... I'm appreciative. I was curious about him too. I thought I might learn something by studying a case he worked on.'

Keyes seemed mildly amused by her restrained passion. He nodded with a slight, condescending smile. 'David has a way of doing that.'

'Doing what?'

'Eliciting loyalty in odd places.'

This annoyed her too; she wasn't a grateful puppy. 'Are you going to elaborate on *your* relationship?'

His smile was contrite. 'You're blunt also. I thought I'd like you.' He sipped his wine deeply. 'We're old friends – and I was his superior at one time. In a footnote you made the point that he was drawn away from an active role on the taskforce by duties of a covert nature, and that as a result his theories were not adequately explored.' Carol's face said, So? 'I was one of his bosses on that covert job. I headed the team that trained and ran him.' He stopped and looked at her. 'How much do you know?'

The meal had arrived by the time she finished telling him. They ate in silence except for complimentary sounds and comments on the food. He paused to lift his wine glass to his lips, and that's when he said, 'David Edge is a Chinese Whisper.'

'You know his reputation?' enquired Keyes.

'I know that he's regarded as a sort of renegade cop. Some think he was a whistleblower. Some think he got too close to the man you were targeting and was corrupted. Some think he's a murderer. Then there are others who think he's as pure as the driven snow, just an innocent victim of circumstances.' She stopped and took a sip of her wine; now he was the one under observation over the rim. 'I think one or two I've met believe he's still working undercover.'

He sat back in his chair and gazed through the window. Two seagulls quarrelled over some flotsam. 'That's a comforting little fantasy for some who care about him. It explains all the contradictions and ambiguities of his behaviour and allows them to invite him to their table with a clear con-science – even with a sense of righteousness. David the martyr.'

'You said you were close.'

'I said I was closer than you. I regard myself as a friend, but I don't know that anyone really gets close to David. Once maybe, but three years undercover left him with an impenetrable shell. No one knows what he has done or what he is capable of, or who David Edge is now. Perhaps David least of all.' His manner had lost its jauntiness. There was a hollow regret in his voice. Carol began to wonder if the tragic clown across the table was here to extirpate some guilt. What was his role in the making of this David Edge he described?

'Is that what you meant by Chinese Whisper?'

He had lost interest in the food remaining on his plate. 'Oh, we cre-ated that,' he said with some bitterness. 'We concocted rumours about his corruptibility and disseminated them through our undercover operatives and informants. It was easy to do that back then. Just like seeding weeds in your backyard. The recent drug squad and corruption scandals, and the underworld killings, brought cop-crim relationships in this state under so much scrutiny that it would be almost impossible now. Inevitably, the stories about David were embellished and distorted. We were so successful we couldn't sort true from false ourselves in the end.' A bleak, dry smile.

'You established his bad reputation.'

'I'm afraid so. When David was approached to cop some quids two things were obvious. One was that someone on the so-called Jogger Murders taskforce had leaked information: the identities of suspects weren't public knowledge. The other thing was that someone with clout was involved. It also indicated that David's suspicions were well founded. Of course when Desmond Poynter died – David's chief suspect – it wasn't possible to establish his guilt. Not conclusively.'

'The murders stopped.'

'They stopped.'

'David Edge was kept undercover to discover who hired Poynter?'

'What? No, no. Something else, something more important, had overtaken us by then. He was part of a whole new covert taskforce. In fact he was the sole reason for its existence. Well him and Jack Barker.'

'Jack Barker. He was a Melbourne Godfather type? There was a book about him.'

'*The Crime Broker*,' Keyes acknowledged. 'It's a good description. Jack wasn't a "Godfather" or "Napoleon of Crime", more a master of ceremonies – a conduit, a facilitator. He kept things fluid and maintained the ecological balance. He knew every game and player – both ends of town. And where the bodies were buried. He was a cop who'd gained so much power through cultivating movers and shakers on both sides of the law that few jobs went down without a green light from Jack. When he was "encouraged" to retire he just went on operating as if nothing had changed. Love him or hate him, Jack was a legend on the force. There still are cops who yearn for the good old Barker days. His apologists claim that he managed crime. According to them, if he was alive today, the recent underworld war wouldn't have happened. But he was corrupt. Jack's "crime management" made him a fortune.'

'You knew him?'

'Oh, yes,' he said, and smiled. 'Jack was charismatic, a charming man. As charming as …' His voice trailed off and his gaze strayed to the window. 'That's where the Chinese Whisper came in. When we linked the attempted bribery of David to Jack we … overreacted – but, it seemed like a necessary precaution.' He paused with a regretful grimace. 'I don't know if you're aware that David's family is very wealthy?'

'I've heard stories.'

'Well, there was a chance David could get close to Jack, but it wouldn't happen without Jack vetting him thoroughly. We were worried that he wouldn't swallow a David tempted by a paltry couple of thousand dollars. So we spread black sheep stories and tales of disinheritance and nasty deeds. They turned out to be redundant. David met Jack, and by a stroke of luck or genius he impressed Jack more than we could have hoped. Jack was convinced that he didn't give a damn about money; it was power that turned him on. Ironically, the fact that he came from money only made this idea more plausible. And of course the benefits of cultivating someone with David's background weren't lost on Jack either.' He looked at the scraps on his plate. 'Would you like some dessert?'

She shook her head. 'Coffee will be fine.'

After he ordered he said, 'I coached David in undercover survival. We were doing it on the run. This had fallen into our laps unexpectedly. But the thing that made it work was that Jack, wily, old, hard man Jack, took a genuine shine to David. I can understand that, but what I never understood was why he came to *trust* him so quickly.' He stared at Carol as if she held the answer. 'David was undercover for three years and we collected a huge amount of intelligence. A lot we couldn't use immediately – not without endangering David. And in the end we didn't use much at all. You know how it is: you start out worrying a loose thread and the next thing you've got a ball of wool and one sock. And when you show it to someone who should care they're angry because you ruined a sock.'

He stared across the water to where an old, bleached quay reposed in decrepit respectability waiting like a faded widow for the kiss of renewal. A fleeting grimace crimpled his face, like a plastic bottle shrinking from a flame. She wondered what memory provoked that inward cringe.

'I have to admit it frightened me,' he continued. 'It felt like we were freaks with eyes sensitive to the invisible spectrum, who'd found a dark city colonising the light one like a hand in a glove, sharing the air it breathed, the water it drank and the bayside views. And no one else could see it. Someone somewhere decided it was all too hard – or too hot. When Barker died the taskforce was disbanded. Of course there was fallout, and anyone too close to Barker was contaminated. There were some resignations and early retirements from the force, two or three pollies decided they wanted to spend more time with the wife and kids.'

He spread his palms and hoisted his shoulders to his ears; his face was an empty knapsack. 'Actually internal tensions were already tearing the taskforce apart. The ever-upwardly-mobile hotshot in charge was a man called Darrell Peach. He wanted to keep David in place indefinitely, even when Jack was arrested. Everyone knew David was Jack's heir apparent. It was Peach's grandiose plan to have him fill the vacuum left by Jack, and then the taskforce would manage the Melbourne criminal establishment through him. It was insanity. Peach couldn't see that we would become the thing we'd spent three years trying to destroy.' He uttered a short cynical laugh. 'If he'd been able to guarantee David's cooperation he might have got funding for that. It would have kept a lid on things.'

The coffee was brought to the table.

'But surely, arresting Barker exposed Edge?' Carol said.

Keyes rolled his head from side to side. 'That's it: the imponderable thing. Jack apparently retained his trust in David to the end. He died of cancer awaiting trial. He left many of his assets to David, and named him executor of a trust fund he'd set up for his daughter. Pat, Jack's wife, walked out when their child was a baby and Jack never forgave her. Jack was a male chauvinist of the old school.'

'Edge was a surrogate son?'

'One of my pop psychology theories.' Keyes grinned.

'Edge does own a brothel?'

'Two actually – plus … other things. And yes, they were part of Jack's estate.'

She watched Keyes watching her. Was he waiting for her to draw an obvious conclusion?

'Despite all this you don't ascribe to the idea that he killed Desmond Poynter.'

'We encouraged that idea. It was a bit of luck. Poynter's death enabled us to paint a picture of David as ruthless and dangerous. It cemented his bond with Jack and gave him a reputation that provided some protection.' Keyes sipped his coffee. 'Whitey Poynter was a name feared in the underworld,' he spread his hands, 'The man who topped Whitey – well?'

Carol studied the sad-clown face across the table. It was a fascinating tale and possibly true, but if the reason for its telling was to demonstrate that David Edge didn't commit murder it fell short. The two propositions were not mutually exclusive. And what's more she couldn't believe that Keyes was unaware of this.

'Why did you invite me here? Why are telling me all this? Really?' she asked eventually.

'I'll pay the bill. Let's take a stroll and I'll point out some of the sights.'

Soft white puffs of cloud were bursting from the horizon like stuffing from the seam of a mattress. They stood at the far end of the quay on the frontier of the development. They were looking through a chain-link fence at old deserted docks that, a huge sign assured them, were eagerly awaiting a place in the Twenty-first Century version of the Australian Dream.

'As you can see it's far from finished,' said Keyes.

'Will it ever be?'

'Depends on the vested interests I suppose.' He pivoted slowly towards her, eyes brushing the remnants of a waterfront history. When they met hers he said, 'In the end there were two schools of thought. You've heard what Peach advocated. David was afraid there would be a bloodbath, he advocated a gradual strategic withdrawal.' Keyes hunched his shoulders and stared at his hands as he rubbed them together vigorously. 'Our masters just pulled the plug.'

There was silence as the ramifications of this sank in. Then Carol said, 'What happened to Edge?'

Keyes stuffed his hands deep in his overcoat pockets. 'Well,' his head gave a small tilt to the side, 'we'd done our job well – much too well. You see it wasn't just villains we had to fool, cops had to believe that David was feral. Jack's old mates were well known, but we had to assume he had new mates doing badness. On the taskforce there were only three people who knew David was the source of the information. The rest knew nothing but code names, we used over a dozen, all of them were David. The taskforce was handpicked, we believed it was watertight – but you can never be one hundred percent. Those processing the information and handling the follow-up investigations were led to believe there were a number of sources. They were also under the impression that the operation was targeting David as much as Jack.' He looked at her glumly. 'So you see, to protect him, we'd painted him into a corner. We couldn't take the Chinese Whisper back: he was thoroughly compromised.'

'So he resigned,' she said staring at triangles of light tobogganing over the water. She realised he was silent and she could feel his gaze on her. She glanced up. There was a twinkle in his eye

'Tell me,' he said, almost coyly. 'You must have formed some hypotheses to explain my motivations. What are they?'

Carol turned and faced him. Very deliberately, she locked with his gaze. 'Are you a practising Catholic?' she asked. Something in his eyes flared; his grin faded then returned at full wattage. She took that as a yes. 'When was your last confession?'

His lips split wider, he bounced on his heels. 'Oooh, you're good. You've got no idea how much …'

'How much what?'

He bustled on without responding. 'You're right. Unresolved guilt: I have to admit that was probably a deep motivation. I worked undercover – in my youth – so when I found myself behind the desk I knew what it was I was sending young men and women into. You train them as well as you can, make sure they know what to expect and that they're as prepared as anyone can be for something like that. Then you sit back, helplessly, and watch it take its toll. The brightest and best can succumb to drugs, alcohol, money, depression or deep, dark cynicism. It's hard not to feel responsible.

I felt a particular responsibility in David's case. He didn't choose the life, it was thrust upon him by circumstance.'

'To what did he succumb?'

'On the face of it, none of the above.' He mimed puzzlement with a fat pout of his lips. 'Which may mean he's the most damaged of all.' His face relaxed into its clown sadness.

'Maybe he's doing what he wants – and always has.'

Keyes gave a dubious, non-committal grunt. 'Most coppers are nine to fivers. It's a job and they do it to the best of their ability and go home and try to forget it. Over the years there have been regrettably few I've met who had it.' Carol's brow corrugated in question. 'Cynics call it crusading zeal or overweening ambition or obsessive behaviour or … other things.' He brushed them away with a brusque flick of the head and flip of the wrist. 'I like to think of it as passion for a vocation.'

'You wanted to be a priest.'

'Thought about it.' His eyebrows bounced in a bashful fashion. 'David had it. Jack – in his twisted way – had it. Someone you acknowledged in your paper, Carol Marks, she had it, poor thing. Even her husband, Neville, although he likes to pretend he doesn't give a damn. But their marriage wouldn't have lasted if they didn't share the enthusiasm. And that's what I thought I saw in your paper. Now I've met you I'm sure of it. You've got it, Carol.' She began to shake her head and make inarticulate sounds of denial. 'You're condemned by your own words, Carol.' He laughed. 'A stranger mentions a name and two years later a large smuggling and trafficking ring bites the dust. I do my homework too. A career like mine builds quite a network of contacts. Got a lot of friends in WA.'

Carol stared at her feet and watched one booted toe tap. 'It could be overweening ambition.'

He ignored her demur. 'Your course finishes in a few days?'

'End of the week.'

'Are you going straight back to Broome?'

'Haven't had any leave in the last two years,' she admitted a little sheepishly, looking at him under her brows. 'I'm taking some and doing a little sightseeing.'

'Crime scenes?'

Her glance sharpened. 'No.' A short self-deprecating chuff of laughter. 'Scenes more picturesque.'

'Well there's a lot of beautiful scenery here, but, just like back home, there are wild things in the undergrowth.'

Her gaze hardened. 'It was just the paper. I wanted it to be the best I could do. I have no intention of pursuing this further.'

There was that grandfatherly patronising smile again. 'It would be best that you didn't. You haven't got the sanction of the law here. And it would benefit no one. It may do unnecessary harm.'

'To whom? David Edge?'

'Oh, David can take care of himself,' he said with a sad smile. He looked around. 'My wife is coming to pick me up. Can we give you a lift?'

'I don't have far to go, thanks.'

He stepped forward and gripped her hand firmly in both of his. 'It was a great pleasure meeting you, Carol. Truly.' He folded her hand around a card. 'Keep in touch with me, please.'

Carol said her farewells and walked away. She was certain Harry Keyes had been on a fishing expedition: under the camouflage of his candid revelations, she had been pumped gently, winningly, for information. She was also certain she had been warned off – in the nicest possible way. Keyes wanted her to know he had clout in WA.

Unless Poynter had gone nuts, if he killed the joggers he was paid to do it by a third party. Barker may have been the third party, but he was dead, so who was left to shield? If Barker's role was only as the broker of the contract, then Poynter's actual client may still be at large. She couldn't imagine Keyes protecting someone like that, but David Edge was another matter. At one time Keyes held him in high regard and still felt responsibility in his fall from grace. She could imagine Keyes shielding his protégé. But which David Edge was he shielding: the one that committed murder, or the one that didn't?

Every cop knows you spend information to buy information. Had Keyes got a bargain or blown his budget? Then she realised he may have given her the answer. What if the Chinese Whisper was the Chinese Whisper? What if police knowingly used a murder committed by its key agent to consolidate a successful covert operation? Back in the bad old days a blind eye might be turned, but these days a new broom was sweeping cop shops in this state. Reputations and careers could still be destroyed if that proved to be true and the truth surfaced.

So, her paper had stirred Keyes to ensure that sleeping dogs would slumber on. His thumbnail of local criminal history was an attempt to discourage her from interrupting their nap. The further she walked from New Quay the more it seemed like a storm in a teacup. Why bother? Why not just let it blow over? Why dip a spoon in? Sometimes imagination transforms a tiny blemish into a huge disfigurement: had a burr of guilt pricked him to over-react?

Harry Keyes was the kind of man who valued his reputation, but there was ambivalence in his attitude that was confusing. Was he an architect or an unwilling draughtsman? Did he know for sure? Did he suspect? Or did he just fear that it might be so? Perhaps he preferred to never know.

That everything he said was designed to encourage her to unravel the other sock, that she did not consider until much later – too much later.

21

He waited until the tram passed, then turned into the narrow side street and swung into the yard behind the building. A clutch of kids leaned against a BMW, smoking and gesturing in animated exchange. They stopped and watched with blank faces and suspicious eyes as the car rolled to rest. A skinny boy with a beret pulled to the back of his head hip-hop style was the first to show any response. As Nev Marks climbed from the car, the boy grinned and stepped forward, his hands in his back pockets, palms to buttocks. His grubby jeans looked three sizes too large.

'Hiya, Sarge,' he said.

'Your Beemer, Brix?' said Nev.

''Er ladyship's.'

Nev didn't get the reference and didn't care. He turned to the man emerging from the passenger side. 'Constable Milosz, this is Brix.' Brix grinned and Milosz nodded, deadpan. Nev scanned the vehicles in the yard. 'Where's the Commodore, Brixie?'

The boy shrugged. 'In the shed, maybe?' He tilted his chin at an old corrugated-iron shed with a youthful Colorbond roller door. Nev strode over and tried the door. It was locked. He glanced at the top floor of the building.

'Is 'e up there?' he asked.

'Ain't seen 'im come down,' said Brix.

'Stay here,' he said to Milosz. 'I'll throw the key down.' He turned and walked back through the gate onto the footpath.

'We haven't got a warrant,' Milosz called after him sulkily, folding his arms across his chest and trying to stare down the kids. Nev ignored him.

There was a door that opened onto the footpath in a side wall which, at street level, was otherwise featureless. Nev pressed an intercom button. When he heard the tinny response he said, 'It's Nev.' There was a buzz and a clunk and he pushed the door open. He climbed the three storeys of stairs to the top floor and walked along the landing to the door at the far end. He entered without knocking. A woman was standing in the middle of the room. She was facing away from him. A hand rested on a shapely hip thrust to the left in a contrapposto pose he usually associated with the man standing behind the bench between kitchen and lounge.

Briefly taken aback, he paused awkwardly and began a mumbled apology. 'I'm sorry I didn't …'

The woman swung around, green eyes flashing. Now he could see her face he realised she was much older than she first appeared, but not as old as he knew she had to be.

'He's hopeless!' she exclaimed, as if he was a participant in the conversation and had just popped out for a pee. 'You're his friend. Tell him for God's sake.'

'Um … you're hopeless,' he said, looking to the man in the kitchen for his cue. All he received was the amused smile of a casual observer. The woman stepped briskly up to him and thrust out her right hand.

'I'm Samantha. You're Neville Marks,' she said with such forceful certainty that if he wasn't before, he was now. 'He's told me so much about you I'd know you anywhere. He's terribly fond of you and your brave wife – Carol? Yes Carol.' She took his hand in both of hers and massaged it.

'Is he?' was all he could say, genuinely surprised.

'How is she?'

'Fine.'

'I'm very pleased to hear that.' She held Nev's gaze. He could see why she was the darling of the women's magazines in her youth. 'I want them for dinner, David. At the house. You arrange it.' He wondered if they were intended as guests or main course. 'Do you think Carol would be interested in talking about her experiences to a group I chair?'

'You can only ask.'

'Good.' She nodded emphatically and smiled. His reply seemed to have answered more than one question. She dropped his hand, pivoted neatly on her toe and swept up a cashmere coat draped over the back of a chair. 'Talk to him, Neville.'

'Not staying for breakfast, Mum?' David Edge asked laconically.

Samantha shot him a sharp glance of love and exasperation. 'I rose some time ago, David.' There was a laugh deep in her eyes when she turned to Nev. 'He calls me *Mum!*' she snapped. Her annoyance was a tissue. 'My idiot boy is going to let her slip through his fingers,' she added, as she hitched her coat smoothly over her shoulders.

'Who …?'

She frowned at him as if he had failed to bring sandwiches to a picnic. 'Catherine Temple!'

He stared at Edge. 'The Counsel for the Defence?' he said.

Samantha stared at him, puzzled for an instant, then she exclaimed,

'Oh, my God! Boys and nicknames. He calls you "Skid", did you know? It's disgusting, don't allow him. And talk to him.' Green eyes like cattle prods as she opened the door. 'Goodbye, Neville,' sweetly; 'David, ring Andy,' firmly. And she was gone.

'That was Mum,' said David Edge.

'Based on available evidence I'd hafta agree.'

'Breakfast?' Edge brandished a pan.

'Ta. Where's th'Commodore?'

'In the shed.' It was said in a tone of mild curiosity.

'Key?'

Edge pointed at the wall end of the bench. Nev strode over, snatched up a key wallet, came back round the bench and crossed the kitchen and opened a door. 'Back inna minute,' he said as he stepped outside. He was on a deck, which was the flat roof of the rear section of the floor below. He crossed to a rail near the fire escape stairs. On the first landing below was a security gate, which could be opened by a push bar from the inside but only by key from the outside. He leaned over the rail and called, 'Milosz!'

Milosz was still leaning against the car in bouncer mode, watching the BMW reverse from the yard. Without unfolding his arms he pushed himself away from the car with his bum and rotated his head left and right. The kids laughed and chorused, 'Hey, Milosz,' as they pointed up at Nev.

When Milosz located him Nev called, 'Commodore's in the shed,' and threw the keys. There was more guffawing from Milosz's audience when the keys eluded his grasp. 'I'm staying for breakfast,' Nev added. 'Take the car.'

'What if the Commodore's marked?'

'It won't be.'

'What about the fuckin' keys then?'

'Give 'em to Brix.'

Milosz glowered suspiciously at Brix. Brix preened.

Nev stripped his outer layer off as he came back inside. 'Might be better you taught those kids a healthy fear of coppers, Dave.'

Edge looked up from a pan into which he was cracking eggs. 'Fear's only healthy if it works to your advantage,' he said smiling.

'Pretty apron.'

'I'd say nice jacket, if it didn't look like a doona with sleeves.'

'Right,' said Nev. 'Ritual insults outta th'way, what's f'breakfast?'

'Protein, fat and cholesterol.'

'Sounds bloody delicious. I'll do the coffee.'

Both men worked in silence for a while then: 'The Counsel for the Defence?' Nev queried.

He was beginning to think that he hadn't been heard over all the hiss and bubble in the kitchen, when Edge said, 'Catherine's getting married.'

Nev watched his friend, whose eyes were on the pan in his hand. 'To whom?' he asked eventually.

'Someone she met in China a couple of years ago.' He flipped the bacon.

'Chinese?'

'No. Australian. Diplomat – something in government.'

'And …?'

'Nice bloke.' Nev stared at him until he returned his gaze. 'Toast?' was all he added.

'Anyone told you when it comes to women you're bloody tragic? Course I'll 'ave toast.'

'Only recently, as a matter of fact. The bread's in the fridge.'

They were seated on stools each side of the corner of the bench, tucking in, when Edge said, 'Has the Commodore been naughty?'

'Hit an' run,' said Nev around a mouthful. 'Not seen the news?'

A couple of mouthfuls later Edge said, 'You'll be the size of several Sumos if you eat breakfast with every Commodore owner.'

'Someone you know.'

'No kidding.'

Nev sat back and wiped his mouth so he could observe his host's reaction. 'Bernie Vargue,' he said. 'Never regained consciousness. Cardiac arrest – dickie ticker.'

Edge finished his mouthful without any discernible sign of surprise. 'Bernie had a lot of enemies.'

'A witness described a Commodore. Didn't get the number. Thought there was an S or five in it.'

'There's an S *and* a five in mine.'

'Funny that.'

'You don't like me for it?'

'If you killed Bernie it'd be with your bare hands. But I gotta touch the end of the pool each lap. When his wife and Maurie Stone disappeared, Bernie insisted you cancelled them. And word is 'e 'ad a contract out on you.' Edge showed more interest in this. There was only a handful of people who would pick it up, and Nev was one.

Edge mopped up some egg with a corner of toast. 'When did you hear this?'

'In the wee hours of this mornin' when I began asking questions. But the noise has been 'round a while, I'm told.'

Edge pushed his plate away, leaned on his elbows and took a bite from the egg-stained toast. He chewed and stared through the wall at the end of the bench. His eyes were placid blue pools – very chilly pools.

'A small cog slip somewhere in th'machine, eh mate?'

Edge's lips tweaked in a resigned smile. 'Can't get the wood, you know.'

They were standing at the sink doing the dishes, Edge washing, Nev drying, when the key wallet came sailing over the rail and landed on the deck. Edge cocked an eyebrow at Nev.

'Brix,' said Nev. 'Milosz didn't find anything.' Edge handed him the last plate and wiped his hands on the end of the tea towel. 'How old is he?' Nev asked.

'Not old enough. Like the rest.'

'Old enough t'know what a condom is?'

'Spade takes good care of their education.' He walked away toward the door.

'It could look like money laundering to some,' Nev said.

Edge paused at the door and smiled. 'Everything needs a lick and promise from time to time, as Aunt Dolly used to say.'

He was tossing the key wallet from hand to hand as he returned. Nev was putting the last plate away. 'Why don'cha get a dishwasher like everyone else?'

'Waste of water.'

'Ever thought that might be why women dump ya?' Nev said, leaving an opening, but Edge didn't move into it. 'But y'might be onto somethin' with Carol. She's the kinda girl who's used t'scourin' tin plates with sand.' This time you didn't need to know him that well to detect the puzzlement. Nev studied him. 'Well, bugger me,' he said in mild wonder. 'She was tellin' the truth.' Edge was returning his scrutiny. 'I'm not talkin' 'bout my Carol.'

'That's a relief.'

'You two really did only meet for minutes.' He could see the question still flickering in Edge's eyes. 'Girl of the Golden West? Pert little copper from Broome?'

Dawn broke. 'Carol ... Parker ...'

'Porter.'

'Porter – that's right. I met her when I was up there a couple of years back. She arrested me.' He opened his palms as if to say give me more.

'She's here.' Edge waited. 'In Melbourne.' Edge's expression said, So? 'She's doin' a course at the Detective Training School. Thanks t'you, apparently.' Now the clear brow furrowed slightly. 'It seems you gave 'er a name an' she parlayed it into a major career move.'

Dawn came up like thunder. 'That big sting that caught Col Mulcahy by the piggies down here?'

'Be my guess,' said Nev. 'Wanna 'nother coffee?'

Edge nodded. 'How did you meet her?'

'She's been pickin' Carol's brains about a case she's analysin' for an assignment. Old one of yours, matter of fact.' He'd turned to the coffee machine with the mugs, so he felt, rather than observed, the subtle change. Cold soup might feel a microwave that way. He turned back, a crease dividing his forehead from unkempt black curls to thickly vegetated brow ridge.

'What case?' asked Edge. Close your eyes and it sounded like idle curiosity.

'The Jogger Murders.'

His eyes were blue icebergs against a pristine Antarctic continent. 'Do you know where she's staying?' Casual question.

Nev nodded. 'Dropped her off th'other night. Why?' he smirked.

'Might stop by and offer my congratulations.'

Nev Marks handed his friend a mug of coffee, and any fantasies of a secret romance, which he may have harboured, he scuttled and allowed to sink silently. He wondered if he should warn Carol Porter what was coming. Nah, why spoil the fun?

Edge took his coffee over to the piano and sat on the stool. 'Handy Bernie dying like that, I was going to call you,' he said. Nev blew steam from his cup and waited. 'Our old mate Terry Varney – what's brewing there?'

Nev took a seat on the couch and a deep sip of his coffee, even though it scalded his soft palate. 'Who told you about Varney?' he asked evenly.

'Friends in low places.'

'Not a leak?'

'No leaks.'

Nev studied his face for a beat or two. 'Varney's worried?' Edge nodded. Nev looked into his mug with a small smile of grim satisfaction. 'Y'cold cases are comin' back to haunt you, mate.' Edge elevated a brow. 'Remember a Customs warehouse job, back in ninety-eight? Musta been one of your first cases. Cigarettes – security guard was beaten to death. Dennis Molten was on it with you.' Edge nodded. 'What d'you remember?'

Edge stared at his toes doing one of their intricate routines, then his head came up. 'The guard was bludgeoned, thrown into a rubbish skip, died of head wounds. His gun was missing – .38 Smith and Wesson – so was his torch, never found. Glass fragments in his wounds suggested that it was the murder weapon. Human hairs tangled in his fingers and blood that wasn't his on a boot. The hair and blood were from different individuals so we knew that there were at least two involved. Considering the quantity of cigarettes moved in a short time we thought three or four. No fingerprints or other useful trace was found. Heavy rainfall after the crime polluted the scene. In fact if they hadn't hidden the body it might have been washed clean.'

He sipped his coffee. 'There had to be someone on the inside and we discovered a storeman with a connection to Varney. We didn't have much doubt about the storeman's guilt, he was a lousy liar, but we couldn't shake his alibi. Neither the blood nor hair was his so we couldn't place him at the crime scene. The blood wasn't Varney's and his head was a billiard ball – alopecia. He didn't have an alibi worthy of the name, but we had nothing to place him at the scene either. We had them under surveillance over a period of time but if there were others involved they stayed well away. Neither Varney nor the storeman went anywhere near the cigarettes or each other. We thought that they either had a buyer lined up to take the cigarettes immediately, or, because of the murder, they cut their losses and dumped them.' He shrugged. 'That's about it.'

Nev waited, gleefully milking the moment. 'Well, Sherlock,' he said with a cheeky grin. 'Y'had the DNA. Y'just lacked the D-A-N.' Edge betrayed neither puzzlement nor understanding. 'A while back one of the suburban stations nabbed someone for a big whitegoods ripoff. When 'e was more than happy to be swabbed they weren't hopeful that 'e was their man, but they took a sample for elimination. These days all DNA donations are gratefully accepted. We ran a check for matches against DNA sampled in similar unsolveds. Takes months for results that don't have priority – labs got a huge backlog. Anyhow, there was a match.'

'Hair or blood?'

'Hair. One Daniel Turoczy. He did a runner – must have twigged that he'd made a mistake. He got picked up in Queensland on a local charge. When we moved to extradite him he started bargaining.'

'What did he have?'

'You'll love this, mate,' Nev said, grinning. ''E says Varney thought the storeman had the security guard in his pocket. Apparently the roster got changed at the last minute – guard might've got cold feet – and Varney didn't get the message. He went ballistic an' beat the shit out of the bloke who sprung 'em loadin' the truck. Our Tez was always too quick off the block. Turoczy claims that, while he and another bloke were trying to pull Varney off, the guard grabbed a handful of his hair and kicked the other bloke in the nose. Varney got the other bloke to help him dispose of the guard, but Turoczy was freaked and decided he needed some insurance. So while they were occupied …'

'The torch,' said Edge.

'The torch,' agreed Nev. 'Fingerprints and all. Varney, greedy bastard that he is, wouldn't leave with half the loot, and he was in such a hurry to load and get to hell out, he forgot about the torch.'

'We didn't find a single unaccountable fingerprint. They had to be using gloves while they were loading.'

'I flew up to Brisbane to question Turoczy. He was very plausible. Apparently Varney was so cocksure he stopped for a smoke. Took off his gloves. Guard appeared.' He swirled the last of his coffee round the cup and tipped it down. 'After the job he wanted to put as much distance as possible between himself and Varney, but Varney was keen to party. He didn't want to get Varney offside by looking too anxious, so he went along until he twigged to Varney's idea of celebration, then he bolted.' Edge raised a questioning brow. 'Pills and porn followed by a bit of festive gay bashing. First time Turoczy worked with Varney. Never went near him again.'

Edge rolled his mug between his palms. 'The others?' he said gazing into it.

'Only admitted to one – no name. Might be a fourth. Either he doesn't want to dob a mate, thinks they won't back his version or he's holding them as bargaining chips. Anyhow the legals are wrangling over it at the moment. Glad to hear Varney is worried. Should be – they'll throw away the key. Couldn't happen to a nicer bloke.' Nev made a show of appreciating his coffee, and watched his host over the rim of the mug. He licked his top lip and said, 'Your turn.'

David Edge took his time taking his turn. He finished his coffee, stretched around and placed his mug on the piano. 'The blood on the guard's boot – your third man, he's probably dark matter. The fourth has had his DNA sampled on other occasions. If there was a match it would be made by now.'

'Got a name?'

The eyes that locked on Nev's were the blue of distant sea under a bruised sky. 'Don't waste time and resources on number four, Nev. There's nothing in it for anyone. He's out of the game and he'll never play again.'

22

'Jeezuz, Macka, where are ya?'

He waved a vague arm, acknowledging the well-deserved rebuke. He couldn't concentrate on the game at the moment. He slowed to a trot and let the pursuit of the ball get away from him. He glanced over his shoulder. That man was still with his dad. They seemed to be arguing. It made him feel anxious and he didn't know why. This only cranked the ratchet of his anxiety. He was sure he'd seen the man here before, he recalled the shape of him: he looked like a torpedo in an overcoat. Fortunately, he'd never know how close this simile came to the truth.

On the edge of the field his dad said to the torpedo standing splay-legged, hands in pockets, blocking his view of the game, 'Jesus Christ, Ernie, do you really think I'd do that? You must have a poor fucking opinion of me.'

'Real big fuckin' coincidence, mate,' said Ernie the torpedo.

'That's what it was, mate, a coincidence. Maybe not so big.'

'Whaddaya mean?'

'Christ this is fucking Bernie Vargue we're talkin' about. Rent-A-Friend's best customer. And why do you think he chose now, right now, to try to top your boss? Eh? He was bored, he wanted to get back into the action. It's crowded, new players, not a lot to go around. No one wants an old kid back on the block disturbing the natural balance.'

Ernie breathed deeply, his head swivelled above his collar. Then he turned to face the field and folded stiffly onto the seat beside soccer dad. 'Yeah,' he grudgingly relented.

'And Jesus Christ, a hit 'n' run! Gimme credit. And I'm not gonna use a fuckin' Commodore! He's gonna be coming to have a chat as it is – if he thought I set him up …'

'Yeah,' Ernie sighed. 'Well – I'll talk to him. An' you know 'e don't go off half-cocked. You'll be sweet.' He began making a noise like a rutting koala. This was his laugh – in chortle form, but his mouth was still a grim line. The man beside him cast a startled sideways glance. 'I got a contact,' Ernie said through his mirth. 'He reckons that it wasn't the car that did the job.'

'Yeah?'

'There's a witness, see. Said Bernie froze in the middla th' road. Didn't try to get outta the way. 'Eart attack just before the car 'it 'im.' The koala rutted again.

Soccer dad began to laugh now, louder than he might have if he wasn't experiencing an enormous release of tension.

'What?' said Ernie, the koala really banging away now.

Between attempts to reign in paroxysms soccer dad said, 'You won't fuckin' believe this, mate, but I knew about Bernie's pump. I was putting together a heart attack. Thought I might have him die on the job. But … Jesus … shit … don't tell … him.' His laughter broke away from him again. 'All that research … and he just needed … a fuckin' good scare.' He nudged Ernie with an elbow. 'The bloke … the bloke in the Commodore … reckon I should … chip in for his lawyer?'

Together both men rocked the park bench.

On the field the boy saw this and smiled and got back to his game.

23

Cheryl put the phone down and left her office. She crossed the short, narrow corridor and entered the reception area through its rear door. She smiled at the bouncing bulk of the woman who joked with a customer at the counter. Cheryl had hung up her garter belt when she found true love; Paula had hung hers up once she'd put her kids through private school, and now worked front of house. Cheryl didn't interrupt. Planting her rump on the edge of the desk she watched the receptionist work her magic.

Paula was one of the sexiest women Cheryl had ever seen. By conventional standards she shouldn't have been. She was a sex goddess, styled not after classical form, but after the most ancient and iconic of models: the Venus of Willendorf. Cheryl had had no idea what that was until Rose showed her a picture in one of her art books (Rose had been an artists' model in her youth). Cheryl saw the likeness immediately. Of course Paula had a face and was taller, but like the eleven-centimetre stone figure, her torso was as wide as it was high, all tits and arse, on legs that tapered to slender ankles and dainty feet. Her mouth was small with lips so full they were obscene. Everything else about Paula was big: her hair, her eyes, her gestures, her heart, her personality. Her voluminous clothes were worn with a panache that women, plump or petite, envied. And there was always a cleavage that men imagined they could swan dive into. She and The Crimson Grotto went together just fine.

The happy customer left the counter and Paula pirouetted, her warm round giggles burbling in her throat. 'Oh, Chers. Sorry, didn't see you there.'

'Customers first.'

'Keith's been coming here for years. Knew him back when I was working upstairs.' She chuckled; her bosom was a tidal swell billowed by a warm breeze. 'What can I do you for, luv?'

'Have you seen, Ernie?'

'Nup. I thought he was at the Garden today? Tried his mobile?'

'No joy. Boof is at the Garden. Ernie was showing the new bloke around, but he should have been through by lunchtime.'

'Problem?'

'Big Boss wants him at the Garden.' She shrugged at Paula's raised eyebrows. 'I'm going over there now myself. If Ernie shows give him the message.'

Cheryl managed The Crimson Grotto and The Rose Garden during daylight hours, which, effectively, made her the day madam. Little Boss – Rose Garden, a nocturnal creature – was the night madam. Although they used both offices Cheryl was based in the smaller office at the Grotto and Rose ruled from her palatial den at the Garden.

She stopped at the Garden reception desk when she arrived and asked Charlotte if Ernie Duggs had shown.

'No-o,' said Charlotte, mouth as round as her eyes. 'And I think he's in the poo.'

'How can you tell?' Cheryl said dryly. It was a rhetorical question, but Charlotte, ever Charlotte, answered.

'I don't know. I think it's his eyes – Mr E's. They sort of change colour.'

'Keep after Ernie,' said Cheryl. She walked away looking over her shoulder and collided with a large body coming through the parlour door. She stepped back, an apology on her lips. It was Boof, Ernie's second-in-command. Cheryl reached up and grabbed an ear, dragged his face down and planted a kiss on it. Boof, ever Boof, blushed, his eyes darting furtively. 'I'll be late tonight, want to cook or eat out?' asked Cheryl struggling to suppress a giggle. God, Boof, we're in a brothel.

Boof glanced at Charlotte, who was ostentatiously oblivious. 'I'll cook,' he said. His voice was deep but whisper-low. He seldom raised it – in anger or joy. It made him seem as shy as he actually was. He was huge, tall and muscled. He was so fair he appeared to lack eyebrows and his face was fresh and button-smooth with a schoolboy handsomeness that was almost pretty.

He wasn't as young as he looked but he was younger than Cheryl. A car accident when he was a child had caused some brain damage. People said he was all brawn and Cheryl was the brain. Cheryl knew better. Boof was intelligent, but his mind milled ideas slowly. His body reflexes, on the other hand, were fast. School had been hell for him. His short-term memory was flawed, it took tedious hours of repetition to retain facts. He emerged from the experience with a magnum of bottled anger. He'd seen things in East Timor, where he served in the army reserve, and still snapped and flipped in the night like a trapped mouse if the ghosts walked.

He met Cheryl when well-meaning friends, believing his virginity was a problem requiring solution, chipped in to buy a bang for his birthday. Cheryl was the solution, but Boof had trouble separating fucking and love. He became her regular customer until she discovered that to afford their Saturday dates he lived on bread and water the rest of the week. By then she couldn't separate fucking and love either. Boof needed Cheryl, there was no doubt about that, but by Christ, did Cheryl ever need Boof.

She could feel the warm beam of his eyes on her back all the way down the hallway to the office door. As she opened the door and entered the office she was wondering about the colour of her boss's eyes. She wasn't expecting to find his body on the floor.

Her own body had barely time to react, when his head rolled toward her and smiled.

'Shit!' she cried, anyway – she deserved the release.

'Sorry,' he said, but didn't move. He was lying on his back in the middle of the plush white carpet with his fingers laced across his belly.

What the fuck are you doing? her mind yelled. He was a bloody law unto himself.

'Shag pile carpets are to be laid upon, not walked over,' he said.

'I think the name speaks volumes for itself,' she retorted dryly as she skirted his feet and crossed to Rose's desk.

'"Shag" and "pile" are two words a nice girl shouldn't dwell upon,' he said.

When she sat behind the huge desk she lost sight of him.

'I spent many a happy hour on the carpet in front of my grandparents' gigantic fireplace reading, thinking, conjuring fantasies in the flames.' A pause. 'Descended from squattocracy, on the distaff.'

She didn't respond, she knew it wasn't expected. If one of the hard men, into whose heart he was meant to strike fear, walked in now, how would he react? He'd lie there and waffle on, she answered herself, and he'd scare the intruder shitless. Because he didn't give a damn – or seemed to not – and nothing fanned fear like that attitude. There was silence as she booted up the computer. She scooped up the notes Rose had left for her on the desk and began reading them.

'Cheryl?'

'Mm?'

'Would you marry me?'

She deliberately misunderstood the question. 'I'm married to Boof.'

'Be brutally honest.'

She pressed back into her chair and stared at the ceiling. 'If I wanted someone to guard hearth and home I'd marry Boof. If I wanted dirty deeds done dirt cheap I'd marry you.'

There was silence from the other side of the desk. 'I had a crush on you once,' she added to leaven the harshness of her words.

'Really?' Genuine surprise in his voice. She thought it had been em-bloody-barrassingly obvious at the time.

'It was my fantasy that you would sweep me into your arms and take me away from all this.'

'That's one of my fantasies too.' Voice sweet as vinegar. She waited – nothing, and was about to go back to work. 'So, a beautiful, intelligent, no-nonsense, common-sensical woman wouldn't touch me with a barge pole?'

'Sorry,' she said.

'Why?'

'She'd never know where you were.'

'I'd keep regular hours if I was married.'

'That's not what I meant,' – and you know it. 'You – you go away to places in your head. You're hidden deep inside. If you understand what I mean?'

With a cupped ear she'd have almost heard the shag pile rustle, then: 'Perfectly.'

Not the stuff of fantasy, but definitely more lovable when he betrayed some vulnerability. Her attention slowly returned to business. There were three sharp raps on the door. She looked up and he rose above the desk with her gaze as if he was a projection beamed through her eyes. He moved like a dancer. Hands in his pockets, he faced the door.

'Come in, Ernie,' he said.

'I'll leave you …' Cheryl began.

'It's okay,' he said, smiling over his shoulder. 'This won't take long.' Ernie Duggs was in the room. He stood with his hands overlapped at crotch level: the contrite boy-child. 'Will it, Ernie?' he added.

'No, Boss.'

Cheryl couldn't see Edge's face but his stance was relaxed. Of course she'd seen him at his most dangerous when (apparently) relaxed.

'Bernie Vargue's carked it,' said Ernie. A dog with a dead duck for his master.

'It would appear so.'

'It was an accident.'

'You can guarantee that?'

'Yeah. Yeah, iron-clad.'

'I heard he'd taken out a contract?'

Ernie dropped his gaze to the carpet. 'Yeah. Sorry, Boss. I thought it'd be better if I handled it.'

'If I want someone dead, Ernie, I'll kill him.'

'Yeah, I know, I know. But it really was an accident.'

'I know. Our friend is a consummate professional. Hit and run is much too blunt an instrument.' Ernie's head wobbled eagerly between the shoulders of his overcoat, a nodding toy.

Cheryl didn't know why she had been allowed to witness this. Perhaps to make it clear that Big Boss had no hand in Vargue's death, a conclusion she may have jumped to if she read about it in a newspaper. Ernie clearly wanted to continue his confession, but Edge cut him off.

'I have a job for you,' he said.

Ernie's polished wooden face struggled to an expression of relief, his mouth creased and stretched into its smile line. He was forgiven whatever his trespass was. Edge drew a photograph from his breast pocket and handed it to him. Ernie stared at it. 'Bit of a looker,' he breathed.

'Name and address on the reverse,' said Edge.

Ernie flipped it over. 'You're fuckin' jokin'. A copper?' He flipped it back and stared again. 'Jesus.'

'She's not local,' said Edge. Ernie glanced at him, expectant. 'Put together a team. Twenty-four seven. I want to know everything she does while she's in town. In the state,' he amended.

'Be a pleasure, Boss,' said Ernie without shifting his eyes from the image in his hands.

'No improvising. And, not a hair on her head, Digger.'

Ernie's head jerked up. 'Hey, Boss.' He tapped the photo with the back of his free hand. 'That'd be a fuckin' crime,' he said with injured gravity. Then he thought of something. The inverted Y between his brows sharpened. 'But the Garden 'n' Grotto – whattabout security?'

'Boof can handle that.'

Cheryl looked up from the stuff she wasn't really doing.

'Boof? But ...' Ernie began to protest.

'You've trained him?'

'Y-yeah ...'

'Then Boof can do it.'

At that moment Cheryl loved the inscrutable son of a bitch. She'd have his child, if she wasn't reasonably sure she was a wee bit pregnant with Boof's.

24

The mobile phone played the opening bars of Grieg's Piano Concerto No 1.

'Meant to tell you,' said Beryl without preamble. 'You remember Francine's oldest – Teddy? Well he's getting married on Sat'dee. Thought I'd better tell ya before I forgot. Just in case, you know, you wanted to go and have a sticky. The Lutheran Church on the corner over from the park. Can't remember its name.'

'Thank you, Beryl, but don't use the phone unless something's happening there,' said Pixie. 'It's poor surveillance technique,' she added. Beryl liked that kind of talk.

'Oh, oh sorry, Pixie. I'm new at this,' said Beryl. 'It's exciting, innit?' she added with beginner's glee. Pixie had proved Beryl's husband, Bert, wasn't screwing around, as Beryl had imagined. Eternally grateful and chronically broke, Beryl repaid her debt in kind.

'Yes it is, Beryl,' Pixie replied, sans enthusiasm. 'Over and out,' she added to smear a little icing on her friend's cake. The phone was on hands-free; she broke contact and went back to her knitting. If Sharon didn't make a run tonight she'd finish this jumper.

Pixie O'Halloran's name was Pixie O'Halloran. Most people assumed that 'Pixie' was a nickname because she looked as elfin as her name, but she was christened 'Pixie' and her family name was 'O'Halloran'. As was that of her late husband, Pierce. This was not the coincidence it appears to be; their first meeting was the consequence of a mail mix-up. They'd got each other's pay cheque. Those were the days when you touched your earnings before the bank did. They were also the days before the paperless office. Some things don't change.

Pierce was a cop. So was Pixie, but her skills with the computer, a much less user-friendly contraption back then, ensured that her feet never hit the street once she'd completed basic training. They were tucked neatly under a desk during her entire career in law enforcement.

He was a first-generation Australian, arriving with his family in his early teens. Pixie didn't regard herself as Irish at all (at all). Her branch of the O'Halloran's weren't on the First Fleet, but certainly the second or third.

Pierce was killed when he attended a 'domestic'. His partner and he had been called to the address on frequent occasions. The husband was a violent drunk. This time his wife had retaliated. He lay on the kitchen floor, life leaking away. She straddled him like a dog over a bone, fending off all comers with bloodied scissors. Pierce, his soft Irish brogue like a lullaby, had persuaded her hand to her side, his fingers were fluttering near the scissors, their eyes were locked only inches apart. Chook, Pierce's partner, said later that he could see the woman's grip on the scissors relaxing when Pierce added a couple of gentle words; no one ever found out what they were. (Pixie said Pierce never knew when to shut up: he'd almost talked her out of saying 'yes'.) The woman uttered a scream and stabbed him in the jugular. Chook shot the woman. Her husband survived.

Now you may have romantic notions that Pixie was sitting knitting on this bleak night waiting for Sharon Kitchen to make a fatal error because of some comic book crusade scenario she was living out. Banish those thoughts. Pixie would be here if Pierce was home tucked up warmly in bed; the bonds of her computer desk had always chafed a little.

She was two and a half lines short of a cable-knit pullover when Beryl interrupted.

'Yes, Beryl?'

'Is that you, Pixie?' Beryl had a phone Pixie had given her. The only number in memory was Pixie's.

'Yes, Beryl.'

'She just came down in the lift. She's looking around real suspicious like.'

'Good. Now remember what I told you – just a glance every now and then. She has to pass you no matter what exit she chooses.' As camouflage, Beryl had a large fake bandage from knee to ankle and crutches. She loved disguises.

'She's taking out a mobile phone,' whispered Beryl urgently. Now, now, thought Pixie, keep your knickers dry, Beryl. 'Now she's … oops …um … ah …Yes, Barry … Well then you know what to do … no … no … yes … no … yes … She's gone. What did you think?'

'Gone where, Beryl?'

'Oh, out your exit. She stopped right next to me. Scared me to me waters. What did you think?'

'Was she on the phone?'

'Oh, yes. Heard everything. She was calling for a taxi to meet her on Swanston at Tin Alley. What did you think?'

'About what?'

'My improvisation?'

'Inspired. Must go. Carl will come and get you.'

'Well,' said Maeve when Pixie called. 'Either we had a rare bit of luck or the cunning little bitch spotted Beryl. She can duck and weave through the uni and either lose or expose a tail real easy. It'd be very tempting just to play safe and pick her up at Swanston Street, but she knows that. Could be the ploy. Follow her, but let her lose you when it gets tight. I'll head to Tin Alley. Keep in touch.'

'She's crossing to the university at the Grattan lights,' said Pixie as she trailed Sharon discreetly. 'I think it's just braces and belt, Maeve.'

'I bloody well hope you're right.'

When Sharon looked at the woman who stepped to the curb beside her she saw a short dumpy figure with a thick knitted hat pulled over her ears. Pixie was cocooned in a long puffy quilted parka. She was wearing an old duffle coat underneath. A backpack tucked around her belly enhanced the effect of rotundity. When the lights changed she scurried across the road like a pygmy hippopotamus in ballet points. Sharon smiled at her bobbing back.

Pixie hurried with tiny knock-kneed steps along Grattan Street until she came to the first ingress to the university grounds. She turned in, then immediately came out again looking around as if confused. Sharon was approaching along the footpath. Pleased that she had guessed right and didn't have to dash back to Royal Parade, she picked her way along Grattan like a plump bird afraid that it missed the worm, stealing quick glances at Sharon's progress. She took the university gate Pixie had abandoned.

Pixie took the next entrance. The tangle of alleys, paths and passages that crisscrossed the campus were a GPS grid overlaid on her brain from student days. She stripped off her bulky coat and cap, shedding kilograms, and threw them behind a wall screening waste bins in a tiny landscaped cul de sac. At night, profile was the give-away. Hitching the backpack over her shoulders and tugging the hood of her careworn duffle coat over her head, she ducked and weaved through the byways. There was an open court Sharon would cross if she remained on track to her advertised destination.

When Pixie got there Sharon was emerging from a Gothic arch of the Old Quad and cutting across the far corner of the court. Pixie chose a course perpendicular to hers. She was beginning to relax. Sharon seemed to be making a beeline, or as close as possible, to the Swanston end of Tin Alley, but after passing under the ersatz arches of the Priestley building into the space occupied by the student union building, Union House, she suddenly changed tack.

The forecourt of Union House was bustling. A banner over the façade spruiked a cultural event. Sharon disappeared into the crowd like a grain in a bucket of sand. Pixie knew the best way to lose her was to jump in the bucket. Maybe she just wanted a pee. Right, Pixie, what now? There were too many exits Sharon could use. If Sharon came out on the north side of the building she was probably still on course, but if the phone call was a ruse she might exit on the south. Pixie knew there was a door on the south that she couldn't cover while watching the doors at the front and north side. She pictured the place in the hospital foyer where Beryl had held vigil. They had put her where a large group of people normally sat or loitered. The odds were that Sharon had not spotted Beryl. To dangle a red herring all she need do was stand in that area and talk loudly. Pixie decided that was Sharon's braces. The Union House digression was her belt. She headed south.

She took up station near the south exit in a motley group stealing a quick puff before the show. If you didn't look too closely, Pixie was now an under-nourished undergraduate clothed by an op-shop, shivering stubbornly for her addiction. She could see if Sharon used the front entrance and retraced her steps, but if Sharon came out to the north, on Tin Alley, she could head back toward Royal Parade, away from Swanston and her taxi, and Pixie wouldn't know until much too late.

She had reconciled herself to losing her quarry, and suffering another cigarette to make sure, when it materialised like a reflection in the exit's glass door. Sharon hovered inside until a small group came to the door. She mingled with them as they passed through. Pixie watched until she broke away from the group and then, throwing her stage-prop cigarette in a bin and groping in her pocket for her phone, she followed. Sharon was returning the way she came. The broad open expanse of the South Lawn would expose Pixie, especially as, now, they both were moving against the general flow of pedestrian traffic.

As she exited the colonnades of the Old Quad Pixie flipped off her hood and turned toward a clutch of people heading for the Union and yelled, 'Sorry, Neil. I'm late, gotta go. See you Sunday.' Then she ran across the plaza diagonal to Sharon's route. As chance would have it 'Neil' was having a night out. Someone in the group yelled after her, 'What? What? Noelene?' Then mumbled something like, 'Silly bitch.'

When Sharon glanced toward the voices she saw a skinny college kid loping over the lawn showing her boyfriend her heels. As she got in the car on Grattan Street she saw a petite middle-aged woman in a white windcheater and black leggings and sneakers jog by, wispy dashes and dots in the air marking her trail.

'Yellow Lexus, Maeve. Personalised number plate T-O-I-B-O-I,' said Pixie as the car lights flickered away between the sidewalk trees.

'That's T for tit, O for orifice, I for insertion, B for bugger me?' said Maeve.

'No, I for incorrigible,' Pixie sighed with theatrical long-sufferance.

'Well, bugger me. Jist like a ticket in Tatts. You've earned yourself an early night my little pixellation.'

Pixie wasn't sure what had happened. She set off to retrieve her discarded clothing. Oh pooh! She'd been enjoying herself.

25

'Harry Keyes? Can't see Harry involved in cover-ups and corruption. He was a tearaway in his youth, I've heard. The face comes from a footy accident in his teens.'

The sky was blue porcelain. There was no wind and the sun had stripped away their winter coats. Yesterday the rain had been horizontal and probably ice when it left the Pole. They had come from lunch at Rosati's and were sipping wine in Federation Square. She liked the place: it tumbled toward you like the Kimberley.

'I partnered an old mate of Keyes once, he worked covert with Harry,' Carol Marks continued. 'Harry had a limited shelf life because of his face. Got out before it became too well known. His undercover experiences made a practising Catholic of him. Faith was his way of dealing with the shitty stuff I suppose. Don said he didn't think he was Catholic before, let alone devout. Harry likes clear guidelines. I can imagine him spooked by any hint of deep systemic naughtiness. When it comes to corruption, he prefers the few rotten apples school of thought.'

'What school of thought does David Edge subscribe to?'

Her wine glass hid the lower half of Carol Marks's face, but an eyebrow arched over an eye, which gimleted Carol Porter. The glass clacked on the faux marble tabletop and she smiled like a mother hearing a timorous, long anticipated confession. 'Davy,' she said, adjusting position in her chair. 'I'd say he favours the breast cancer school.' She smiled at Carol's frown. 'Eternal vigilance and regular self examination.'

'This is a man who profits from prostitution and may have committed murder?'

The reply was delivered with camp pomposity. 'Zero tolerance is a declaration of war on your enemy before it's born, and it makes society impossible.' Carol Porter made her eyes and lips round. Carol Marks gave a full-throated laugh. 'I actually heard him say that once, back in the days when we'd all meet at the pub after work and get as pissed as a barbie of philosophising Bruces.'

'It's difficult to imagine the person I met in a situation where he's in less than complete control of himself.'

'You're a bright girl, Constable Porter, and perhaps you're still young enough to believe that human motives are simple, but I think you'd be quite contemptuous – rightly so – if I suggested your interest in David was just a romantic one.' Carol Marks cast a gaze like spider silk on Carol Porter.

Carol's eyes felt its pull and didn't struggle. She used time sipping her wine. 'Is that what you and Neville believe?'

Carol Marks shook her head. 'No. And we don't think you're just trying to rack up more brownie points by solving an unsolved. But – do you know why you're doing it?'

Carol Porter flopped back in her chair and gave an unconvincing incredulous chuff of laughter. 'Doing what? I'm not doing anything. I wrote a paper and I did a … a weeny bit of extra homework because … because I'm … an obsessive perfectionist. There, I confess.'

'Carol Porter …' grinned the other Carol, waggling a finger.

'Carol Marks …' a mirror finger tick-tocking before wide-eyed innocence. Then her composure dissolved and the two women laughed together, neither sure what they were laughing about, but enjoying the release. 'Okay, okay,' she sighed. 'I don't know what the hell I'm doing. Or why. At this point in time I'll accept any and all ideas.'

'You didn't invite me to lunch just to thank me, or to get advice on your sightseeing itinerary, did you?'

'I hate bloody sightseeing.'

'You want to follow the thread as far as you can?'

'It's not about him; or truth or justice or the Australian way of life. It's about me.' She swirled her wine slowly and watched liquid ruby oil the wall of the glass. 'I'd been briefed about David Edge before I met him: crooked cop, hard man, whoremaster, perhaps cold-blooded killer. And what's he look like? Surfer Blue the all-Aussie boy – Ginger Meggs in long pants. Then I see him behave in complete contradiction to the warning on the packet. I learn later – from the lady herself – that he crossed the continent to help an ex-prostitute he barely knew. Hadn't so much as fucked. Why? Because she asked him.' Her voice rose in pitch. Its inflection demanded to know what kind of idiot believes crap like that. 'Doesn't that sound like atonement for past sins?'

'You're a very beautiful woman, Carol. I imagine men are attracted to you for all the wrong reasons. As a paranoid schizophrenic I have some insight into your situation.' Carol Marks grinned.

Carol Porter laughed sardonically. 'Pretty perverse, eh? Wanting to know someone who you hope will tell you to peddle your pretty arse elsewhere.'

'But, if you pull one of his cases apart piece by piece you can get to know him, and never have to meet. Eh?'

She stared at Carol Marks. Was it as simple as that? It must be. She felt a constriction flush from her body, as if released from inner hooks and wires. It was her permission to go ahead.

'Yes,' she said. 'I want to follow the thread to the end; see the face of the Minotaur, but I don't want to slay it. I want to know why Theseus didn't.'

'You don't think it was Poynter?'

'Oh, he may have been the instrument, but …' She faltered as the subtext of Carol Marks's question rose like swamp gas. She eased back in her seat and studied the chiselled ascetic face. St Paul's, in the final phase of renewal, draped it like a mantle. Laughter chimed like a bell at another table and a waiter paused to ask if there was something more they wanted. They said 'just the bill' simultaneously. When he was out of earshot Carol said, 'You know who killed Desmond Poynter.'

'Pretty sure,' said Carol Marks airily. Her nose wrinkled and her lips pursed in a moue of dismissal. 'Not know in any sense recognised under law. More of a … feel for the Gestalt.'

'Does Neville know?'

'Good grief. Can't tell him, he's a Homicide cop.'

Carol regarded Carol. A shadow slid across the table and fell in her lap. Both Carols glanced up. One lonely, tattered shred of grey fleece in the blue, and it blocked the sun.

As Carol Marks's gaze dropped back to earth it brushed a familiar shape. She focused, and saw that man again.

'I'm twining a thread on my finger,' said Carol Porter. 'I want you to tell me if you think it's the right one.'

'I have a feeling it is,' said Carol Marks, as the shadow skittered away across the square. 'Assuming you're going with the statistics.'

26

Maeve said, 'There's the name, address, phone and email.' She tapped the slip of paper attached to the photos with a stout finger. 'Shame we didn't credit Varney with a subtle sense of humour.'

'The criminal mind never ceases to amaze me.'

'Bullshit,' said Maeve.

They were in a Vietnamese restaurant that she favoured, for lunch. She was tucking into a large omelette. He poked his food around the plate, watching it cool.

'Well, "toyboy" – sounds like a snide reference to a relationship. Course it was – as well.' Maeve mumbled around a mouthful. 'He's a lot younger than our Sharon. An' they are shaggin' – no doubt about that.' Her mastication slowed and her black marble eyes studied her lunch companion. He was staring at the food fleeing his fork as if calculating how to head it off at the pass. 'Pixie rang last night. Spelt t-o-i-b-o-i, the word rang a bell. She's gonna look into it.'

'Good.'

'I left Sneaky in place so Sharon won't catch on that we caught on.'

He seemed to notice that his food had been harassed but not eaten. He took a mouthful. 'Tasty,' he said, nodding.

'Whattahellsamatter with you today?' asked Maeve with her signature circumspection.

His food was abandoned again. 'I had a case once. Elderly woman with three adult offspring, all intellectually challenged. The youngest, the son, was in his thirties but a mental ten-year-old. One day, a couple of weeks before Christmas, when the mother went to collect the eggs, he laid siege to the chook shed with chimney bricks. Neighbours couldn't get near him.

When the cops arrived she was dead. It was handed over to Homicide. Not touched by a single brick, she'd died of a heart attack. His motive was the only question. Eventually it was teased out. He attacked because he suddenly remembered Christmas was coming, and he thought she was going to kill a chook for Chrissie dinner.' He tapped the plate with his fork. 'Now they'd slaughtered a bird every Christmas of his life, and he loved to watch the process, from axe to plate. Had begged to swing the axe. But, this year there was a runt chicken in one of the broods that was getting hell from its brethren. His mother encouraged him to take care of it until it was fit enough to survive alone. It wasn't a pet. He seemed to forget all about it once he'd finished nursing it. A couple of weeks after it was returned to the pen, his mother coaxed him to show the chook to his uncle. He didn't have a clue which one it was.'

'Well, fancy that,' said Maeve, as dry as a peanut-butter smoothie.

'And he loved roast chicken, Maeve. Eat it every meal if they let him.'

'What the fuck are you on about?' dismissed the obdurate Maeve, but she felt a tiny worm of apprehension wiggle in her core.

As if on cue the brightness in the street dimmed, then the sparky flicked the switch and the stage was flooded again. When she looked back at her employer he was tucking in.

'Just a little something between us and the sun.' He grinned over a forkful of stir-fried squid.

27

Cat burglars are a rare breed of crook.

They tend to be solitary creatures and therefore seldom prowl in typical criminal haunts. Their contact with the underworld community is mostly limited to that part which converts theft-specked items to spotless cash. And in most cases this association is a simple matter of necessity rather than choice.

Lin Flowers was even more isolated from what might be considered his natural milieu than most. He came from a respectable middle-class background and was led to his disreputable profession by a cocktail of romantic desire and morbid curiosity rather than base venality. Of course, those motives didn't make him any less a thief or his occupation any less unsavoury. Initially he stole to extinguish the voyeuristic nature of his trespass in private spaces and to repudiate the inference – levelled by himself at himself – that his actions were symptomatic of obsessive compulsive behaviour. In other words: a little bit kinky.

So far, curiosity had not killed this cat – nor incarcerated it.

He was now financially independent and semi-retired and took on jobs only as a challenge, a sop to boredom or, as in this case, a favour. These days he possessed a cleansing facility of his own and could wash, rinse and dry the accumulation of filthy lucre that had been mouldering in the Caymans. Ironically – or appropriately – his laundry was a business that sold and installed security systems. He relied on a comparatively small and efficient staff to manage its day-to-day operation, but he assumed the burden of product testing.

This, in a sense, was what he was doing now.

He was standing in the centre of a lounge room in a four-bedroom suburban house on a relatively large suburban block. It was in the heart of Elwood, one of the older bayside suburbs. The original house would have been built a little over one hundred years ago and had undergone several extensions or renovations in its lifetime. The security system was a recent addition and, obviously, an improvement installed by the present resident.

Improvement was not a word that Lin would apply in this case. The product was an inferior one and Lin felt righteous not being its supplier. In fact he had formed a strong conviction that the occupant was paying lip service to security for insurance purposes. Neighbourhood Watch was active here and it wasn't a crime hotspot by any stretch. No, if this householder had any secret hoard it was tucked away in one of the plastic boxes in the second room off the hall to the left, approached from this end. The door to the hall was directly behind him.

There had been a lock on the back gate – easy pickings – in a high wooden fence of fairly recent construction. It ran along three sides of the property. The backyard was a pocket forest with a small wedge of lawn skewered by a Hills Hoist near the back porch. A security mesh door and a deadlock on the back door had given him only slightly more pause than the gate. There was no alarm, which suggested the occupant didn't want police or neighbours bursting in uninvited. There were a few low-tech devices employed, such as the odd hair stretched across gaps between doors and jambs, and inconspicuous alignments, the displacement of which would escape the unwary displacer, but was obvious to the placer.

Lin felt the buzz even on a walk-through like this: he was inside, in a forbidden space, it was kind of sexy. He was moving at a swift but leisurely – for him, luxurious – pace. He had backup. Someone was watching his flanks and rear. He didn't know who and didn't need to – that was his employer's business. If the resident returned unexpectedly he would have ample warning.

There was a single resident and he was male. The bathroom said so. He had female visitors, but there wasn't a resident woman. Interesting, because for a bachelor pad this place was neat as a pin. He was either Mr Sheen or had a little woman who does, in whom he had absolute trust. Judging by the paraphernalia in the first room on the left it certainly wasn't his mum. Of course, someone must have a mum who's a swinger. How else could the existence of discos be explained?

Thoughts of wife abusers with manicured lawns crossed his mind as he took a mobile phone from his pocket and selected a number in memory.

'All clear, Dave,' he said.

He pocketed the phone and went through a door opposite the hall entrance into a small vestibule. He guessed the hallway originally bisected the house, but sometime in the past a wall had been removed to enlarge the lounge room. The vestibule was in darkness but he didn't turn on the light, and flicked off the exterior security lights before he opened the front door. It faced onto a wide verandah. He went back into the lounge room and waited.

It was about five minutes before he heard the front door close.

'Spick 'n' span,' said David Edge, after his eyes had done the walking on entering the room.

'I don't think he's a big reader,' said Lin indicating the wall of books at one end of the room. 'Leads to dog ears.'

'Are they real?'

'Yup. Delivered by front end loader I'd guess.'

'Any nasty surprises?'

Lin knew he was referring to security devices not literature. 'The CCTV cameras are hooked to his computer. If they're nobbled ...?'

'His computer's convinced it's molested by a power spike and has eyes squeezed tight and fingers in its ears. So I'm assured.'

'Then nothing worth mentioning. Show you before I leave. He's cocksure that he's below anyone's radar.' He beckoned with a wiggle of a raised index finger, and moved towards the hallway. 'Bedroom's there,' he said. He inclined his head to the right. 'There's a camera and a light in there, but ...' and he ushered Edge into the room on the left, '... this is where they put the wood in Hollywood.'

They stood side by side just inside the doorway. The room was a white cube. If it ever had windows a flat wall now covered them. There was a metal structure with pulleys supporting rolls of backdrop scrims in various colours at one end and floor-to-ceiling inbuilt cupboards at the other. An assortment of lights, cameras on tripods and other photographic paraphernalia strayed across the floor between.

'It could be the studio of a keen amateur,' said Lin. 'Or it could be a low-budget production set-up.'

'For internet distribution?'

'The cameras are digital, not analogue. There's CD and DVD stocks in the next room down. But I'd reckon the web would be his outlet of choice.'

David Edge went to one of the cupboards. He looked back at Lin and raised an eyebrow in question. Lin nodded to indicate it had been checked for booby traps. Edge hooked a gloved finger in the D handle and tugged. His eyes went up and down the shelves.

'Everything the well-dressed dominatrix is wearing this season,' he said.

'What's the masculine of "dominatrix"?' Lin inquired.

'Really?' said Edge, looking at other cupboard doors.

'The one with the lock is the most interesting,' said Lin. 'I took the liberty of opening it.'

Edge tugged on that door. He stepped back while his eye grazed over the contents.

'Hobbits,' he said.

'It's a small world after all,' Lin agreed.

'You can lock this again,' said Edge, closing the door.

As Lin did his magic with the lock he said, 'Any more dark secrets this boy has will be locked up in his hard drives.'

'Which are …?'

'Next door down the hall. But virtual locks aren't my thing, you need a virtual cat burglar.'

'It just so happens, Lindsay, I have one.'

'My guess is any real security's there. The front door could be booby-trapped.'

'There's a back door that might be left ajar from time to time.'

'I bet you never go to a picnic without an opener,' said Lin. 'I'll make myself scarce. Don't forget to lock up and turn out the lights before you leave.'

28

A small bird was squeezed in winter's icy fingers. Hungry and exhausted it fell to earth in a farmyard. The farmer's young daughter found it, close to death behind the milking shed, a quivering puff of feathers. There was a steaming cowpat nearby and she gently placed the bird neck deep in it to keep it warm. The kind girl then went to the farmhouse to fetch some warm milk to feed the starving bird. She was gone only a short time when a fox crossed the farmyard. Discovering the bird snug and warm in its bed of pasture pâté, he promptly ate it.

The moral of the story? It's not always your enemies that drop you in the shit, and it's not always your friends that get you out.

This old joke was the content of Ben Bovell's last thought.

Ben always believed he remembered his mother's face. It was possible, but highly unlikely. He was eight months old when she died. The authorities located distant relatives who came and fetched him. They fed and clothed him and ensured that, materially, he wanted for nothing, but remained distant in every other way. They were Christians who prosecuted their Christian duty with stainless-steel severity. In their eyes Ben's mother was a whore and Ben was steeped in original sin. He was never formally adopted, and in lieu of affection he was given things. When he committed his first crime he was summarily judged and his sentence was abandonment to the system for life. He was five years old.

This Christian home where he was raised was on the outskirts of a country town. The next-door neighbour lived almost a kilometre down the road. She was a widow whose husband and only child had died on the same day. She'd found father and son floating in the dam. It seemed one had attempted to save the drowning other. She never knew which was which.

She bounced Ben on her knee and smothered him in her bosom. In her kitchen he drank homemade lemonade in summer and Milo made with hot milk in winter. A string of paste pearls adorned her neck. Ben stole it on one of the rare occasions she removed it. The widow was distraught. She felt betrayed by the small boy she had dared to love; the necklace was of deep sentimental value. No one understood that it held the same value for Ben. His guardians, arrogant with virtue, knew his sin must be greed and his crime venal.

Ben lost count of his foster homes. He was incorrigible of course. The system and the many families he passed through on the way to adulthood concurred in this. He was a natural born criminal, habitual thief: a recidivist. He stole when his appointed guardians wanted him for his weight in gold. He stole when they wanted him as a surrogate for their dreams. He stole when they wanted him for their carnal gratification. He stole when they wanted him as an answer to their prayers. When his mother's face came to him in memory or dream, pearly teardrops looped below it like a fractured halo.

When Ben was fourteen he loitered outside a suburban pub. The latest manifestation of parental care was inside drinking. It was eight-fifteen pm. They had been there since five. Although he could never look at this knowledge in the harsh light of day, he knew he was beer money. In his room he had a TV, a video, a stereo boom box, several transistor radios and myriad other gadgets that popular wisdom deemed necessary for a boy.

These were all presents from foster aunts and uncles and assorted observers of his life's hard reality who, unwilling to initiate change, offered things to soften its edges.

Next to the pub was an electrical appliance store. Ben went to the bottle shop, took a bottle of Mateus Rose from the fridge and walked out undetected. He threw the bottle at the store window. When the glass shards stopped falling he reached in, picked up a transistor radio and a four-slice toaster and went home. He shoved his booty under his bed and forgot about it. When asked why he did it, he told a policeman that he didn't know, probably just bored. He told a sympathetic teacher that when he was feeling bad, stealing made him feel better, not good, but better – for a while.

As foster families went this one wasn't bad, neglectful but benign. He scored small bribes from time to time, and while he was no trouble he was left alone. Now that he was trouble he was an institution's problem, yet again.

In these institutions, 'dog pounds' to the inmates, he learnt that his overwhelmingly negative experience of foster parentage was not necessarily the norm. Many good stories were told and the tellers deeply regretted the stuff-ups that lost them a little paradise. Once back in an institution Ben regretted the act that had brought him there. He was bullied and abused in these places, but if he made no complaint, curled contritely in a corner and showed he was harmless, eventually another place was found. He didn't know it, but his life had assumed a pattern, vicious and cyclical. He was trapped in a demolition derby clutching a stolen wheel, but all it could do was steer him around the circuit.

His next family was even more benign. They embraced their responsibilities with missionary zeal. In their spirited hands foster parentage was a social obligation, a righteous self-indulgence and a cottage industry. They were fostering seven children of various ages when Ben was taken in. One of these was his undoing.

Like a lost puppy, hope crept up to Ben on its belly, but he feared its teeth. As time passed his caution seemed justified. The household began to feel like a petting zoo for crippled and wounded wildlife. The keepers were earnest and caring and they distributed affection conscientiously in meticulously measured amounts. Each day each child received an equal portion of TLC with the regularity of vegan bowel movements. He began stealing small things. Nothing that would be noticed and get him ejected, just the odd thing to perk him up when he felt down.

Ben was fifteen now and in this house he had his first sexual encounter. To be accurate, his first consenting sexual encounter, and his first with a girl. Tyla's biological parents had devoted more brain cells to her name than her welfare.

There were three bedrooms in the rambling old weatherboard house: the adults' bedroom, a boys' room and a girls'. Each of the children's rooms had four bunk beds. When Ben and Tyla came down with chicken pox they were quarantined in the sleepout, a lined and insulated prefab garden shed reserved for emergencies like this. They were sleeping on their mattresses on the floor, but compared to the cramped dormitory conditions in the house, this was luxury. Ben wondered how often he could get sick.

The first night he woke from a febrile dream to find Tyla investigating his pyjamas. She looked up at him with an embarrassed little smile. Then they both looked at the stiff object in her hand. 'Oh, Jeezuz!' breathed Tyla. Ben was about to apologise when she flipped up her nightie and slung a leg over him. She dropped on him as if she'd found the last seat on the tram and yelled, 'Ow! Shit!' but kept bouncing her bum. He apologised profusely for hurting her, but she seemed distracted. She stopped suddenly, came to her knees and lifted her nightie. She stared at their loins and uttered a disgusted, 'Yuuck!' Ben apologised again but she got up, grabbed the box of tissues and disappeared through the door stuffing sheets between her legs. He lay spent and sticky where she'd abandoned him in a state of guilty confusion. He assumed she'd gone to the toilet. He couldn't remember ejaculating.

The next morning Tyla didn't acknowledge the night's activity by word or gesture. If not for the blood spots on his pyjamas he would have believed it was a wet dream. Three nights later Tyla was back. And she kept coming. She said it was 't'rific, the best fun I ever had'. And it was the best fun Ben had ever had – when he got used to it. For a while he didn't steal. Unfortunately Tyla was insatiable and reckless and demanding; if Ben betrayed reluctance she would sulk and simmer in a way that invited exposure. As time went on it began to feel less like sex and more like rape to Ben. He was relieved when they were caught en flagrante on the bathroom floor. Ben had assumed that Tyla was the older, more experienced, of them, but her thirteenth birthday was weeks away.

When clearing his things from the two drawers he'd been allotted they found the purloined items. As usual, he had forgotten he had them. His fate was sealed.

He accepted that he was a thief, but he didn't know why. Back in 'the pound' he decided to go with the flow: if he must steal he might as well do it properly. It seemed to be his only chance to get free of backwater eddies. And so he opened the floodgates and the torrent deluged the channel his footsteps had worn in the earth.

For the first time in his life he initiated an action. He fled to the streets and discovered drugs. And so, instead of taking it into his hands, he delivered his life into the coils of the pattern. Addiction fed on addiction, two snakes, each devouring the tail of the other. Pounds made way for prisons. It wasn't until Sharon that the cycle took on meaning and found its purpose.

Sharon was a wreck when he found her. Almost as big a wreck as he. He'd been looking for his dealer. Someone told Ben a whore called Sharon Kitchen was letting him shag her for a supply and she might know his whereabouts. She didn't, and when he had stared at her mutely for longer than is comfortable, even for someone whose tits and arse were extruding from opposite ends of shrink wrap, she demanded, 'What's it gonna be, sport: fuck or fuck off?' He didn't hear her words, just the sound of her voice – whether it was the green fire in the large feline eyes or the sense that only cosmic cataclysm could diminish her. Ben fucked off, but he was smitten.

From that moment he moved in eccentric orbit of Sharon Kitchen. He found a new bolthole a few blocks from the scabrous building she lived in. From a legal standpoint, he was stalking her; but from Ben's perspective he was a self-appointed guardian angel. He began to wean himself off chemical dependency and to plan a big score that would finance his scheme to whisk Sharon from her squalor. He learned her routine and managed to bump into her quite often. He'd say 'G'day', or just smile and nod. Sharon's response was distant but cordial. She grew accustomed to seeing him around, like a stray dog that turns up now and then for leftovers.

It was no coincidence, therefore, that he was on the spot when Sharon's drug dealer accosted her on the street, slapped her silly and began to drag her away by the hair. The drama had a (numerically) respectable audience, but Ben was the only one who acted. Yelling at Sharon to run, he charged at her assailant and pushed him over. Then he was at a loss for what to do next. He didn't know how to fight, so he let the hulking slab of muscle kick the shit out of him as a distraction, while Sharon made good her escape. Fortunately for him Sharon paused in her flight to review the situation from the shield of a skip full of demolition rubbish. She selected a length of three by two impressively studded with rusty four-inch nails and, swinging it over her head, screeching like a banshee, all boobs and legs, cork soles and pink hair, she bore down on the site of Ben's demolition. Abruptly alert to the attention he was drawing, and favouring discretion over valour, Whelan the Wrecker retired from the fray spitting expletives, which all but smothered his intimation that, like Arnold Schwarzenegger, he would be back.

With the help of a couple of the girls, Sharon got Ben to her room. He was bloodied and bruised but nothing was broken. Salving somehow segued to celebratory sex. Sharon didn't like being beholden, especially to a man. She insisted, to herself and to him, that this was due reward for the poor little bastard; but a discovery was made. Ben, who knew only how to gratify others – and who had been taught what women want by the ravenous seeker of sensation, Tyla – was a great lover.

'Christ!' exclaimed Sharon in convulsive climax. 'You're one helluva fuck, you little fucker. An' I oughta know, I've fucked 'em all! You're a fucking bobby dazzler!'

Ben was pleased he pleased her. Because it was unexpected, festive and frantic, a prophylactic wasn't a participant in the party.

They moved in together – Ben's place. With Ben it was undying love. With Sharon it was the fact that the dealer knew where she lived. Companionship was an incentive, but she would never admit to anything more than sex. Sharon still couldn't allow a male within arrowshot of her heart.

True to his word, the drug dealer came back – unfortunately, in the form of a corpse. Ben was arrested for his murder. That was when the other significant other entered his life.

They had heard about the dealer's death and expected a knock on the door sooner or later. The street incident three weeks earlier had entered neighbourhood folklore. When they came, Sharon was out. Ben panicked and dug a deeper pit of guilt with every shovelful of ill-considered bullshit he uttered. There were two reasons for this: he always disintegrated in the presence of authority, and his alibi involved a crime against property perpetrated roughly synchronous with the crime against person. If push came to shove he didn't mind doing time for theft if it got him out of a murder charge, but it meant dobbing in mates to prove his story. Too late to get together to concoct a plausible tale.

He was in an interrogation room. There was the usual tag team of coppers doing the usual Stiffy and Mo routine. What got him arrested was his reaction to the suggestion that Sharon was involved. The older cop, the one who seemed to be in charge, asked where Sharon was at the time of the murder, and what does dickwit Ben say? She wasn't there. Jesus – not, she was home with me, no – she wasn't there!

The senior cop kept going over and over everything. Standard procedure, but Ben had lost the thread of his lies. The young cop said nothing. He just stood loose, relaxed, balanced on a leg, hands in his pants pockets, a surfie in a suit. The cannonade of questions became meaningless sounds and it was the oppression of the young cop's silence that began to weigh on Ben. He looked at him and felt a sudden stab of fear. The cop didn't look much older than Ben. His boyish face couldn't be less threatening. It was the eyes that bothered Ben; they were studying him as if his secret history was printed in bold on his body.

The boss cop paused and pushed back from the table; he looked up at his partner with a sour expression that said feel free to jump in anytime. The young cop didn't take his eyes from Ben as he stepped forward and said, 'I'm sure Ms Kitchen will be wondering what happened to you, Mr Bovell. I'll see if we've located her, shall I?' The older cop's head moved reluctantly in approval. Ben spluttered and stammered ineffectually. The old cop pursued the young cop from the room. Ben caught the tail end of an exchange as the door cracked open on his return.

'… may be the way it's done in the sticks, but you're in the big smoke now.' Voice laced with irritation. 'Little Lord fucking Fauntleroy,' he muttered as the door exhaled heavily behind him. Then his eye snapped to Ben and anger had another target.

He said they had witnesses that saw the fight; witnesses that saw the victim leave the building Ben and Sharon lived in; witnesses that saw Ben on the street trailing a hundred metres behind the victim on the night of his death. Ben had abrasions on his knuckles, a bruise on his forehead and a scratch on his nose (due to some clumsiness during the unmentionable robbery).

The problem was this: someone had knocked on the door just as he was about go out on the job. Bloody inconvenient, so he lay doggo. It must have been the dealer and Ben followed him unwittingly. Ben didn't know where Sharon was that night. He was caught in a pincer. The old cop could smell his dilemma. He pointed out that Ben would get a lot of sympathy for protecting his woman from a notorious piece of shit like the victim. And a full confession would help. Ben began thinking about caving. He was charged, brought before a magistrate and denied bail. He had form for absconding.

Sharon came to see him while he was in custody. 'He gave me the third degree and I gave him the full three hundred and sixty. Eyes strictly front and centre. Mummy musta told him not to take eye candy from strangers. Real polite and cute as quiche. And that ain't the only queer thing about him. Asked about the fight with scumbucket and what I was doin' the night he was topped and I told him I was home with you and he smiles and writes it down no quibbles and then just wants to know all about you. You know, how we met, where you come from and stuff – the full catastrophe. Well don't know much, do I?' Sharon said about her encounter with the young cop. 'Looks wet behind the ears, but I dunno, scares me a bit. I can usually figure out what's goin' on behind a punter's eyes – but him? An' look at this.' She slipped a card across the table to Ben. 'He gave me that. She's a lawyer. Expensive but does freebies.' It occurred to Ben that it might be part of the softening process.

His solicitor was a spectacular, statuesque redhead called O'Connell. She looked like she'd stepped out of an American soap about family dynasties. She said a date for his committal hearing had been set and the Crown was willing, in return for a full confession, to consider a plea of manslaughter. She counselled against this. She said they had the services of a good barrister, a young but talented woman called Catherine Temple. A recent case of hers had attracted some notice in the news; Ben may have seen it? Ben said he didn't read the papers much. She said the case against him was circumstantial, she believed reasonable doubt could be easily established. For instance, Sharon Kitchen had as strong a motive as he and couldn't account for her movements on the night either.

Ben said he'd plead guilty.

O'Connell studied him closely. She recommended he think about it and she would see him again in a few days.

The next day he was brought to the interview room, the young cop was there. He said, 'Ben, do you know what I am?' Ben didn't know how to answer. 'I'm a Homicide detective, Ben.'

'I'm not an idiot,' said Ben, who feared he was.

'No, I don't think you are,' said the blond cop. 'But I'm in the Homicide Squad, not the Drug Squad or Fraud. If there's a robbery, say, it's none of my business – unless someone dies during it. No one died in your robbery, did they, Ben?' Ben didn't know how to respond. His head ducked around as he tried to avoid the searchlight gaze. 'You see I have to eliminate you as a suspect. You're static that's breaking up the picture. There's two ways I can do it. I can give your name to the boys handling the computer thefts.' Ben flinched. 'And they can go through your known associates one by one. You impress me as someone who'd stick with old mates.' Ben almost protested he would never do that, and as good as gave him the names: his 'old mates' would fill a phone booth. 'Or you can give me their names and I can have a quiet chat with them and we can keep it between us.'

For the first time he didn't feel simply processed by the system. An individual with power was treating him as an individual; in Ben's mind, an equal. It could have been a trick – cops were cops weren't they? As he looked into the eyes across the table that didn't occur to him.

He was released from custody two days before the hearing.

It was Ben that flushed the culprit. Back on the street in his fifteen minutes of fame a clear whisper rose from the noise around the murder. He wasn't a dog: he didn't dob. And larceny was a matter of survival – but murder was something else. And he didn't want them loading up Sharon to close the case. He passed the whisper on to Detective Constable David Edge, and so began a lifelong association.

Ben had never had a mate. Through life he'd bounced between friendly and hostile encounters like a pinball. He had workmates: blokes he'd pull the odd job with, and not all those were friendly. It was beyond anyone's comprehension, none more than Ben's, why he bestowed the mantle of mateship on this man. Ben had a mate. Ben had a mate and a mate. What more could a man want?

He could want a body.

Another old joke: it tells of a boy who is born as just a head. He lives a happy life. He has lots of friends. They carry him to school in their back-packs and, tucked up their jumpers, sneak him into the cinema for free. They include him in their games, usually as the ball; but he desires above all else to be like other boys and girls. He prays every night for this. Eventually, his prayers are answered. Ecstatic with joy, he runs out into the street to show his friends his new body and is hit by a car.

The moral of this tale? Quit while you're a head.

Ben has a body, but it is irrelevant. He knows it's there, he sometimes thinks he can feel it. Itches, tingles, jabs of – not exactly pain – sensation, a weighty thing pulling on his neck, holding him prostrate, binding him to the earth. His body never returns his calls. An irritation harasses his nose, salt water dunks his eye and no ready hand swoops over his brief horizon to fall upon and rout his tormentors. He is abandoned at last by even himself.

It's time to quit while he's ahead. And, contrary to appearances, he is ahead.

Time concertinas, yawing in and out. He can't measure it or feel its proper rhythm. He can't tell a single day from multiples. He can no longer tell the chicken from the egg and it no longer matters in which order they come to him. And they must come to him. He is trapped in a private theatre of cruelty of his own making, a scumble of images chafing his ret-inas, impotent before them and powerless to look away. He can no longer tell if they are thrown on the widescreen of the ceiling or burned directly on his brain. Often they are just pale fugitive shadows, avatars of presence and movement. A sound and light show lacking rhyme and reason. The glimmer on a Holland blind of passing traffic has more meaning.

A Gingerbread Man, he is outfoxed and diminished, and so is his world. It is an intimate cinema. A cast of characters enter and exit, their dialogue is alien and lacks subtitles. Sometimes they are properly aloof in their shadow play. Sometimes they violate the integrity of the membrane and invade his Plato's Cave. Faces balloon to fill his visual field and shrink to distant orbs. He doesn't know who they are. Reason tells him they are something med-ical, but this means little to him now. They are as irrelevant as his body, precisely because they tend it and insist on its corporeality.

Only two faces have any meaning now: Sharon's and that of his deliverer. Sharon's face is the only fixed point in his meagre hemisphere, the moon of his twilight sky. She is there again and again, always waxing never waning.

But he doesn't come.

When will he come? When will he come?

And then he is there.

I know what you want of me, Ben, he says with his gunmetal-blue regard. Ben grasps for the breath to make the voice that will give sanction. He feels a feeble breeze in his becalmed throat, salty and fleeting. He doesn't know if the word that gives it shape wafts beyond his lips or is lost in the caverns of his skull. The word is 'Yes.' And another, stronger, is sucked after it. 'Please.'

Shadow plays flicker on his planisphere. Celestial bodies pulsate in his heaven. The moon and sun come and go.

And finally, the dome of his world descends like a hand cupped, and light and dark are folded into one.

Somewhere in the universe stars are dying, planets spiralling down into black otherness. And who is to say they are uninhabited?

29

Rose and Cheryl were going over the weekend receipts when they heard the faint commotion of raised voices. The office door was being hammered upon before Charlotte's distraught voice issued from the speakerphone. 'I couldn't stop her, Rose! She's a madwoman! Keep the door locked! I'll get Boof!'

The office door locked automatically on entry. The lock could be operated remotely from Rose's desk. Cheryl was already halfway across the room. The doorknob was jiggling frenetically and guttural cries, some recognisable as references to female anatomy, were assaulting the heavy, reinforced door. Cheryl turned at the sound of her name. Rose had taken a can of mace from a desk drawer; she tossed it to Cheryl. When she reached the door Cheryl placed her eye to the spy hole. She looked back at Rose and shook her head.

'Say when,' said Rose, a finger on the remote lock release mounted beneath the desktop.

Cheryl gripped the doorknob with one hand as she felt for the button on the mace pack. Then the verbal onslaught subsided and she thought she heard a familiar sound; she looked through the spy hole again. She could see a fisheye version of Boof's face, his lips moving in submarine mono-logue. 'Boof's there,' she said.

Rose released the lock and Cheryl pulled the door open. The mace can was held low to her side. Her finger was still on the button. Sharon Kitchen must have been leaning her weight against the door; she staggered backwards into the room.

'Sharon,' said Rose, coolly. 'What a surprise. To what do we owe the pleasure?'

Off balance and disoriented, Sharon struggled to recover what physical and moral momentum was possible. This amounted to buggerall. Her cheeks were streaked with mascara, her eyes parched, shrunken billabongs; vestiges of besieged vitality swam in their green centres. She staggered a few paces into the room turning jerkily as she sought a point of reference. Her distracted gaze found Rose. She placed her feet firmly apart and, chest heaving, squared off. Her hair was a storm-stranded haystack. She was wearing a tracksuit that was probably something she slopped around in doing housework. It looked slept in. A lace on one sneaker trailed on the snowy carpet.

'Where the fuck is he, Rose?' she demanded. It came as a low, choked snarl.

'Sit down Sharon,' said Rose gently (for Rose). 'You look terrible. What's wrong?'

'I don't wanna fuckin' sit down,' Sharon yelled over Rose's words. She hunched her shoulders and swung her head and arms as if trying to free herself from a net. 'Where the fuck is he?'

Cheryl glanced at Rose, whose composure was stately. She stood behind the desk in her familiar ramrod posture, fingertips of both hands splayed on its satin top. 'Take a seat, Sharon. Cheryl will get you a drink. Have you had bad news about Benny?'

'Ben!' Sharon screamed. 'Ben, Ben, Benbenbenbenbenben! His fucking name is Ben!' Her clenched fists were pumping before her forehead as if they gripped a monstrous jackhammer.

'C'mon, Shaz,' Cheryl persuaded. 'Sit down and tell us what's going on.'

'Fuck off!' Sharon spat. Abruptly the vibrating ceased and she glared sidewise over a raised upper arm. Only the green blaze of pain in her eyes saved her from looking like a comicstrip evil genius. As Cheryl watched, calmness seemed to wash in trickling descent over her face. Taking this as a sign of the storm's easing she started toward the wall panel that concealed the liquor. As she skirted her, Sharon's pants pocket became as lively as a sack of cats. Cheryl realised she was fumbling for purchase on some object. She pivoted on her toes and lunged, as Sharon shook free of the snag of clothing. She was too late. Sharon's hand came up grasping a small silver pistol. Her attention was focused on Rose and her other hand was moving to form a classic shooters grip.

Then there was Boof. Cheryl hadn't known he could move so fast. And smooth. Old slow-and-steady-wins-the-race Boof. He didn't seem in any particular hurry. He stepped up beside Sharon from behind, and took the gun from her hand as if she had removed it from her pocket specifically for that purpose. He even said thanks, his arm, almost protectively, around her shoulders. Well, whaddaya know, thought Cheryl, who's the master's good little apprentice?

Sharon seemed to concur. She stared up at Boof's earnest schoolboy face, not surprised, not defeated. Cheryl thought she said 'Fucking clown' but in fact she said 'Fucking clone' as Boof steered her to the large low couch. She refused to sit. 'I wasn't gonna shoot,' she said defiantly.

'I know, Sharon,' said Rose, who hadn't budged during the brief scuffle. She glanced over her shoulder to locate her chair and lowered herself into it. She reposed as unruffled as royalty behind her desk, her eyes on the uninvited. Sharon stood with her shoulders slightly hunched, her chin thrust belligerently, fists clenched in her sagging sleeves, as if calculating her chances in a dive across the desk.

Cheryl's gaze flicked back and forth between them as she poured a stiff drink for Sharon. Boof retreated to the end of the couch. His attention never strayed from Sharon. Cheryl brought the glass and a box of tissues to Sharon. Sharon sniffed and stripped a handful of tissues from the box, stuffed them in a pocket and took the drink. 'I suppose he's taught the lotta you how to kick the shit outta everyone else,' she said, and tossed the liquor down.

'What's this about, Sharon?' asked Rose.

Sharon stared into the mouth of the liquor glass. It was hidden in the bundle of her fingers, but Cheryl was sure it must be empty. 'You think you're so fucking safe in this fuck factory of yours, with your fucking lord and fucking protector, your fucking ... fucking ... heat-seeking missile. Well ... fuck ... he's just a man just like the rest of the fucking pathetic pricks that come through your fucking door looking for an open cunt to dump their slime in.' She waved an arm wildly at an invisible airborne irritation. 'You ... you're a fucking cold bitch, Rose, in your,' she twisted at the waist and swung the arm in a loose-limbed arc, 'fucking ivory tower ... your sterile ... frigid, fucking cell. You wanna know why I got outta here? I wanted to live! This is a ... a ... fucking monastery ... or ... something.'

Rose made no attempt at a rejoinder. She sat and waited with more patience than Cheryl had seen her display before. Sharon took a few steps toward the desk. Boof followed as if he shared an umbilical cord.

'But it's gonna happen to you, Rose. 'Cause I've still got friends here … an' I hear things. It's gonna happen to you. He's got a lotta enemies … on both sides … a lot. 'S only a matter of time before some cunt twigs how killable he is. Jesus … Jesus …' She turned and looked at Boof. 'He doesn't carry a gun. Know that? Everyone knows that. She,' her thumb jerked over her shoulder, 'fucking gave him a gun once.' She turned back to Rose. 'Didn't you?' And back again to Boof. 'I heard that. Gave 'im one … but he don't carry it. Every fucker knows this. It's all fucking bluff. It's all bullshit. But he is a fucking killer. Toucha death. That's true, that's not bullshit. You can see it in his eyes. Can't you? Who are you?' she said suddenly to Boof. 'Are you hers?' She pointed at Cheryl, then turned to face her. 'It's gonna happen to you too, Chers. It's gonna happen to you.'

'Sharon,' said Rose. 'When did Ben die?'

The question severed the strings of rage that were holding Sharon erect. She sagged, sticks and hinges in a worn sack. Boof supported her to the couch. She slumped with her face in her hands.

'He …' her muffled words came at last, '… I … he was … I didn't … he was …' She looked up at Cheryl, and she was desolation itself. Cheryl felt something like piano-wire pulled screamingly through her body from the base of her throat to her crotch. She pressed her fingers into her belly as if in physical pain. Boof crossed swiftly to her. She muttered she was okay, her eyes locked with Sharon's. 'Y'see, Chers, y'see? I didn't … I didn't know …'

'You didn't know what?' said Rose.

Cheryl raised her palm abruptly to silence Rose. 'I see, Shaz, I see,' she cooed soothingly as she freed herself from Boof's touch and crossed to the couch to embrace the shrunken woman. They rocked in each other's arms for some time. Boof stared at his boots. Rose studied the two women with sympathy, if without empathy.

'Ben died last night.' Sharon spoke from somewhere far away. 'I'd just left, they said.'

'Does David know?' asked Rose.

Sharon burst away from Cheryl, flinging her back on the couch. Her thighs thumped against the desk before Boof could launch an interception. 'Of course he fucking knows, you silly, shrivelled old cunt! He killed him!'

Now Rose was on her feet. Their eyes were hard-wired across the desk. The steel of Rose's voice keened with anger. 'You're hysterical, Sharon, but that's ridiculous, even for you.' She relented a little. 'David's protected you and Ben as much as me. My God, your children call him uncle.'

'Yeah,' hissed Sharon, bitterly. 'Well, good ol' Uncle Dave killed his brother Ben. My … Ben. That was their deal. Th-their bargain … or, or whatever. Their fucking secret men's business! They didn't let me … let me l-let … me …'

'Let you what?'

'Let her look after Ben, Rose,' said Cheryl.

30

Col Mulcahy was the eldest son of Grace Mulcahy. Grace was generally described in the media – somewhat melodramatically – as 'the matriarch of Melbourne's most notorious crime family'. This translated in Grace's terms to 'a notoriously bad judge of men'. And she readily admitted it. If adolescent Grace had ever made a list of things to accomplish, crime family matriarch would not have been on it. Her list, never committed to paper, was limited to three items: find a good bloke, get pregnant as quickly as possible and live happily ever after. Marriage would be okay too, if it happened. The thing was she was as plain as porridge, and her single-minded determination, worn like a full-forward's guernsey, scared the hell out of nice boys. This didn't deter her. She spared no contempt for males so easily discouraged. Grace was tough, and to make a romantic impression on her a bloke had to be tougher.

There had been three such men in Grace's life. All led colourful lives – short, violent – and died messily. The first, Kev Mulcahy, Col's father, was the only one she married in church, or any place else for that matter. She gave birth to seven children, five to Kev and two to her second mate; five survived. Her second child, a girl, was stillborn and Kev accidentally killed her third, a boy, in a drunken rage. Grace, pregnant with his fifth, dispatched Kev with the electric iron. She'd been ironing his shirts just the way he liked them, when Kev had given Michael a careless backhander. He forgot his wanton fist was holding a bottle. If she hadn't loved him so much she might not have hit him so many times. Despite her interesting condition she received a gaol sentence. Perhaps if she hadn't told the court that she'd happily do it again to any bastard that laid a finger on a kid of hers …?

Unchastened by internment, Grace remained prepared to protect her children, with extreme prejudice if necessary, even from the men she loved. If she truly became a matriarch, therein lies the reason.

Col was considered incorrigible from an early age. He had no respect for authority, nor fear of law and order, and was contemptuous of the justice system. He was six at the time of his mother's incarceration. The possibility cannot be ignored that this had some formative influence on a lifelong attitude. And Fitzroy was a great little petri dish for certain cultures.

Col was in gaol. The first time for a long, long time, but not the first time. The only family member that had not been a guest of the state was his sister Bernadette, the youngest of his siblings. She had a university degree, and had never run foul of the law. See – it's got little to do with genes.

Technically, Col's first crime was aiding and abetting in his father's demise. When he saw his little brother felled he clamped onto Kev Mulcahy's right arm like wax on a Brazilian. Kev, stunned by the consequences of his actions, didn't notice until he found the limb encumbered as it moved instinctively to protect his head from Grace's blows. His left hand held a full glass.

Col went on to solve most of his problems and answer most of his critics with direct, often pre-emptive, action. He didn't enjoy violence, but he wasn't going to fuck around splitting hairs either. He didn't like killing – not good for business for one thing – but cripes, some cunts had it coming. His garish reputation had him down for many more murders than he'd actually committed – broke a lot of bones, but. The two or three blokes he'd actually topped 'n' tailed – he wasn't sure of the exact number – were bad, bad bastards, much worse than he considered himself, and he'd had to jack himself up with drugs to do them.

Not like this bloke, the one on the other side of the security glass. He didn't need tiger tea in his veins to get him that last yard. That's probably why Col, grudgingly, liked him. No, that was why he respected him. He was what Col wanted to be: cool, surgical, without malice or self-righteousness. Why he liked him was because he didn't hold your badness against you. You were just someone with whom he begged to differ. And he didn't bullshit. He might not volunteer the full story, but if you asked straight questions you got straight answers. Col knew it was as much his stock-in-trade as native honesty, but fair enough, straight up was straight up. He treated you like he knew his shit stank as much as yours. He should have been Col's natural born enemy: by birth, breeding, bank account, by chosen profession they were diametrically opposed on the wheel of life. He was even rumoured to favour legalising drugs of addiction; a direct threat to Col's right to profit from his labours for fuck's sake! Of course, push come to shove, one would have to kill the other.

Col wondered why he couldn't hate the cunt. As he studied the face through the glass, that girl, years ago at the school social, foxtrotted into his mind.

You didn't dance voluntarily with girls at those things, unless you wanted to spend the next day skinning your knuckles on every dickhead in the playground. That girl though, every grubby little bastard wanted to ask her to dance, give the code the finger, but no one had the guts to chance their thick tongue. It wasn't her looks that grabbed you by the balls, it was her poise; but that was what put her on the top shelf too, way beyond sticky-fingered reach. And you wanted to hate her guts, and you clustered with your mates and made foul jokes under your collective breath to bring her down. Then a nun grabbed you by the figurative ear and dragged you over to her to sacrifice grammar on the altar of invitation. And you felt blessed and damned by the same hand. And she smiled and took your hand and she held up both ends of the conversation and thanked you when the music stopped. And she sought you out at ladies' choice and you couldn't believe your fucking luck. She laughed at your pathetic joke and smiled when you stepped on her toes and apologised to you! And she seemed interested in everything you said. And when you asked her out to the pictures she said yes and when she kissed you lightly on the cheek at her front gate you knew it was goodbye. And even if she went out with you again and you became friends you knew your bed was something she'd never get into.

Col had a head as scarified as Mars. The fissure below his nose crag suddenly split wide and the hammered plains of his face cracked into a hatch of canals and gullies as he raised the intercom handpiece to his ear.

'Didn't think you'd be this pleased to see me.'

'Fuck,' said Col, wryly amused at the tenor of his thoughts. 'I've been in 'ere too long, even you remind me of pussy.'

'Whatever works,' the other replied, smiling.

'Mum said you'd be coming. An' I hadda talk to you. She said.' He scratched the taught, leathery muscles of his biceps in a show of indifference.

'Mother knows best.'

'I don't dog on me mates, Mr Edge.'

'Not why I'm here. And I'm not a cop anymore, you can call me David.'

'And you're not a fuckin' mate, neither.'

'Oh, never that.'

'If you're not a fuckin' cop, what are ya?' drawled Col as if quizzing himself. He stared thoughtfully at his visitor, who sat placidly permitting the scrutiny. 'Working for Prisoner's Aid now?'

Amusement curled snugly in Edge's lips. 'In a manner of speaking.'

Col's searching eyes continued to roam and probe. 'The bite that bit the Barker,' he mused. 'What the fuck keeps you down the shit end of town?'

'Big end's the shit end at least once a day,' Edge said. 'Don't worry, Col. I'm not some sort of Super Stinger.'

Fuck, unsolicited information. Col stared at a class of person he didn't understand and therefore his whole life experience screamed at him to distrust. 'You sayin' you're fuckin' freelance?'

'Free as a lance in flight.'

Col stretched out in his chair and locked his fingers behind his head. A creeping moss of dark hair was blurring the lines of the tattoo on his skull. 'I mean fair enough, someone left me a shopful of cunt I'd hang around. But you don't dip your wick, I heard. Zat true?' he said after another leisurely study of the man on the other side of the barrier. 'What's the fuckin' point?'

'Over familiarity with the product you push earned you this gig.'

Col's chuckle was a stick dragged along a corrugated iron fence. 'Yeah, give y'that. Fucked me judgement a bit.' He swivelled his eroded gully grin back and forth. 'Not a total loss, but. Gettin' clean and,' he winked cheekily, 'makin' a few new contacts.' Then he leaned forward. 'For some fuckin' reason I can't fathom, Mum thinks we're in your debt. By my count the score favours the home side.'

'Harks back to Gavin Pretsch. Remember him?'

Col stared, as much inward as outward. 'Jesus Christ,' he said at last. '*Mum* brought you in on that? I couldn't figure how y'fuckin' knew.' He slumped back again. 'Shit! The cunnin' old bitch. Trine to save me from meself, eh?' Another corrugated rattle and shake of the head. 'Dicko saw ol' Gav in Brisbane, back a bit. Goin' to uni again. Gotta nice little limp.' He smiled slyly. 'Left leg I think.'

'Some blokes will stoop to any ploy to pull.'

'Always a desperate, was Gav.' Col glanced at the clock on the wall above the guard. 'What d'you want?' he said, abruptly down to business.

'I want you to think about this before you say yes. You'll need a small crew. And I don't want anyone serving extra time. Green light only if it can be done with *minimal* risk.'

'And, *it* is?'

'Are you acquainted with Terrence Varney?' Col's face was flat, his eyes adamantine. He turned his head slowly without shifting his basalt gaze and spat. 'I see you are,' said Edge.

'You want 'im flushed?'

Edge raised his right hand. It clutched a large carry bag. 'A little hamper for you from Mum. I slipped in the latest issue of *Ralph*.' He winked and four fingers tapped the bag twice – page forty-four. 'A bloke a lot like Varney features. Let me know what you think. No hurry.' He glided to his feet and took the parcel to the guard's station and passed it through for inspection. As he returned he paused and reached into a pocket. His hand emerged with a mobile phone; he poked its face and read a message. He slipped the phone back in his pocket and approached.

'Apart from bein' a maggot a dead sheep's clacker'd reject, what's Varney's crime?' Col asked when he picked up the intercom again.

'He offended a friend of mine.'

'Pay back.'

Edge cocked his head thoughtfully to the side. 'Mmm, pay forward perhaps. He may offend others. I'm sure if he's made aware how saddened I am by his behaviour he'll modify it. The devil's in the detail, of course, as any well-read man would know.' He hadn't resumed his seat. 'I won't be back. Let your mum know what you decide.'

'Shit, I'll do it. You got any idea how fuckin' boring this hole is if you're not on the quoits team?'

'I'll look in on Grace from time to time.'

'Think the old girl can't look after 'erself?'

'Might have her hands full if the Yanks decide she's hiding WMDs in her laundry basket,' Edge said, grinning. 'Anyone on the team, I'll see his family right too.'

'Would'n expect any fuckin' less,' said Col by way of thanks.

Edge glanced at his cranium. 'Good luck with the crop,' he said, by way of farewell.

'Most of the cunts in here have heads like half an arse. The rest of us,' Col grinned at the oblivious guard, 'are complete arseholes.'

31

Carl Fokker – 'Sneaky' to friends and foes – needed to piss. He was groping around the dim floor behind the driver's seat, amongst the greasy detritus of the fast-food lifestyle pressed upon him by the circumstances of his present employment. His nostrils were cloyed with the subtle reek of rancid fat and at least eleven different herbs and spices. He didn't recognise his own stale sealed-capsule funk. He sought, with some urgency, the plastic two-litre orange juice bottle. His knees were on the seat and his bum mooned over the steering wheel. The fabric of his designer jeans had a slight sheen and they were artfully faded in patches to coincide with convex parts of the human body. To an impressionable pedestrian, approaching in the fading light of a late winter afternoon, the parked vehicle might appear to be in the control of an enormous blowfly.

Carl was a petty thief. The constabulary, if they mentioned him at all, described him, somewhat indulgently, thus. This meant he was generally regarded more as a nuisance than as a serious threat to the fabric of society. Hence, he had often been questioned, sometimes harassed, rarely arrested, but never, quite, charged. Carl pictured himself differently.

In his imagination – a two-dimensional space stacked with flat black and white boxes behind a glossy cover of lurid hue – Lamont Cranston, Simon Templar and Don Diego de la Vega sported his precipitous profile. From the deep philosophical well of his beer glass he frequently drew laconic scorn for the meek, myopic punter that kowtowed to society's restrictions, sanctions and interdictions. Carl, according to Carl, did not possess a plebeian soul.

Of course he wouldn't express this in these specific terms. He had never seen the word 'plebeian' written anywhere. He had heard it once, part of a conversation in which he was but a marginal participant. A solicitor uttered it and, because of the source, Carl heard 'plea bargain'. Therefore the sentence in which it was embedded was completely incomprehensible, and the conversation from that point on gathered into it a perplexing density. Earlier parts of the discussion began to shift beyond his ken also. Unabashed, he generously contributed his usual response in such circumstances: 'Yeah. Heh. heh, heh, fuckin' oath, squire.' Carl, according to Carl, was an outlaw, a desperado, a bit of a rascal – but a nice bloke with it.

Just adequately educated, hand passed from relative to relative when mum and dad were ambushed by the pokies or the bottle, always generously fed and clothed and well treated but never quite belonging, Carl didn't complain, nor blame anyone for his lot. In fact he had only the vaguest perception of what his lot was. Whether he was born with a gregarious nature or had it thrust upon him is hard to tell, but he rather enjoyed social variety. He meandered through life much as he began, casually, almost accidentally, attaching to group after group (gang after gang); and if asked about his lot he would say 'Fuckin' orright'. In respectable middle-class society he would never be described as bright. And he wasn't; but Carl was street smart. Cunning as a shit-house rat is a phrase that springs. And Carl was in his milieu.

He'd had a bit of a fright this morning. He'd decided to start his shift later than usual, picking up the subject of his attention after she had completed her routine morning chores. He had been watching long enough to know that these were duties she wouldn't or couldn't shirk just to steal a jump on her shadow. He was in position by the time of her normal return from dropping the boys at school. According to Maeve, the last week or so she'd been looking after the kids of the black woman a few doors down, who apparently worked an early morning shift somewhere. This woman would turn up about ten fifteen, stay for a cuppa (he guessed) then take the kids home. The little sex bomb he was watching would take her girl to play group or kinder or something, and after that she was a moving target. The real work began.

This morning, though, he sat and waited – no show. The black woman arrived, knocked and couldn't raise anyone. She must have had a key, because she got inside. When she came out after a while, she looked concerned. She stood at the decaying front gate looking up and down the street. Then, as she seemed to come to some decision and head for her own house, she got a call on her mobile. At first an expression of relief flooded her features. It was replaced by one of concern, then sadness. When she began dabbing at her eyes with a handkerchief and miming words that were clearly commiseration, the penny dropped. Carl drove straight to the hospital.

He was at his vantage point when the black woman arrived and half an hour later drove off with her kids and his mark's unhappy daughter.

Sharon Kitchen didn't emerge until after noon. Not a moment too soon: Carl was running out of games to play to keep him awake. Even from the distance that he was observing her, she looked eroded. Her appearance almost convinced Carl he had waited the ten years it felt like. She led him on a meandering odyssey. Her driving was erratic and oblivious of other road users. Carl was seriously considering forcing her over to the curb to prevent an accident, when she suddenly arrived at a destination – The Rose fucking Garden of all places.

It was hours before she emerged and that cute little brunette – what was her name, Shirley? Cherry? – was with her. Shirley-Cherry drove her to collect the boys from school, stayed an hour or so, drove off in Sharon's car, then returned a few minutes before nature called to Carl, hefting two full supermarket bags.

His fingers touched plastic. 'Ah, there y'are y'little bugger,' said Carl. He twisted back and bounced into the bucket of his seat. He fumbled his zip down, the top off the bottle and manoeuvred the ol' ladies' request into the opening. One or two tears sprang to his eyes as he waited. It had just begun to function as a conduit when there was a sharp rap next to his ear on the misted window. Carl jumped and the dragon escaped. He hastily pursued the beast, choked off its complaint and shoved it roughly into the folds of its den. Breathlessly he wound down the window trying to make up his mind which mask his face should be wearing: guileless curiosity, offended innocence, patient condescension?

'Carl.'

'Jesus!' His sphincter almost opened again. What kind of shit had bloody Maeve dropped him in?

'You okay, Carl?'

'Yeah, yeah ... I'm ... jist ... jist ...'

'Watching Sharon Kitchen as you were asked to do.'

'Ahhh ...'

'It's alright, Carl. You're working for me.'

'Shit! Am I?'

'Yep. And you can have an early night. You're relieved.'

Of course he wasn't. He went home anyway and forgot that he wasn't – until the first sip of beer. Halfway through the second can he began thinking about the juice bottle – had he put the cap back? And he began wondering about the choice of the word 'relieved', as he scooped up the car keys.

32

'How is she?' he asked Cheryl when she opened the door.

'Did Rose reach you?' she said, as she stepped back to let him into the narrow hallway.

He nodded. 'She filled me in. Do you know when it happened?' He led the way. He seemed familiar with the house.

'Sometime late last night or early this morning. Sharon hasn't been all that coherent. She said the hospital needed to reach you. Something about power of attorney.'

'They only had my home number.'

'Don't you go home?'

'Where is she?' he asked. They were in the doorway of the cramped living room. The carpet was threadbare but a thick rug decorated in slabs of bright colour covered all but its perimeter. The rug looked new and it looked expensive. Evidence of children was strewn on every horizontal surface in the room, almost obliterating visual evidence of the furniture. A pile of technology, of the type described as a home entertainment centre in junk mail catalogues, clambered up one wall. A plump black woman came through the opposite doorway with a handful of coloured mugs and a teapot. White teeth flashed when she saw him.

'G'day, Ruby.'

'G'day, Dave.' She managed to find a place on a low, cluttered table for the things she carried then she came straight to Edge. She wrapped her arms around his middle and with her cheek on his chest she said, 'Za bit sad, innit?'

What you see when you don't bring a camera, thought Cheryl. She'd known this man for seven years in the context of brothels and sex, drug and alcohol-fuelled parties and she couldn't remember witnessing a scene like this. She had seen girls approach and drape themselves on his shoulder, hoping for some sort of vacant possession, but they'd wander away sulkily when a polite smile was the only response. She'd tried it herself, back in the Barker days. He was Jack's fatal right hand after all, the power next to the power. Now here he was in a woman's arms at last.

His face looked like the bridge of the Enterprise under attack with the shields down: a stoic shell humming with synaptic action. She could almost hear Scotty's 'She canna give ye any more, Cap'n'. She knew the touch of another could shake the pillars of your universe, but not this touch, not the touch of simple spontaneous affection.

His arms folded hesitantly around the woman and the fingers of one hand stroked her thick black hair. Was the mystery of him as banal as that? The girls at the brothels, the escorts, the refuge, Rose, Sharon and Ben, Ruby: he collected surrogate families like parking tickets, but shrank from their warmth like nightshade from the sun. Were they a clutch of warm bodies that needed him, but had no claim on him ultimately, something that couldn't be taken from him, because it wasn't his? Since Boof, Cheryl had learned what family was. It was commitment and compromise, and if you wanted to stay true to yourself you redefined yourself in family's terms. He had no trouble with commitment, but she could see he might choke on compromise. If his game was to have one without the other, it didn't work with Ben Bovell. The dead hand of Benny had a fistful of his short and curlies.

'It's a bit sad, Ruby,' he agreed.

'Don't think she'll be 'appy to see you though, Dave,' Ruby said stepping back, liquid brown eyes lapping at sharp blue.

'I don't suppose.'

'I gotta get back to me kids for a bit.' She glanced at Cheryl.

'I can stay with her tonight, Ruby,' Cheryl said.

'Y'sure, luv?' Cheryl nodded and walked with her to the front door. 'I'm off, Shaz luv. See y'first thing tomorra,' Ruby called at one of the hallway doors. There was a muffled response. When she returned Edge was in a familiar pose, hands in pockets, head lowered, watching a toe beat its cryptic tattoo.

He looked up. 'Rose said Boof handled things well.'

'Like you'd left a clone.'

Just a faint smile with a touch of rue.

Cheryl hooked her head toward the hallway. 'An old friend?'

'I arrested her husband for manslaughter.' Cheryl mouthed an 'Oh'. 'He hanged himself waiting to go to trial.'

They both turned their heads to the sound of an opening door from the hallway. Sharon Kitchen wandered into the room, her chin on her chest. Her hair was pulled tightly back, secured with a rubber band, revealing dark roots. Her head came up slowly, but her eyes held to the pot of tea. She shambled in a beeline to it as if there was no one else in the room. When she poured a cup she wrapped it in both hands and hugged it to her chest as if it was the only source of warmth in the world. In fact, the room was very warm. Cheryl was feeling uncomfortable in her polo-neck jumper. Edge unzipped his coat and dropped it on some papers littering the corner of the table. Nothing in Sharon's demeanour admitted the presence of others. Her face was pale, washed clean of makeup. Misery becomes her, Cheryl thought.

'I'm not mother,' Sharon croaked.

Neither of the other two caught her meaning immediately. Then Edge said, 'No tea for me, Sharon.'

Then Sharon's head swivelled slowly towards his voice. Cheryl had read the word 'baleful' in bodice rippers, but now she thought she saw just what those two syllables described. Sharon's green eyes seemed to be both dead and glowing with a sulphurous light, hot coals beneath ash. And Cheryl was way behind the play. To her right she sensed rather than saw Edge's movement. He seemed to retreat into her peripheral distance, like a trick with a telescopic lens, before Sharon moved. Then her field of vision was slashed with an amber sickle. The arc hung in the air, the ectoplasm of a furious screech, tearing the fabric of the room. Its tail struck her shoulder as it fell and her cheek was splashed with scalding tea. Belatedly, she flinched away. She glanced at Edge. He seemed untouched.

Then Sharon was laying siege to him like a berserker at a castle keep. She clubbed on his chest with the bottom of the empty mug, again and again. Apart from the original scream and rhythmic sobs of effort she uttered no sound. Edge stood and took the blows, staring down at Sharon with a mixture of puzzlement and pity. The mug broke. Sharon looked at the jagged shard snarling from the back of her hand like a ceramic knuckle-duster. Then she glared up at Edge's face with a raptor's eye. Cheryl cried out, she had the sickening feeling he was going to let her maul his face. She needn't have worried. What followed was a macabre dance: Rogers trying to destroy Astaire before the music stopped – *The Gay Divorcee* meets *A Clockwork Orange*.

Sharon weaved, ducked and leapt, swinging her taloned fist at his elusive flesh like a child trying to draw blood from a butterfly. Edge backed away, leading her around the room. Every thrust, swipe and parry seemed choreographed, gestures perfected in hours of rehearsal. Edge's calm was uncanny, the casual ease and litheness of his movements was confounding. He made no attempt to restrain Sharon, but she was a marionette attacking the puppeteer who was manipulating her strings. He drew her into exhaustion, as she beat at spaces he ceaselessly ceased to occupy. Eventually, Sharon could barely raise her arm but she kept lunging; her breath was coming like gravelly sighs of anguish. It stopped abruptly with blood. Cheryl wasn't sure if Sharon had found her mark and her satisfaction, or Edge had seen the last blow was about to fall and put his hand in harm's way. Sharon staggered, and her arm looped like a poor swimmer in a woollen jumper. Edge displayed a hand before her eyes, where blood was welling from the fleshy cushion on the outside of his left palm.

Sharon slipped to her knees. Her shoulders heaved. 'It's not enough,' she croaked.

Cheryl had no idea how long this had taken. It seemed like the longest pas de deux she'd ever witnessed. She caught the direction of Edge's gaze and the concern on his face and swung around. Sharon's children huddled at the dark mouth of the hall. Their faces were studies in confusion and desolation. Today the man they called father was dead, and they found their mother and the man they called uncle in mortal combat.

Cheryl rushed to them uttering nonsensical denials to soothe the pain she saw in their faces. 'Oh no, no, no-no-no-no. It's alright … it's alright … darlings … darlings …' She tried to shepherd them back into the hall, but they had knotted together and it was like pushing against a deeply rooted stump. She felt them flinch as one. She looked over her shoulder. Edge was withdrawing a hand, his eyes were electric-blue pain.

'It's okay, kids, Mum's a bit upset with me. I'll go. See you in a couple of days, eh?' he said. He stooped and picked up his coat from where he'd dropped it on the cluttered table. He sidled past the wide-eyed and tearful children, touching Cheryl's shoulder. 'Will you be okay?'

Cheryl nodded without looking up. 'Boof's bringing my things and some food.'

'Thanks,' he murmured, and was swallowed by the hall.

Alone with the sound of a closing door, Brie's small creature whimpers, the boys' puzzled monosyllables and Sharon's harsh moaning breaths, Cheryl couldn't take her eye off the table top. She was sure there had been no empty space on it apart from the one Ruby filled with the mugs and teapot. Now there was a gap in the spot from where Edge had removed his coat. She had been about to clear the table for Ruby when Edge knocked. The stuff from that corner of the table was in her hands and she put it down again to answer the door. She tried to remember what it was. She chastised herself and vaguely wondered why she allowed this trivia to distract her in the midst of the misery that needed her attention. Was David Edge able to go coolly about his business, whatever that was, even in the fraught centre of a small human tragedy? That question disturbed Cheryl more than she cared to admit.

It was answered an hour later, when Boof arrived. Cheryl had cleared the table and stacked its contents in a corner. Boof, carrying her overnight bag and a pile of pizza cartons, glanced at the table. His smooth brow wrinkled fleetingly, his glance bounced from the table and flicked around the room. He put the pizzas on the table, crossed to the corner and placed her overnight bag on the floor next to the stack of stuff from the table.

Later, around midnight, all ministrations and chores complete, Cheryl was preparing to bed down on the sofa and went to collect her bag. Next to it, sitting on top of the pile of table jetsam were papers she recognised, and which she hadn't placed there.

Oh please, Grasshopper, was her prayer as she switched out the light, don't become too much like the Master.

33

The doctor was in. And the doctor was in unfamiliar territory – for him.

He was in his office. His office was very familiar territory, well marked out with his spoor: his degrees and diplomas, his awards and trophies and testimonials, an eclectic scatter of items sampled from his priceless collectibles, and of course, his photographs of family, nuclear and extended. This familiar space had become momentarily unfamiliar. Some delicate turn of the screw, a skewing of the ambience, a prismatic shift in the light perhaps, had made of the room that he'd cluttered and scuffed into well-worn comfort a strange and difficult place. It had something to do with the person who faced him from the other side of his desk.

The doctor was a man of average height and lean frame. His head was large, bestowing his body with childlike proportions, and he had a short, neat beard and bright, brown eyes. If he was plump and jolly he might be described as gnomish, but he wasn't. He was in the latter part of his fifties but his hair was a luxuriant, curly, brown crop. He was very proud of it. Yes, he had grey hairs, but not enough to be obvious across the width of a desk. He was proud of that also. He endeavoured to keep the width of a desk, if not the desk itself, between him and most of humanity most of the time. Of course professional activities dictated closer approximation and even physical contact with some on a daily basis, but one needn't be intimate. He was a good doctor, brisk, and efficient, and therefore able to keep the duration of such encounters minimal. Any intercourse with a patient, or the associates thereof, he limited resolutely to the realm of his medical expertise and pragmatic responsibility; none of this psychology or pastoral care and their messy like.

The doctor asserted his authority without raising his voice, and assumed effortless command of situations or left the room. He determined, by force of character, the length, and breadth, of each professional or social encounter. He was polite, direct and reasonable. He was willing to listen while his interlocutor was polite and reasonable, but terminated the discourse when those too stubborn or obtuse to perceive the percipience of his views persisted. Some mistook this esteem for moderation in all exchanges as arrogance. Actually a lot of people did.

He had acquired a knack of seeming much taller than he was, without standing on a chair. Subtle orchestration of posture, gesture, masterful facial cast, unwavering eye contact and dynamic modulation of the voice were key elements in this illusion. Although he wasn't a man given to self-reflection the Thespian implications of the stratagem did not elude him. Admittedly, it could be defined as acting, but it was method acting: he was a doctor playing a doctor, he was being himself.

For some reason he was having difficulty being himself at the moment. Someone else had assumed effortless command of the situation and he couldn't, in this instance, leave the room. The room was his office. The man on the other side of his desk was taller than he was, many people were, but this man was taller than the doctor's stratagem as well. The doctor had a feeling that standing on a chair would not help.

Dr Throsby, for that was his name, contrived to look relaxed. He lay back in his chair, made a church of his fingers and, resting his wrists on his chest, touched the tip of his nose with the steeple. He stared across the knuckled roof with his bright brown eyes.

'I don't know what else I can tell you, Mr Edge,' he said through the nave. He thought of how his voice might have resonated in a cathedral if he hadn't been agnostic.

'You can tell me,' said the younger man, bright blue eyes staring straight back, serve and volley, 'if Ms Kitchen specified me as Mr Bovell's murderer.'

This man had the deceased patient's enduring power of attorney but had not presented himself as a lawyer or a policeman. Nevertheless he behaved with such effortless authority that he must be operating within the sanction of some civil establishment. He was polite and reasonable, but much more direct than was desirable. Throsby was having difficulty determining the limits of this encounter in any dimension.

'Now, now,' said Throsby, feeling firmer ground beneath his figurative feet. The man was just worried about the wild accusation, after all. 'Ms Kitchen was – quite understandably – extremely distraught. In her grief she was clutching at straws for something or someone to blame. I've seen reactions like this many times before.'

'So have I,' said Edge. 'What I'm trying to understand is the context in which she made the accusation.'

Ah, thought Throsby, he has a medical background. He began to feel the proximity of his comfort zone once more. 'It was simply an angry outburst, quite spontaneous, quite irrational, on hearing of Mr Bovell's passing.' He frowned and relocated the church to his desktop. 'Did one of my staff tell you about this?'

Edge gave a perfunctory shake of the head. 'Just a guess.'

For some obscure reason this shocked Throsby. He shrugged it off with a spasm of his shoulders. There was obviously some history here. He didn't want to be involved in any messiness.

'There was nothing said to her that suggested irregularities surrounding Ben Bovell's death?'

'No, no. She was told the simple fact that he passed away peacefully in his sleep.' Throsby decommissioned the church and threw wide the two halves of it. 'The shock, the relief from tension, the anger just boiled over and found its expression that way.' He smiled reassuringly. 'Everyone concerned with Mr Bovell's case was upset, Mr Edge. The team was feeling quite optimistic – about his survival, that is. Even a hardened campaigner like Dr Plotell, who had the least contact with the patient, was visibly upset.' He was confident that he was back on top of the situation again. 'No one takes her accusation seriously, Mr Edge. A death certificate has been issued. You needn't worry.'

'Why?'

'W-what? Why? I'm afraid I don't understand.'

'Why does no one take her seriously? Are you absolutely certain that his death wasn't assisted in any way?'

Throsby's comfort zone slipped through a wormhole to another part of the universe. 'Mr Edge,' he administered a prescribed dose of wooden chuckle, 'if you persist in this way you'll have me accusing you of nefarious deeds.'

'Perhaps you should.'

Throsby pushed his chair back and began to press on the armrests to raise his body. 'I'm a very busy man, Mr Edge. Your next step is to arrange with an undertaker for the disposition of the body and ...' He paused. The man hadn't moved. In fact he seemed to settle back further in the chair. Throsby always thought they were too damn comfortable. The blue eyes seemed to pin him suspended over his chair neither sitting nor standing. The eyes shifted and Throsby's were tugged along with them. He was looking at his appointment book open on the desk.

'Your daily diary is organised in half hour blocks,' said the man who called himself Edge. He glanced casually at his watch. 'I've only taken ten of your minutes, Doctor, and I won't keep you much longer.' He waited.

Throsby lowered himself slowly into his chair. He was trying to recall what his response should have been. He was certain he was acting out of character. He wasn't being himself.

'I was under the impression that Ben was making progress. Aren't you curious why he took a turn for the worse? If only for purposes of best practice.'

'Mr Edge, people die in this hospital every day. We are required to carry out a postmortem when a patient dies within twenty-four hours of an operation, but Mr Bovell was operated on many days ago. We can't perform an autopsy on every one. Pathology is overworked and under-staffed. There are protocols and criteria. Hysterical outbursts by the grief stricken are not sufficient reason for a postmortem examination.'

'Humour me, Doctor.' Edge rocked forward, recrossed his legs and rocked back. 'Would it have been possible for me, or another visitor, to have done something that could result in Ben dying sometime after we left. He died between – what – three and four am?'

'Mr Edge, Ben was making progress, yes that's true.' His comfort zone was returning from the far side of the galaxy at hyper light speed. If the man wanted a first year med lecture he'd accommodate him. 'He was stabilised and we were preparing to transfer him to the spinal unit at the Austin Hospital. However, although his condition was no longer considered critical, it was still extremely fragile. His system had endured acute trauma. Three bullets had been removed, any one of which might have been fatal. His spinal cord was severely, probably irreparably, damaged – a confident prognosis was difficult to establish. All his vital functions were under extreme stress and being maintained artificially. Under those circumstances the slightest variable could send him into seizure or provoke the failure of an organ. A total collapse could be set in train with one organ after another failing. And I must say this, unpalatable as it is: he wasn't fighting very hard, Mr Edge.'

'A variable. Could someone have … facilitated such a variable?'

'With sufficient medical knowledge,' Throsby conceded with a sigh. Then, for some reason he didn't understand, added, 'Or a little research.' He could feel the candid blue eyes probing like searchlights in the swarming caverns of his cranium. 'But who, apart from yourself and Ms Kitchen, had access?'

'If I told you that Ben Bovell indicated to me a desire to be released from his misery would you perform an autopsy?'

Odd, formal way to put it, thought Throsby. His lips tweaked upwards in his most patronising smile. And he knew it was patronising. 'I doubt anyone with a throat full of tubing could communicate that clearly.' Under a corrosive gaze his smile dissolved. 'Mr Edge, enduring power of attorney may mean you can turn off the machines when all hope is gone, but it doesn't constitute a request for euthanasia.'

A small dimple curled into the man's cheek just above the left corner of his lips and his eye glittered with an unvoiced chuckle. Throsby's world wobbled a little; he sobered and became very earnest. 'If, however, Mr Edge, if you informed the proper authorities that such a request was made of you and you acceded to it, I have no doubt an autopsy would be performed.' There, that showed him. Put up or shut up.

The man suddenly came smoothly to his feet. Throsby lurched back in his chair but managed to convert the reaction into an awkward arousal from his chair. He stared at the hand suspended above his desk.

'Thanks for your time and forbearance, Doctor.' Edge smiled.

Throsby clasped the hand firmly and found his pressure subtly matched. He looked into the eyes again but found himself distracted by that little comma at the corner of the mouth. He wasn't going to win that contest either. 'It wasn't time wasted if I have allayed some of your concerns,' he said with another wooden smile: blackheart sassafras.

When he had his office back again, and his comfort zone had decanted between the four walls once more, he sat behind his desk and made another church. He stared at the steeple. How extraordinary! Over the years these walls had witnessed some odd encounters with the grieving and grasping, but that was a doozey. That was an Americanism, he believed, and he preferred not to use Americanisms, however sometimes that nation's vernacular was apt.

He tapped the tips of his steeple together several times then pressed it to his chin. What if he had just been very cleverly manipulated by an extremely daring and cunning criminal? What if he had been milked for information and for reassurance that there were no suspicions about the death, using some sort of reverse psychology? No, ridiculous, that was much too Agatha Christie. Of course he could arrange an autopsy, he had the authority. It was well within his power to do so. But, no! Why give the arrogant bastard the satisfaction?

34

Ernest Philip Duggs, Ernie or 'Digger' to his friends – which he could count on the fingers of slightly less than two hands – and his many acquaintances, was taking a risk. At this point in time he didn't know how big a risk. There was no way that he should or could know.

Ernie had been Jack Barker's toecutter. If 'Blackjack' said remove some piggies or break some bones, Ernie asked, how many? He didn't enjoy hurting people, but was yet to meet a punter who didn't dislike some aspect of their job. He'd served Barker with a diligent consistency that was presumed by everyone, including Ernie, to be unswerving loyalty. He was in fact a simple pragmatist. The circumstances of his nature and nurture had convinced him that he existed in a perpetual urban war zone; and it was shrewder to be part of an elite cadre of mobile mercenary guerillas than stuck in the trenches with the foot soldiers of one of the hostile factions. And Jack had clout where it mattered – a plus there.

Then something happened.

He was witness to an act of breathtaking ruthlessness. Jack Barker was a ruthless man, and it had never occurred to Ernie that he himself was not. He had witnessed Jack's hot-blooded variety many times. This was an act of another order. This was passionless and discriminating and arctic in its pristine purity. It was surgical. It was pragmatic in a way that Ernie could only admire and aspire to but never emulate. And although he couldn't describe its essence nor articulate its effect on him, the fact of it penetrated his soul like a particle at light speed. Embedded there, it was parcelled in nacreous secretions of the psyche to shield his soft moist centre from its gritty certitude. Masked from the hard shell of his awareness the grain transmuted into something far beyond diligent constancy, into something unswerving and unquestioning, something which Ernie would never put a name to, even if he could.

And when Jack fell like a rebellious angel there was no hiatus. There was no dislocation, no ruction, no rudderless disarray, no starless wandering in search of a new true north. His fealty, all without his bidding, was foresworn. It found instantly a new home because it already lived there.

The risk he was taking was prompted by something else that had happened. Something similar yet something quite different. He had been pierced yet again by a sub-atomic particle and he was as ignorant of this event as he was of the other.

Ernie knew his function was supervising the surveillance, limiting his active participation to an absolute minimum, and then preferably after dark. The reason for this was the singularity of his physiognomy. Ernie was neither handsome nor ugly, he was neither fat nor thin, neither tall nor short. His face was smooth and firm as an apple, his hair a gunmetal bruise. He had the proportions and crude, compact conviction of an artillery shell, and gave the impression that, if discharged, he would arise unscathed from the rubble at ground zero. As plain as his individual parts were, their aggregate drew the casual eye and dragged in more than its fair share of personal space. It was never necessary for Ernie to step aside or swerve to avoid a sidewalk denizen, unless said denizen was walking backwards. Ernie looked ballistic.

The thing was, she wasn't moving around much after dark. All her excursions, alone or with that cop friend of the boss's, the one that went troppo for a while, were in daylight, mostly during business hours. At night, when she did venture out, he couldn't get a good look at her. Getting close was out of the question, and he could only use the binoculars or telephoto in the car. Entering the places she did was too chancy, unless it was a crowded corner pub or its ilk. Catching a glimpse of her bathed in light was rare. The best he could manage was distant snaps and flashes and silhouettes. The silhouettes when she removed her bulky coat were cameos etched on his brain. Shit, she was a corker.

He found himself allotting himself all the night shifts.

Then something happened.

A face he recognised turned up in a car outside her digs. It was a cop. One he didn't like much. There were a lot of cops he didn't like – but there were a lot that he did. The boss had been a cop once, and he'd liked him as a cop as much as he did as the boss. He didn't like Ricciardelli. Ricciardelli pulled up on the opposite side of the road a few parking bays down from Ernie's vantage point. He double parked, the smug prick, and called someone on his mobile. A poor fucking punter'd be done for that.

Ricciardelli had daytime television looks and fancied his chances with the ladies, which was one of the reasons Ernie didn't like him. Well, it was two reasons. He had a plateful of marriage, wife, kids, mortgage, but he liked a side dish or two. He had one of the girls at the Grotto doing a bit of moonlighting once, personal services. She thought he was serious, but he was sucking the juice out of her, until the boss had a word in his ear.

The Ricciardelli charm didn't seem to be having instant success if that's what was going on. The facial expressions suggested the call was social rather than professional – unless he worked part-time flogging toiletries or time-share. It had to be a coincidence. It couldn't be connected to her – could it? Jesus this girl couldn't be taken in by something like Ricciardelli. Nah!

The call lasted for at least fifteen minutes. Then Ricciardelli ran a comb through his thick dark hair, hooked his left arm languidly over the back of the seat and relaxed into the curve of its bucket. He looked like he'd committed the perfect murder of a canary. When the focus of his fantasies appeared and climbed in beside Ricciardelli, Ernie didn't know why the sudden void punched in the pit of his stomach rang, fleetingly, with the hollowness of his doggedly forgotten adolescence. He almost didn't follow them. Serves the silly little bitch right if Ricciardelli dicked her and ditched her. He thought she was different, she'd have more sense. In fact he had no objective reason or material evidence for believing that she was any wiser than anyone else in matters of the heart, but that wasn't the fucking point. Just what the point was he didn't bother to consider. He had a job to do, and, after all, she wasn't much more than a kid. He hit the ignition, slipped the car into gear, swung a tight U-turn and set off in pursuit.

They led him to a pub in North Melbourne. There was live music belting from the first-floor windows. From across the street he could see terpsichorean action and clusters of drinkers. It looked like a private bash. A few rozzers he recognised rolled up in glad rags. He went into the front bar, bought a beer and complained mildly about the racket upstairs. The woman who served him was happy to fill him in, chapter and verse: some cop's fiftieth. He took his drink to a corner and nursed it. It was a hell of a lot warmer in here, but he couldn't soak in it for too long. There was no clear view of the exit for one thing.

His faith in his pin-up girl was rebooting. Ricciardelli had used a cop party to get her to go with him. Probably persuaded her it was a good opportunity to fraternise with her East Coast jack (and jill) colleagues. He was warmed by these thoughts back in the chill of the car.

There was no real reason for him to hang around. She wasn't doing anything of interest to the boss – anything that he had hope of finding out about. Boys in blue surrounded her. It was only sensible to call it a night. If he hung around he was in for a long cold wait. And his girl wouldn't invite a sleaze like 'Dick-a-deli' up for a nightcap. What the fuck did it matter if she did? He wasn't her fucking mother. What could he do about it? Shoot the bastard? With honey buns like hers she must be used to swatting flies like Ricciardelli. She must have had lots of blokes. This stray unwelcome thought made him feel like the glass of beer was repeating. He was so engrossed in his inward tug-o'-war that he almost missed her.

She burst from the doorway that opened directly to the upstairs access. Shrugging her coat over her shoulders she stepped to the curb and looked up and down the street. Shit, she'd been in there barely two hours. As she turned uncertainly and looked towards the light of the front bar, Ricciardelli came through the door. He was in his suit, no overcoat. Ernie couldn't remember if he'd worn one inside. What the fuck was the matter with him? He usually noticed those details.

They weren't happy little Vegemites. 'Dick-a-deli' obviously wanted her to go back inside, she seemed intent on being somewhere else. They paced up and down in front of the pub like bickering panthers. She kept coming to the curb, glancing up and down, looking for a taxi, Ernie guessed. He had the crazy idea, for a split second, of posing as one and whisking her away. Then at the end of one of her paces she disappeared around the corner. Shit! Ernie scrambled from the car and tried to hurry, inconspicuously, along the footpath to keep her in sight.

As he got to a position where the pub didn't obscure his view he saw Ricciardelli catch her wrist and spin her around to him like some sort of tango dancer. He pulled her against his chest and pressed her there with a large hand in the small of her back. He couldn't see the other hand, but he feared it was somewhere near her breast. Her face came up to his. Ernie couldn't see her expression, but the gesture was real *Gone With The Wind*. Ricciardelli's face came down on hers. Her right hand snaked around his neck. Her left hand seemed to be groping around his arse under his jacket. Ernie's heart plunged into the chasm his bowels had vacated earlier. He thought he heard himself sob and it shocked him into some semblance of self-awareness. He looked down and saw his gun in his hand. He shoved it hastily away.

And that's when the something happened.

She stepped back and Ricciardelli followed in the clinch. They were slow dancing towards a parked car. Oh Christ, he wasn't going to do her on the bonnet? The illusion of dance was reinforced bizarrely when she did one of those over and under manoeuvres. Next thing Ricciardelli's on his arse at the foot of a parking meter. She steps back and starts to walk away. Ricciardelli's laughing, struggling to his feet and following her. Ernie heard his voice: something like, 'I knew you'd rock 'n' roll.' Then Ricciardelli stops dead, one arm stretched behind him. He looks back curiously as if his sleeve is snagged. He must be pretty pissed because it takes him a little while to realise that his wrist is hand-cuffed to the parking meter. 'Very funny, Carol,' he calls when the information swims through the booze, and he looks at her retreating back, laughing. Carol Porter turns the corner, an airy, 'Good night, Frank,' wafting behind her. Ricciardelli starts patting himself down for his keys. Next time the bastard'll go home and get out of his work togs before playing up, sniggered Ernie as he tracked the woman.

Ernie saw her safely into a taxi, then went home. He lay in bed in the dark for a very long time, staring at the place where the ceiling was when he flicked the switch to off, and where common sense said it should be still. Ernie resisted the urge to turn on the light to make sure. Something had happened.

The next morning, before official business hours, he sat in the parlour of The Crimson Grotto at one end of the huge plush couch. At the other end the boss read the names and addresses and blunt words of his report in a small notebook.

'Did you recognise any of these people?' asked David Edge, tossing the notebook back to him.

'One or two, Boss.' The boss had given up asking him to use 'David' long ago.

'She's picked all the right ones to interview.'

Ernie couldn't comment. Only two of the names were familiar to him.

'She's circling, Digger.'

'That'd be my guess, Boss.'

'She has a theory and she's testing it against the facts. She's good.'

Fucking separated at birth, thought Ernie, but said nothing.

The boss grabbed him with his eyes. 'As soon as she makes a move in their direction – either of them, Digger – I want to know.'

'What're you gonna do?' Ernie asked, and didn't like the way it left his lips.

The blue gaze that held him in its grip tightened. Ernie blinked to keep his eyeballs in their sockets.

'That's an odd question from you, Digger,' said Edge.

It was an odd question, but sometime last night he had stepped through the looking-glass.

35

'Y'didn't tell me who we were workin' for,' Carl Fokker said reproachfully when he opened the door. He wore baggy boxers and a navy singlet, its front polka-dotted with cigarette burns.

'Good mornin', Maeve, nice to see ya. Come on in an' have a cuppa,' said Maeve and waited.

'Orright,' said Carl, turned a grudging back and led her deeper into his apartment.

Maeve had a good sticky on the way through to the kitchen at the rear. It was a small two-bedroom place. The first thing that impressed her was the quantity and quality of the furnishings. Here was everything the larcenous man about town could wish for. Of special note was the comprehensive catalogue of white goods, household gadgets and electronic equipment. It was a museum of recent pilfering history, exhibit A to exhibit Z. Domesticity fallen from the back of a truck.

The next thing that impressed her was its neatness. If Maeve had an image of Carl Fokker's pad (and she couldn't imagine picturing Carl Fokker at all) it was a squalid shamble. This put her domestic arrangements to shame. Maybe he was shacked up with someone or lived with his mum. She found it difficult to imagine either of those arrangements too.

'Nice digs, Sneaky,' said Maeve dryly, eyeing the flat plasma screen, bigger than a window, on the lounge-room wall. 'Bit crowded. No cat I suppose.'

Carl's head tortoised around the doorjamb from the shell of his kitchen. He glared suspiciously, said nothing and pulled it back in. Maeve could hear tinklings and clatterings.

'Wake you?' she asked.

'If y'want coffee or breakfast or anythin' get y'bum in 'ere,' snarled Carl. The affable, laconic, wait-till-it-falls-on-my-plate Carl was notably absent this morning.

'Not a morning person, Sneaky?' Maeve grinned as she entered the kitchen. It was just as neat as the rest of the house. She wondered if IKEA had been knocked over recently.

'Get grumpy when I don't get enough sleep,' Carl replied from the other side of his hunched shoulders. He was at a bench in the corner with his back to her. His straw hair sprayed like a cartoon explosion above his shoulder blades. 'An' get snaky when I get bullshitted.'

'Now don't pout, pumpkin. You'll swallow your face,' said Maeve as she slid a chair away from the table. 'I didn't bullshit you.'

'Y'didn't tell me who the fuck I was workin' for.' He turned around with a bowl of cereal in each hand.

'Now come on, sulky socks, you know how it works – need to know. It's safer all round.'

He put the bowls on the table and wrenched open the refrigerator. He gave her an eyeful of his backside, then turned back and plumped a plastic two-litre bottle of milk and a banana in front of her. He sat opposite, reached around to an open drawer and scooped up a selection of cutlery. There was silence while they assembled their breakfast in the bowls.

'I've worked for 'im before,' Carl mumbled, after a few mouthfuls. 'I know it can be dangerous. It's jist … I'd like a bitta credit.'

Maeve's hand froze in the midst of a muesli delivery. She cleared her throat and said, 'Credit? You get paid. D'you want a plaque?'

'No! Jeeeez,' Carl glowered. He wiped some milk from his chin with the back of a hand. 'Credit for some nouse and gumption.'

'*He* suggested using you, Sneaky,' she said. Jesus, if she'd known this gig entailed playing mother, she'd have had second thoughts herself. 'He must have a bit of faith in you.'

'Yeah …' he said grudgingly. 'I never know what I'm fuckin' doing it for, but.'

'Well, like I said – it's safer. He's thinking of your best interests.' She watched him wrap his forearm round his bowl like an urchin in a thief's kitchen and shovel in a few more spoonfuls. Then he suddenly looked up.

'Are we doin' good?' he said with injured belligerence.

Maeve just stared.

'Well?' he demanded petulantly.

'Jesus, Sneaky, I didn't know y'gave a stuff,' said Maeve, struggling to assimilate this little twist.

'I know about him. 'E might kill people, but 'e does it for good reasons. I know 'e tries to fix things. An' 'e looks out f'people like me. You're a tough old bitch dyke but you wouldn't be in bed with 'im if 'e weren't straight.'

Maeve wedged her tongue firmly in her cheek and bit down on it. She couldn't trust herself to speak so she just stared.

'I-I know I'm not as good as youse. I'm a bottom feeder,' Carl continued, faltering, when he elicited silence. 'I'll probably never be anythin' else. But, y'know, it … sometimes it's nice to know y'skills – pissant though they may be – are good for, you know … somethin'.'

Well bugger me, thought Maeve, insight from the internally blind. You forget the Carl Fokkers of the world might have as good a view of the stars from their gutter as you do from yours. Shit, she knew bottom feeders who lived at the top.

'Jesus, Sneaky! I'm an alcoholic.' Christ! Why did she say that?

Carl flashed a disdainful glance up from under the crag of his brow, as if to say: Shit, every bastard and his cousin knows that. He retreated morosely to tucking away his breakfast.

Maeve stared at the dishevelled crown of his bobbing head. She was about to break a personal rule. In the short term it could be dangerous, but it might reap long-term benefits.

'We're doing good, Carl,' she said at last.

He looked up, like a dog at her feet that's heard its name. His face was watchful, but uncertain. Are we going walkies, or is it just another false alarm? 'Who we helpin'?' he ventured, suspecting his audacity would earn him a slap across the nose.

'The kids – we hope.'

'Benny Bovell's kids?'

'Did you know Benny?'

'A bit. We did a job together once.' He sat back and grinned. His face compressed into folds like a concertina. He rubbed his fingers in his hair with enough vigour to chase snakes from the canebrake. 'Wanna cuppa coffee and some toast?'

As Maeve spread butter thickly on a hot slice she said, 'Your job's been important, Sneaky, even though you were just a decoy. We needed her to lead us to someone, and then keep her away from him.'

'How come I got that job?'

'You're a man of exceptional appearance, Carl.'

'Y'mean I'm an ugly prick?'

'That too.'

'You find 'im?' He was making some sort of toast sandwich, filled with gobs of peanut butter and honey and something brown. Maeve tried not to look at it.

'We've been watching him for a week. Took a look around inside his house. Bugged it, his phone. Hacking into his computer.'

Carl's head nodded up and down as his maw opened around the abomination in his hand. 'Lin Flowers,' he said with approval.

'Need to know, Sneaky,' she reminded him.

'I know.' He grinned knowingly, squirrel-cheeked with toast. It sounded like 'Oimoe'.

'David's flying to Brisbane today. He thinks someone up there might help us join the dots.'

'Inna foonra tmor?' Isn't the funeral tomorrow?

'He'll be back. But I don't think he'll be welcome at the funeral.'

'Roy.' Right.

'Yasmin Glover is doing something for us. There's a bit of risk. We want you to ride shotgun.'

'Fuuug!' Carl sprayed in crumbs. 'Seesa orbug.' She's a hornbag.

'I take it that's a "yes"?' She brushed her sleeve as if he'd spat ants.

'Fuginoh!' Fucking oath!

'After Benny's put to rest we want to drive a wedge,' Maeve said. 'There's a house in Box Hill Sharon doesn't know we're onto. We'll use you again to keep her away from there as well as her toy boy when the time comes. It'll be your last job. And the possum will be stirred.' She took a loud sip of coffee. 'That's when it might get dicky. The more we learn about him the less benign he appears. You're the only one of us that Sharon can identify – as far as we know. She's complained to him about you over the phone.

She feared David's interest and figured your connection. We were counting on that.' She removed an envelope from her pocket. 'The balance of your retainer, and a nice fat bonus.'

His cheeks rolled like a sackful of kittens. He swallowed, his head dipping like a bellicose rooster. 'Y'want me to piss off for a while?'

'We don't know how he'll react. It'll be safer.'

'I'll be bait. Don't mind.'

'We do,' said Maeve. She sank back into her chair, bunched like a frog waiting for its dinner to move, and studied him with hooded eyes.

'Wha'?' Carl demanded warily.

'Nothin'. Just thinking.'

Well, there it was. Why Edge had faith in no-hopers like Carl Fokker had been a bit of a poser over the years. She'd also been unable to fathom why he took it for granted she'd stay away from the turps long enough to get a job done. Now she glimpsed what he saw in Sneaky. What did he see in Maeve Maguffin?

36

'You don't remember me, do you?'

'Your face is familiar.'

'Shed a few kilos since.' Avery Diderrich took a furtive peep at himself in the rear-view mirror. He wouldn't recognise himself if he'd stayed in Melbourne and only travelled north to meet himself today. He looked like Mr Squiggle with a goatee. Had his nose got bigger, his face grown smaller or had he simply shifted the mass (and the glow) from his cheeks to his proboscis?

'Your voice, more so,' his passenger added. 'You cross-examined me once or twice, I'd hazard.'

'Got it in one.' He passed a singularly slow taxi and manoeuvred the VW convertible back into the left lane. He'd chosen to drive with the roof up. It made conversation easier. The fact that a small skin cancer had been removed from the dome of his forehead two weeks earlier also influenced the choice. 'Little good did it do me.' He glanced at the man beside him. 'Cross-examination. Cross-examination.' He chuckled. He tried to get a few chuckles out early in any attempt to establish rapport. He had a bubbling, joyous, little-boy chuckle that had charms to soothe judge and jury alike – and he knew it. 'You earned quite a reputation.' There was no response. 'Amongst my brethren.' Chuckle. 'Know a brief or two threw his client on the mercy of the court soon's he learned the arresting officer was you.'

'A tad defeatist, everyone makes mistakes.'

'Well prepared – you had 'em bluffed. Knew your law, didn't you?'

'Did law at uni.'

He felt the satisfying burble of an I-knew-it chuckle in his chest. 'Only one gave you a real run for your money was that tiny brunette. Fragile looking little thing, lame in one leg – spina bifida or cerebral palsy or something – but slung mutton like a shearer's cook. Destined for big things. What was her name? Always think cathedral when I'm scratching for her name – Church? Kirk? No, no – Temple.'

'Catherine Temple.'

'Tha-a-at's it. Now she shook you, didn't she?'

'To the darns in my socks.'

'Abby Kirk: that was the name in the story.' His passenger glanced at him, mildly curious. 'Used her in a story once. Well, not her exactly. Based a character on her, called her Abby Kirk.' The passenger's blue eyes held his. That's how he remembered him – the eyes. In court they never strayed from yours, no matter what you threw at him. The answers were always succinct, measured, delivered in mild reasonable tones – Mr Let-me-help-you-to-the-truth himself. I've got the chuckle, you've got the eyes, he thought. 'I write between gigs now,' he added, dragging his attention back to the road. 'Just take the cases that really interest me, these days.' He grinned ruefully into the burnished aluminium sunlight. 'Or the ones that might make good raw material.'

'Did you come up here for the climate?'

'Had a bloody heart attack, didn't I. Tryin' to get to the top of the rubbish heap in record time. Didn't notice wife was an alcoholic and kids hated my guts. Stuffed up a case or two: high on pills that promised to deliver a thirty-hour day. Leaped up to object one day and fell on my instructing counsel. Dead for a coupla minutes. Makes you think.'

'So you transplanted to rewrite your life?'

He grinned. 'Yeah. Mara beat the booze, but she divorced me. She likes me again though, and the kids give me the time of day. Write scripts for TV. Mostly cop shows. Published a book of short stories – cases I had. Names changed to protect the innocent. Wrote a screenplay. Tryin' to get the movie up at the moment. Bugger of a process. Defending child molesters is a picnic compared.'

'Are you Turoczy's barrister and solicitor?'

'Switched to solicitor – can't be both up here.' He chuckled, wholeheartedly this time. 'Shrink – fell into the maw of one in my enfeebled condition – said I was an addict and my chosen substance of abuse was performing life 'n' death dramas before figures of authority.'

'It can be a turn-on.' The blue eyes swung to the road ahead. 'And a habit hard to break.'

'You're not a cop anymore?'

'No.'

'Whatcha doing? Security? PI stuff? Or something completely different?'

'Fiddling at the fringes of a PhD.'

'No kidding? What about?'

'Trying to apply the science of networks to an analysis of criminal organisation.'

'Ooo, makes my literary endeavours sound pissweak. What the hell's the science of networks?'

'It's a way to explain how chaos becomes order. Gets the dry-as-dusts all damp and unnecessary these days – after Kylie's lingerie, of course.'

He glanced at his passenger's profile. Probably true, but it had the ring of arcane crap designed to mask the man's real business – couldn't make a buck out of that. Then he remembered.

'You know why you stuck in my mind?' he said. The blue gaze brushed the side of his face. 'During one of our encounters I questioned the honesty of your testimony. You know what you said?' He looked across. The gaze rested, patient, waiting. There was a tiny curl of amusement in the left corner of the mouth. 'You said: This isn't important enough to waste a good lie.' He chuckled loudly. 'That was good. Bloody good. You won me as well as the jury with that one. I used it in a TV script. Tell me, was that a line to get the jury onside, did you use it a lot?'

'Can't remember ever saying it. But, if I did, I meant it – at the time. Lies complicate life too much. I'm a simple bloke.'

Bull-fucking-shit he thought, but said: 'We'll turn off at the next ramp. I organised the interview to suit your flight.' He flicked a glance at his watch. 'Should have time for a coffee. And you think you can help him?'

'If I'm right, the benefits should be mutual.'

Daniel Turoczy was a career criminal of the old school. He prided himself on never having done harm to his fellow man – just relieved him of the twin burdens of wealth and property. He too was a simple bloke. The psychological subtleties of victim trauma never hove over his horizon. If they had he'd have – simply – told the sufferer to get a grip, it wasn't fucking cancer.

He limped into the concrete-blocked, concrete-paved – concrete-bloody-roofed, as far as he knew – hollow box of the interview room. Fluorescent light robbed the flesh of warmth and the space of shadow. No wonder the legal eagles kept visits to a minimum. His cell was a cosy nook compared to this. It had an ambience that made his bloody arthritis play up a treat. He took Diderrich's proffered hand. He liked his lawyer, probably because he pitched a genuine interest in his client's fate.

As he shook his hand and half listened to Diderrich's encouraging yabber he stared across his shoulder at the person on the far side of the metal table that was bolted to the floor in the middle of the room. Life was fucking funny, wasn't it? There was his nemesis: the living embodiment of the nightmare that had nipped at his heels for ten years. The situation had been bad enough. He probably would have gone on the square a while anyway, but when he learned this bloke was on his heels he went bush as well. This bloke had a reputation for persistence – and pulling rabbits out of hats. Now here he was, maybe about to pull a rabbit out of a hat for good old Daniel Turoczy.

His visitor held a small backpack and was dressed in a corduroy shirt and jeans. He probably thought the weather was warm, but Daniel had been here more than long enough to acclimatise. It was bloody cold. And the bloody pipedream peddlers that ran this state were so convinced it was a tropical paradise they refused to acknowledge the existence of central heating.

'Danny,' Diderrich was saying, retaining his grip on Daniel's hand and tugging him to the table. 'This is David Edge. Have you met before?'

'Almost,' said Daniel, as his attorney passed his hand across the table. 'G'day, Mr Edge.' He winced a little as they shook. Edge turned his hand over and held it in his palm, maintaining a firm but gentle grip with a thumb. The hand was sheathed in a fingerless woollen glove. He looked up into its owner's face. Daniel wondered how long he'd last under interrogation from those eyes. 'Arthritis,' he shrugged. 'Avery reckons you might help me.'

Edge gave a flick of an eyebrow and an almost imperceptible shrug of one shoulder in reply. He twisted slightly, reached for a chair, hefted it to the table and sat. Daniel took a seat opposite. Avery Diderrich stood at the end of the table and studied them both. Here was an instant rapport between strangers, established without any apparent gimmicks. He wondered what esoteric knowledge or experience they both drew on to make it possible. If they had anything in common it was invisible to the indifferent eye.

One was tall, fair, young, fit, a lean face, casually but smartly dressed. The other was short, slight, at the Gothic end of middle age, and when he wasn't in an oversized daggy windcheater, a small pot was visible, tucked in his sunflower-yellow prison trousers. Today he had a thick woollen beanie pulled tight on his large round head. He looked like a sock puppet of the Magic Pudding.

'Is there going to be anything said I shouldn't hear, gentlemen?' Diderrich asked.

'At this point only the truth is going to help anyone,' said Edge. He put his eyes on Daniel and leaned. 'I need the truth. If don't get it I've got no straw to spin into gold for Mr Turoczy.'

Daniel's eyes slipped sideways to Diderrich – who was lowering his bum into a chair at the end of the table – then back to Edge. They narrowed in naked calculation. He sat, bowl-backed, like a geek in thrall to his PC.

'I asked around,' he said eventually, his eyes like polyps lurking in coral.

'Always wise, ' Edge agreed.

'They say you run Barker's business now,' he said slyly and watched the man across the table closely. Wrong answer here, thought Diderrich, and all bets are off.

'Ben Bovell is dead,' said Edge.

Who the bloody hell is Ben Bovell? Diderrich could see Turoczy struggling to maintain a poker face while spilling his cards face up all over the baize.

'Ah, oo's Ben Bovell?' Daniel asked. A beat or three too late, and he knowing it.

'Ninety-eight. The fourth man on the Customs warehouse job.'

Turoczy was unconsciously recoiling from each statement as if the words were gusts of wind. Diderrich wondered if he detected the implications of 'fourth'. Edge was letting him know he held a winning hand – or a bloody good bluff. Daniel had divulged to him no more than two cohorts. And then only one name: Terrence Varney.

'F-fourth?' squeaked Daniel, trying to muster a derisive laugh, but it ducked and ran away.

'The one who didn't bleed on the guard.' Edge let himself fall lightly back into the chair as he took something from a breast pocket. He cupped whatever it was – a photo? notes? – in a hand resting in his lap. He seemed to become oblivious to the rest of the room and studied it the way teenagers on trains study mobile phones. The suspense was getting to Diderrich, so he wasn't surprised when Turoczy broke the silence.

'What?' It was an offended yelp.

Edge looked up under his brow. He rocked forward and placed what Diderrich now believed was a photograph face down on the table and tapped it in Daniel's direction. It was Daniel's turn to rock backward and stare at the blank white oblong.

'That's the man who bled on the guard.' Edge smiled. 'As he is now, somewhat older. He was only a kid then, wasn't he, Daniel?'

Turoczy's head rotated back and forth like a performer's in a quaint German slap dance, dividing its attention equally between Diderrich and the rectangle of wire-hatched glass in the single high window. Can't make that jump, Danny boy, not with your arthritis. The oscillation of his face decayed and ceased, to centre on Edge's as if held by its gravity. He had evidently chosen stubborn silence as his response for the time being.

'You're one of the old school, Daniel,' said Edge, ignoring the tactic. 'You don't dog on your mates if you can help it. Neither did Ben. He was a dog that only barked at murder.' Turoczy was hanging on every word now. 'He had nothing to offer on this one. I didn't think anything of it at the time. It's only TV cops who have informants that know everything. Right, Avery?' he grinned at Diderrich.

'Not wrong there,' Diderrich agreed.

'You've got the torch Varney used – with his fingerprints,' Edge continued to Turoczy. 'But Varney's vindictive, a sociopath – no code. He'll say you held the guard while he hit him. Won't he?' No reply. 'Ben's dead.' He reached over and tapped the back of the photo. 'There's only this one witness left to corroborate your version.' Pause. 'Will he, Daniel?'

Turoczy's mouth opened, but Edge raised a palm and it dropped shut like the hinged lid on a municipal bin.

'Hear me out,' Edge said. He dipped his forehead at the photograph. 'Friends of mine are involved with that man. He doesn't have a criminal record. He may have been a kid looking for excitement who was freaked out by his first criminal experience and was never naughty again. Then again, he may be a nasty piece of work who never got caught. I need to know.'

Turoczy's body foreshadowed another response and he was silenced again.

'I want you to tell me exactly what happened. No glossing over details like you did with the cops. If you tell the whole truth, I can help you. If you don't, you're on your own.'

Turoczy dug at his interrogator with his eyes for a long time. He was using a toothpick on titanium. He gave up and scowled a question at Diderrich. He was a man torn between running for hearth and home now, and waiting until the storm passed – doubting that it would pass.

'My professional advice is to 'fess up, Dan,' said Diderrich, voice deep, serious, leaning forward over clasped hands to underline his earnestness.

Turoczy's attention drifted back along the table and hovered over the inverted image. Diderrich expected him to pick it up and look at the face on the other side. He poked at its corner, nudging it in a rotation to the left. Was he afraid it wasn't the third man and he'd be left with no leverage? Or was he afraid that it was?

'I supplied the truck and the plan and brought Benny in on it,' he said suddenly. 'Varney got the inside info. He had something on a storeman – dunno what.' He gave several small, abrupt jerks of his shoulders as if chasing a chill from his spine. 'The storeman was supposed to see a security guard sweet. Dunno what went wrong, the guard was a no-show.'

He stopped while he poked the photo clockwise until it was approximately where it started.

'Anyhow, Varney gives the green light. I didn't know anything about him, never worked with him before. A mate,' here he grunted low, dry, humourless laughter, 'put me his way. Heard him brag about his "Customs mole" – he called it – in a pub. Varney turned up with this young bloke on the night. Said he was breakin' him in. Kept teasing the kid, calling him "virgin". And said stuff like he was his "toy boy", wind him up and he'd do anything he was told.'

He paused and studied Edge to judge the effect of his words so far. Edge was resting his elbows on the table and his chin on his interlocked fingers. If he was reacting, Diderrich couldn't see it. He seemed to be waiting patiently and politely for the monologue to run its natural course. Turoczy ploughed on.

'The kid might have been sixteen, seventeen. Looked a bit chingchong. Real pretty an' knew it. Always flexing, doing them Kung Fu-ee kicks and poses. Catchin' a look at himself in anything shiny. I say "who is he?" to Varney and he laughs like a hyena and says "that's right". Didn't get the joke at the time.'

He stopped and gazed at the rectangle of sky divided into bite-sized pieces by the grid of its reinforcement. It had turned blue. It would be hot in the lee of sunlit walls, but chilly in the slice and dice of the westerlies. He pulled his pudding bowl tighter.

'I was in the truck stackin'. The others were handin' the stuff up to me. It was one them U-Hire removal vans. I nicked it and got it back before anyone twigged. Done it before, coupla times. We'd almost loaded it all. Varney gets cocky and decides to have a coffin nail while we finish up. I'm muckin' around trying to get the load balanced right and I hear this kerfuffle. Look around and no one's there. Hear Benny yellin' at someone to stop something. When I stick me head out I see these bodies wrestlin' around on the ground and someone circlin' them like a ref. It's Benny, really screamin'. The young bloke comes outta nowhere and shuts him up with a chop across the throat. You know …?' He ran his fingertips along the edge of his palm. Diderrich and Edge nodded.

'Anyhow, when I get there Varney's on top of the guard, got his knee on one arm, stranglin' him with one hand and tryin' to get the torch outta his grip with the other. The kid's sayin' "get off, I got his gun". I think it must've been knocked away an' the kid was lookin' for it when I stuck me head outta the truck. Anyhow Varney ignores him. 'E's got the guard beat an' knows it. Benny's coughin' an' splutterin'. Then Varney gets holda the torch – one a them big ones – and starts layin' into the guard.' Turoczy stared at the back of the photo and shook his head. 'Shit! He's yellin' the fuckin' storeman's name – callin' him for everythin' – and beltin' the fuckin' guard. Can you believe that?'

Edge obviously could, but he said: 'If the guard wasn't in on it, why did it take him so long to notice you? And why didn't you twig that your man wasn't there? How did you get in? We assumed that you'd been let in, then cut the fence later to cover the inside man.'

Turoczy grinned like the keyboard on a Wurlitzer. 'Aah,' he said. 'It was all done to fit the guard's routine. Like – whatsit? – choreography. 'E wouldn't be in it otherwise. Our bloke – the storeman – got the gate code from him and the timetable of his movements. That spot in the corner of the compound was used temporary-like when they were pushed for space. The guard knew stuff stacked there caused a blindspot in the security system: camera blocked one way; too much shadow the other. On the right night, fence was anybody's. We did everything as if the guard was square. One of us went through the fence and waited till he was due to patrol the far side of the compound, then opened the gate. Course, we could move fast 'cause he was turnin' a blind eye an' a deaf ear.' An ironic snuffle. 'There was this other compound next door and the guards useta stop at the fence to have a little chat in the wee small hours. Our guard was supposed to delay there as long as possible to give us plenty of time. He was gonna put a flat battery in his watch so he'd 'ave an excuse for dropping behind schedule. That was my idea.' He tapped his temple with a finger and winked.

Edge acknowledged the cleverness with a tiny smile and an inclination of his head.

'Later o' course,' Turoczy continued, 'he's supposeda patrol the other side and – I'll be buggered, we're bein' ripped off! He helps us finish loadin' then we tie him up.' He shrugged regretfully. 'Bitta bad luck – f' all of us – the ring-in, poor bastard, didn't stick to the script.'

He stared at what might have been for a deep drawn breath. 'Anyhow, I latch onto Varney's arm, but 'e's a strong cunt and I lose me balance and end up tangled with 'em. Next thing someone's got a handful of me hair. Can't get up, on me back tryin' to dodge the torch. Varney's hammerin' the poor bastard like he wants to slip him under a door. The kid grabs me and yanks me away. Felt like I'd been scalped.'

His hand went up to his beanie and moved it around on his cranium in soothing circles. 'Anyhow,' he said, and stared into a distant place that was gaining on him with the momentum of tomorrow.

'Anyhow. The kid waggles the gun under my nose, threatenin' like. I thought 'e was tryin' to help the guard. And maybe he was. But he's leanin' over 'em and the guard's legs are thrashin' around like crazy. 'E cops a boot in the face. He stares at the blood drippin' on his hand for a coupla seconds an' then he drops on the guard's legs an' pins 'em an' starts stabbin' the barrel of the gun in his balls. By the time I get to me feet Varney's stopped swingin'. Bloke's head looks like a melon dropped from the top o' the Rialto.'

'What happened to the guard's gun?'

'Dunno. Can't remember layin' eyes on it again. Forgot all about it. Kid might have souvenired it. He was a nasty little mongrel, 'f you ask me.'

'Who hid the body?'

'Varney and the kid. I refused to touch it or let Benny near it. Benny wasn't much use anyhow. He was dry retchin'. Least I didn't see any spew. I emptied me guts once we were outta there. Anyhow, Varney snatches the keys from the ignition and won't give 'em back until they get rid of the body and we get all the fags. That's when I see the torch and decide I need a memento.'

'Didn't Varney notice it was gone?'

'Thought 'e would and had a story ready. But once the body was outta sight he acted like the whole fuckin' thing was outta mind. Didn't mention it. Neither of 'em. Wanted to party that night, both of 'em. C'n you believe it?'

'Had Ben met either of them before that night?'

'Nah.'

'You're sure?'

'Pretty sure. But ... funny ...'

'Funny?'

'You know how Benny rattled on when he thought he'd found a new friend? Like a bloody stray puppy. Drove people nuts. He just clammed up, hardly said a word – 'cept to me. Took an instant dislike to them two. Shoulda paid attention, shoulden I?'

Turoczy had been leaning forward, eager to be believed. He flopped back into his chair, his hands resting one each side of the photo. He watched Edge for a while then his gaze leafed down. With a deft movement of his right hand he flipped the photo over. His face was impassive while his eyes and mind adjusted to changes the years might have wrought.

'That's the cunt,' he said.

'You're sure?'

'Put on a bit of condition, but 'ardly changed.' He stared at Edge, patiently waiting.

Diderrich lifted his battered briefcase onto his lap in anticipation. Edge looked at him and nodded. He reached in and brought out the Ziploc sandwich bag. He dangled it from a corner at the end of an extended arm so Turoczy could see its contents. Daniel frowned and his face swivelled inquiringly toward Edge.

'Ben Bovell left an envelope for me,' said Edge. 'One of the things it contained was a microcassette recorder. Probably liberated from a Dick Smith's. That tape was in it.'

Turoczy eyes hopped to the tiny cassette in the bag and became mesmerised by its pendular sway.

'With a few minor differences – which a good lawyer can easily account for – it tells the story you just told me.'

'Shit,' said Daniel.

'Ben doesn't mention names – it was a private confession for my ears alone – but he identifies time and place. There's no doubt he's talking about that robbery. He doesn't identify himself, but his fingerprints are all over the recorder, and the tape. Hence the plastic bag.'

'Shit,' said Daniel.

'Ben's dead. The only physical evidence of Varney's presence is the torch. And I don't think our friend in the photograph will back your story, do you?'

'Shit no,' said Daniel.

'I think Avery can make good use of that on your behalf.'

'Shit yeah,' said Daniel.

'I need a favour.'

'Shit yeah, no fuckin' worries,' said Daniel.

'Toy Boy's been active. When the wallopers wallop him the splatter will touch a few shoes. I need a little time to get someone into galoshes. A window of, say – a week?'

'I stalled this long.' Turoczy grinned eagerly, cocking an eye at Diderrich. 'Long as you like. Colder'n Disney's dick down south now.'

'Thanks, Daniel,' said Edge, and stretched his right hand across the table. Turoczy appraised it from a distance, then lunged and grabbed. 'Detective Sergeant Marks is on the square. He'll look after you.' When he extracted his captive hand Edge pushed his chair back, scooped up his backpack and stood. 'I'll wait for you outside,' he said to Diderrich.

'Hey?' Turoczy called to his retreating back. Edge turned. 'Why th' fuck did Benny do this?' Diderrich wasn't sure what 'this' was.

Edge lowered his head and contemplated a toe tip. 'For a man who hated prison, Ben always seemed remarkably reconciled to his stints in gaol. I assumed that with a childhood spent in institutions, he found life simpler there: a sort of respite. Some truth in that I suppose, but more and more I suspect that, to him, it was like paying off a debt – not for his petty crimes, for some original sin. Maybe the sin of being born Ben.' He looked up and his eyes were grey as mist. 'I think Varney got wind that you'd been tagged and tried to persuade Ben to back his story. There was the prospect of a long prison term, and … there were other things. In Ben's mind he faced a future he couldn't endure or evade.' He paused and looked up at the window that had earlier engaged Turoczy's eye. 'Ben was an informer, but exclusive to me – a Homicide plod. Ironically, the only murder he actually witnessed, he couldn't tell me about.' Edge hooked a strap of the pack over a shoulder. 'He wanted to bow out on the square?' He shrugged. 'Part of the picture.'

'Bit more to ol' Benny than met the eye, eh?' said Daniel philosophically. 'Odd little bugger, but all wool and a yard wide.'

The two men held each other's gaze. Diderrich tried to picture the traffic in the subliminal interchange.

Then Turoczy said: 'I useta play the cornet once. Fair dinkum. Mum made me learn.'

Edge smiled, tapped an adroit Astaire routine to the door. 'Dad,' he said, and left them together in the bunker.

Diderrich was impatient to finalise things with Turoczy and get to his notebook. Jesus Christ, he'd collected some fiction fodder today.

37

Carol didn't know why she was here. The crowd was small, so she, presumably the sole outsider, had drawn attention: the mysterious uninvited guest. Perhaps that was the part written for her: to spice up proceedings with a little intrigue. She didn't know why Carol Marks was here, but most of the others seemed acquainted with her.

The 'here' was a small chapel attached to a crematorium in a large Melbourne cemetery – she thought she'd heard the word 'Fawkner'. As such places went it had ambience. Architecture: tasteful, intimate, with the requisite gravitas. But, when you came down to it, all architecture could do was keep out the rain. Devotional elevator music was insinuating its presence: the odd hymn, some gospel, a smatter of classical and (God preserve us) 'The Wind Beneath My Wings'. Carol's ears had little to do but play spot the pop.

If shedding a tear was an accurate sign, the nearest and dearest seemed to be a small group consisting of two women and seven children. The most visibly upset woman was plump and black. Three of the children appeared to be hers; they were subdued, but awkward and uncomfortable rather than sad. The four children who displayed the most grief belonged to the other woman. She was short, buxom, earthy, with blonde hair as bright as a freshly-minted dollar coin. Her makeup was hard-edged and heavy, as if to plaster over grief, or encase frailty. The green eyes that glowered from the shell saw everyone in the chapel – apart from the tight-knit clutch around her – as hostile.

The two rows of seats behind her little cluster were left empty. Four people occupied the next row. One of the men and the two women had arrived together. The other man came later and was greeted warmly by the first. Body language suggested that the first man was the partner of the young woman and the older woman was her relation: an aunt or grand-mother. The two men were mates, each head leaning to each, catching up. The latecomer was a Noongar – no, a Koori over here. This made Carol look more closely at his fair-haired companion. None appeared to be known to the bereaved, but when the old woman, supported by the young woman, approached to offer condolences she said something that almost shattered the mask.

Directly across the aisle from these, Carol Marks sat talking in low tones to two men. Carol Porter guessed they were former colleagues, but only one looked like a cop. The other had an island of thick long hair on an otherwise bare scalp, the remnants of an archipelago when the mainland retreated towards his ears. Every time the door opened it wafted on end and he smoothed it down with an absent gesture.

The air shifted, the topknot lifted, a palm slid over his cranium and Carol twisted toward the door. A tall, broad-shouldered young man was holding the door for four women to enter. His fair hair was shaved short as a lawn in a gated estate. He shrugged and tugged at his clothing, uneasy in a suit. It hung on him baggily, the way off-the-peg items did – once upon a time – on Arnold Schwarzenegger. One of the women, an attractive brunette in a chic grey suit, touched his arm lightly and smiled up at him. He glowed as if she'd switched him on. He showed deference to the four women, and three of them showed deference to the fourth.

They were an odd assortment. One was the most magnificently bosomed and voluptuous XXOS Carol had ever laid eyes on. Her barely contained flesh cascaded down the aisle like an erotic ice-cream avalanche. Her billows engulfed the bereaved. A slim, sensual brown woman, who might have been the love child of Sophia Loren and Sidney Poitier, proceeded more sedately. The brunette in the smart suit hung back beside the remaining woman. Their escort, his eyes never still, hovered behind them. The fourth woman, though, was the study.

She was petite, almost a head shorter than her companion. She was ageless and of another age at the same time. Standing two or three metres from Carol her face betrayed no obvious lines or sagging of flesh. If she was wearing makeup it was cunningly applied. Her complexion was as cool and delicate as porcelain and her profile as hard-etched and regal as a bas-relief of Nefertiti. Her clothing was black. A long coat, cut with the spareness of a cassock, was buttoned to the throat and reached below the calf. Wide bottomed slacks revealed only the toes of black boots. A grey silk scarf was draped over her head and fell in loose folds around her shoulders. It was held in place by a black hat with a round crown and a flat brim. Sans scarf, from a distance she might be mistaken for Father Brown.

Carol was overtaken by a sudden conviction. She glanced at Carol Marks. Carol's arm rested along the back of the pew, her gaze was alert over the bunched shoulder of her coat. An eyebrow flicked, an eye twinkled and her attention returned to her conversation.

The woman's head turned slowly and she gazed frankly at Carol, then it turned away until her gaze touched the other Carol. It swung languidly back and her regard lingered, measuring and assessing. One gloved hand raised her hat as the other slipped the scarf from her head. Her hair was bobbed and a colour that can only be achieved naturally, and which disguises well the signs of aging; but her exposed neck gave away a little more. Her head may have tipped in a curt nod then she swung crisply on a heel and entered the row of seats at her elbow.

The woman's acknowledgement (if it occurred) hinted at a prior awareness of Carol Porter's existence. Carol was feeling paranoid. She wondered why she was here. She wondered what Carol Marks was up to. She wondered what the hell she was discussing with those men.

Those men with Carol Marks also had the new arrivals on their minds. 'Who's the woman that looks like Mary Poppins's aunt?' whispered Gareth Nile, flattening his forelock.

Don Collison, arms folded on his chest, glanced over his shoulder and grunted.

'That's Rose Garden,' said Carol Marks.

'That's actually her name?'

'I have it on good authority.'

'You got it from the whoreson's mouth, haven't ya, Caz?' said Collison archly. 'Speaking of which: where is the boy?'

Until this point the conversation had been about Carol Marks's health

– Gareth had been the first to recognise her symptoms – and her cute auburn-haired companion.

'The boy isn't Sharon's favourite little Vegemite at the moment.'

'I heard she's trying to get the coroner interested in Benny's demise,' Collison said.

'She's hurting. Wants to blame someone.'

'But he'd do it, wouldn't he, Caz? For a friend.'

The organ muzak swelled and began to fade.

'I'd better get back to Carol,' Carol said. 'He'll be pleased to know you were here.'

'D'you think I give a fuck?'

She slapped a hand on his shoulder and levered herself to her feet. 'See you, Don. Give my love to Amber, Gareth.'

Collison watched her make her way back to the Kimberley cop.

'Two fucking Carols,' he said. 'You think she's taking this schizophrenia too seriously?'

'Not funny, Don,' said Gareth.

Mercifully, the service was short and sweet. It was obvious that the minister or celebrant or whatever he was – the officiating presence – had received scant intelligence about his subject, but he was a trouper. He trowelled over the chasms in his knowledge with a thick mix of platitudes, which he managed to refresh with good humour and professional sincerity.

The partner of the deceased provided the drama. When she stood to deliver her eulogy she choked. Her mouth opened and for the first time in her life – Carol Porter suspected – there was nothing on the tip of her tongue. For an interminable time, excruciating for her audience, emotion gurgled pitifully in the back of her throat, her body quivered, finally a single intelligible word issued from her lips: a defeated, desolate 'fuck'. By then her children were wrapped around her and the oldest, a boy no more than thirteen or fourteen, pried the crushed ball of words from her twisting fingers and delivered them with tremulous dignity.

There was a long hesitation between his opening 'I'm' and 'Dee', as if tasting or testing the name for the first time. No bloody wonder: Carol learned later his given names were Delphi Apollo! A future heartbreaker that one. All of them for that matter, with their honey skin, mops of dark hair and big green or brown eyes. The boys favoured the mother, but the little girl could have been amongst the flowers on the coffin, smiling from her father's photo.

After it was over, Carol stood apart from the awkward mingling and observed. The two cops nodded to the family and left immediately. The two men accompanying the elderly woman and her young carer hovered uncertainly then swooped recklessly on the bottle-blonde Carol now knew as Sharon Kitchen. Sharon listened to their story then clasped them in a fierce hug. The two men looked embarrassed, but pleased.

Carol Marks was chatting with the four women under the watchful eye of the tall, boyish 'Arnie'. She glanced over and beckoned to Carol.

'Carol Porter,' she said as Carol approached. 'I'd like you to meet Rose Garden, Cheryl Brown, Yasmin Glover and Paula Ginley, friends of David's.' She indicated each in turn.

'I'm his business partner,' the woman called Rose said, extending a small gloved hand. She'd donned dark glasses. Perhaps she was needed in *The Matrix*. 'In point of fact,' she added. Up close Carol could see most of her life was behind her.

Paula's full lips twitched, she cocked an eye at the one called Cheryl, who winked. The exotic Yasmin took her hand as soon as Rose released it.

'He's more than a friend,' she said bluntly. 'He keeps the jackals at bay.' Her voice was pure ocker, her words pure Desert Song.

Before Carol could formulate a response she was grabbed by Paula and a wet kiss slapped on her cheek. 'Don't mind us, luvvie,' was stage-whispered in her ear. 'We get a little possessive.'

Cheryl chuckled. 'He's our boss, Carol,' she said. 'He and Rose.' Her eyes were probing, gauging the extent of Carol's knowledge. 'We sort of look after each other.'

They'd confirmed what she'd guessed on their entrance: madam, working girls and minder. That, or the cast of Chicago.

'And this,' Carol Marks added, 'is—'

'Boof!' said the minder plunging forward and grinding the bones of Carol's hand together. His eagerness to block the utterance of his given name caused her to speculate what sort of abomination it could be. The situation was amusing Cheryl no end.

'Um, nice to meet you all,' said Carol.

'Don't say it unless you mean it, Constable Porter,' said Rose.

Carol locked eyes with her. What the hell did these people know? 'I mean him no harm, Ms Garden.'

'I have scars from people who meant me no harm.'

'We have to get a move on,' said Carol Marks hastily. 'Rose, girls,' grabbing Carol by the elbow and steering, 'we'll catch up some time soon.'

'Have they registered their rights in all First World countries?' Carol Porter asked as the chapel door hissed shut behind them.

Carol Marks chuckled. 'I wanted you to get a feel for the loyalty he attracts.'

'If they've all got marriage certificates they'd better burn them.' Where was this anger coming from? 'Bigamy is still a crime. That's a fucking harem!'

'That's what Skid says.' Her chuckles were laughter now.

'They know something,' said Carol Porter, her anger ratcheting an increment with every step towards the car park. 'What's going on, Carol? What'd you tell them about me? Why did you bring me here?'

'I don't know what that was about. I just said you met David in the Kimberley two years ago.'

'Why did you bring me here?'

Carol Marks was about to answer when the attention of both was drawn by the clack of running steps on the bitumen behind them. They turned as one. Sharon Kitchen was on their heels. She halted, breathing heavily.

'Who are you?' she demanded of Carol Porter. She didn't wait for an answer. 'Is she welfare or something?' she demanded of Carol Marks. 'Did he send you here today?'

'Ms Porter is a friend of mine,' said Carol Marks gently. 'And no, he just made sure I knew about the funeral.'

Sharon stepped back and glared with triumphant vindication. 'Feelin' fucking guilty, is he? Fucking good for him. Well you tell him, Senior Constable fucking Marks, he won't get away with it. I'm gonna fucking fix 'im.' Tears began to well, she spun away before they could fall and walked away with the clumsy dignity of someone who realises the coat hanger is still in her jacket.

'What the Christ am I doing here?' said Carol Porter to the seeping heavens. She drew heavily on drama-queen experience from her teens.

'Sorry,' said Carol Marks. 'I wanted you to get a glimpse of David's world.'

'Has he slept with all these women?'

'None of them, I'm willing to bet,' Carol Marks said with a laugh. 'Sharon blames him for Benny's death.'

'So, what? He assumed you'd stand in?' Carol Marks pushed her bottom lip out and arched her brows in reply. 'And what? This is supposed to dissuade me from going any further?'

'Does it?'

Carol Porter threw her a bald, disdainful glance and turned towards the car.

'Hey,' said Carol Marks before she'd gone a few metres. She turned back with deadpan sufferance. 'Catch,' said Carol as she threw the car keys. 'Won't be long. I have another little chore, then we can go and have coffee.'

The world of the horizontal, like the world of the vertical, was divided along ethnic boundaries. Carol passed through the shadows cast by the

Italian highrises to the Latvian section of the cemetery. And there he was.

'Thought I might find you here,' she said.

He looked up from some grave-tending. 'Did I hear more than one version of "Wind Beneath My Wings"?'

'You did. I'm surprised there wasn't a video clip.'

'Why is the expression of our deepest and truest emotions always so bloody kitsch?' His hands brushed each other as he stood.

'Can't keep tears in a string bag, I guess. Sharon was a mess.'

'She's heard her screen door slam.'

'The significance of "I Was Born Under a Wand'rin' Star" escaped me?'

'Ben was a Lee Marvin fan.'

Her lips made a well-you-learn-something moue. 'I knew you couldn't resist checking the faces.'

'You're good, Harpo,' he grinned. 'You should've been a detective. Why don't you go back to the force?'

'I'm not cured, Davy. Just under control.'

'None of us are cured. We're all just under control.'

'This is your stepfather's first wife?' she asked, nodding at the brass plate mounted in a small granite slab, almost indistinguishable from those surrounding it.

'Mmm.'

'I thought with all his money there'd be a family mausoleum.'

'Not the Latvian way. As Andy says,' he swung his arm in an arc, 'they all came here with the same dirt under their fingernails and the same holes in their shoes. He'll be buried here.'

'How are they? Andris and your mum.'

'Firing on all eight.'

'What's going on, Davy? I thought I was having an episode. Same faces kept popping up everywhere I took her.'

'You *are* good.'

'Don't spread it too thick.'

'Can you head her off?'

'Even if I can, I don't want to.'

'What will it achieve?'

'We'll know.'

'If you want to know, ask. I'll tell. Who did which and with what and to whom. Just ask.'

She gazed at him for a long, long time. Was this a bluff: truth or dare? Dare, dare, double dare. No, he would give it all up. Now. Right now, here. The sadness on his face said it.

'No,' she said. 'I have to find out for myself.'

'Everything's … in equilibrium, Harpo. Don't muck it about.'

'What kind of bargain did you make?'

'The kind that keeps angels in heaven and devils in hell.' He compressed his lips in a resigned smile.

'We've got to finish this, Davy. Carol and I.'

'Why is she doing it?'

'I think she wants to find out what kind of man gave her a leg up the ladder.'

'Why doesn't she just ask me out on a date?'

'Why don't you ask her?' She studied his face. 'That's got you stumped, hasn't it, spunky?'

'Couldn't I fill out one of those quizzes from *Cosmo*? How do you rate as a leg-upper?'

'Oh, she doesn't want a profile. She wants the Full Monty. Wide screen, 3D, surround sound and glorious Technicolor. She's a lot like you: needs to see the corpus delicti.'

She saw something on his face that was rare: genuine puzzlement. It was endearingly reassuring. He hunched his shoulders, raised his open palms to his ears and said in atrocious John Wayne, 'A gal's gotta do whatta gal's gotta do.'

Carol Porter reclined in the passenger seat and stared at the slab of slate sky visible between the edge of the windshield and the tops of the trees that bordered the car park. Strung across the glass, beads of water, a rosary abandoned by rain, absorbed its light and transmuted to pearls. She was becoming paranoid. Her gut said that Carol Marks was playing straight. She wanted to trust her, but what if she was as much Edge's creature as those others? She couldn't risk it. He was every-fucking-where. She now realised she had seen him on the TV news in those scenes of the siege of that poor bastard who was being chargrilled at this very moment. No, she was going to do this by herself now. And now, she knew how to do it. The means had always been there; but was the end still sufficient justification?

38

The pub was unwittingly retro. Its public bar entrance faced a corner. Inside, anything that wasn't brown was cream. A flyspecked menagerie of sporting livestock grazed on the walls. Rare and endangered AFL species were on exhibit, but sadly, no poker-playing canines. Falling-down drunks still encountered the odd fleck of sawdust in cracks and crannies of the floor – or their face the next morning. It was a rough beast that hadn't slouched anywhere to be born, just crouched in its own shadow and waited for its time to come (again) at last.

Or perhaps it was stubbornly retro. The toilets had been refurbished – compelled no doubt by health regulations – but the paper towel dispenser had not been screwed to the wall and the warm-air hand-dryer – never connected to power – was yet to do a blow job.

The inevitable TV glowing from the inevitable brownout above the end of the bar was tuned, inevitably, to a sports channel. Somewhere in the world, it silently pledged the punters, someone was belting the hell out of someone. As a result, somewhere someone was going for broke and some-where someone was going broke – as reassuring an arrangement as retro itself.

Gareth Nile and Don Collison, half the clientele present, hunched over the bar. During the hour they'd been there, greater quantities of fluid than words had passed their lips.

'Mind if I join you, gentlemen?'

Gareth turned hopefully. The silence had been growing oppressive. Don's head dropped towards the counter rather than raised to the voice. It was David Edge.

'No, sure, take a seat,' said Gareth. He thought he heard Don mutter 'fuck' and made a fuss with the barstool to mask it.

'Thanks – Gareth? Is that right?' said Edge as he sat. 'Not many of the old crowd about, Don?' The other two souls in the establishment, unless they were undercover, weren't cops. The eyes of one were glued to the ceil-ing; the eyes of the other glued to the floor.

Don lifted his beer, dragged on it noisily and put it down. 'A lot of cops don't drink in the old haunts these days,' he said, eventually. 'Might catch something that'd get 'em quarantined from promotion.'

'Can I get you something?' Gareth asked.

'My round,' said Collison, almost belligerently. He slapped some cash on the bar and signalled the bartender. He looked a challenge at Edge.

'A beer thanks, Don.'

Collison ordered three beers and poured the dregs of the glass in his fist down his throat.

'Lemme guess,' he said to the rows of spirits and liqueurs protecting the mirror behind the bar from shattering truths. 'You were out there checking the mourners for the face of the killer in the crowd.' It had the melodra-matic cadence of a TV promo voiceover. He chuckled without humour. ''S bullshit that. But I can tell y'this time, one way or another, the culprit was there for sure.'

'You're probably right.'

'Only three weeks ago. Hard to believe,' said Gareth, for something to say. Collison shot him a sour glance.

The barman lined up three beers. 'Once upon a time there were three beers,' said Collison.

Edge scooped one of the beers his way, but didn't lift it. Collison was resting on his forearms, almost lying on the bar. He raised his shoulders laboriously and twisted to stare past Gareth to Edge.

'Well?' he said.

'It occurred to me, when I saw you out there, that you were involved in the investigation of the gay assaults ticketed to Terrence Varney.'

'The poofter bashings, you mean?'

Gareth shifted uncomfortably. Don was going out of his way to be obnoxious. His glass was almost drained again.

'That's the technical term, I believe,' Edge said amiably.

'The second lot,' said Collison. 'Not the first.'

'There were two series of assaults?'

'Uhmm,' Collison grunted. 'About eighteen months, two years apart.'

'Mind telling me?'

'Shit, got nothin' better to do. Have we, Gareth? We'd put aside the arvo to mop up organised crime, but,' he looked at his watch, 'there's buggerall left of it.' He flapped a hand. 'Do it tomorrow.' He pushed his empty glass towards Gareth and gave him an empty stare. 'Tryin' to impress our guest with your restraint, eh?'

Gareth reluctantly ordered another round.

'When did the murder occur? Or was it murders?' Edge prompted.

'Murder, singular, uno. Last of the first spate of attacks. Probably scared shit outta himself. Then padded up for a second innings when he got his nerve back. Mightta been in gaol for a while. Dunno.' The beers arrived and he took a gulp. 'I wasn't on that investigation. Read the reports when we thought there might be a connection. The attacks started with a bit of punchin' and kickin', boys just bein' boys, then increased in savagery until someone died; same escalation was happening in the second wave. Course, once there was a homicide, your lot stepped in and took over. Didn't get far.'

'Was Varney a suspect then?'

'There was a list. Despite being a bit old to fit the typical profile, he wasn't far from the top.' He took another gulp from his glass. 'Hey. Shame you weren't on the case. You could have just erased the lot of the bastards and saved us all trouble.'

'Don ...' said Gareth.

'Oh, take a pull, Gareth. ''E loves this kinda talk. Don't y'mate?'

'Can't get enough,' Edge agreed. 'Paradoxically, it reminds me both of my clay feet and my stainless-steel teeth.'

Collison laughed dryly, grudgingly. 'Fucking son of a bitch.'

'How did you come to Varney?'

Collison gave Edge the hard, flat stare now. 'You could buy this shithole. You got shares in the dump over the road?'

Edge ordered a round.

'Got the word from some of his acquaintances about his ... inclinations. I decided to bump him to the top of the list and put him under surveillance. Then we got a very specific tip about a dunny safari that he was embarking on. We set up a sting. And got him.' He lifted his glass to toast past glories.

'Was he alone?'

'Varney? Was there one Beatle? Gutless fucking wonder.'

'How did you connect him to the earlier assaults and the murder?'

'George's toy – or was it Ringo's? Dunno.' The next glass was making its way to his mouth.

The other two waited.

'It was the camera,' he said when he'd wiped the foam from his upper lip with a thumb.

'Camera?'

'Yeah. One of his mates brought along a video camera. That got us a search warrant and we found the trophies of the hunt in his cave.' He grinned at them teasingly.

'Trophies?' Gareth prodded obligingly.

'A videotape with various encounters in the wild on it. Fucking beautifully edited. And a soupçon – lovingly preserved in a Vegemite jar.' He grinned again, but his face was melting a little and it was more like a leer. 'Deadshits in your squad had been trying to pin it on Mike Tyson,' he sniggered.

Gareth thought the grog had finally caught up with Don and he'd lost the plot. He turned quizzically, apologetically to Edge. Edge's eyes were narrowed and he was frowning at Collison.

'He bit off his ear?' he said.

'Left lobe.'

Gareth swung his gaze back on Collison, who added, 'Best cut o' course. Other part, lotta cartilage, sticks in your teeth.' He was as vainglorious as a little boy revelling in the aftermath of his fart. And then, abruptly, he became sombre. 'Little detail that was withheld from the media.'

Gareth could see it was true. 'A total stranger? Who he believed was homosexual? In the nineties?' he asked incredulously.

'Thought you could only get AIDS up the arse.'

Gareth took a long pull at his beer.

'Also thought that if you were a gun dung-puncher in stir you were a real man. But outside, you're a fairy.' He finished that beer and held up a finger to the barman. 'Ain't the human mind a fine 'n' delicate thing? A nice little case study for you there, Gareth.'

'The murder was on the tape?' asked Edge.

'Would I lie to you?'

'Who held the camera?'

'Russell fucking Boyd for all we knew. Different crew to the one we nabbed.'

'The tipoff? Who was that?'

'Anonymous phone call. Public phone. Male.'

'Recorded?'

'We're talking years ago, not centuries.'

'You heard his voice? Did he have an accent?'

'The experts said his voice was homogenised. He'd trained away most identifiable ethnic traces. Spoke English as it's spoke nowhere. Probably born here but raised in a non-English speaking home. Not enough on the tape to even make a guess.'

'You said you studied the files from the earlier spate of attacks.' Edge reached in his jacket and took out a photo and pushed it along the bar. As it passed under Gareth's nose he saw the head and shoulders of a slightly prettier, slightly more oriental Keanu Reeves, caught by a telephoto lens. 'Does this face do it with a bing bang bong?'

'Shit, David.' Gareth glanced at Collison. It was first time he'd heard Don use his name. 'This was years ago. Varney had a taste for the exotic. But not too obviously foreign – if you feel the lean of the land, see the way my piddle trickles?'

'Is he a possibility?'

'This bloke looks like a lot of them. But he is cute, ain't he?'

Edge stared at Collison. Collison stared at Edge. The staring match was stretching into time-on and Gareth was about to cut in, when Collison sighed heavily and theatrically. He picked up the photo and slipped it in his pocket. 'Fuck. Orright, I'll take a look.'

'Thanks, Don.' Edge started to push himself away from the bar. 'And thanks for the drink.'

'Hey, wait a minute!' said Collison. 'A name?'

'If you make a match, you'll turn up a name, won't you?'

'Not if he's an unknown from surveillance photos.'

'Make a match and you'll get a name – and, with any luck, a pinch. I'll be in touch. Thanks for the drink, Gareth.'

'Hey!' called Collison, halting him a few steps into his exit. 'What kind of father does something like that in front of his kid?' It was an accusation.

'Brie didn't see anything. That was one of the reasons my presence was requested.'

Collison's rejoinder was a flinty stare.

'Ben had trouble distinguishing between Clark Kent and Superman,' Edge added.

'Fancy you in tights, did 'e?'

Edge made a little moue with his lips. 'Fishnet body suit for the real action.'

As Gareth watched him walk to the door, in those slacks, that jacket, he felt an overlay of deja vu. 'You know I think I've seen him 'round the uni. I think he runs some tutes in criminology or something.'

'Well at least students won't be bored to death. It'll be quick and pain-less.' Don poured the last of his beer down his throat. 'You see that,' he said nodding emphatically at Edge's glass as if it provided definitive proof of something.

'It's his glass, Don.'

'It's full, Gareth.' His brow arched like a ribbed cathedral portal in munificent sufferance, a martyr to his disciple's obtuseness.

If a full glass had significance, Gareth failed to see it.

'That bastard's got one of his little projects on, Gareth,' Collison nod-ded with tipsy sagacity.

Gareth sighed under his breath and worried his topknot with spidery fingers, a long-suffering Laurel to Collison's Hardy.

'Oh well, waste not, want not,' said Collison reaching for the beer in question.

The face in the photo might be shrouded in mystery, but, as he watched the liquid amber slip down Don's throat, Gareth was in no doubt about the identity of the designated driver.

39

After he delivered his son and his mates to training he hung around to make sure the lights were turned on and that the coach turned up. Then he began to walk across the park. Night began to nip at his ears. He ducked under the single metal rail of the boundary fence and followed the thread-bare jogging track lined with melaleucas. He crossed the road before he reached the bend, driven from the path by peak-hour fervid foot traffic with zero tolerance for the plain perambulator.

Segmented worms of motor traffic, released from the thraldom of red lights, slid by in sluggish bursts. He entered the cemetery through the West Gate turnstile. He'd have to come back the long way; the gates closed in about five minutes. He liked Melbourne cemetery: it was one place he felt unobserved. He experienced it as a landscape, never dwelling on what lay beneath. He followed the serpentine avenue through the stone gardens to the East Gate and emerged on Lygon. It was clogged. The street he wanted was directly opposite and the traffic lights were a major digression. He made a dash to a tram stop in the middle of the road when the lanes cleared on the near side, then another to the safety of the pavement when the far lanes cleared. Two more residential blocks down the side street and another turn right and he was at his destination, a modest but popular café in a strip of similar establishments.

Contrasted to the smoky blue air he'd left, the atmosphere he entered was amber. He saw her immediately, but paid her no special attention. His gaze fluttered idly over the interior, its patrons and furniture. When it touched a vacant table near the front window he pointed to it and raised an eyebrow at a waitress. She nodded and he made his way to it through the clustering tables, chairs and diners.

He sat back to a wall and with a clear view of the street through the window. He could observe the woman with a slight turn of his head as he perused the menu. She had followed instructions; taken the table he told her to and had the agreed objects of identification in place. She should have been waiting about twenty minutes now and was showing signs of impatience and doubt. There were no names in this transaction, but he remembered her as blonde during her fifteen minutes of unwelcome fame – if she was who he thought she was. She was a brunette now, but her hair had that buffed, fresh from the bottle look. Her makeup failed to gloss rumpled darkness around her eyes and sallowness in her cheeks: a striking woman even so.

Now that he saw her he was almost positive it wasn't a set-up, but the day he dropped the precautions would be the day he was dropped on. The fact that on first contact, less than a week ago, she was emotional and uncertain, reluctant to give the green light, and now was suddenly in a hurry, made precautions essential.

He had provided the address of their rendezvous a mere fifteen minutes before the prearranged time, so the opportunity to organise electronic surveillance on site was minuscule. He checked the street. There were no convenient delivery vans, there were no lingerers in doorways and no one had relocated to maintain an unobstructed view. His subtle scrutiny shifted to the interior. He recognised most of the staff. They had worked this shift last night and the night before. There was only one new face and she was so efficient, relaxed and familiar with the routine, the space, other staff and many customers that he was sure she wasn't a ringer. When it came to the customers you could never be one hundred percent sure, but some of the faces he recognised from his reconnaissance. Body language and social interaction suggested most were regulars.

A waiter approached his table, he gave his order and as the man was about to leave he said: 'Oh, I just noticed an old friend sitting alone.' He indicated the woman. 'Bring my food over there, please.' He stood and made his way to the woman's table. She was seated with her back to one wall, nursing a glass of wine. When her green eyes caught his approach they sharpened in caution and calculation, weighing aggression and discretion like a hawk straddling carrion.

The table was set for two in the establishment's Siberia. It was tucked in a corner and isolated by the natural geography of the café. A door, both emergency exit and access to the toilets, on one side, and a large Victorian sideboard, a station for various housekeeping tasks, on the other, conspired to keep the clumps of patrons at bay and gird the table with a moat of privacy.

Am I waiting for you? her feline eyes asked.

He paused by the table. 'Is this the way to the little boys' room?' he said. It was half the security code.

'The little girls' too, I believe.' Big smile (with the mouth – eyes micro-surgical instruments) and correct response.

'I have an umbrella like that.' That was the other half.

'So do I.'

Check. He went through the door, down a narrow passage past doors marked Female and Male and through the exit at the end. He found himself in a tiny concrete courtyard with an anemic security light. Wheelie bins jostled the fence on one side. A quick glance over double gates at the rear revealed a bluestone-quilted lane that was void of life signs. He slipped a pack of cigarettes and a lighter from his pocket and waited. She appeared in a minute or so and faced him, hands in slacks pockets, feet spread, silent, poised to spring or flee. A low-cut cashmere jumper advertised her breasts and the green scarf she'd suggested for identification looped loosely around her shoulders and scooped into her cleavage.

'It's fucking cold,' she said. He lit two cigarettes and handed one to her. 'I don't smoke.'

'Pretend you do.'

Her gloved hand darted like a wagtail.

'Slip your jumper up.'

'I'm not wired,' she said with indignation in her voice.

'That's for you to know and me to find out.'

Gripping the cigarette between her lips and huffing an exasperated sigh she hooked the hem of her jumper and lifted. A few moments later, as she shrugged back into it, she said, 'Cop a nice feel?'

He took the cigarette from her lips, stubbed it out on the brick wall with his and put the butts in a pocket.

'Jesus,' she said.

Inside he removed the umbrella from where it hung on the back of a chair and leaned it against the wall beside her. He shifted the chair around the table, draped his jacket on it and sat with his back to the other wall, took his time surveying the room. He felt her eyes the way a blind man feels light. Their narrow shafts jabbed at his retinas when he fully engaged them.

'I think we can dispense with James Bond 101,' he said, and smiled. The response was a turquoise ceramic stare. He pushed the corners of his lips upward with a finger of each hand. Her lips reproduced the required smile. Her eyes were still vitreous splinters. 'But let's maintain appearances. Have you eaten?' he asked glancing at the menu.

'I've ordered,' she said. 'Just an entrée. I thought it would be less suspicious.'

'Good,' he nodded approvingly. 'I've done the same. I'll leave first, when we've completed our business, so you can continue with your meal if you wish.'

'They say you're the best,' she said bluntly. She was impatient to get it done. His clients usually were. 'In this town, at least,' she added. He smiled. Let me know if you're not overly impressed, lady, he thought.

'I'm one of the few true tradesmen operating in this country,' he said with Discovery Channel authority. 'I'm not a Mickey Mouse Mafioso collecting brown-nose bonus points. Unaffiliated.'

She nodded and took a sip of her wine to hide her distaste. A waitress delivered her entrée and asked if he wanted to order. As he explained his situation he watched the woman. She was tense but not nervous, a novice in forbearance.

'You didn't canvass the question too widely I trust?' he asked when the waitress was gone. Her glance was dry with scorn. 'Have you done this before?'

'Sort of,' she said enigmatically, and didn't elaborate.

'But you've not used professional help?'

She shook her head and speared a garlic prawn.

'I'm very expensive.'

'I can afford you.' Her voice was flat as a mortuary slab. He guessed she would find a way to afford this no matter what the price.

'Half on my acceptance of the contract, the rest on completion.'

She snapped a nod. 'I know how it works. How much?'

'A sliding scale, depending on the complexity of the job.'

'Complexity?' For the first time, she looked a little alarmed.

'Some clients want accidents, some want to send a message. High-profile targets can be surrounded by security. Each case involves degrees of difficulty. It depends on who it is and what you want done.'

'I just want him gone.'

He glanced at his watch. 'If you give me his details, we can take it from there.'

She twisted around and took her bag from where it hung on the back of her chair. She slid a folded sheet of notepaper across the gingham table-cloth to him. He let it lie as the waiter approached with his order. He declined the suggestion of a glass of wine but asked for a coffee. The waiter retreated and he took a few bites of food. Then he picked up the paper. It enfolded a photograph with an address printed in blue ink on its back. He didn't look at the address. He refolded the photograph into the paper and pushed it towards the woman. She frowned.

'Well that simplifies things,' he said. 'I can't take the contract. And you can't afford it.'

'Why the fu ...' Her voice was rising in volume. She checked herself. 'Why the fuck not?' she hissed over her garlic prawns.

'Do you know who this is?' He tapped the paper with a gloved finger.

'Of course I fucking know who 'e is. D'you think I pick punters from the phonebook?' she whispered hoarsely. 'Whatsamatter with you? Do you believe all that crap about him? He's as killable as anybody.'

'Of course he is,' he said. 'If you don't attempt strangulation,' added dryly as an aside. 'Arranging his demise is not the problem. It's the aftermath.'

'Aftermath? He'll be fucking dead, that's the aftermath.' She stopped as a waitress went to the sideboard and collected another table setting.

'I don't think you do know who you're dealing with,' he said when the waitress moved on.

'Oh I know him, believe me.' She sounded like a woman scorned.

'Fully appreciate, may be a better way of putting it.'

'Oh yeah? Please explain,' she growled sardonically.

'If I kill him I'll need to be paid enough to retire and move to the far side of the planet. Another planet, preferably.'

'How the fuck will anyone know you did it?'

'When they get around to asking you, you'll tell them ...'

'I don't know who you are.'

'That's if they haven't already asked *me* who *you* are.'

'Who the fuck is "they"? He's not some fucking Mr Big with an army of goons.'

'No, he's not. More like a virus. He has …ah … spores in places high and low on both sides of the law …'

'Jack Barker's network.'

He was impressed. He nodded. 'What's left of it. The thing is, these leftovers will take his death personally. Even if I knew them all, I would have to carry out a small massacre before they got me. That's not feasible – practically, politically, professionally. What's my name?' he asked abruptly.

She looked confused. 'Wha— I don't know.'

'Who'd you ask for when you put out the word?'

'Joe Black's mechanic.'

'Right, *mechanic*, I engineer deaths. I'm an instrument that people utilise – sort of a smart bomb. The cops might not know my name, but they know my signature.' She was batting at a prawn with simmering exasperation. 'But knowing and proving are two different things. That's why it's in my interest to *never* reveal my client. If I do, means and motive are linked and we both end up trashed.' His eyes grabbed hers. '*You* know how long secrets survive in Squizzyville.' He noted her reaction. 'See, you're not anonymous. To the good guys I'm just forensic evidence. To the bad guys I'm a tool: something to keep well oiled, in a dry place, for use in an emergency. Everyone uses me, I don't take sides, nothing's personal; that's the rules. But him?' He flicked his chin toward the paper-enveloped photo, which still lay near her hand. Her fingers flinched away as if it was hot. 'He doesn't use people like me, he handles things himself. It's nothing *but* personal to him: different rules. And he does unto others as he would have them do unto him.'

Her face skewed in quizzical distaste. To his own ears, he sounded as if he was channelling a fundamentalist bible-basher.

'D'you get it?' he persisted. 'He doesn't pay *back* he pays *forward*. There are people out there *queued up* to balance the books before we raise a finger. You've heard of Rose Garden?' Disdain fell well short of describing her expression. 'Good. Then you have an inkling what she's worth. How much do you think she'd put on our heads?'

Her lips were sullen. 'The besotted old bat.' It was a bitter snarl. 'His mother's worth a fuckin' lot more.' Clearly she knew enough to glimpse the size and shape of the elephant.

'You and I are much too well acquainted.' He studied her. There was defiance simmering behind the green veil of her gaze; this was very personal. She had asked around for the 'Mechanic'; if she persisted with her vendetta she'd be a threat. He preferred not to kill women. 'You've heard of Bernie Vargue?'

'He was a cunt.'

'Bernie took out a contract on him.'

Now there was a flicker of fear, like a cold stone thrown into a flame.

'Look, you weren't committed when we made first contact. Why not drop it?'

'No,' she said tossing her head as if to shake something from her hair. 'He's gotta go.'

Shit, she's got guts and she thinks she's a jihadi. He looked at the espresso machine but stared at his thoughts. He should have walked away as soon as he saw the face in the photograph, but he'd always had a soft spot for feisty women. And she had kids. Perhaps he could dissuade her with a different tack.

'Look, this is my advice. Anyone with a gun and nerve can kill him. He'll be alert to someone like me, but a new face could get under his radar. Use a virgin, someone eager to make his mark and someone too green to understand the consequences. Just make sure he can't be linked to you. Never meet face to face, and use public phones. Arrange a drop for instructions and cash. Make sure there are no fingerprints.' He wiggled sheathed fingers. 'Don't trust him to cover his trail. He's expendable. They'll get him, and if he hasn't got a pro track record they'll probably assume it's personal and look no further.' If they're cops, he thought. 'As I said, to reveal that he has a client is an admission of guilt.'

Neat white teeth scraped colour from her plump bottom lip. Her gaze flashed around the room like a trapped swallow, then alighted on him. 'Can you give me a name?'

'Always boys who want to leave the Gameboys and join the game.' He pulled the folded paper back towards him, slipped a pen from his shirt pocket and wrote. 'I heard a whisper recently.' He gave her the paper. 'That number is someone who might put you in touch. Ask for Mr Cassidy. He will say they have no employee of that name. Say you're looking for a bodyguard and one of the boys at Bar 20 gave you the phone number. He'll suggest he may be a member and ask for your contact details. Give him a number and wait. If he asks for a name, you're Mrs Black. *Don't* use a phone traceable to you. Eat that once you've memorised it. And I'm not joking.' He glanced at his wrist as he stood and retrieved his jacket. 'Good luck.'

Family came first. He was running on time, he'd be back before the coach finished his obligatory (for the coach) pep talk. He'd done all he could to keep her alive. He didn't look back. Poor bitch.

40

Clack-clack-clack-clackety-clack-clack.

She ran a thumbnail along the spine of her spiral-bound notebook.

Carol Porter could see the problem quite clearly.

She had nothing of substance. She didn't have access to the original files. She had not been present at the original crime scenes, had not viewed the physical and forensic evidence, had not interviewed the usual suspects at the time. The material she used in the course was abstracts of reports and notes, summaries of evidence and interviews. She was working almost exclusively from secondary sources: hardly world's best investigative practice. And she'd just graduated from detective school. Shame, Constable Porter. Still, Nero Wolfe never left the house.

What did she have? She had a hypothesis. A hypothesis that wasn't her own: a secondhand hypothesis. A recycled hypothesis; that had a better ring.

Let's assume these weren't serial murders of randomly chosen joggers. Let's assume that the three girls were victims of a cold-blooded killer's plot to murder one of them. Let's assume that one was the second victim, Ariel Buchanan Castleman. Let's put the serial killer investigation to one side and forget about it, except that a thread of it led to a contract killer. Let's ignore all the mystery and intrigue accreted around the death of the alleged killer and regard him simply as a murder weapon. The question then becomes who aimed him at Ariel and why?

The original detectives on Ariel's case had only just begun to address the question when they were deflected by the assumption that she was only one of the killer's victims. Once the investigations moved down this fork an individual personal motive was automatically ruled out. Her similarity to the other victims, her conformance to a type, which only existed in the killer's mind, was assumed to be the factor that singled her out for murder.

The investigators had done a lot of the groundwork. They had, for instance, verified the alibis of family, friends, lovers past and present, and possible enemies. Of course, if you accepted the premise that the deed was carried out by a hitman, that didn't mean much. They had made some progress on motive before the case veered away on its new trajectory, but only in the negative sense. They had eliminated a number of people and established that none of those close to her had an obvious motive.

Ariel Buchanan Castleman was twenty-six years old, fit, attractive. She had independent means, inherited from her mother, but worked hard for an international aid organisation. Her circle of friends was modest in size but close, and she was well liked and highly regarded by her colleagues and employers. She had not had many boyfriends and her last known one, although admitting to being surprised and hurt when their relationship suddenly ended, did not appear to bear a grudge.

The two Carols had tracked him down. He was married with two children, in love with his wife and obviously happy. Rather than being annoyed by the intrusion of a past unpleasantness into his present life, he was eager to be interviewed. He said that Ariel deserved better than she got from the investigation. His sentiments seemed strong and genuine. He confessed to feeling guilty that he hadn't fought harder to hold their relationship together. He felt she'd be alive today if he had succeeded.

'Why do you believe that?' Carol Marks had asked. 'You know, having a boyfriend hadn't prevented the other girls from being killed?'

'Well, when I read about the serial killer … I have to admit to feeling … um, relief,' he'd said.

'Is there something you hadn't told the detectives at the time?' she'd asked.

'It was … it was vague. I hadn't mentioned it because I was afraid it would look like I was trying too hard to divert suspicion from myself. You know? Make myself look less guilty by cooking up a mysterious stranger.'

'Did you see her with someone?'

'No.' He'd shaken his head emphatically.

'Had she mentioned or hinted at someone? Is that why you didn't persist?'

'No. No. It's difficult to understand … to explain. It was because she *didn't* that made me think there was.' He'd looked from one to the other. 'You see why I didn't say anything to the cops. It's … it's silly.'

'How did you break up? Presumably she initiated it, what were her reasons?'

'There were none. She just sort of … cooled. Almost snap froze. It was like, like … you know when … Have you ever been in a rowboat and you're trying to get ashore? You know, pull in beside the jetty? And the more you try, the more you push the boat away?' Both Carols had nodded. 'I just felt this … distance. And it just got greater like ice floes cracking and moving apart.'

'She said nothing?'

'Just … she was sad and she was sorry and it wasn't my fault and she'd been happy with me, but there wasn't a future for us and it was best for both of us if we ended it quickly while we were still friends.' He'd shrugged.

'She gave no other reason?'

'Nope.'

'Did this happen gradually? In retrospect, did you realise it had crept up over a long period of time before you noticed?'

'No. It all happened in the space of a couple of weeks, maybe less. I suppose it was the contrast that made me so sensitive to it.'

'The contrast?' she had said.

'On a Sunday night I went to her flat to pick her up. We were going out to dinner. Her father was there. She was really happy. They were good mates. More like brother and sister than father and daughter. It was the first time I'd met him; he'd been out of the country a lot. He'd been an MP until he lost his seat. He'd come to tell her the party had wooed him back home with the offer of a seat. They'd been drinking champagne in celebration. She was really happy. Then on Tuesday, when I saw her next, she was … well she wasn't unhappy, she was sort of distracted, sort of inside herself …' He had stopped, thinking, then he'd poked the air with an index finger. 'I know, I know what it was like. It was like my wife when she was pregnant. You know that Mona Lisa thing that woman get. And she was, like, there, but drifting away. By the end of the week I sort of knew it was ending. But I hung on, hoping.'

'What made you associate this behaviour with a secret lover? Or – what did you say – "mysterious stranger"?'

'After some time had elapsed, when I got some distance from it, I realised … Have you ever been with someone who seems perfect for you, too good to be true? You know? All the qualities you could ask for in a life's partner – beautiful, bright, funny, kind, similar interests – and yet you don't quite believe in it. Something's not meshing somewhere in the machinery. I didn't know this until I met Jenny. I mean we, Jenny and I, didn't like each other much at first sight. But there was this something, like … like an ember that sparked a bushfire. I realised that Ariel had never opened herself to the possibility of that. I came to believe that she'd kept that part of her well sheltered from anything that might fan it into flame. It was like she was keeping it for someone.'

'Maybe she was saving herself for Mr Right?'

'It felt more like she was *preserving* herself for Mr Right.'

'You suspected there had been someone – or was someone – who was unavailable at the time, but she believed, or hoped, would become available again? Like … a married man?'

'In hindsight.'

'How long was it between your breakup and her death?'

'Um, don't know exactly, eighteen months at least.'

'Eighteen months?' said Carol Marks. 'I can't recall that being recorded in the files. That's a long time. Why were the investigators so sure you were her last boyfriend?'

'Oh there's no doubt about that. We were still friends and our social group was a tight-knit bunch. Jenny was introduced to me by one of the crowd. We've all sort of dispersed now, but back then, if one of us sniffed the rest blew their noses. Ariel's love life, or lack of, was community property. If she had a lover he was the Phantom of the Opera.'

'What about a "her"?' asked Carol.

'Hah! She was so hetero she made me feel gay at times.'

Clack-clack-clack-clackety-clack-clack.

Her thumbnail played the notebook spine like a washboard. She had a feeling it was playing a well-known tune but she couldn't recognise it.

'Well, we know her secret lover was male,' Carol Marks had said sometime later as they sat around brainstorming over the information they had collected. 'The traces of condom lubricant indicated that she'd been sexually penetrated by two different partners the night of her murder. One was the murderer, the other unknown.'

'That's not conclusive by itself.'

'True, but what are the alternatives? She'd used a condom on some object to pleasure herself, or the murderer raped her, changed condoms and raped her again. One is more plausible than the other, but both are a real stretch.'

'I agree. The way they were murdered – if David Edge's theory is right, and we're working from that assumption – was extraordinarily risky. If he changed condoms – say to confuse the police, play with their minds – even if it was just on some hand-held object, the risk was astronomical. But ... what if that was his turn on?'

'You mean he couldn't get it up unless he built some risk into it? It was the danger that he found erotic.' Carol Marks liked that. 'But you would expect that to escalate. This was the second murder. The third one showed no sign of that. It was closer – in risk – to the first.'

'It's consistent with Desmond Poynter as the killer. Poynter lived with his mother. The local cop I talked to said the girls in the district thought he was a catch, but he showed no interest. There was speculation that he was gay.'

Carol Marks really liked that. 'I like that. Poynter wasn't the cold-blooded mercenary everyone assumed. He'd always been in the game for the erotic jolt. The money was just icing on the cake. Maybe it even provided him with a rationalisation for his kinky desires.' Her voice trailed off and her eyes lost their focus as she stared into some distance that had nothing to do with space. 'And if Davy discovered that, then ...' Abruptly she was back in the room, her gaze fell on Carol and her face closed down. But Carol could see that wherever she'd been she'd found something she really, really liked.

Clack-clack-clackety-clack-clack-clackety-clack-clackety.

Of course there was a boyfriend. She had to operate on that premise.

Still she was sure – *they* were sure – that the erotic thrill of the game was Poynter's primary motivation. It would explain why he might become a liability to someone like Jack Barker. A ruthless contract killer is one thing but a psychosexual sociopath, who's showing signs of losing the plot, is another thing altogether.

There was a joke about a golfer who played with cricket bats, baseball bats, hockey sticks, bent pipes, and always won. When the other golfers asked why he used these objects, he replied that he was such a natural at physical activities he had to make each one as difficult as possible or he got bored. Inevitably in such jokes the question of sex will be raised. Standing up in a hammock, the natural said.

Poynter was used because he could do it standing up in a hammock. He was discarded when he couldn't do it without standing up in a hammock. A man standing up in a hammock drew too much attention.

A neat little scenario, but pure speculation, no matter how much she liked the fit.

Clackety-clackety-clack-clack-clack.

Ariel Buchanan Castleman was born Ariel Kristin Buchanan. Her father, Murray Buchanan, was a Collins Street pastoralist. His properties were far flung. Although he was not a man of the land, but an investor, he took a personal interest in all of them. This required frequent air travel, mostly in light aircraft. He died shortly after obtaining his pilot's licence when his plane came down not far from Goondiwindi. Ariel was three years old.

When Ariel was five her mother, Kristin Forbes Buchanan, married Simon Beaumont Castleman. Although Simon was seven years younger than Kristin and his family fortune, compared to hers, was a little thread-bare, it was still substantial, and those close to the couple were convinced theirs was a genuine love match. And Simon proved to be a more doting dad to Ariel than Murray had ever been. He wasn't constantly flying off into the wild blue yonder on the slimmest pretexts, for one thing.

When Ariel was seven, to everyone's delight her mother became pregnant again. The normal body changes attending this condition brought – what Kristin feared to be unusual – discomfort to one of her breasts. Cancer was diagnosed. The pregnancy was terminated and the breast was removed. The cancer was aggressive and neither the mastectomy nor the chemotherapy nor any other measure could check its charge. Kristin died two days after Ariel's eighth birthday.

Although there had been no lack of devotion before Kristin's death, following it Ariel became the recipient of the love her stepfather could no longer lavish on her mother. Simon was greatly admired for the way he raised the girl. No nurses, no nannies; of course there were relatives and the household staff, but they too were admiring of the way he retained responsibility for all but the most pragmatic trivialities in her upbringing. Things like keeping an eye on her if he was called to the phone while she was playing in the pool, or the occasional sleepover at a cousin's.

Even those who could not be called close – bank managers, business associates, lawyers – were impressed by his attention to the girl's welfare. He wasn't very good with money, because he took it for granted and wasn't very interested in it. He was of that generation that loses the wealth his forebears have so scrupulously (or unscrupulously) accumulated. He quarantined the inheritance Ariel received from her mother's estate and a substantial amount of his own money in a trust fund, so that he could not be tempted to touch it in lean times.

Simon had political aspirations. He had worn away quite a lot of his personal fortune on these. And Kristin had invested some of hers as well. It was considered a measure of his devotion to Ariel that he put his ambitions on hold while she was a child. When she was older and more independent he began working his way back into the game. Despite his background, Simon's politics leaned to the left. The values he'd instilled in Ariel, and which would later earn the admiration of her friends and colleagues, derived from this leaning.

Simon was handsome. He was physically fit and trim. He was still relatively young and had the Cary Grant trick of appearing youthful and mature at the same time. Until Ariel was sixteen he was never linked romantically to any woman, but then suddenly he was wooed and won by Hebe Bancroft Soames. That this coincided roughly with a cranking up of his interest in a political career was a point lost on no one.

Hebe was a woman who fancied she was a kingmaker. She was not beautiful enough to have the stereotypical female power derived from feminine allure. She'd seen her siblings, much prettier than her (even the boys), wield that kind of power as she grew up and she'd envied it – not the looks, the power. She had wealth and brains and that would have to do. Men managed more with much less of these than she. When Hebe and Simon met she was a widow. Her husband, Cornell Soames, the shadow minister of a very minor portfolio, had died when a car in which he was passenger ran into a tree outside of Rutherglen. The driver was a young lady well known in the district as an entertainer of visiting dignitaries, minor celebrities and rock bands.

Hebe and Simon made a good team. The only issue of discord, as far as anyone knew, was the raising of Ariel. Hebe had no children and the only model she had for motherhood was her own mother. Her mother was something of a control freak – a remote control freak. Hebe considered Simon to be far too indulgent and Ariel to be far too pampered. Ariel, however, was Simon's daughter so she held her counsel and, applying the formidable self-discipline for which she was renowned, left what remained of her upbringing to him. Although Hebe constantly sang her praises, usually as the remarkable accomplishment of her husband, she and Ariel never became close.

While Ariel completed her school days and entered her university years, Hebe and Simon organised Simon's active participation and meteoric rise in state politics. By the time Ariel graduated, his faction was grooming Simon for party leadership and he was touted as a future Premier.

The playing fields of politics were more of a wilderness than Simon anticipated and he lost sight of many of his ideals in the undergrowth. He was the type of politician who felt a need and a duty to serve but lacked a distinct vision of the service. Like a guide dog or a St Bernard, or one of those cadaver dogs, he required training and a leash. He began to drink more than was required for social and professional purposes and lost his seat in a massive swing against his party. The old Simon, the one that had entered politics, would have just snuck in, but he didn't try very hard. His party wasn't pleased, but Hebe's money and influence weren't something they could lightly discard. He was slipped into the back of the political drawer until he got his priorities right and proved useful again. They kept him busy behind the scenes and in trade missions and other junkets and, when convinced he was the old Simon once more, offered him a marginal but winnable seat. He won, and Simon was back on the Premiership path again.

This of course, all fell apart when Ariel was murdered and Simon fell apart. He was devastated and, as natural disasters never respect borders, Hebe was swept into his devastation. This metaphor probably paints an inaccurate picture. It would be truer to say the foundations of their relationship were swept by devastation, and later began to crumble. To everyone's surprise Hebe was the one who fell through to the cellar. She was in a delicate condition for a long time, and seldom seen in public on Simon's arm for even longer. But Hebe, being Hebe, bounced back.

Clack-clack-clack-clackety-clackety-clackety-clackety-clack.

Her thumbnail plucked the spine of the notebook in which this information was written. Not written as above, in a much more abbreviated form: dot points. They were gleaned from newspaper reports and magazine articles and Carol Marks's recall.

'Physical evidence is the best evidence' was the motto of the Detective Training School; had been since 1937. The physical evidence in this case had been around for a long time. It had been interpreted and reinterpreted by some of the best. All she had were motive and a hunch: not the motive of the murderer, the motive of the victim. Ask yourself, Carol, what motive in this day and age would an educated, intelligent, independent – in the personal, intellectual and economic senses – young woman have for concealing the identity of her lover? Concealing even the fact that she had one. This wasn't Shakespeare's Verona or Bernstein's New York. In the early days of the third millennium Carol could think only of one motive.

Clack-clack-clackety-clackety-clack-clackety-clackety-clack.

Carol Porter decided she couldn't continue sitting here playing a tune she couldn't identify on a notebook spine. Time was running out. Her leave was running out. She had to drop a rock in the pool or drop the entire silly business.

To be or not to be, that was the question. Wasn't it always?

41

A Calais entered the yard behind the drop-in centre from the side street. It rolled to a standstill beside a Commodore in the far corner from the building. As the driver climbed out, closed the door and activated the remote lock, a man exited a door in the rear of the building and strode towards him. Bent forward at the waist as if in a rush to get through life, he was tight and wiry with the desiccated leanness of an addict or ascetic. Someone running on empty but never quite drained.

'David!' he called.

'Spade? How's things? Blue goose weather tonight.'

So, it's a jaunty mood we're in, Spade thought as his forward propulsion terminated under the other's nose. He straightened his back. His gaze pinioned his quarry. His actions were spare and sudden, jump cut by the blink of an eye. 'I've been looking for you for a couple of days.' His delivery was clipped and curt, his tone not that unfriendly.

'I've been out and about. Up north. A problem?'

'I don't know,' said Spade. 'You tell me. Brix and Krystal haven't shown for some time.'

'That's not unusual.'

'They were last seen in your company.'

'That's not unusual either.'

'David?' His voice assumed an admonitory tone.

'It's okay. They're on a small job for me.'

Spade's large nobbled fist clamped his forehead then was dragged down his face. A bony finger and thumb seemed to plough crevasses from the crags of his cheekbones to the jut of his jaw. The furrows remained when his hand dropped from his chin. 'Tell me they aren't surfing – whatever the jargon – the bank accounts of some Mr Big?'

'They aren't surfing the bank accounts of Mr Big. I think the word you're after is "hacking". But, I have it on good authority, that this is a much-abused term. And technically inaccurate in this particular ca—'

'David. I'm not in the mood for your warped brand of humour. Or your evasions.'

'Sorry, Spade.' Contrite. 'That's a nice tee shirt. Must be warm.'

'And save the coy contrition. Tell me, he … she … it isn't dangerous.' Silence while a blue gaze lapped over him. 'David?'

'He may be an accessory to murder.'

'My god.' He cinched his arms in a knot across his chest and turned in a complete tight circle. When the black eyes swept the face before him again he sucked air noisily and said, 'There's something else?'

Edge shrugged. 'Maybe pornography, sex slavery, blackmail, internet infractions … and he might be a paedophile. Otherwise, just a regular bloke.'

'Jesus Christ Almighty. You're not using them as bait?'

'Only in the virtual sense.' Edge studied the moist warm clouds of their conversation, stygian under the orange security light. 'Why are we standing out here?'

Spade spun on his heel again, and pushed the sharp prow of his nose through the billows of his breath three long, quick paces away. He halted and whipped around. 'They shouldn't be hacking.' He spoke as if the word tasted sour.

'What we digitally challenged like to call "hacking" – "cracking" in this case – is all they care about, Spade.'

'My point, exactly. My point.'

'Don't worry. They're safe. And it's for a good cause. D'you find it a bit nippy tonight?'

'Good causes can ruin a life just as easily as bad causes.'

'Are we talking about Brix and Krystal or you and me?'

'David!' His voice was wired with exasperation. 'We're trying to help these kids turn around. Get back to some sort of normality.'

'Normality, or a badly transmitted facsimile of it, is what most of them are running from.'

He allowed himself a deep, exhausted sigh. Here we go, off around the circuit once more. 'I know. I know that. But, pandering to … to … an addiction is not going to advance their social adjustment.'

'Prohibition doesn't prevent addiction, or cure it. And there are a lot worse addictions than theirs.'

'They're on good behaviour bonds. If not for your pull with the Federal Police they'd be in the nick now.' His palms met under his chin and his hands beat like a metronome. 'I appreciate that. I do. But if either of them is caught again, it will be a prison sentence. Is that what you want?'

'Of course not. They're secure. Look, would you prefer they were plundering cyberspace from coin laundrettes and internet cafés? They're in a controlled environment. They're using our equipment, our addresses, in our premises. Nothing can be traced back to them. Their role is a sort of ... consulting one. And the law is the last thing our subject will resort to.'

'Our?'

'A little team of ... volunteers.'

'Volunteers?' His upper body convulsed in a sardonic chuff resembling laughter. 'Bullshit, David. Not fair. These kids think the sun sleeps in your corn flakes overnight. You're the romantic mystery man upstairs. You're what their fathers were supposed to be.' He waved his hand around. 'These streets are the Deep Woods, this building is the Skull Cave, they're the Bandar and you're the fucking Phantom! It's not voluntary. When you ask, it isn't a request. For them to say no is unthinkable.'

'I'm dense, Spade, but not that dense. I choose my words with utmost care. And I rarely involve them in my escapades. You know that.' He rubbed his hands with vigorous ostentation under Spade's nose and tucked them under his armpits. 'Delicate instruments. Tools of the trade.'

'I know that, do I? When were you going to tell me?'

'Listen to yourself. This is a refuge, a drop-in centre. They *drop in* – when they need to or when they feel like it. Food in the belly and a pillow under the head. You're not their parents. What they get up to outside these walls, you've no responsibility for, have no influence over. You can only touch their lives when they wander within reach. You do what you can when you can. That's all I'm doing. Maybe I'm providing these two with an opportunity to see that cyberspace isn't just a place to hide, and their skills can be used for something other than self-indulgence.' A pause. 'You know all this. You throw these wobblies when someone's OD'd or contracted AIDS. Who?'

Cunning bastard, thought Spade, but was determined not to be deflected. 'You're a dangerous role model, David. They have no idea of the cost and consequences of being what you are.'

'At the last audit, about the same as the cost and consequences of being you, Spade. You don't think you're a role model? Why do you think they keep coming back? They like the architecture? The coffee?'

'What's wrong with the coffee? It's a perfectly good caterer's blend. It's Brazilian.'

'That explains the taste. A toucan pissed in it.'

'I'm not laughing.'

'Me neither – I'll buy the coffee from now on.'

'It doesn't get you off the hook.'

'They're safe, Spade, they're safe. Do you feel the cold at all?'

'I wish you wouldn't intrude in the lives of others.'

Edge burst into peals of gleeful laughter. 'Our conception is an intrusion in the lives of others – in the best laid plans of the whole bloody universe.'

'Don't try and bull me with your *Star Trek* philosophy.'

'Spade, neither of us is as pretty as a butterfly's wing, but we're both as dangerous as one. Unless, of course, we don't flap. Are you going to stop flapping, eh? Eh? You old Franciscan, you. I think it's going to snow. May even be a blizzard. Come on. Come on up and have a drink.'

'I don't drink, and you know it.'

'Coffee. Real coffee. Coffee that tastes like coffee. Hot coffee. It'll be educational.'

Both men turned and walked to the fire stairs that zigzagged up the rear façade.

'You know we appreciate what you've done for us, David,' Spade began. 'This building, your mother's donations – but ...'

'My mother has given money to the Foundation?' Edge's foot was arrested on the first step.

'You didn't know?' So, we're not omniscient. Spade allowed himself a smidgeon of smugness.

'I didn't know she was aware of its existence. Huh. Sneaky old ... benefactress.' Edge was staring at the building; the corner of his lips twitched at a private thought. 'How long has this been going on?'

'A year or two. It got us out of the red. But could you ask her to make the cheques out to the Foundation and not me, personally?'

'You are the Foundation. The rest of us are paper soldiers.'

'You know what I mean.'

'I'll try. But Mum has more faith in defrocked priests than institutions,' said David Edge as he began to climb.

Like mother, like son, thought Spade as he climbed after.

'Some institutions,' Edge amended.

'I actually don't like coffee,' Spade confessed.

'You surprise me. Fear not, my pantry boasts a plethora of beverages.'

42

Pixie O'Halloran had raised a family and she had no intention of starting all over again. She was making hot chocolate in her kitchen for the two juveniles who'd usurped the room she called her office. She didn't know why her home was being thrown into turmoil. The last time she'd done this sort of investigation for him she'd used David Edge's office and equipment. She suspected he was trying to foist these waifs on her, that he imagined by spending time together in her home, all nestly and cosy, they might bond or something. Not bloody likely: they were arrogant little twerps.

They were arrogant little computer geniuses. Maybe that was what was getting up her nose. Pixie was not of a generation born into the wide web world. The only laptop she got on exiting the womb was overlapping flannel secured with a safety pin (you couldn't count on it, but it contained less shit). Her computer skills were won the hard way. It was difficult to get up close and personal to even the smallest computers. They filled a room and you had to wait until you went to university or you joined a corporation to find a portal into cyber space. In her case it was the police force that provided her opportunity.

She learned fast, she was good at it, but she would never have the intuitive facility of these kids. They addressed the keyboard like PC Paganinis. She stirred the chocolate. They'd even told her the 'right' way to make that. She suspected it could be cut into bars when it cooled.

There was a sound behind her. She turned. The girl was in the kitchen doorway. Her hands were behind her and she rolled her body back and forth on her backbone, which rested against the jamb. Her turquoise eyes watched from black-smudged sockets. Kohl and mascara weighed down her lids and lashes: Pola Negri with a buzz cut and chromium trim. She wasn't particularly tall but the short, studded bomber jacket, snug leather mini, and the platform soles of her knee-length, buckled boots lent her the height and heft of Madam Lash. The only relief from the black of her body was the pallor of her face, but her cheek was too pink and her figure too robust for the average Goth. The K shaved into her crown was not visible from Pixie's viewpoint.

'Your chocolate will be ready in a minute,' Pixie said.

The girl kept staring and said nothing. Pixie thought she detected slyness in her eyes. Then, she thought she saw that all the time in the eyes of both. They whispered and giggled and shared secret communications by word, gesture and through some sort of telepathy. They had barely spoken to Pixie except about the nuts and bolts of their present domestic arrangements or the project they were working on together – and then, mostly in monosyllables. Based on the quality of her clothing and the educated patterns of her frugal utterances, Pixie guessed the girl was from a good home. Well, an affluent one. The boy certainly was not, neither an affluent one, nor good. They had come to the streets by very different paths; or perhaps, in some ways, tragically similar.

The girl slowly withdrew a hand from behind. It held a gilt frame that Pixie recognised instantly. A surge of anger seasoned with fear burst from her centre and scraped at her outer shell like an exploding population of tiny rodents. She bit her tongue, literally, and took her time to respond. Her voice, when she spoke, surprised her with its calm.

'You've been in my bedroom, Krystal,' she said.

The girl didn't reply. She endured Pixie's gaze, which would have withered the optic nerve of anyone else at that time. Then she looked down, but not in shame or embarrassment.

'That's a personal, a private place, Krystal. I don't intrude in your rooms.'

The girl didn't look up. 'You clean them.'

She was about to say if you cleaned them I wouldn't have to, but she said, 'This is my house and you are my guests. I have a duty of care. I don't touch your things.'

The girl's gaze came up slowly. Her expression was still enigmatic, studied. Pixie suspected that she practised it, long and hard, in mirrors.

'Is this your family?' she asked, holding the framed photograph face out towards Pixie.

Drop that, thought Pixie, and I'll slap that face so hard the muck on it will decorate the back of your head. 'Yes, that's my family,' she said. Clamping her eyes on the girl's she stretched forth an arm and opened her hand. 'Please.'

Krystal turned the photograph back to her own scrutiny. Nursing it in the crook of her arm, her eyes perused it, as she walked around the island bench. She trailed the fingers of her other hand along the polished wood. Pixie followed her path like a sunflower. When the girl reached Pixie she placed the photo in her hands, but didn't surrender it. She held it by one corner and moved beside Pixie to look at it with her. Pixie felt their shoulders touch and she fought an impulse to recoil. The girl didn't pull away in the conventional reflex either. In fact Pixie thought she detected a subtle increase in pressure as the girl leaned into her. Now what?

Krystal's finger circled and landed on Pierce's grinning image. 'That's your husband?'

Who else would it be? 'Yes, that was my husband.' Pixie tugged with gentle pressure, but the girl's grip on the frame was firm.

'What's his name?'

'Pierce.'

'Pierce? Like James Bond?'

'More or less.'

'Where is he?'

'He died. Many years ago. Killed in the line of duty.' Get it all out of the way at once, Pixie.

The girl looked at her. Her eye level was well above Pixie's. She didn't express sympathy, but the Mona Lisa death mask went slightly out of focus. 'The kid's married an' all that stuff by now?'

'Patricia is. She has a two-year old son. Sean is overseas. The Europe thing.'

'Well. Grandma,' said Krystal and let the corner of the photo go. She swung away, placed her palms behind her on the bench top and hoisted her bum onto it in one smooth move. Her thighs bulged from the tight, narrow band of her skirt. The photo frame imprinted Pixie's breasts as she folded her arms across her chest and faced her. There was definitely colour under that white gunk on her face.

'Are you fucking him?' said the girl.

'I beg your pardon?'

'Are you fucking David?'

Pixie chuckled. 'No! No, I'm not. And it would be none of your business if I was.'

'I'd fuck him if he asked me.'

'Well … well … um.' She didn't quite know how to respond to this revelation. It wasn't an issue that had arisen with her daughter.

'Brix would too,' Krystal added.

Although the brittle shell of her swagger hadn't softened, there was a gravity about her now that checked Pixie's brusque curtailment of this tête-à-tête. She knew the boy was gay, and she hadn't been sure about the girl. 'Well, David won't be asking,' she said. As soon as she uttered them, she saw how her words might be misconstrued. There was no need to worry.

'Nah. He's straight.'

'He's also nearly twenty years older than both of you.'

The girl actually smiled. And her face didn't fall off. 'You fancy him?'

'He's nearly twenty years younger than me.'

The smile widened. 'What the shit does that matter? Turn out the lights. C'mon, d'you fancy him?'

'He's an attractive young man, Krystal, but definitely not my type.'

'Is the butch one – Maeve – your type?'

'I'm not gay.'

'Do you think I'm his type?'

'Krystal, if he … slept with you – or Brix – how would he be any different from the man we're stalking?'

'He's the straight wire, isn't he.' It was stated, but a ghostly question mark hung on the end, like the shade of past poor judgement.

'Straight wire?'

'He helps you just 'cos you need help?'

Pixie studied her face then said, 'Yes. And because he can't help himself.' It was said without emphasis, each word deployed on a level playing field. She was conscious of the ambiguity. Two furrows appeared like back slashes between the girl's eyebrows. Then she nodded sagely. Pixie wasn't exactly sure what she'd meant, but Krystal seemed satisfied with her answer.

The girl's expression had become unreadable again. She levelled her gaze and held it as if to drill through to Pixie's thoughts. 'You don't like us, do you?' she said.

There it was. What should she do? Lie point blank? Rattle off the conventional platitudes? She had a feeling the girl possessed a finely calibrated bullshit meter. Damned if you do, damned if you don't. When in doubt, honesty was probably the best policy. She was about to say a flat 'No', then she realised that wasn't the truth either. 'I think … I resent you,' she said.

The back slashes reappeared.

'I'm jealous,' Pixie added.

'Jealous?' Krystal was baffled.

'Mmm. Jealous of your computer skills. I've been working with computers for thirty years and I'll never be as good as you and Brix.' Krystal was grinning. This time her face might fall off. Pixie repressed an urge to rub it vigorously with a Steelo pad. 'When I watch you two in action my brain feels like frozen tripe and my hands like pig's trotters.'

'Yuk!' said the Goth. 'Maybe I shouldn't tell you then.' Her eyes gloated impishly. Her grin was testing the architecture of her face. Even her nose and eyebrow studs seemed to sparkle. She hauled her shoulders up to her ears and sort of hugged herself with straight arms.

'Tell me what?'

'We – well, Brix – slam dunked.'

'Slam dunked?'

'We found his records. Lists 'n' stuff and … something else.'

'Here,' said Pixie. She shoved the photograph into Krystal's startled hands. 'Put that back in the bedroom for me.' And she almost ran from the kitchen. 'The chocolate, the chocolate! I forgot it,' she yelled over her shoulder.

She hurried across the living room and down the short hall that led to the small, light room that held her IT equipment. 'What have we got,

Brix?' she said from the doorway to the back of the boy nestled in a bower of boxes, screens, wires and cables.

He was hunched over the keyboard of her most powerful unit. He was rocking back and forth like a dipping-bird toy on the rim of a glass. He was muttering: an incoherent mumble at first, which resolved into intelligible words as Pixie drew closer.

'Fuckincuntfuckincuntfuckincuntfuckincunt …'

'Brix?'

He kept rocking as if he was unaware of her presence. 'Fuckincuntfuckincuntfuckincunt …'

She was beside him now and put a hand on his shoulder. There was no reaction. He stared at the screen like the little girl in that movie Sean loved: *Poltergeist*, was it? Her eyes slid along his gaze. There was nothing but an email page on the screen. It was addressed to their target. One of their pseudonyms was in the sender box. The subject was 'FYEO'. At first she thought it was otherwise blank, then she noticed an attachment. She didn't recognise the file name. It wasn't one of the programs they'd been using. She looked back at Brix's transfixed face. His eyes were glazed, his nostrils were pinched and his lips bluish, as if he'd forgotten to breathe. He always looked slight and fragile in the out-sized op-shop trawlings he wore, but now he looked like a bird, crushable in a child's hand.

'Brix? What's wrong?' she pleaded as she knelt beside his chair.

There was no reaction to her voice. Then she noticed his mantra had altered.

'Dieyafuckincuntdieyafuckincuntdieyafuckincunt …'

She glanced at his right hand. It was a pale moth hovering over the keyboard. Her eyes flicked to the screen again. 'Send' had been selected. Her eyes bounced back to the keyboard. A finger hung, crooked, over the 'Enter' key.

'Die you fucking cunt!' Brix said suddenly and decisively.

Pixie grabbed his wrist. 'No, Brix!' She didn't know what he was doing, but instinctively, she knew it wasn't productive.

His left hand darted at the key. She deflected it with her wrist and pinioned his arms in a bear hug. He sat in a typical office chair and her momentum thrust him away from the console on its castors. She anticipated a struggle and clutched him tight, but she realised he had dropped his head to her shoulder and was simply shivering with a sudden release of tension.

'There, there,' she soothed. 'Brix, Brix-brix.'

'Twenty years younger is too old, eh? Cradle-robbing's the go?' Krystal was standing at the door with three mugs of hot chocolate in her hands. 'He might look thirteen or fourteen but he's actually almost eighteen, you know.'

'What's that?' said Pixie, pointing at the computer display.

Krystal sauntered across and leaned to the screen. 'Oooh, Brixie. That's not nice,' she said over her shoulder.

'What is it?' said Pixie, even though she had a pretty good idea.

'A weapon of mass destruction.' Admiration burnished Krystal's voice.

'Disarm it,' said Pixie.

Krystal found a place for the mugs on the desk. She trashed the email and ejected a disc.

'Why did you do that, Brix?' said Pixie, relaxing her grip on him.

'He wanted to hurt the bastard. Punish him,' said Krystal. 'And the other bastards.'

'That virus would have destroyed all his files?'

'Right down to his screen saver. And anyone linked to him. Turn their hard drives to soft fruit.'

'Banana smoothies,' mumbled Brix into his chest. They spluttered into that excluding giggle – Brix weakly, Krystal with malevolent glee.

'Shit!' breathed Pixie. Evil little cybernauts.

'Oooh, wash your tongue,' said Krystal.

'Brix. Brixie, I know how it might seem to you that that's the worst thing we could do to him, but those files are evidence. Without them we can't prove what he's done. We need them to stay right where they are so we can stop him for good. The worst thing that we can do to him is put him in gaol. They don't like his kind in there. Believe me.'

'Here, cowboy,' said Krystal as she knelt at his knees and handed Brix one of the steaming mugs. 'Fairy godmother made it. Not bad.' She handed Pixie a mug.

Pixie got to her feet. 'But it sounds like you've done it for us, Brix. Krystal said you'd found his records.'

'And his gallery,' said Krystal.

'Gallery?'

'Sick stuff. He didn't have it on his hard drive. It was stored in a "secure",' she wiggled two fingers each side of her head and giggled derisively, 'site on the web. All these porno pics of kids. An' we know how he disguises his hyperlink hot buttons now.'

Pixie took a deep breath and let it out slowly. 'Then we've got him, Brix.'

'Should thank her,' said Krystal. 'You could have stuffed David up real bad.'

Brix's thick soft brows tented like a beagle's above his large eyes. His upper lip was hooked over the rim of his mug. It lifted. 'Forry,' he said softly.

Pixie sipped her hot chocolate and looked down at them looking up at her. She guessed they were the same age, but there appeared to be the same age difference between them as between Patricia and Sean. The expressions on their faces tugged at a memory. Look at them: two street kids with mouths that wouldn't melt butter. Oh Jesus no, Pixie, don't even think it – that way be too much drama.

'Did you get a copy of the stuff?' she said.

'Oh der,' said Krystal, rolling her eyes.

'Okay, then let's not push our luck. Put the horse back in its stable before he's alerted.'

The pink tip of Krystal's tongue chased chocolate from her lip. 'Anyhow, what kind of name is "Pixie"?' she said.

'What kind of name is Krystal Sett?' Pixie challenged.

43

'What do you think?'

'I think you make a marvellous team.'

'I think you should dismiss any little ideas of yours along those lines, forthwith. That's not what I meant. And you know it.'

'I think we've got everything we need.'

'What next?'

'Now we make sure that you and Krystal and Brix are out of harm's way and can't be connected to this little scheme. I'll take it from h …'

'What's the matter?'

David Edge tapped the page before him on the table. 'Plotell. That's an unusual name, wouldn't you say?'

'Can't say I've ever come across it. Hang on.' Pixie stood up and left the room. She returned with the L to Z volume of the Melbourne phone book. 'I hope those two aren't hacking into the Pentagon or something,' she said as she sat down.

'I'll take them off your hands when I leave.'

She thumbed through the pages. 'Where will they sleep?'

'They have their little nooks and crannies.'

'Here it is. Plotell. Only one in Melbourne. Dr J D. Is it important?'

'To me.'

'They can stay tonight.'

'It's okay. I'll take them to the shelter.'

'They can stay tonight.'

Edge gazed admiringly at the materials arrayed on the kitchen bench top: sheets of lists, accounts, images, web pages, emails, chat room dialogues, uploads, downloads. 'How did you do this?'

Pixie, chin on her chest, folded her arms across her small bosom and looked up from under her brow. She could feel the backrest of her stool hugging her kidneys. There was a dry smile in her eyes.

'You have no idea how we did it, but you expected us to deliver, nonetheless?' she said. 'Has it ever occurred to you that you act on very little but faith?'

'Well look,' he gestured at the bench top, 'it can move mountains.'

'Don't push it.'

'How?'

'To put it in terms even you will understand: we infected his computer with a nasty little virus we'd … customised. A program that cuddles up to his hard drive and looks and listens and tells all.' Pixie topped up her coffee. 'More?'

Edge shook his head. 'Like a trojan or – what's that other – a zombie?'

'More like a whistleblower. Basically it's spyware. In the form of adware it's used legitimately, if sneakily, by software companies as a marketing tool. The programs do no damage, so no one complains. Or calls them a virus. A lot of people overlook them when organising virus protection.' She took a sip. 'This bloke's computer literate, but no geek. His encryption is pathetic: a numerical version of the letters in TOIBOI in reverse order. What's this obsession with that epithet? He's either arrogant or plain stupid when it comes to security. And that's what I don't get. Paedophiles are paranoid about security. How did he penetrate these rings?'

'I suspect he may have had a leg up, courtesy of his stepfather.'

Pixie considered this with a thrust of her bottom lip and a hitch of her shoulders.

'Anyhow,' she continued, 'Sharon's computer was his Achilles heel: no security worth the name. Our program piggybacked in on an attachment to one of her emails. He opened it and the program installed itself.' She took another sip. 'When he logged on, each transaction – chapter and verse – was recorded. While he was online we owned his computer.'

'I thought Brix would have goodies like that tucked away in his knapsack.'

'Nothing quite benign or discreet enough,' Pixie said laconically. 'I would have tracked all this down in time, but they knew a few shortcuts. They're sharp, those kids.'

'I'm sure you taught them a thing or two.'

Pixie strafed the no-man's land between them with her don't-play-the-charm-card-on-me stare.

Edge began to shuffle all the papers together. 'Thanks, Pixie. I'm forever in your debt. And so is Ben Bovell.'

'Do you think he knew about all this?'

'Knew a little, guessed a little, feared a lot.'

'Has it occurred to you that, to Benny, the distinction between enduring attorney and eternal vigilance was far too subtle? That he expected you to watch over them for the rest of your natural?'

Edge chuckled, shaking his head. 'Ben was brighter than people gave him credit for.'

'Brighter, perhaps. Less naive, I don't think so. I've been giving it some thought. His little plot was pure comic book. Who – other than an incurable optimist with a childlike mind – probably in a depressive state – would believe they could solve their problems post mortem?'

'I think there's an oxymoron in there somewhere.'

'What did a small-time thief like Benny do to deserve this? For you to go to all this trouble? Rescue you from a burning building in his teeth? Risk life and limb to deliver a vital clue?'

Edge chuckled like a priest who can't help forgiving an incorrigible sinner. 'Truthfully, most of his information was useless or redundant. Ben was more nuisance than assistance.'

Pixie sat back and stared at him. 'You do know,' she said eventually, 'that stuff about saving someone's life making you responsible for them for the rest of yours is pure bull?'

'You don't drag someone out of the torrent and leave him standing in the rain.'

'He's gone now. Any obligation you imagine you had is void.'

'On the contrary, his death sealed the pact. Why do you think he made sure I was witness to it all?'

'Now you're really letting imagination get the better of you. You're making a martyr out of a simple crim.'

'We do what we can, when we can, with what we've got. All Ben had was the skin he stood up in to keep him – and his – dry.'

Pixie grunted with exasperation and stared out the window. When she turned back she said, 'You know why he could read you so well? You're alike: you're children. The naivety of your good intentions has led both of you to do badness.'

'The only computer crime Ben committed was nicking one. How did you know him?'

'I didn't. Pierce had a few Benny stories. He arrested him once or twice.' She shrugged. 'It's just a theory.'

'Everywhere I go lately someone filters me through psychobabble.' He pulled a sad-clown face.

Pixie ignored him. 'You know who else you're like? Pierce. You'll get too close one day and someone you think you're helping will kill you. Get out of it all, David. Go back to uni. Do your PhD.'

'I was surprised that you let Maeve recruit you in this. I thought the Jack Barker business put me in your bad books.'

'Oh, it did. But I trust Maeve.'

'She's very trustworthy – for an old dipso dyke.'

'I'll tell her you said that.'

Edge made exaggerated gestures of supplication.

'It's hard to trust someone who can conceal thoughts and feelings as skilfully as you. In fact it's not rational to trust such a person. But, I do have a … um, an appreciation of some things you've done.'

'Oh?'

'That poor woman, the one that killed Pierce, she didn't deserve to die; but if they'd given her fair warning then shot her, there would be only one dead, not two.' She placed her eyes firmly on Edge's and locked them down.

'Situations, solutions,' he said eventually, flipping a hand back and forth, palm up, palm down. 'In the heat of those moments you don't crunch numbers. Rules, procedures: a rough guide, at best. You usually do what you think will work at the time – SOP or not.'

'You *are* handing all this over to the appropriate authorities?' She glanced down at the document-littered tabletop.

He smiled and nodded. 'Once the collateral is removed beyond damage.' He cocked his wrist and looked at his watch. 'With a bit of luck, e'en as we speak, Maeve and Co are at the Box Hill house tying a nice neat bow on some of that.'

44

Yasmin Glover had not been a pretty child. The biological chronology of her life had been tumbled in a bingo barrel and extracted randomly. She'd been born a wrinkled crone, and by the time she was in nappies she was a brown Cabbage Patch Doll. It wasn't until her early teen years that the severe planes and curved ridges of her brow, cheeks and nose found their proper proportion and rightful place in the cosmetic order of things. Flesh and bone contrived with such economy that the resultant beauty was both austere and delicate. It was described as regal – when it became apparent. The child had the face and form of a woman. And the trouble started.

The trouble didn't end until she'd been picked up off the streets and placed in a brothel. She was an addict by then, still a teenager, and a prostitute to pay for her habit. Of course she couldn't use and stay at The Rose Garden for long. Rose was a wowser and wouldn't tolerate drug use inside the Garden's doors. Yasmin was given a special dispensation and a strict time limit to get her act together. Which she did, although she really couldn't remember how, exactly. It must have been the kind of hell memory suppressed.

It was a man she'd only ever known as Spade, and David Edge, who'd got her off the streets. In her mind – rescued her. Spade shepherded her into the shelter. Edge engineered her rehabilitation.

He was accused of using the drop-in centre as a recruiting ground for his brothels – even by Spade – but Yasmin knew she'd still be plying her trade in alleys if he hadn't offered her an 'honourable' solution. She was a pig-headed little bitch – freely acknowledged. No man was going to lay claim to her salvation. She'd save herself even if it killed her. Her father had instilled in her the pride of Icarus and when she fell (and he shunned her) she clung fiercely to it and swung it like a club. It was useless as wings. But it was her body and soul that bore most of its bruises.

She was still proud, but it wasn't the old shallow, arrogance. It was something annealed, tempered, beaten and burnished. Something nobler. Yes, she had saved herself, and, in the end, you are the only one that can do that. But she hadn't done it alone. She had been held afloat until she could swim again and knew where the shore was.

That's why she was here. She had a debt to repay and an opportunity to repay in kind.

Here was Box Hill Central, the shopping town on Whitehorse Road. In particular, *here* was the fresh food market of Box Hill Central. This part of the complex was a small undercover China Town. The faces behind and in front of the counters were mostly Asian. That's the other reason she was here: her face was Asian. Subtly Asian. There was something Caucasian in her muddy gene pool – hence the surname – but most of it from the middle bit of the East rather than the West. The Far and Near were in the recipe, but it was difficult to specify the ingredients in her ethnic stew.

Her targets were easier to identify.

It had been decided to use Yasmin because they would be less likely to take flight if approached by a non-European face. It was also a plus that she was a prostitute. She had made her first approach here in the market and they had met here, or at the house, regularly. This was planned to be the last meeting. She had won their confidence and, finally, convinced them to run.

Her targets were three women and two children, a girl and a boy, who lived in a house in a quiet leafy Box Hill street. They spoke little

English and ventured out of doors during daylight hours only to do the shopping. At night their excursions were business-related. The business was fucking men for money – or letting men fuck them. The men who fucked them were men with 'exotic' tastes, so they rarely worked close to home. Asian women aren't all that exotic to Asian men. Or so it is said. Of the money they earned they saw little. They were working off a debt. The debt was the cost of smuggling them into a wide brown land. And, with accrued interest, it probably wouldn't be met until they weren't so 'exotic' anymore.

Yasmin, over a series of 'serendipitous' meetings, had told a version of her own story, gained their confidence and persuaded them that she could introduce them to a man who would take over their debt and protect them from the lawful and the lawless. She was with the older woman – the one the others deferred to – at the fishmongers, the place she had first 'bumped into' them. They would go and have a coffee and make final arrangements.

They were sitting at a table in a sunken eating area in one of the complex's pedestrian hubs doing just that, when the design of the grand plan and its execution parted company. Yasmin wasn't aware of this at the time.

Nor was Maeve.

Maeve poked at the digits, audibly lamenting the commercial world's marginalisation of the large woman in terms pithy and personal. She looked as if taken with a sudden toothache when she jammed the tiny mobile phone to her cheek. 'Sneaky' Fokker was supposed to be watching Yasmin's back while Maeve was at the Box Hill house to ensure she wasn't surprised on the premises by an unscheduled visit from the proprietor.

'Snea … Carl!' she snapped.

'Struth, whassa matter, Maeve?'

'Sorry. Something on my mind. Just letting you know Sharon's taken a detour. You've got a bit of time up your sleeve.'

'No worries. Nothin' worth watchin' on TV this time of day.'

'Right.' Maeve wasn't sure if he was joking. 'Is Yasmin still inside?'

'Nah. Went out a while back with a Chinese chick.'

'Thai,' she corrected him. 'A woman from the house?'

'How the fuck would I know. There's bloody Chinese all over the place. Where they come from?'

It had been some time since Carl had visited Box Hill it would seem. At least he didn't say they all looked alike to him. 'Did they leave in Yasmin's car?'

'Yeah. They ain't got wheels. Took 'em to the shops probably. Gave me the sign to not folla.'

Yasmin had chauffeured them shopping on one other occasion that she knew of, so there wasn't anything odd there. 'Okay,' said Maeve after a small pause. 'I'll let you know soon as Sharon's moving your way again.'

'No worries. If Yasmin's not back I'll tell 'er to drop the chick off a coupla blocks away.'

The brief bristlies on the nape of Maeve's neck should perhaps have stirred, but they didn't.

And they didn't stir when Sharon Kitchen returned to her car in the car park of the Box Hill Central shopping complex, drove down the ramp into Station Street, turned left into Whitehorse Road and returned the way she had come.

They did thrash around like a field of corn with a stiff southerly through it when her revised destination became apparent to Maeve.

45

'She got him out of the house as soon as she got there?'

'Yep.'

'And they stood in the middle of the oval to talk?'

'I had my glasses on 'em.'

'What were his reactions?'

'She seemed worried – trying to convince 'im of something. He seemed to be brushing it aside. He laughed and shook his head a couple of times. Then he got thoughtful at something she said.'

'If Yasmin was at Box Hill Central around the same time as Sharon we have to assume she was seen.'

'Big place, big bloody fluke – but yeah.'

There was silence in the room for a while.

'Shit, this is good stuff,' Maeve said breaking into his thoughts. 'Well, it's pure shit, but for our purposes … How did Pixie find these?'

'Hyperlinks – she said. Apparently you can select a few pixels in an image and make them a "hot button". Click on one and it links you to another website. The chat room he set up to attract blackmail targets was one. Our boy favoured hiding the links to his more … illicit offerings in vaginas.'

'Virtual G spots, eh? So the three soft-core sites were fronts to his real business. Sharon's in on the illegal prostitution and soft-core porn, but d'you think she knows about these?'

Edge's brow lifted and his lips pressed on the moot point. They were sitting on the couch in his office: the room at the head of the stairs that had

'David Edge, Research Consultant' emblazoned on the door. The materials that Pixie had given him were piled in Maeve's lap.

'A bit of luck Pixie recallin' the "Toiboi" site from one of her old cases.'

'We'd have teased out that thread eventually, but she saved us a lot of time and shoe leather.'

Maeve held up a page. 'This looks like his extortion hit list. The name second from the bottom is the target we watched him entrap. If it's chronological he's hit on another one since. Busy boy.'

'He's hit on another one,' Edge confirmed.

The tone of his voice drew sharper scrutiny from Maeve. Before she could ask how he knew, he added, 'There's a cryptic email in the printouts, similar to one he sent others. That suggests the list is chronological. Which helps us to decipher the coded stuff next to the names.'

'It's an odd name. The last one.'

'Yes, it is an odd name. Fortunately.'

She was about to quiz him further when he raised his fists in a double thumbs-up gesture. She realised she'd misunderstood its meaning when he spoke.

'How are yours, Maeve? Mine are pricking. We've stirred the jelly too long. It's going to set before we get it in our mould.'

46

The sultry siren sashayed up to the bar and within minutes the intended victim of her allure was sidling over to light her cigarette or buy her a drink. That was the way it happened on the silver screen.

Hitchcock said movies were life with the boring bits edited out.

Alfred had left Carol with the scenes from the cutting room floor.

She had lost count of the nights she'd sat taking bee sips of a cocktail as its temperature slowly rose to the ambient. Perhaps her perceptions were slave to a sexist stereotype: handsome, trim and urbane didn't necessarily translate into philanderer any more than her image into nymphomaniac.

She had lost count of the number of approaches and passes she'd parried. There was a book in it: a book of bad pickup lines. The regulars had given up trying. The semi-regulars seemed to suffer from short-term memory loss, or perhaps there was an arcane house rule stipulating the number of tries, and it took them twice as long to reach the cut-off. He was an irregular, but as far as she could discern, this was his watering hole. Parliamentary sittings and party business probably regulated his partaking of the waters.

The barman claimed there was a local legend growing around her aloof presence and solitary vigil. He was quite excited about it – but then, he was gay.

She wondered if her prey had heard the legend or contributed to it. She had noticed him notice her. So far the character of his attention had been no more than you would expect from a male in the company of males observing a solitary attractive woman in a bar a Whip's whistle from the hub of government. As far as she could tell she was the only one – well, the only female – who might be angling for an MP, so this wasn't, typically, an establishment frequented by political groupies, if there was such a thing. He shouldn't be harbouring the kind of suspicion that might give him pause.

It was best, for her purposes, if he made the initial approach and she was resistant – not too resistant – but time was running out. Her waders were filling with water as rapidly as the bottom bell of her hourglass, and not a nibble from the honourable fishy member.

She attempted another cast.

Rotating her rump ninety degrees, away from the bar toward the room, she slipped her right foot from the rung of her barstool and stretched it to touch the floor with the tip of a lightly clad foot. The high heel of her left shoe remained hooked over the hooped rung. Her left leg remained bent and held high. At the same time she twisted her torso back towards the bar and reached out to grasp the small leather handbag sitting near her cocktail glass. The impression she hoped to give was of a woman about to go to the little girl's room suddenly, in mid action, remembering her bag. The visual effect she hoped to deliver was one similar to a hosiery advertisement: an artless cascade of limb and silken promise.

An old boyfriend had told her that women who were innocently unaware of their decolletage were infinitely more sexy than women who brazenly flaunted the highs and lows of their topography (his words: 'put it on display next to the check out'). She hoped this was a general rule and not just an articulation of his particular kink. If she judged her man correctly, subtlety and sophistication would work best. The dress she had chosen was simple and as economic of cut as possible without being sluttish. Fortunately, these days, the difference between sluttish and not was measured by quality not quantity, and less was more. Still, it was stylish and cunning in design and there were more silk handkerchiefs in it than you'd imagine. It had better work: it cost a fortune.

The tableau her manoeuvre was intended to trap in the amber of the male mind's eye should, if she got it right, have highlighted her best attributes. The twist of her torso should have narrowed her already fine waist, accentuating the firm sweep of her hips below and the firm swell of her breasts above, and raised her rippling hemline on her silken thigh like a curtain on opening night. She hoped her timing was right and the rhythm of the gesture would be read as natural languor and not theatrical pose.

If it didn't work she'd just have to spill a drink in his bloody lap.

She slipped smoothly from the stool and walked across the room with a relaxed, measured stride – something between a slink and the march she'd learned at the Academy.

Carol Porter wasn't adept in the arts of seduction. She'd never had to employ them. The art of dissuasion was her forte. She was making this up as she went along – well really, she was appropriating it from old movies, *Bridget Jones' Diary* and *Sex and the City*.

She could feel eyes skittering over her flesh like lice and, with a small shock, understood why she felt so comfortable in uniform. The eyes of the two men in the booth licked at her as she passed.

Taylor Payne screwed around in his seat like a perished balloon. When the door closed behind the redhead he turned back to press a muffin top of belly to the table.

'Now there's a set of shanks that take their time getting cheeky. Howja like to play Snakes 'n' Labias with that?' He leaned forward with the same confidential urgency he had, only a moment before, applied to branch stacking and other tactical matters. Never shy to press a point he added, 'Wouldn't mind poking around under that verandah. Eh?'

Simon Castleman took a protracted sip of his scotch to avoid any reply. He knew Payne wasn't finished and would hurry to get it all off his chest.

'Not often you get the trifecta.' This time he waited.

'Trifecta?' Simon eventually conceded the response Taylor wanted.

'Tits, arse *and* face. That one, that one,' hissed Taylor Payne, connoisseur of female flesh, one of the boys, life and hack of the party. 'She don't need the clothes and makeup, believe me! How old d'you reckon she is?'

Simon opened his mouth with a bromide poised on his tongue – the older I get the younger they look, or something like – but Taylor had the answer to his own question.

'Eighteen to twenty – tops. Whaddaya reckon?'

The assessment, Simon guessed, was based on subjective desire not objective observation.

'I don't know, Tay. She seems too poised and confident for someone of such tender years,' he said, knowing he sounded like an Edwardian uncle, and meaning to.

'Shit. They pop out of the womb ready to rock 'n' roll these days, Simon.'

Simon acquiesced with the constrained, jaded smile of a whore enduring pious platitudes. Still, he had to admit to himself, Ariel had had – or seemed to have – that almost eerie self-possession in her teens. It occurred to him then that what had seemed so familiar about the woman was exactly that: she reminded him of Ariel. Her features, colouring, size, shape were nothing like Ariel. It was her poise, her gesture, the way she comported herself: a sort of dignified, good-humoured and gracious muscularity that said 'muck with me at your peril', but sweetly.

Tay suddenly shoved with his palms against the table edge and his body rocked back and sagged against the soft leather padding of the booth. For one disconcerting moment Simon thought the sibilant hiss issued from his torso not the upholstery. He looked at the much too ruddy jowls, the mottled cheeks, the muddy eyes isolated in chalky divots of flesh below dry spiky bushes like dams in a drought. Despite the recent display of crassness Simon liked him. He knew that Tay's boy talk had become cruder and more frequent in inverse proportion to his waning ability to act on it. Not that he ever had practised what he now preached. He was sad that his old friend felt it necessary to taint the well of his past with macho slag from his present tongue.

'Well,' said Tay suddenly. 'We clear on all that?'

Simon assumed he was referring to their conversation before the red-head's promenade had scattered their thoughts and stampeded their dialogue south. 'Very clear, Tay.'

'Wanna lift?'

'You're not driving?' said Simon, trying to swallow the alarm that had crept into his voice.

Tay stared at him as if he had suggested he'd joined One Nation. 'Taxi. Can drop you. 'S not far outta m'way.'

Tay's internal GPS went down when he had a few. 'Thanks, Tay, I'll be fine. See you Tuesday.'

Taylor was suddenly in his face. 'Saw how you looked at that redhead,' he hissed loudly. 'Don't do nothin' I would'n.' He winked lewdly and lumbered toward the night.

Simon watched the pendulous ovoid of Taylor Payne's departing posterior, reminded as always of Lewis Carroll's Walrus. When Lilith, Tay's wife, accompanied him the Carpenter was there too.

Tay's wink was still flashing before his eyes like a caution light at an intersection in the wee small hours. Why was he still sitting here?

When the redhead appeared at the door from the amenities he realised he had been waiting on the vision like the hopeful (or hopeless) at Lourdes.

As she passed his booth one of her ridiculously high heels, the one on the foot nearest (the one Constable Carol Porter had gone to some trouble to loosen in the toilets), buckled under her and she staggered and fell into his lap.

Just like that.

47

'Good morning, Mr E.'

'Morning, Charlotte.'

'You've got a few messages. Someone called McCluskey from something called the AFP phoned to change your appointment from two to one. Cheryl says the safe house is ready. Yasmin says the consignment is ready to move. She and Boof are waiting for you on-site …'

'Tell them I'm on my way.'

'… and there is a policeman in the kitchen. Shane is minding him.'

'Minding him?' The corners of Edge's eyes tweaked the corners of his lips.

'You know, making sure he has enough tea and bikkies to keep him occupied.'

'Thank you, Charlotte. Very efficient. We'll miss you if you leave. Not planning to?'

'Of course not! Why would I?' Charlotte was offended.

'Recent experiences may have prompted second thoughts about the job.'

'Quite the opposite, actually. It's a great job. Like living in a Graham Greene novel. I'll never give it up.'

'The man you marry may have something to say about that.'

'Not if I marry someone who works here.'

Charlotte felt the satisfaction of her words raising one of his eyebrows and drawing a fleeting, but definitely sharper, scrutiny. 'Small pickings – if you're interested in the opposite sex,' he said.

Charlotte willed her features into – what she hoped was – an inscrutable arrangement. 'You'd be surprised,' she said.

He smiled and began to turn away, then paused.

'You read Graham Greene?'

'One of my all-time favourites. So totally wicked.'

'Totally,' he said, and continued on his way.

That's it, Charlotte, thought Charlotte, keep him guessing. She was sure she was beginning to learn what drew his attention. 'Safest workplace in the world,' she called and felt the satisfaction of the brush of another glance.

David Edge walked down the narrow passage that would have led to the servants' quarters in the century of the house's heyday. Then again, perhaps the house thought this was its heyday. You never can tell. Now, the passage led to Rose's office, the small general office, the security and surveillance room, a storeroom, a bathroom and the kitchen.

In the kitchen Shane Clarke sat on the forward edge of an otherwise comfortable lounge chair in the tiny sitting nook to the right of the kitchen door. It was divided from the rest of the room by a large bench. The functional part of the kitchen took up the remaining three-quarters of the space. Shane still looked alienated from his suit, but it was gradually taking on his contours. His eyes were fixed on the occupant of the couch against the wall opposite him.

Don Collison sipped delicately on his tea and nibbled a Tim Tam with the nonchalance of a lap dancer on a lunch break.

'Morning, Shane. G'day, Don,' said Edge.

Shane stood. 'That bloke was there again last night.'

'Just another tourist. But, good work.'

Shane nodded, cut a parting glance at Collison and slipped away like a noon shadow.

'They get very cheeky when they come to work for you,' said Collison inspecting the teeth marks in his Tim Tam. 'Think that's in their best interest?'

'Shane's employed by Rose.'

'Oh, that's okay then.' A politician's non-core promise might have got a more sarcastic response.

Edge sat in the chair vacated by Shane and smiled.

'Have you ever sucked coffee through one of these?' Collison asked.

Edge shook his head. 'I'm a purist.'

Collison slumped back into his chair and studied the features across the table. He reached inside his coat with ponderous world-weariness and tossed a grainy ten by eight photograph on the table. 'Found the face in the background of a surveillance video of Varney. Hadn't turned up anywhere else, and Varney's such a bigoted cunt, no one picked it for anything but a casual acquaintance or passerby. There was no attempt to identify him.'

Edge placed one finger on a corner and moved the image to see it better.

'I take it,' Collison continued, 'that you think he was the mystery caller?'

'Probably. But, having surveyed his interests over the last few weeks – and viewed his portfolio – I'm more confident that he was the cameraman.'

'And you've got a name?'

Edge nodded.

'What do you want?'

Edge ignored the question. 'He and Varney have a relationship that goes beyond gay bashing. They're both implicated in another old homicide. Have a chat with Nev Marks. You might be of use to each other.'

'He does have a name?'

'Hu.'

'Clint-fucken-Eastwood in *A Fistful of Dollars*.'

Edge chuckled. 'Talk to Nev. You have a video and a tape, Nev has a witness and a name: between the two of you, bugalugs here and Varney can be spliced like noose rope.' He flipped the photo over and wrote two words on the back. 'Just tell Tezza "Toyboy" sent you.'

'Toyboy?'

'Oh, that reminds me.' He slipped a piece of notepaper from his pocket, placed it on the photo and slid it across the table. 'This website is worth a peek. You'll love the camera work. Now, I hate to rush off, but no rest for the morally challenged.'

48

At four minutes to two Jacinta McCluskey returned to her office: a dreary little cube with two chairs, a small battle-scarred desk, a metal filing cabinet and an uninterrupted view of a mottled brick wall through a window only slightly larger than a porthole. Its solitary saving grace was the state-of-the-art computer that perched on the desk like a ballerina on a beer crate. It was the only thing that drew her back to an office she found the most tenuous of excuses to leave. Fortunately it was a temporary arrangement. She normally worked out of Canberra, where the water closets were more palatial than this box and her office was a home away from home.

She shook the droplets of a brief rain shower from her coat and hung it on the hook behind the door. She ruffled her short dark-red hair and felt a light sprinkle on the back of her neck. Suspecting that she might now look like a Raggedy Ann, she pressed it as if moulding foil over a cantaloupe. By now she was behind her desk. In this room, simply entering placed you behind the desk. She tugged at her skirt to smooth it over her hips and opened her suit coat for comfort as she lowered herself into a marginally ergonomic chair. Her bum had barely touched the seat when the phone rang.

'Your two o'clock's here,' said the voice of Helen from reception when the receiver reached her ear.

She was about to demand what bloody two o'clock, but bit it off. 'Thanks, Helen,' she sighed. She replaced the receiver by dropping it the last ten centimetres, sagged back in her chair and stared at the door. Bugger! She should have known. She wondered now why she had even bothered.

With sudden purpose she sat up, buttoned the jacket of her suit and woke her computer with a flick of her finger at the mouse's nose. When a light tap heralded the opening of the door she was staring at the screen through glasses that teetered on the snub of her nose. Her eyes slid along the metal rims of her spectacles like green bubbles on a silver ripple.

'Not too early, am I?'

'You're an hour late,' she said, as if noting a simple fact.

'Now, Jac, we both know that's not true.'

'The appointment was changed to one. Didn't you get the message?'

He looked through window with that private almost-smile that was just a disturbance at the extremities of his lips. 'Oh, I got the message.' Then he looked back at her, all ingenuousness. 'Which one?' he added. Bastard. He sauntered across the room – the whole step and a half – spun the visitor's chair at an angle to the desk, slipped off the backpack that was hanging by one strap from his shoulder and sat. 'Didn't know you were in town till I spoke to Darrell.'

'Good.'

'Cosy office.'

Her eyes rolled toward the ceiling. 'They're renovating the floor above. Space is a little scarce.' I'd probably have scored this kennel anyway, she didn't add.

He gazed through the window. 'Still – a nice view of Tierra Del Fuego.'

She glanced at the ancient stain on the brick wall. 'I thought it was Haiti. But I failed Rorschach.'

'How are you, Jac?'

'I'd be a lot better if you had turned up at one.'

'Would you have been here?'

'No.'

He chuckled.

She let it annoy her. 'Darrell told me you were delivering a package. We have reception to handle that.'

'Darrell said I should talk to you.'

'Darrell seems to think we have some special bond,' she said as she tugged off her glasses. 'There are others here just as competent to handle your … business. Anyhow, I'll be back in Canberra in a couple of weeks.'

'Not a commander yet?'

'The ceilings are just as hard and transparent in the Feds. But I knew that.'

'Darrell said you were handling sex-slave investigations?'

'Mmm. It's a girl thing.' She intended to be flip, but could taste the dry bitterness in her voice. She hoped he didn't hear it. To recover, she leaned forward with proficient dispatch. 'What do you want, Edge?'

He studied her frankly. She knew he could see the eyes were still green, the complexion still creamy, the freckles still there – a peachy splatter. His head dipped down and came up as he hefted the backpack onto his knees. He unbuckled straps and reached inside. 'I want to give you this.' He withdrew an expandable file secured with an elastic band and placed it on the desk.

Jacinta regarded the package without moving. 'And what is that?'

'Information I've obtained that is pertinent to your investigations.' He grinned with the guileless guile of a cheeky schoolboy who knows the teacher knows where the apple came from.

'Legally obtained?'

'Of course not,' with mock affront, 'I'm not a policeman anymore.'

'And whose fault is that?' Oh shit, Jacinta, why go there yet again?

'Mine entirely,' he said. His contrition was as openly false as the former affront. 'Mea culpa, mea culpa, me—'

'Okay, okay.' She sighed. 'What good is illegally obtained material to me?'

He sat back and gazed at her with sly discernment. 'Jac,' he drawled. 'You're an alchemist. It may be dross now, but you can transmute it to gold.'

'Alright,' she relented. She inclined her head at the file. 'Is this a confession or an autobiography?' Damn! She'd slipped into his bantering mode. She was surrendering control of the transaction already.

To her mild surprise he was abruptly serious. He tapped the file. 'This boy is much more entrepreneurial than me when it comes to packaging and marketing the product.'

'The product being …?'

'Sex, Jac.' He lurched forward, placed his palms on the file and gloated like an evangelist across a bible. 'Sex. The ultimate post post-modern commodity: portable and potable, easily appropriated and globally negotiable; cheap and simple to produce, propagable in any soil, adaptable to any climate; exploitable and exportable, no trade barriers or tariffs, obsolescence inbuilt, infinitely recyclable; desired by young and old, rich and poor, and available in any format – imagined or imaginable.'

Jacinta felt her resolve soften. 'You and Phillip Marlowe: always posing as cynics.'

'How is Phil these days?'

'His author is dead.'

'So is mine. Now I'll never have closure.'

'Derrida's dead too.'

'Jacques? Surely not: just eternally deferred.'

Jacinta found herself giggling. She and Carol Marks and Edge had been the only university-educated recruits in their group at the Academy. They often played these silly undergraduate games. Well, not too often and seldom in earshot of the others: it excluded them. Nev Marks was the only one who didn't resent it – but then Carol could do no wrong in Nev's eyes. There was a time when Edge could do no wrong in her eyes.

'Alright, you can switch off the charm,' she said sobering rapidly. 'Can I have a digest?' She rolled a palm toward the file. 'Then we can begin the bartering.'

He didn't bother denying the implicit accusation. He relaxed back into his chair – insofar as it was possible to relax in that chair.

'His name is Hu, Lionel Hu. His father was a Vietnam vet. His mother is Vietnamese. His father went back to Vietnam after the war, married her and brought her here. The children were born here. Lionel was the youngest child, the only male. His father had struggled against drug addiction for years and his mental health took a nose-dive shortly after Lionel was born. He committed suicide. Hu is the name of Lionel's stepfather. He was a fifth or sixth generation Australian Chinese. We suspect he was a child abuser.'

'We?' Jacinta smiled. She'd caught him in a rare faux pas.

'Oops!' He grinned.

'Let me guess,' she said. 'Sophie Demetriou? Maeve Maguffin? Vaughn Peake? Carol – if she was feeling up to it? An assortment of crims and cops and some of the girls who don't mind a bit of rough trade for the cause? Am I close?'

'Out by miles,' he said. 'All my own work. Just making sure you're paying attention.'

'Yeah, right.' She flipped the back of her hand, a pedestrian giving way to traffic. 'Don't let me interrupt.'

'Lionel is a conflicted lad. He's running a small stable of illegals from Thailand. He's distributing porn on the internet. He's using chat rooms – and his websites – to ferret out paedophiles, lure them into the light and then blackmail them. This is the interesting bit – the reason I think he was abused as a child – he is only blackmailing homosexual paedophiles; he's supplying the heterosexuals with kiddie porn. He's used images – they're all in there,' he indicated the file, 'images of the daughters of two of the Thai women …'

'Sex slaves with kids?'

Edge shrugged. 'He may have got 'em at a good discount. Anyway, that's why they'll be willing to cooperate. He may have used the girls … in other ways – I don't know.'

'Small change.'

'Winning tickets are bought with small change.'

Jacinta discarded her protective shell and hunched over her forearms. 'Are you suggesting what I think you are?'

'Mr Hu offers a window into parallel universes: people smuggling, sex-slave trade, internet child porn, a who's who of paedophiles in prominent places. He's done some serious research – mostly with a profit motive, unfortunately.'

'What's in the file?'

'Hard copy. Print-outs, downloads, discs, lists: a map of the multiverse. And this.' He slipped a disc from the file and held it up.

'And that is?'

'A piece of software that will put you in touch with our little man in his computer. After you obtain a warrant, of course.'

She ignored the coy sarcasm and shook her head gently at the inevitability of his thoroughness. 'Still using braces and a belt, I see. A bit of Hollywood tape these days as well? Which reminds me: the Thai women, where are they?'

'In a safe place.'

'Of course.'

'Of course.'

'And we're talking about immunity?'

'And about permanent residence.'

Her laugh was a sardonic grunt. 'Even if it's possible, you know I haven't authority to negotiate anything like that.'

'Darrell has.'

'Darrell's not here.'

He smiled. 'In my fevered imagination this is what happened, Jac: Darrell told you to meet me, evaluate this material and report to him. You didn't want to meet me, so you rang the Garden to change the appointment, not my private number, which I know you have. That way you could avoid talking to me. You left someone here to collect this if I turned up at one.' He paused for her reaction. She offered none. 'The thing is, Jac, this is good stuff, but you need these ladies to nail him down. They aren't going to turn anyone over if they're afraid they'll be sent back home. They're not suicidal. Darrell will arrange things and then I'll make the introductions. They'll have a good lawyer.' He stopped suddenly and studied her. 'To be honest, Jac, I would have respected your sentiments, and dropped the file off at one – and I'm happy to leave it with you to peruse at leisure – but there's something else …'

'*Your* price,' she said. She felt smugness stretch her lips. 'The immunity you want applies to someone else.'

He washed her with an appraising smile, a sad smile. 'Sharp as ever, Jac. You'd have made a good Homicide cop – you and Harpo – if I hadn't stuffed things up for you.'

'It's water under the bridge,' she said, tiredly. 'You stuffed things for yourself too. I wonder what you think about that now?'

'We're all expendable.'

'Then there's no point to apologies and regrets, is there?' The glimpse his words allowed of the ruthlessness, which you could forget too easily in his company, had put an edge on her rejoinder. 'Who's your candidate for immunity?' she added brusquely.

'Her name may never come up, but …'

'Her?'

'Sharon Kitchen.'

'Oh, Jesus Christ. You did all this,' she slapped the file, 'for that slut?'

She glared at him like an exasperated matron. He said nothing. Nor did he look contrite.

'Darrell would expedite your application to the AFP – if you applied. You know that. And you persist in playing games in the gutter like the miscegenate issue of Ned Kelly and a Boy Scout.'

'Even if I signed on, Darrell would want me to stay in the gutter; that's my value to him.' He pointed his nose at the file. 'Look at the intelligence that just falls in my lap.' His smile was wry, resigned; he lifted his shoulders and dropped them. 'But, our agendas – Dazza's and mine – diverge, radically.' His eyebrow arched. 'I didn't think you'd want me as a colleague?'

'Oh *please*, join us. It'll guarantee I'll see a damn sight less of you than I do now.'

He chuckled, then sobered. 'Slut or not, Sharon is a mother with four kids; her immunity is the trade-off. And I have an obligation.'

'You had an obligation to us.' She regretted the words as soon as they were uttered. They sounded carping. And she realised instantly how he might misread them. 'To Carol and me,' she qualified.

'Unfortunately, I had a conflicting and more pressing obligation.' He stood, looped the backpack over his shoulder and turned toward the door.

'You're leaving this?' she said incredulously. 'Without something signed in blood?'

'I have absolute faith in you, Jac.' He smiled with those candid blue eyes.

'Fuck you, David.' As he tugged the door open she said, 'Why didn't you handle this yourself?'

'It would be best if you handled it, Jac. You can tender mercy with justice: you have the resources of the state. Mercy's a luxury in the justice I can afford.'

'I … I heard about the Counsel for the Defence,' she said hastily. 'Carol told me.' Her eyes got a monkey grip on his. 'I do … appreciate … the full cost. Of your obligations.'

His eyelid snapped a resigned, conspiratorial wink and the door closed quietly on his absence.

For a span of time she neglected to measure, she stared through the fat file to a place far beyond it. Then her eyes drifted to the water-stain on the wall: verdigris, rust and efflorescence. It could be Tierra Del Fuego.

49

A misty rain was washing like smoke through a canyon when the boss left the building that housed the Australian Federal Police in Victoria. Ernie, snug in a heated capsule, watched as he sheltered in the doorway to pull a waterproof of some kind from his backpack and slip it on. He was probably going to catch a tram home. Ernie's head shook in bemused mystification. 'Shook' is not the appropriate description: it moved back and forth above his collar like the dome of a Dalek. In Ernie's humble opinion the boss didn't travel the way a man in his position was supposed to. He should be chauffeured around in a fucking BMW or, at the very least, a Toorak tractor – with minder muscle (Ernie) in the front seat. But then the boss didn't do anything the way he was supposed to, and he was still alive, so if it works why fix it?

Ernie did another Dalek to check the road was clear: it wasn't. As he waited for a gap in traffic his thick, blunt fingers on the wheel tapped a tune its composer would never recognise, then he swung out of the loading zone in a wide U. A strident bleat of horns bounced by his ears like peanut shells. Get fucked, Ernie acknowledged with mute affection.

For a moment he thought he'd lost the boss, but then he saw him crossing to the safety island at the next tram stop. Ernie felt the satisfying warm fizz of knowing someone – at least enough.

The intersection lights changed to red. He stopped behind a taxi, activated his window and thrust his head into the drizzle.

'Hey, Boss!'

The boss was waiting for some women and an old fart to get aboard a rattler that had been painted to look like a full colour magazine layout. His eyes flicked away from the queue, along the line of vehicles to the source of the cry. He vaulted the safety barrier and threaded his way to the passenger door of the car.

'This is fortuitous,' he said as he fastened his seat belt. 'Or were you looking for me?'

'Charlotte,' said Ernie by way of explanation.

'Is there a problem?' asked his boss, who could read between his absent lines.

'Dunno.' The light changed. 'You goin' home?' There was an affirmative. The car surged smoothly across the intersection. 'Just reportin'. Slept in, di'n' I.'

'Uncharacteristic, Digger.'

'They're keepin' late hours.' His normal flat delivery had a pucker. It sounded like prudish disapproval in his ears. He wondered if the boss picked it up. Of course he fuckin' did.

'How many nights is it now?'

'Three – not countin' first contact – two in succession.'

'Where do they go? His place or hers?'

'Neither.'

There was no response but Ernie visualised blue spots of light near his ear. His head pivoted. He met the waiting eyes. 'They meet at that bar an' go to clubs an' dance an' stuff. Fuckin' casino last night.'

'They got a room?'

'Nah. They stay up till sparrow's fart.'

'Not even a nightcap?'

'If they're shaggin', I don't know how. He drops her off at 'er car.'

There was silence. Ernie twisted his head. The boss had gone to that place in his head again. 'Sumpin' wrong?'

'Is there a chance that he knows where she's living?'

Ernie's thick coat pumped to his ears and back like the action on a sawn off shotgun. 'She mightta told 'im, but she ain't showed 'im.'

Silence again.

'What?' he said. He felt a prickling of anxiety. He'd missed something?

'It's okay,' the boss said from that other place. 'It's what I would do.'

Ernie was confused momentarily. Who was the boss referring to: him or the woman? He realised it had to be her. 'Whaddaya think she's up to?'

When there was no answer he glanced across. The boss was writing on the back of one of his cards. When he finished he reached over and tucked the card between Ernie's thumb and forefinger where they gripped the wheel. 'If they go to that address I have to know immediately, Digger.'

'What is it?' he asked as he slipped the card in his pocket.

'It's where best-laid schemes gang aft a-gley.'

When the boss went oblique on him Ernie took the hint. The drizzle, at least, was clearing. He turned the wipers off.

'There's another thing,' he said eventually. 'Someone's watchin'.'

'Shane's told me and so has Boof. I wouldn't worry about it. They're just new and keen.'

Now Ernie was confused. 'How the fuck would they know about …? Um, I think we're talkin' about two different things, Boss.'

'Ah. You mean we aren't the only uninvited guests at Constable Porter's party?' Ernie grunted assent. 'Are they aware of you?'

'Bo-o-oss,' he admonished.

'My apologies, Digger. Carol Marks?'

'No sign of the sarge's missus.'

'Anyone we know?'

Ernie tapped the glove box. The boss took a digital camera from it and began to scroll through the images on it. If he recognised a face he made no sign.

'She's a bright girl ...'

'Fuckin' bobby dazzler.' The fault line of his smile forced a path across his jaw.

'... and a trained cop. It could be backup.'

'Who she know around here she could use?'

'Carol Marks could organise it. And she'd make sure it was someone we wouldn't tag easily.' Ernie gave a neutral grunt. 'I take it you've put a watcher on the watcher?' Ernie Duggs's smooth turret swivelled. 'Of course,' said his boss, smiling.

An inverted Y pressed into the smooth, tight flesh above Ernie's brow. 'This other thing? 'S there a stalker at the Garden?'

'Don't worry about it. He'll either materialise at reception or fade away. Just another tourist.'

50

He was nervous. He was excited: even a little bilious. This was his debut. This was the beginning of the rest of his life: his real life, his *professional* life, not the false start of his birth. When he completed his mission he'd be on a whole new level of the game. He'd be in *the* game not *a* game. Out of the arcade and on the street. Toecutters would surrender their place to him when he bellied up to the bar.

Secure in his fastness of shadow, he checked the object in his hand again.

It was a lovely thing, blue-black, gleaming with a dull lustre in the fish-belly light like the scales of a snake. He'd touched a snake once; it had moved under his fingertips, the frisson was exquisite. So was the touch of the gun. He'd stripped it, cleaned it, oiled it and polished it in the days leading up to this moment of truth, many times. He'd made – no, crafted – the silencer himself from a design he found on the web. He'd toiled on it in his dad's old shed – where his mother didn't venture, even when the old man was alive – measuring, cutting, grinding under the silent approval of disciplined ranks of alert and burnished tools. He'd tested it out in the bush: fired into the fat bodies of trees, the perfume of each explosion entwined lacily with eucalyptus. It wasn't silent, but it didn't sound like a gunshot. It sounded like a sneeze in a drainpipe. He was very proud of his work. By just thinking about it he was suffused with professional effulgence.

He slipped the gun into his jacket. His jacket was long with deep pockets, deep enough to accommodate the modified weapon. The jacket was bulky, not the best if he needed to get the gun in a hurry; but he wouldn't need to get the gun in a hurry. It would be snug in his gloved hand close to his thigh, shrouded in the folds of the jacket, as he walked up to his victim and popped him – just like that. Too easy. He was a little disappointed that it was so easy. He had pictured his initiation as a blazing gun battle à la John Woo.

It was a cold night, cloudless but no moon. His jacket was dark. His gloves were soft Italian leather, kid-skin, black, expensive. Women's gloves, large size. They fit like a second skin – fine, elastic, excellent grip, and warm. It wouldn't do to have fingers stiff and clumsy from the cold. He had spent the down payment on the job on these little refinements – you gonna do sumpin', do it proper, his dad would say.

Ski mask rolled up like a beanie, dark jeans, soft soles with plenty of tread: he'd prepared well. He'd studied his target for a few days and knew his routine. Everything was perfect, even his prey was cooperating in his own assassination. The poor bastard left his car on a quiet one-way street, bordered by houses with narrow but leafy front gardens and faced by a small, heavily-treed park. At one end the streetlight was out, and at the other end overhanging trees from the park blocked light from three-quarters of the street. The target's car sat around about the middle. Perfect.

It was a classic set-up: he'd wait until the target emerged, around midnight usually; he'd walk ahead of him so he didn't suspect that he was being stalked; he'd pass the target's car, step through the gap between it and the next car as if approaching the door of his own vehicle; then, as the target climbed behind the wheel, while most vulnerable, isolated in a bubble of light, he'd walk up and, pop pop, ruin the upholstery. He felt his cock stir at the thought. He'd shoot him in the eye and the soft .22 calibre pellet would bounce around in his skull until his brain was baby food. He frowned at the brothel across the road. He felt his flesh harden and press against fourteen-ounce denim. If he was the type that had anything to do with women like that, he would come back after he finished the job and pork those sluts until they sizzled like shish kebab.

Hey, wait a minute: that was an idea. That would be an ace alibi. Not that he needed one: there was no way he could be connected to his target.

Didn't know him from Adam, but, you gonna do sumpin', do it proper. There'd be no way anyone would suspect him of bumping the boss – pimp or madam or whatever his title – then visiting his whorehouse. No way. And that wouldn't be paying for sex with filthy slags, that would be clever, professional strategy. It would be a wise business investment. And he could afford it.

That had surprised him – the amount he was paid. He hadn't expected that much for his first contract. He'd been prepared to discount his fee until he'd made his reputation and could demand top dollar. Of course the woman didn't know that – or that it was his first job. Still, she must hate this bloke's guts. Or maybe it was her first time and she didn't know the going rate any more than he did – probably that. Maybe she was some rich bitch with more brass than sense – didn't sound like money though. Then again, maybe this bastard was some sort of big deal. Fuck, that'd be totally great. The story could be all over the papers and TV. Yeah, good thing he'd decided to play safe and use the brothel to bolster his alibi. Shit, and they were whores, weren't they? And he was paying. There's all sorts of stuff he could make them do. His knob hurt, it was pressing against his belt buckle. He looked at his watch – shouldn't be long.

He wondered now, for the first time, about the identity of his victim. He might be someone important, but it didn't matter, he ran a brothel, he was still scum and probably deserved what he was going to get. That made the whole thing even better. He was cleaning up the environment and getting paid for it. His hand moved up and down in his pocket, his fingers encouraged his flesh, the contours of the gun brushed his knuckles.

Yeah, he was scum. The man was always alone, probably had no friends. A moth of panic fluttered through his intestines. If the target hadn't left the brothel with anyone before, there was a greater statistical probability he would tonight. Jesus! No, there he is. Shit, there's a woman with him. Jesus! No, no, she's not wearing a coat. She's going back inside, one of his harlots. Fucken excellent.

He hesitated until he was sure it was his target. The man paused under a streetlight to pull a glove on each hand. That was him: tall, blond, moving in a relaxed long-legged stroll, a dead man walking the other pavement. He abandoned the shadows and reached the intersection where his target habitually crossed at the same time as it arrived at the opposite corner. He turned left into the adjoining street and this placed his prey about the width of a city road behind him – just right. He resisted the temptation to look back. The night was crisp and hollow, footsteps had the clarity of bells. He paced himself to match the sound, tracking his prey blindly like a U-boat. As he crossed to enter the street where the car was parked, he took an opportunity for a quick peek. He was gratified to see the distance had barely altered. Houses bordered the park along the street he was leaving, so he knew his man couldn't cut the corner. Perfect.

As they approached the scene of the crime-to-be his head echoed with the beat of footfall and his heart syncopated the rhythm. He drew level with the target's car and his body began to quiver with anticipation. He reached the space between its nose and the rear of the next car and swerved to pass through. To the unsuspecting it would appear as if the next car was his. He withstood the urge to check that his quarry kept to the choreography. He stopped at the driver's door groping for the gun in his pocket as if for his keys. He glanced casually to his left – as one would – and received a shock.

The tall blond man was standing at the driver's door *two* cars back. Somehow he'd mistaken the car or, in his hyped state, miscalculated and gone one car too far. It meant he was further away than planned when the target opened his door; but it was a minor glitch. He'd just have to move faster.

The target was fussing with his keys. For fuck's sake, why didn't he open up and get in? He knew he could stand there like a faggot in a public dunny for only a few more seconds before raising suspicion. Then he had a minor secular epiphany: the flip side of this was an opportunity. While his prey was engrossed with the drama of his keys he'd stroll over and do him. In his pocket his fingers embraced the grip of the gun and he began walking victim-wards. At the driver's door of the car between he paused when he realised he'd attracted the man's attention. He turned toward the car to shield the action and began drawing the gun from his pocket, saying, 'All these bloody cars look alike.'

That was when the car beside him woke up. Its lights flashed and it gave a perky electronic cry of arousal. He hopped to the side, the weapon in his hand pointing in reflex at the vehicle, exposed. Too late, he understood this was the target's car. The gun ejaculated prematurely as he swung it around, wrist jarring, arm jumping with the recoil. The tall figure was no longer silhouetted against the dim wash of light at the end of the street. It flashed through his mind that he'd dived for cover behind the car. Then he saw the low shadow in shadow boiling toward him. A horrible possibility dawned.

He was in one of his bad dreams now, one of those that unfold in a crystal atmosphere denser than porridge. As he waited for his left hand to sweep ponderously to join the right in a two-hand grip he watched his target dive to the road a few feet away. Automatically his feet sought the stance, but they moved in syrup. He pulled the barrel of the gun down on his target. It was as stubborn as the second hand on a Swiss clock. He fired, and heard the bronchial cough of the suppressor and distant whine of a ricochet: echoes from an abyss. The target was closing, rolling toward him in a lazy somersault. He strained on the recalcitrant weapon dragging the barrel down, down through jellied nightmare air. He squeezed the trigger again. The flash, when it eventually came, lit the target's face as it came over, up from the bottom of the roll. He listened to the bullet push protesting space aside, bounce off the bitumen and spin down the road, and watched the face it failed to find rise moon-like to his. He saw cold will in blue eyes, and the man burst like a bottlenose dolphin through the triangular hoop of his arms. Energy cupped like an offering in the man's palms exploded under his jaw and he was looking at the sky.

Indigo velvet.

Pinpricks in the fabric winked at life after the universe. And through one he fell.

He didn't hear the gun clatter off the hood of the car onto the nature strip. He didn't see his target kneel beside him, didn't hear him swear softly, then rise, casually strafe the sleeping neighbourhood with his gaze, retrieve the cherished weapon and toss it in the car.

Propped on his arms, the tall man leaned back on the bonnet of his car and gazed up at the perforations in the sky. His chest rose and fell.

In the ink blot staining the base of a Moreton Bay Fig a man removed night-vision goggles and began to disassemble an Armalite sniper's rifle. He placed the components in snug silhouettes hollowed for each in a slim black case open at his feet; that done, he left the shadow, stepped from the fringe of the park and out onto the road. He was thickset, trim, with steel grey, short-cropped hair, taut posture and spare gesture.

'All things considered,' he said. 'I think that went well.'

'Less than perfect,' said the man leaning against the car.

'Well your reactions were a mite slow, old son, and the forward roll was only a six point five.' He sat the gun case on the bonnet of the car. 'Swap the gymnastics for the ballistics next time?'

'Maybe – if I'm threatened by a barn, and you don't have arthritis.'

'Don't knock arthritis, it keeps me out of trouble.' He squatted, with a theatrical groan, beside the supine hitman, tugged a glove from his left hand and pressed two fingers to the neck below the ear. 'Oh, I see why you're less than pleased with your performance.' He lifted the head and rotated it. There was a sound like Rice Bubbles rattling against bone china. 'Broken neck.'

'Fear and adrenalin,' said the other, as a latecomer might say 'heavy traffic'. 'Backup?'

An emphatic shake of the head.

'Amateur.'

'Professional enough to wait for a headshot, or you might not be alive to cast such slurs.'

'I'm alive because you taught me well, Obi Wan.'

'Obi Wan is jealous.'

'Jealous?'

'I've always wanted to do that.'

'Do …? You've never *done* it?'

'It's a manoeuvre that demands certain conditions for success, which, in the mayhem of battle, seldom occur. They were perfect tonight.'

'My eternal gratitude to the evening.' Uttered with a five-G irony.

'Don't worry, if *you'd* fumbled or frozen, *I'd* have shot him. Boys with guns count on you running or freezing.'

'Was he old enough to count?' He sighed. 'Any identification?'

The older man slipped his hand back in his glove. 'Did he shit his pants or is that you?' he asked, sustaining the banter as his hands dipped in and out of the dead man's clothing.

'If it smells like vindaloo it's me.'

'You ate curry *tonight*?'

'It might have been my last meal.' He pushed himself from the car and dropped to his haunches beside the older man. 'It's Church?'

'One Carroll – Jesus, what we saddle our kids with – Christian Church,' he read from a driver's licence with the aid of a keyring light.

'We should have spanked him and sent him home as soon as he was spotted.'

'No history of violence, no criminal connections. He was in a pistol club – so what? We had to wait till he acted. Don't knock yourself about over this. I watched the little prick tonight: thought he was tugging the slug. But it *was* a gun in his pocket, and he was *very* glad to see you.' One hand gripped the younger man's shoulder briefly. 'An embryo Whitey.' Shoulders rose and fell. 'An abortion that's all.' He shot a quick glance past the other, whose head swivelled in reflex. A car was turning into the street.

'Put him in coma position,' said the younger man as light cast them in stark relief. He stood and removed his jacket, passing it to the other as he turned to the approaching vehicle.

The car hopped jerkily then nosed forward slowly. The young man smiled benignly into high-beam glare. It drew alongside and a tinted window descended on the passenger side. A woman's face was unveiled, eyes dilated with a cocktail of trepidation and anticipation.

Her gaze fixed on the corpse. It looked like a man sleeping peacefully on the road. 'Has there been an accident?' she said, somewhere between querulous and curious.

The young man blocked her view as he approached and stooped to her eye level. An exhalation she had been unaware of suppressing escaped when she saw the candid blue eyes and tousled sandy hair of an urchin underlined warmly by a smile. 'You're good Samaritans,' he said. 'But thanks, everything's under control.'

'Is he drunk?' asked the driver, rubbernecking above the wheel.

'No, he's epileptic,' said the nice young man. 'Overdid it a bit tonight and had a small seizure.'

'Oh, poor dear,' said the woman. 'Should we call an ambulance? We live just a few doors down.'

'No, thanks very much,' big smile, 'but that's not necessary. We're used to looking after him. He'll be okay in a couple of minutes, then we'll get him into the car and home to bed.'

'Are you sure? You could bring him to the house. I could make a cup of tea …?'

The driver was tugging the sleeve of her coat. 'They know what they're doing, Marge. We're just holding them up.' He started the car rolling. 'Good luck, young fella. I hope your friend feels better in the morning. Make him take his medication. Some of 'em are a bit slack on that, y'know?'

'Oh Wayne, I feel like we should …'

'I was a safety officer at Tippets, Marge. I did first aid – remember? I know this stuff. They're doin' all you …' and instructions on the management of epileptic seizures were guillotined by the window.

'Jesus, I had boyish charm once, I coulda done that,' said the epileptic's grey nurse. 'We have a disposal problem. Maybe you can flash that grin at ER and they'll swallow your crap too.'

'Be nice if there were places of precipitous elevation within plausible range of Mr Church's domicile, where he might pull over for a pee and fall and break his neck,' the urchin said as he watched the car fade into a driveway. 'Shame he lives out west.'

The other waggled Church's licence between two fingers. 'Could be worse.'

'Yeah: Geelong. Let's move him before we have a lividity problem.'

The body was buckled securely in the rear seat. 'Where did he leave his car?' asked the younger man.

'Other side of the park. I've got his keys.'

A few minutes later their car stopped behind Carroll Christian Church's '94 Hyundai. The Melways was consulted and a likely location was identified. As his passenger climbed out the younger man said, 'Don't touch anything you don't have to, make sure your shoes are clean and don't remove your gloves.'

'Sir! Yes, Sir!' The older man saluted.

The other's gaze alighted briefly and sombrely on the mortal remains in the rear seat. 'I suppose it wasn't a total disaster, Hutch. We delivered him from evil.'

'David old son, we philosophers in the SAS had a saying: if you call up death, expect death to answer.'

'Can you get that on bumper stickers?' said David Edge.

51

'Nice,' said Carol Marks as she stepped across the threshold. 'How did you find this?'

'A friend of my sister,' said Carol Porter. 'They worked together in Perth before he was transferred to Melbourne.' She tagged behind Carol Marks as she stickybeaked from room to room.

Except for a pinkish beige and an almost yellowless yellow, the décor was black, white and numerous greys. Stripes – horizontal, vertical, oblique, sometimes zigging sometimes zagging – harassed the solid and spatial geometry of every room. The furniture, velvety slabs and wedges of cream cheese, was accented by a bar here, a chevron there. Spare, but strategic, horizontal surfaces were colonised by anthropomorphic objects: souvenirs of exotic travel, perhaps. Many had three lower extremities, one generally raised in a high kick.

'He's gay …'

'No kidding.'

'And he thinks he's met Mr Right. At present they're on a trial … conjugation? Mr Right's apartment is much larger – and there's a pool – but Neil doesn't want to give this place up until he's sure they're domestically compatible.'

'Mondrian meets the African Queen,' said Carol Marks. She glanced sideways at Carol Porter. 'That quip, I take it, isn't original.'

Carol gestured at the wall above the Neufchatel bed. 'Neil took Kate and Bogey with him. Coffee?'

'Ta.'

Carol Marks sat in a dairy product chair. At her elbow on a polished grey marbled block was an ebony figure that gave new meaning to looking oneself in the eye.

'What's going on, Carol?' she said when the coffee tray sat on the low black glass table between them and they were sipping from white porcelain.

Carol Porter's eyes widened over the rim in innocent puzzlement.

Carol Marks mimicked her and said nothing. When her prolonged silence failed to draw her young namesake she relented. 'I can't believe you've suddenly lost interest in this business, yet I haven't heard from you in days.'

'You said that you had an earlier obligation to take care of.'

'I also said it would take one or two days at the most.'

She watched Carol Porter, moving with deliberate precision, take two sips of her coffee then lean over the table and place her cup on its saucer before she replied: 'We've gone about as far as we can, haven't we? I mean, without the sanction of the law to … um, persuade people to answer our questions. The people we need to talk to now will just tell us to pull our heads in as soon as we broach the subject.'

'The "cold case" ploy has worked so far. No one has queried our authority.'

'If we're right, those remaining have the most to lose. They'll ask what new evidence we have to warrant reopening the case. Even if we bluff, and it works, they'll lawyer up and we'll be stuffed.'

'If they do that we can be pretty confident we're on the right track.'

Carol Porter was wearing a WA Police windcheater over jeans. She shrugged then hitched up each sleeve in turn. Without raising her bum from her chair she stooped over the table and picked up her cup between thumb and forefinger.

Carol Marks studied her openly, then said, 'I'd accept that anyone else might have lost the ticker for a speculative undertaking like this – but not you. What's really going on?'

'I have to be back in Broome in three days. Time's run out – that's all.'

'Oh, bullshit!' Carol Marks slammed her spine into the soft cushions of the chair. They were surprisingly soft for something with such sharp edges. 'Look, I like you,' she said after a heavy silence during which both avoided eye contact. 'I flattered myself that you liked me. This is about confidence. You don't trust me anymore. Why?'

'Those women at the funeral knew too much.'

Carol Marks shook her head.

'They had to,' Carol Porter persisted. 'Why be so belligerent if they didn't think I was some sort of threat? What did you tell them?'

'Nothing.' Carol Marks leaned forward and studied her fingers folded on her knees. They opened and closed. She sighed. 'Look,' she said. 'David's relationship with those women is … unusual – for a … a context like that. He really looks after them. And they get very … protective of him. And … well,' she paused. 'David knows.'

'You told him.'

'No.' The utterance was as hard and dense as fact. She nursed her coffee tightly, wary of spotting the spotless.

'Harry Keyes. He must have told Edge and then was sent to warn me off.'

'I doubt it. Harry is no man's messenger boy. And I think he's as interested as we are in some sort of closure on this.'

'Interested in keeping his reputation intact. Interested in keeping a lid on police stuff-ups on his watch.' She took a deep breath. 'They decided to red-light a murder investigation, and green-light an operation that would earn more Brownie points … with …someone.'

Carol Marks shook her head emphatically. 'Those sorts of decisions about priorities are made every day. Why would it bother him now? He's retired: it can't affect his career. No, Harry has a very Catholic conscience. It's guilt that bothers Harry, not shame. He wants this brought to light for personal reasons. And he knows better than most that any evidence that connected Poynter and Barker and the person who wanted those girls dead is long gone, so there'll never be official action.'

'It's long gone because they used it as barter. Suppression of evidence connecting Barker, Poynter and Mr X was the price of entry to Barker's club.'

Carol Marks nodded and cut in hurriedly. 'True, but at the time, Harry had every reason to believe that it was an investment, and the conspirators in the murders would be included in the returns when they got Barker. He may regret it now, but I don't think that's what's pricking his conscience.'

'Well, it doesn't matter. As long as it wasn't you that told Edge.' Her eyes lowered as she took a sip of coffee, then dark copper lashes slowly unveiled her emerald gaze. 'How do you know he knows?'

Carol Marks grinned apologetically. 'He told me. He was at the cemetery the day of the funeral. He wanted me to dissuade you.' Her words were met by a level stare. 'He's my friend, Carol. He doesn't want to harm us. He's afraid we'll stir something up that might have … ah, um, unfortunate consequences.'

'You believe him?'

'What is he risking? Barker's dead, Poynter's dead, he's not talking. The only chance we have is to get a confession from the person who paid Poynter. But …' She shrugged and watched with a sly smile. 'You want to pack your bat and ball and go home.'

Carol Porter turned her face away from the scrutiny and let her eyes rest blankly on the grey-wash painting that almost covered one wall. It had a black smear like the tide line on a bath creeping along the bottom and a fat pink stain the colour of mould on sour cream just left of centre. It looked like sweet corruption: the kind that seethes with life, the kind the world can't do without, the kind that is almost beautiful. Depending where you stand.

'I went to Poynter's place in the Otways,' she said when she turned back. 'I spoke to the cop that found his mother's body. Did you know David Edge was there – solo? That he took physical evidence away from the house? Including Poynter's loot.'

'I didn't know much of what David was doing by that time.'

'I think it's safe to assume that it was delivered to Jack Barker. And Barker kept what was harmless or useful and destroyed the rest. Or Edge used it to control Barker.'

Carol Marks was looking at her friend with open compassion now. 'You wanted to vindicate David, didn't you? But, every fact you turn over damns him more. Is that why you're tossing it in?'

Carol Porter didn't reply. Her attention had drifted back to the painting.

'What set you off on this?' said Carol Marks after a while.

The face that floated back from regard of the painting had a wan smile. 'Have you ever fallen in love with a character in a novel?'

'All the time.' A soft chuckle. 'But you know what they say about what we take from what we read?'

'I know, I know, probably only what we take *to* it. I'm as much to blame as the author.' She grinned weakly. 'You fall in love with them because they're what you want to be. When he crossed my path he wasn't a policeman anymore – some said he was the antithesis – but he was still a Cop. Know what I mean? That's what I wanted to be: a Cop with a capital C.'

Carol Marks gazed into her cup, her head slowly bobbing, and swirled the dregs in the bottom making random patterns. 'Back to my original question: what's really going on?' she asked softly.

'I've been watching Simon Castleman,' Carol admitted reluctantly. 'Where he goes, who he talks to.'

'Ha! I thought so!' There was triumph in her voice. Then there was mild alarm. 'You haven't approached him?'

'No, of course not.'

Carol Marks studied her, with a modicum of suspicion. 'Good. Let's do it tomorrow. I'll ring his office, do my cold case act, and arrange an appointment.'

'Day after would be better for me.' Carol Porter smiled apologetically. 'This time *I* have a prior engagement.'

52

Sharon Kitchen hadn't slept well since the funeral. She'd hardly slept since Ben was shot. She thought she would find rest when he finally did. But she didn't. On her rack in the dungeon depths of night she felt doom gathering around her house. It blanketed doors and windows, buzzing like wasps.

The luminous display on her clock radio glowed twelve forty-three.

She would get up and have a hot shower. For a while she could wash her cares and sins away. Even if they sucked back and clung like bacteria as soon as her foot touched the bathmat, the hot deluge would relax her physically. That's what she'd do: she would get up and have a hot shower.

Eventually she did.

She was towelling herself off, rubbing her hair vigorously. She'd decided to stay brunette – she was a brunette after all – just enough dye to hide the grey. There'd be more of that now. She was towelling herself off when she heard the noise.

Even though it wasn't the direction of the sound, she glanced sharply at the sweating window. She pulled the towel slowly away from her ears. It was her only movement. Her blood was being thrust into her head in hot gushes by a pounding heart. She struggled to hear what she heard (or thought she heard). Adrenalin was cooking into anger – those bloody kids. One of them had snuck out and turned on the TV. She was still frozen in the pose. The sound was soft and metallic. It sounded like voices, but voices in a box. The silly little buggers. Her bedroom was the closest to the television, her door opened directly onto the living room. What made them think they could get away with it? Of course she had no idea how many late night sessions she might have slept through in blissful ignorance in the past – when she did sleep.

She finished drying her hair, made a turban of the towel, wrapped her thick bathrobe around her and switched off the overhead light-cum-heater-cum-fan thingy. As she closed the bathroom door behind her she could see the swamp-light glow leaking through the living-room doorway. Little bugger – or buggers. Her mind was occupied trying to guess which little bugger – or buggers – it might be as she approached the living room on tiptoe. She was going to give them the shock of their short lives.

The living room was a flickering aquarium and her eye was distracted initially by the screen. An old movie was showing. A beautiful woman was trying to justify her transgressions to a badly wounded man with a gun. 'Lady,' he said apologetically, 'I don't have the time.' And shot her.

There was something familiar about it.

It was one of Ben's old favourites. She thought she'd got rid of those old tapes of his. The little buggers must have kept some. Her face swung towards the viewer sunk in the big fat armchair. And that's when her heart lodged against her soft palate and conspired to rob her of oxygen.

The wasps had found the gap under the door.

'We were an unlikely pair: Ben and I,' her intruder said. He pressed a button on the video remote and the sound muted but the image rolled on. 'What on earth could two characters as disparate as us have to talk about? I know my copper colleagues were puzzled. I'm sure you wondered from time to time.'

Sharon was gulping her fear down in choking lumps, trying to breathe, trying to speak around it. 'Y ... yo ... you ... you? You! You fu ... fuc ... fucking ... What wha ... what ...'

'It's okay, Shaz, it's an impertinence. You can vent your – quite justifiable – spleen. I've taken the precaution of closing the kids' doors, as well as the door to the hall.' He turned slightly in the chair without uncrossing his legs and gestured over his shoulder. 'See? But use some restraint.'

Sharon's voice dropped in volume instantly. What's the matter with me? I should be screaming blue murder: the thought that stumbled after the reflex.

'There it is,' he was continuing as if there'd been no hiatus. His hand brushed towards the screen and fell back in his lap: the host of Armchair Theatre. 'Old movies. That's *The Killers* – Don Seigel's version. It's the end. Almost everyone's dead by now. I was just flipping through while I waited for you to finish your shower.'

'Thank God it isn't *Psycho*,' she said.

He chuckled. 'You're sweeter than fiction, Shaz: the living embodiment of the hard-boiled femme fatale.'

'You're not going to kill me under the same roof as sleeping kids,' she said with more confidence than she felt.

He studied her with the detached familiarity a scientist might regard a favourite lab specimen. 'No, I'd never do that,' he said.

She took a deep breath. 'You wanna take the kids, don't you? You think I'm a rotten mother.' There, it was out, stated: her fear and her challenge.

He may have looked surprised. It was hard to tell in this light. It was hard to tell in any light. 'Quite the contrary, I think you're a good mother. A tad primeval. Most mothers these days don't kill to protect the nest – or mate to that purpose. Or dabble in the slave trade.'

She had been standing, bathrobe tugged tightly, trying to maintain some authority, some high ground, moral or not. Now she slumped and seemed to pile on the couch like hip-hop laundry. 'Sneaky Fokker,' she sighed.

'Amongst many others,' he agreed. 'But Carl was just a decoy. He was there to be seen. He had no idea what it was all about.'

Sharon pressed her fingers to her temples and said, 'Shit!' into her chest, when she saw how she had been manipulated. 'You knew I knew you were comin' and turned it against me.'

'You're intelligent and tough, Sharon, but you have a fatal flaw: you think you're smarter than any man – which may be true – but you tend to hold your own sex in contempt as well. Your sisters stalked you. We came up on your blind side.'

She sank into the corner of the couch. She was a crippled canary caught in a corner of the cage; the cat could preen and pounce at will.

'Do you want part of the action?' she said with faint hope. Or all of it, she thought.

He chuckled over there in the glaucous light. The DVD had finished but the TV was still on. 'No,' he said.

'What're you gonna do to me?'

'I'm going to break your heart.'

Her brow knitted in puzzlement. Then she felt the skin on her skull tighten as a possible meaning slithered across her mind.

'Remember when we met, Shaz?'

She nodded, afraid to trust her voice to any utterance.

'The bloke who killed your drug dealer? He confessed but he was very confused about why he did it. The dealer was a bad man, he said. Seemed to be his only reason. He couldn't explain why he was a bad man. He had no motive – not in the legal sense. In fact we couldn't connect him to his victim in any way other than the fact that he killed him. He said he didn't mean to kill, just punish him; for what, he didn't seem to know. Of course he never went to trial: diminished responsibility. He was sent to a place where he could be cared for and has probably been happy there.'

'What has this got to do …'

'Hear me out,' he said, affably. 'The case was closed, officially, but you know me: anal retentive, daggy ends annoy. I looked into his history. He'd beaten the hell out of someone once before, in a little town up north. The same little town you were born, according to your record.'

'If you knew this, why wasn't I arrested?'

'We had a crime and we had a culprit. I was the new boy. I was told to invest my enthusiasm in more important investigations. But I did ask him a few more questions. He wouldn't budge. He'd clam up and say nothing: not a peep, if your name was mentioned. And it was self-defence – of a sort. At the time, it was reasonable to assume you would never need to resort to something like that again, so I dropped it. Of course,' he added, cat to canary, 'times change.'

Now he had her attention.

'Did you know his name?'

'What? Who ...'

His hand flicked from his lap and a package bounced on the couch near her thigh. She flinched and stared at it as if it was alive and venomous.

'Carroll Christian Church,' he said. 'So many carols in my life and over one hundred and fifty shopping days to Christmas.' His tone of voice, the rhythm of his words, his demeanour didn't change. She could never tell when he was joking. 'That was in his car. I don't think he spent any. Fifteen hundred. He was ripping you off; he was a virgin. Put it to some good use – like the kids' education.'

'David ... I ... I ...'

He raised his hand and she swallowed the words fluttering in her throat – whatever they were going to be. 'Forgive me for the tedious exposition, but we need to know where we stand. We're renegotiating a relationship here, Sharon.'

'Relationship?' She'd heard of blood running cold – who hadn't? It was a cliché. Now she felt the intravenous fact.

'Ben asked me to keep an eye on you ...'

She had refused to accept this since he had first suggested it at the hospital, but it was too – too Ben not to – in the end. 'The silly little bugger ...'

'Not in so many words. Unfortunately.'

'The attorney ... whatchamacallit.'

'That's part of it.' He leaned forward and placed his elbows on his knees. 'The real disparity in our relationship – Ben's and mine – was in Ben's mind. He saw himself as useless, stupid, incapable, and he saw me as his antithesis. We were a yin and yang, a Jekyll and Hyde, of competency. He had so little faith in himself that he couldn't believe I'd carry out his wishes simply because he asked. So he set up a mystery. Sprinkled clues like a paper chase. I couldn't convince myself of this: too far-fetched. At first I thought he'd brought me there that day as a witness. I still think he did. Well, we all want that, don't we: a witness to life's inequities and iniquities, to our finest moments and our final moments?' He looked up with an almost wistful smile. 'Ben had bundled all of his into the one occasion.'

She wanted to stopper his mouth. The more she heard, the more it sounded like Ben and the more condemned she was by the words.

'The scheme was bizarre enough for Ben, but it was far too subtle,' he continued. 'And who, even a simple soul like Ben, would arrange a few vague hints then take his life, with any expectation that his intentions would be carried out? As an explanation of his actions it was implausible. It wasn't until I had done everything he wanted that I realised it had worked just as he must have imagined. Right down to the shielding of Brie from the sight of her father's death. Pure blind luck of course, but all the faith he lacked in himself he invested in me that day.'

There was something like wonder in his voice. Sharon shifted awkwardly, a goat fearful of drawing the tiger's gaze.

'Ben might not have known much, but he knew you and me like the back of his hand. Better than the back of his hand – much better.'

Sharon felt something splash on her hand and realised she was crying.

'The bomb was to get my attention. His death was the key, of course, it was meant to be the first clue – well, the catalyst really – a plea to be taken seriously. I should have seen it – the whole melodrama of the siege.' He gestured toward the blank blue TV screen. 'Do you remember the plot of *The Killers*?'

She shook her head.

'Two hitmen are so puzzled by the stoic way one of their victims dies that they decide to investigate his past to find out why. Did you recognise the actor?'

She shook her head.

'Lee Marvin.'

'Oh ...'

'He played a similar role in *Point Blank*: a thief trying to find some sort of rough justice. In *Prime Cut* he's an enforcer who saves a young girl from the sex-slave trade. You see a picture building? Where Ben might have got his idea from and why he might have thought it would work?'

She was sobbing now, face averted.

'You were Earth to Ben's moon,' she heard him say. 'He was going to spin off into space without you and he knew it.'

'You d-don't understand. I ... I ... it was ... is my last chance. I ... I hadn't forgotten the kids but ... but it was ... it's ...' She couldn't explain it – not to someone like him. Her body sagged forward and her hands covered her face.

'The grand romantic passion?' he said. 'That fabled thing that you stumble across only once in a lifetime – so they say – if at all? So familiar, so inevitable, like two atoms in a vacuum. Seems so right, but even if it's wrong it seems a sin against creation to deny it, doesn't it?'

Her face rose slowly and she stared at him with her lips cracking open and closing silently. Then she said, 'He was so ... so ...'

'So young and beautiful and clever and he wanted you like mother, sister, lover – goddess?' Although he was a watery blur, she could feel him studying her grief-raddled face. 'Ben understood, very well. Or he wouldn't have done what he did,' he said. 'Which brings us to the problem of Mr Hu.'

'Who …?'

'Don't bother, Sharon. It's an old joke.'

That's when she knew she'd run out of rope. It was no use dissembling.

'Ben knew anything he said to you about Lionel Hu would be put down to jealousy or desperation. He obviously thought that would be my reaction too. So he sent me off on a voyage of discovery.'

'Lionel …' she began.

'Lionel is dead to you,' he said.

She didn't hear the last two words. With a sound like a kettle boiling in her gullet she lunged across the space between them. Her fingers were tines aimed at his throat. They found only space and the rest was almost a pleasurable experience; rather, she imagined, like being tossed and twirled in amniotic fluid while your mother completed a gymnastic routine. When the blind rage subsided like the tide, she was stranded flat on the floor with him straddling her hips. Her breasts were heaving, but he showed no sign of exertion. Her turban was unravelled.

'Go on! Fuck me!' she spat. 'You've always wanted to!'

He smiled wearily as he released her wrists and got to his feet. 'I have no doubt that would be a pleasurable experience,' he said. 'But lady, I don't have the time.'

Her eyes flicked toward the TV screen and back to hold his. He reached down, she cringed away, but he grasped her wrist and pulled her to her feet. He tugged the lapels of the bathrobe together across her breasts and stepped back.

'You can't go near Lionel anymore. He's under investigation by state and federal police. By now he is being watched and his phone is tapped. Sneaky Fokker's job was to keep you separated. But you're on your own now. As well as the money, that package contains information about Lionel's activities. The police have the same stuff – and a lot more. If you don't believe what I'm about to tell you, open it. All you need is there.'

She was still trying to keep him, his words, his lies, at bay with the radiance of her searing anger. She wanted to put her hands over her ears, but hugged the bathrobe about her.

'Lionel,' he said, beginning to hammer the nails in her temples, 'is an accessory in at least two murders and a robbery. You know about the illegal prostitution. How many websites does he have?'

'Three,' she said defiantly. 'And they're …'

'Legal? Perhaps. What about the other six?'

'What …?' She gave a weak humourless giggle.

'He has nine – that we uncovered. You know about the chat room and male child porn, I'm sure. You were using that to lure your blackmail victims.

We watched one of your stings,' he added in response to a silent question. 'What were you thinking: a little punishment, a little profit? Did you feel righteous? But what about your bait, Shaz: the children?'

'Those cunts never touched those kids!' she flared. 'I saw to that!'

'I believe you, but who wrangled the tethered goats before you met him?' He waited for an answer. She had none. 'In that package,' pointing at the couch, 'are downloads from his websites. Check the images. Check the sites. The positions of the hot buttons are marked. You'll find the children from the Box Hill house and … Do you have pictures of Brie, naked, building sandcastles at the beach?'

She wanted to scream 'No!' – but no to what?

'They're on the web now. Where did you park your brain? These people are paranoid about security. How do you think he penetrated a ring? Found it under P in the Yellow Pages? You can't just Google paedophiles-R-us.' He paused and pushed a finger from the bridge of his nose to his hairline. 'Do you remember a Dr Plotell? Did you meet him? He was on Ben's medical team. He's on Lionel's blackmail list now. A recent addition. Appeared just before Ben died. Look at the material, Sharon, it's all there. Don't speak to Lionel again. He's dead to you. He killed Ben, as sure as you killed the drug dealer.'

The words came at her rapid-fire – she had never heard so many from his lips – delivered with anger neither hot nor cold but with a thrusting force of deep tectonic release. Her body was rigid but her head thrashed back and forth in a vain attempt to deflect each projectile. Her mouth twisted in silent denials. His last words brought a sudden stillness to her.

'Are you sayin' I killed Ben?'

'We all bear some responsibility. No one can cast the first stone.' His voice dropped and hardened. From him, his next words sounded like a snarl. 'If Ben wanted to end his life it was his decision; the choice of the instrument was his, and he should have died in the arms of a mate. He was ours, Sharon, ours alone. We were the witnesses to his life.'

'You would have killed him,' she said as if it was a revelation, as if she had never slated blame to him.

'If he'd wound up a talking head and couldn't endure it – yes.'

'You killed him,' she whispered coldly. He'd opened a chink. 'You did. He wanted to be like you.'

'If so, for one reason only. He thought someone like me could take better care of you and the kids. But we know who the better man was, don't we?' he added as if to himself. 'No, I think, in the end, he wanted to be what he could be. He wanted to be the real Ben. The trouble is, he was Ben: Ben didn't believe in Ben. He believed he could sustain a sprint but not a marathon. So he arranged to pass the baton.'

She studied him closely. 'You're not going to kill me?' She hadn't asked till now for fear of conjuring the deed.

He said nothing.

'You're going to kill him? That's what Ben wanted, isn't it?'

'He asked me to kill someone. But it's Ben, remember? He didn't want a murder – I was stupid, didn't see it soon enough – he wanted a coup de grâce.'

'He wanted you to find out what Lionel done then kill 'im,' she persisted.

He sighed like an old popstar asked to sing the number one hit he'd never wanted to record. 'You've heard the name Whitey Poynter bandied about, I presume?'

'I've heard of you,' she said, flat and dry.

'Whitey wasn't promoted for what he had done, but for what he would do. If he'd survived, perhaps one day more, another innocent would have died.' He stepped forward and his gaze grasped hers like lawyer vine. 'Do we know where we stand now, Shaz?'

She knew. He was telling her: mission accomplished. Lionel, beautiful, golden Lionel, was as good as dead. He didn't need to kill him. She watched as he turned to the DVD, popped the button and removed the disc. 'I've always liked this one, myself,' he said, smiling.

At the door he said, 'The police may come to ask questions, but don't worry, I've arranged immunity. Just tell the truth. I'll get a good lawyer for you.' She felt their eyes were opposite ends of bungee cord stretched to its limit. 'The kids are the best of you and Ben. You're within a gnat's nut of losing them. Moral endangerment. Straighten up and fly right, Shaz.'

'I didn't throw 'im out,' she pleaded. 'I said 'e could live here, look after the kids. I'd earn the money.'

She flinched from the parting stab of his sardonic gaze.

Ben, Ben, bloody Ben, she thought when she was finally alone. Ben was the vegetarian who bought McDonalds for the pickle, then ate the whole fucking burger because he didn't want to offend Ronald. Yet, he sorted us out.

She chuckled, off-key and brittle, dabbed her eyes with the sash of her bathrobe and flopped onto the couch. Her head fell back against the cushions and her eyelids dropped like the shades on a bank at four. Her hand crept out of its own volition and grasped the packet.

After a while – a long while – she roused and, pulling it into her lap, set about the thankless task of opening it.

'Well?' said Maeve Maguffin.

'Don't let her out of your sight,' said David Edge.

'Seems pretty straightforward,' said Milosz. He stood at the crime-scene tape watching the forensic team go about its business. 'He pulls in up the top there for a piss.' He hooked his chin upward, indicating the flat parking area at the top of the ridge. From their vantage it was completely screened by trees. 'Finds the dunnies locked. Comes across to the edge. He's a bit shy – probably a pimple dick – so he goes into the trees a bit to splash, it's dark, slips over the edge, boom-boom-boom and breaks his neck.' He turned around. 'It rained last night. Grass was wet. Happen easy.' He threw his hands up to show how easy.

'It wasn't rainin' the night before. He's been dead two days.'

'Doc's just arrived. How do you know?' asked Milosz. He always seemed offended by another's opinion.

'I've seen a few corpses.'

'Anyhow, his dick's hanging out.'

'His fly is open,' the other cop nit-picked. 'More than one reason for that.'

'Yeah … well.' Milosz turned toward the grey bulk of the other detective, knocked a drip of water from the tip of his nose with a finger and scowled up at the dishwater sky from under the hood of his police-issue parka, as if the fine drizzle veiled smirking heavens. It always rained on Milosz. 'Shit!' he muttered. 'Car's open. Key's in the ignition. Doesn't look like anything's been touched or taken. No sign of a struggle.'

His sergeant flapped the deceased's wallet. 'He lives on the far side of the city.'

'So, he's been to the snow for a long weekend.'

'Bit outta his way. No skis. No chains. No luggage.'

'He's got a squeeze over this way.'

'Boy from the western suburbs, girl from Kew?'

'Some blokes'll poke anything.'

'I'll defer to your authority.'

'Get fucked.'

'No one's reported 'im missing.'

'Lives alone and only shags her on Mondays,' Milosz volleyed smugly.

The sergeant looked down at the wallet so his partner couldn't see his expression. 'His address is in Altona.'

'So? A lotta people live in Altona.'

'Altona is very flat.'

Milosz didn't say 'Oh, der', but he looked it.

'Hard to break your neck having a piss in Altona.'

Milosz screwed his face laboriously into an expression of agonised sufferance. 'Shit-a-brick, Nev, we've got enough on our plate without lookin' for the crime of the century in this.'

Milosz, young and ambitious, *was* looking for the crime of the century. He was smart and could be a good detective – one day, perhaps – but he was too eager to drop the little death in hand to grab at the big killing in the bush.

'The queue's been jumped on this poor prick, Millie. He deserves due diligence at the very least. It's what we're paid for.'

Milosz sulked. 'Don't you have to catch a plane north?'

'Not till this arvo.'

A cop in uniform approached.

'Did you get the jogger's statement?' Nev asked. The uniform nodded. 'Anything new?'

'He said he ran this way, same time, yesterday, Sarge, but didn't have the dog with him,' said the constable manoeuvring his body to shelter his notebook.

'Thanks, Geoff. Go up top and see if Tanya needs more eyes or legs.'

'So what do we do – besides hang around in this brew like teabags?' asked Milosz as he watched the constable skirt the crime-scene tape and begin to scale the steep embankment.

Millie could be funny – when he was in the mood – but there was something stunted and grudging about his broader outlook. 'We make sure everyone here is doing their bit for truth, justice and the Australian way,' said Nev. 'We check out Mr Church's address. We find next of kin. We seek out the usual suspects and ask the usual questions. We wait for autopsy results and Tanya's crime-scene reports. *Then* we decide if this is the crime of the century or the fuck-up of the fortnight.'

55

'Where are we going?'

'It's a surprise.'

'We could have taken a taxi.'

'I had one light beer, two hours ago. If anyone in this car is over the limit – and one of us is – it's you.'

'I do imbibe a little more than I should.'

'Why is that?'

He took a while to answer. She glanced across at his patrician profile. It was being scanned by streetlights like a photocopy caught in a loop: printed with raw, grainy contrast against the bling of urban night.

'I'm trying to forget.'

'Oh? What?' That it was around this time that Ariel died?

'I can't remember.' He laughed at his own joke. It was a desiccated sound. 'Seriously,' he added. 'I can't remember – when I look at you.'

'I'll bet you say that to all the girls.'

There was silence and she thought she'd gone too far. Then he said, 'There haven't been any girls. Not for a long, long time.' When he'd had a few his mood was a pendulum that could swing between morose and frivolous several times in a short conversation. She suspected his present state of mind was provoked by a phone call from Carol Marks.

She flicked her eyes from the road once more. He was staring into the darkness or reflections in his window glass. Or perhaps he was staring into one of the crystal balls scattered across it by mercurial explosion in the last abrupt shower. In the flaccid light between flash and flare the planes of his temple and cheek were razed to a parchment cutout.

Her eyes came back to the road and she almost missed a turn. She had to concentrate. She had studied the Melways until a map of her route was etched on the rat maze of her brain. It wouldn't do to lose her way 'home' tonight. She checked the rear-view mirror again. In wet, neon night detecting a tail was like finding a shard in a kaliedoscope. She chose to assume she was followed.

'I know what the surprise is,' he lilted with deliberate smugness.

'Do you, smartypants?' Smartypants – where did that come from? Thank God this was her last pass at the target; she was turning into the monster she'd created. Poetic justice, no doubt.

'I'm actually going to see where you live. Mmm? I was beginning to think that you turned into a pumpkin at the witching hour.'

'Nothing nearly so good for you.'

'Oh no! Not a member of the opposition!' His eyes widened, aghast. The tips of his fingers fluttered at his lips.

She laughed despite herself. Unfortunately, in the brief span of their acquaintance, she had taken a liking to him. If nothing else came of this escapade, she had at least gained insight into the soggy pitfalls of undercover work.

'A potato of the press gallery, actually,' she said, stoking the silliness.

One dry run in a taxi, but her finger had navigated the maze again and again. Queen Rat: she knew exactly where she was. Now the tributaries were funnelling down with the inevitability of a sewer system. They were only a few blocks away and she wondered when he'd catch on. Perhaps, if she could keep him in this mood, she could distract him until the penultimate moment.

'Tell me about your wife.'

He smiled that charming smile, the bright, candid one that was a mask. 'You're sure that I have a wife, aren't you?'

'Positive.'

'You are rare among young women,' he said, wistfully – then nothing. She didn't look, but knew he was staring into the window glass again. 'Hebe, my wife – well, Hebe is more of a partner, but not in the sense it is used in marital relationships these days. More like the traditional sense. Hebe is more of a business partner than a wife. Actually,' and he gave a dry snort of mirth, 'she's more my business manager – or has been for a long, long time.' He turned to her and the false bright note was there. 'But don't get me wrong, she loves me in her … Hebe way. And we deserve each other.'

'You don't make your marriage sound like something made in heaven. Why have you stayed together?'

'Because we deserve each other.'

'Does *she* turn into a pumpkin after sundown?'

'She's been staying down the peninsula. We … she has an interest in some boutique wineries. They've been entertaining a potential overseas buyer. But I think she's got a charity thing in the city tonight.'

The annoying thing about older parts of Melbourne was the paucity of visible street signage: it always seemed to be playing peek-a-boo. On this occasion she blessed its playfulness. Not that he had been taking much note of their passage. Suddenly something outside their bubble caught his eye. He followed its retreat, head swivelling and craning back over his shoulder. Some landmark she supposed, but he settled back in his seat without comment or further curiosity. With luck the final byways had the same anonymous suburban homogeneity for him as they had for her.

'We are going to your little nest, aren't we?' he wheedled, probing for their destination.

She gave him the sort of arch smirk expected on these occasions. Just wait and see – smartypants, she hoped it said.

'How long have you had it?' A new ploy.

'Hardly at all,' she said, turning the last corner and seeing the cheese ahead.

Her words had the effect she sought. He had no interest at all in their surroundings. His eyes and mind were on her, his little triumph in their silly game and the unfolding night ahead. He didn't even look at the building when the car pulled into the parking space. He was too busy fumbling with his seat belt to free himself so he could lean across and kiss her. She turned off the motor, snapped her belt free and was out her door before he accomplished the action.

A car passed. It didn't slow. The driver remained in profile.

Simon clambered out and grinned at her over the bonnet of the car. The building loomed behind him and both were reflected in the gleaming, bedewed duco. He, a dark absence pastry-cut in the bland façade. It occurred to her that she might be able to keep his eyes on her all the way to the door. And the internal passages had no singular features.

Another thing occurred to her: if the significance of his whereabouts hadn't impinged on his consciousness by now, perhaps they weren't significant, and she – they – Carol and her – were completely wrong. The arrogance and futility of her recent behaviour began to press on her like a hand determined to force her to her knees and and rub her nose in her childish silliness. Shit! What was she thinking? She should call it off now, save herself from ignominy, settle for embarrassment.

'What's wrong? Not having second thoughts?' His words were playful but his eyes were probing, like a boy who knows everyone's pretending to have forgotten his birthday, but won't relax until he's blowing out the candles.

Oh well, Carol, in for a penny. She allowed herself to smoulder. 'I've never had second thoughts.' Liar, liar pants on fire. 'Not since I fell into your lap.' She moved slowly and deliberately along the BMW. He mirrored her. They met when they ran out of car. She let him kiss her.

There was a sudden squall of rain and, head down, they dashed and splashed across the asphalt. They entered the building without his eyes straying to the sign bearing its name. As they climbed the stairs she noticed his brow pinch and she moved to distract him. On a landing she tugged his tie and drew his lips to hers, then giggled and ran to the top of the stairs as if outwitting him in some unspoken contest.

Simon cast his eye around the corridor walls without curiosity. Like any other in the brick and concrete constructions of its era, it was a bland, rectangular tube. Carol began fossicking in a bag with more surface and volume than the rest of her attire combined.

'Let me hold that for you,' said Simon, reaching for the straps.

Carol relinquished it. Good, that'll keep him busy a little longer. She sidled along the corridor, rummaging.

'It weighs a ton,' laughed Simon. 'What on earth have you got in this thing?'

'Artillery,' said Carol, nose over the bag. She had found the keys, but maintained the pretence of searching.

'Feels like a battery of Howitzers.'

'Just a girl's usual ordnance,' she vamped up from under her lashes. 'Makeup, mace, manacles and Magnum .357, the most powerful handgun in the world – feeling lucky, punk?'

By now they were at the end of the corridor. His back was at the last door. As she spoke she withdrew the key and moved around him to the lock. His smiling eyes were pulled into her orbit and his body rotated. The door number floated into his field of vision.

It was a simple brass number, number twelve, attached by screws, available in any hardware store, but someone had added personal embellishments. It was embroidered with a bouquet of pink and red hearts outlined in black: coloured marker on blond wood. The gravitational field of the door captured him now. And, as she swung it inward, he moved after it like a child whose tongue is stuck to a frozen gate.

He was across the threshold and that was all she could have hoped for. She'd thought she would be lucky to get him as far as the street address without awareness dawning. She'd been luckier than she thought. His inebriation, the splash of shadows, the brief veils of downpour, the disorienting scintillation from wet roads had conspired with her.

She'd been much too lucky for one night.

56

Ernie had shadowed the shadow. It made life simpler. Like being sucked along in the vacuum of a semi-trailer's wake and its driver's ignorance.

He'd had faith in the shadow. He'd had him checked out. In fact the 'him' was a 'them': a reputable private security firm. Big – lots of staff, wealthy clientele and high-tech equipment. And they were only present when the man and girl were together. Their interest was in Castleman not Carol.

When he'd reported this by phone, dropped the firm's name, there was dead air at the boss's end. Then: 'Let me know the instant they go to that address or they look like doing more than kiss goodnight.' The boss used that tone: the one that dragged its nail down the chalkboard of your spine.

He'd had faith in the shadow because it was professional. He'd had faith because the shadow was hanging so far back from its target vehicle that detection in a rear-view mirror was impossible on a night like this. So far from its arse, in fact, that it was obvious that Simon Castleman's car had a radio-transmitting suppository. Ernie could sit a safe distance behind with some confidence that the shadow, intent on his receiving unit and his driving, would lead him to the destination of their mutual quarry in blissful ignorance.

He'd had to close the distance when they began snaking through residential streets and had been lucky enough to see the shadow's stoplights glowing at the far end of the block before he turned right into the street. He'd turned left and parked at the curb. A sharp flurry of rain had needled his face as he got out of the car. It swirled like an insect swarm in the glow of security lights from an apartment block midway between him and the shadow.

He tugged up the collar of his thick coat.

The shadow was shadow in shadow flickering back along the pavement like a form glimpsed through a picket fence. It took human form in the far fringe of the light from the apartments, watched the façade for a few minutes, wrote briefly in a notebook and retraced its steps.

Ernie walked back to the corner and looked up at the street sign. He crossed the road and noted the blink and glow of lights as the shadow's car started up. He padded softly in the black lee of a tall hedge. The shadow's car turned out of the street and was gone. Ernie crossed over a footpath leading to a poorly lit bridge, along the apron of a brief strip of shops, beside a high, concrete-block fence and stopped short of its end at the entrance to the residential parking lot of the apartment block. He took several steps back toward the road until he could see the name above the door of the apartments and most of the parking bays. There was Castleman's car.

He took a mobile phone from his pocket and thumbed its buttons. Scowling at the building as if it had jumped a queue, he rammed his fist at his ear.

'Boss? Ernie. They're at that fuckin' address an' they don't look like leavin' real quick,' he snarled.

Ernie was, unaccountably, extremely angry.

57

'How … this is … how long … how long have you lived here?'

Simon Castleman turned in eccentric, staccato, heel and toe revolutions in the centre of the room. His face was that of a man sluiced clean of all knowledge and understanding, save that the meaning of life really was forty-two. He bobbed all at sea, clutching Carol's bag to his chest as if it was the sole piece of flotsam from the wreck.

Carol observed him from the firm shore of her certainty.

'H-how long ...?' he stammered, locating her at last in his spinning universe, striving to lock in her coordinates.

'Not long,' she said. 'Only days. As you can see I haven't had time to furnish it.'

He stumbled in another circle, a goldfish forever discovering the bowl.

'But it's got the essentials,' she said. 'A queen-sized bed, a mini bar and tea and coffee makings. A bit like a *motel* suite,' she added, lewdly.

Slack-mouthed, his eyes were on her but his scrutiny was inward, as if he could make sense of things by watching each synapse fire. She reached out to take her bag back, but he frowned and wrenched away like a child claiming a toy. Rallying scraps of command, he strode toward a door behind him, pushed it open and said, 'The bedroom!' The words held both the ring of vindication and the rattle of perplexity.

At his shoulder she said, 'Here, let me take that.' And attempted to ease the bag from his grasp.

Again, he spun away. He stopped unsteadily on the far side of the room facing the kitchenette. His right hand relinquished bag duty and rose before him. An index finger beat a soft tattoo on a point in space where hung some crucial encryption.

'No ... no ... no, no, no,' he said, assurance and resolve firming with each repetition. 'No!' He turned to face her. 'Who rented this to you?' He was tugging anger from somewhere in his tangled skeins of emotion. The hand gripping her bag sagged to his side.

'A real estate agent.'

He grimaced, teeth gritted, and scratched violently over his right ear as if her reply was a physical irritation. 'No, no,' he said, with curt impatience. 'Who? Who? Which individual?'

'I don't know,' said Carol, and gave a shrug that said, who the hell cares?

'Male? Female?' He took a step toward her, hand outstretched, palm up, bouncing air.

'Both. I dealt with different people at different times.' She feigned rising annoyance.

He stared at her in disbelief. 'Jesus Christ! What are they ...?' He clamped a hand on his forehead and rubbed. 'That can't be. That can't be. They had express instructions not to rent this flat under any circumstances.'

'Do you own this place?' said Carol. She injected as much surprise, disbelief and wonder as possible into her question.

Perhaps too much: he paused and really looked at her for the first time since entering the building.

'Huh?' she hawked an incredulous laugh. 'You're totally kidding?!' She hated that use of 'totally' but she was in character.

'Who are you?' he frowned.

'I'm the girl whose bag you've stolen.'

'What?' Distracted.

He looked down as she moved smoothly forward and eased it from his grip. 'Small world,' she said gaily. 'But why on earth didn't you want to rent this?' she added, but his disbelief was already dropping out of suspension. Like faux snow in a glass dome the scales were falling from his eyes, he could glimpse the world beyond the bubble.

'Where's your furniture?' he demanded.

'Pardon?'

'This isn't your furniture.'

'You wanted the furniture preserved in aspic too?'

His jaw became pugnacious and his eyes cunning. 'Who are you? Are you one of *his* … his protégées?'

'What?' she said. Her voice sounded as if she thought he was going mad, she hoped her face showed it. 'Who?'

'I don't understand … Why would he …? If you're not his, you must be hers,' he said with sudden conviction.

'Who?' she said, and this time her bafflement was genuine.

'I'm getting out of here,' he stated flatly, but there was alarm in his eyes.

He skirted her as if she was decaying, wrenched the door open and turned toward the rear exit. Old habits, thought Carol. His shoulder careened off the corridor wall as he corrected and stumbled back past the doorway in a headlong charge along the passage they had just taken together. His footsteps rang in the stairwell as Carol turned out the light and closed the door.

When she crossed the lot he was pacing back and forth at the car, circling it, away from it, back again, irresolute.

'You've got the keys. Give me the keys,' he barked with bravado that was less than convincing.

'Not in your state,' she said quietly but firmly. 'I'll drive you home.'

His gaze wavered and flitted to her bag. 'You don't know where I live,' he said, defiantly drawing his shoulders up, bulking out, but blinking like a man who's noticed his fly is undone.

'The Honourable Simon Castleman, MP?'

'I'll call for a taxi,' he conceded, the eye skittering around her bag again.

She thumbed the electronic key. The car jumped to life and so did Simon. 'Get in, Simon. I won't hurt you.'

The only movement was his eyes, up and down.

She reached into her bag and he flinched. She brought out her identification wallet and flipped it. Just a flash: enough to see its authority but not its jurisdiction. 'I'm a cop. I won't hurt you.' Why would he be so apprehensive about violence?

He uttered a cynical snigger. 'You're wired,' he said.

Carol slipped out of her coat and pirouetted like a Hills Hoist: coat hanging from the end of one arm, bag from the other.

'This dress barely conceals *me*,' she said.

She was surprised to see the slick dorsal of lust break the surface of his liquid gaze, fleetingly.

'These days,' he said, sceptically. 'You've got pins and buttons ...'

'We're not that high tech, believe me. And no one is sticking a battery up my arse. Not on my salary.' She gestured. 'Get in.'

'Could be in your coat. And that bag ...'

'Let's make a deal, before I freeze. I'll put them in the boot, if you let me pat you down.'

'Pat ...? My God! You thi— I don't carry weapons!' He was genuinely offended.

'Nevertheless ...' said Carol, biting a smile from her lips.

She did know where he lived, but only had the vaguest notion of how to get there. He packed down in the corner, as far from her as possible in the front seat of a BMW. Half of him appeared to be jammed in the door pocket. His only utterances were corrections to her navigation – until:

'You're not from around here, are you?' Dawning realisation.

'Secondment.' While he thought she had backup she was reasonably safe. If nothing else, the events of the night so far suggested he wasn't a nutter.

'And I suppose you're name isn't Gaylene Kiss?'

'No one believes "Gay Kiss",' she said. 'My parents were Methodists.'

She could feel his eyes on her.

'How long?' she said.

'What?' Startled. Mildly.

'How young was she when it began?'

'What?' Weaker. A hint of capitulation.

'You and Ariel? Before her mother died? After?'

'I'm not a *paedophile*!' He was sitting up now. Straining against the seat belt. 'That was accepted ... established! I loved her mother. I wouldn't do that to her while ...'

'While she was alive. But she was young, wasn't she? And so much like her mother.'

'I … I don't understand.' He raked his his face from hairline to jaw with clawed fingers. 'Why are you people bringing all this up again? I was wrong, I was weak, but she needed me as much as I needed her. I … I …'

'Did you have her killed because she was going to expose you? Wreck your regenerated political career?'

She heard a series of soft expulsions of breath through puckered lips. She looked at him. He looked like a goldfish again – a hyperventilating goldfish.

'Wh … wh … wh …' His eyes were round and confounded. He eventually found a vowel. 'What is going on here? No one has ever suggested I had anything to do with her murder. The police know I didn't do it. Who in hell are you? Who are you working for? Who sent you? He didn't … he wouldn't …'

'He being …?'

He searched her face with sly suspicion, a rat that can see the cheese and the trap. He was about to press 'mute'.

'He being David Edge,' she prompted.

'David knows I didn't do it,' he conceded, with something like relief. 'For Christ's sake! What's going on? He was the one that determined I didn't do it.'

Now, there was an intriguing little wrinkle in the record.

58

Ernie's mood had improved.

In fact he was deliriously happy. And it showed. The sharp Y inverted between his eyebrows had smoothed to a pale stain. His mouth almost curled at its extremities, and his apple-firm jowls had a slightly pearish look. He felt the satisfying ache of little-used muscles.

His mood began lifting when he saw the Honourable Simon scurrying from the building. He checked the time and his lips pressed and stretched. Even *his* quickest quickie wasn't that quick, and he left the bam out of 'wham, bam, thank you, ma'am'.

As Carol Porter waltzed Castleman to her tune, dancing him to exhaustion while barely raising a glow, he watched admiringly from the shadows of a garden across the street. She was controlling the show; there was nothing to fear.

As he followed them, he knew not where, his mood was positively euphoric. They were at least fifteen minutes into their mystery tour when he remembered that the boss would be on a wild goose chase to that block of flats. He pulled out his phone and thumbed the buttons. He cursed when his thick blunt digit misdialled the second time. The boss's phone was busy. He left a message, an apology and said he'd be in touch when he figured out where they were going.

They were heading up St Kilda Road when he guessed she was taking him home. He waited until he was sure, then rang the boss again.

'Boss. Ernie. Sorry about the false alarm.'

'That's okay, Digger. Better safe.'

'Heh, heh, she's a corker, Boss.'

'So you keep telling me.'

'Shoulda seen 'er handle 'im.'

'I'm sorry I missed it.'

'Looks like it's gonna be a quiet night after all.'

'Good.'

'She's tuckin' him in for the night.' He couldn't keep the grin from his voice.

'What?'

'She's deliverin' him home. They're turnin' into his street now.'

'Don't let her go inside.'

'Boss?' The inverted Y branded his brow.

'Rear-end them if you have to.'

'Too late, Boss. They're turnin' into his drive.'

Dead air at the boss's end, then: 'Digger, if she doesn't come out straight away, I need you to go in and keep an eye on things.'

The words were delivered placidly but with a mean temperature that always had a Pavlovian effect on Ernie. 'No worries, Boss.' He was galvanised; but, this time, he felt something unfamiliar in the mix. His bowels melted in a way they had never before: not even when all two and a half metres and one hundred and ten kilograms of Tich Morris came at him with a cleaver.

'I'll be there toot sweet. And Digger – don't wave it around – but take your gun.'

Ernie paused to throw a switch on his train of thought. 'I don't think she's that dangerous, Boss,' he said with a tiny, taut smile. Boss just being the Boss: one for each person, one and for the pot. 'Not if she ain't got someone to do 'er dirty work.'

'Humour me.'

'No sweat.' Fuck, this was getting serious.

The elaborately wrought metal gates were still wide open as he drove past.

He drew into the curb two doors down – big doors, custom-made – and began walking back. Halfway there he noticed the gates move.

As a rule, Ernie preferred not to run: an image thing. He liked scaling walls less, so he made an exception.

'Ow, shit!' he muttered when elbow and gate collided, but he was inside.

He was halfway up the long drive, kneading his biceps to chase away the electric eels corkscrewing from finger to shoulder, when he heard the gate whir and grind into action again.

59

It was a four-tennis-court garage: one court, presumably, for each car. With the one she had driven, it was three-quarters full.

Simon clambered out the moment the car stopped and stood two paces from its open door. His arms hung at his sides and when the garage doors hummed he shuffled in a desultory semi-circle to watch their descent without interest. He didn't move while Carol closed his door, got out and closed hers, retrieved her belongings from the rear and locked up. When she dropped his keys into his palm he stared at them with even less interest.

Carol stepped back, watched and waited to be given the boot.

His head came up tortuously, as if cranked by a windlass driven by a three-legged donkey. It rotated torpidly as he scanned the garage's cavern. For all she could tell from his expression he might have been wondering why Tennis Australia had turned it down as a venue for the Australian Open.

He turned and climbed a few leaden steps to a door, which he pushed open and passed by without acknowledging her existence by word, glance or gesture. It occurred to Carol that she had, in some unforeseen way, wounded Simon Castleman.

Perhaps he expected her to find her way off the premises, perhaps he expected her to make herself at home, or perhaps he was looking for a shotgun with which to dispatch her as a trespasser. Whatever, she trotted up the steps into Castle Castleman.

She passed through a grot-lock: a room where wet clothes, dirty boots and such were cast off before entering the living areas – you could even have a shower. There was a security control keypad next to the door leading to the rest of the house. Simon had disarmed it. She saw him shamble around the corner at the end of a long, wide hall. Its walls were adorned with what she suspected were second-string artworks. In pursuit of mine host, she passed doorways beyond which were kitchen, laundry, pantries and sundry other utilitarian spaces.

The house seemed to be lighting Simon's way and she found him in a huge room with a view over a broad patio and submarine-lit pool the size of a small lake. Several echoes away he was pouring himself a drink at a bar that would accommodate a chorus line of pole dancers.

Carol crossed a floor representing the remains of a modest rainforest, wondering if she had the resources to make it to the other side. As she hiked by, she dropped her bag and coat on a chunk of cunningly upholstered solid geometry resembling a famous bank logo. Base camp: she didn't think she'd need mace, manacles, Magnum or makeup for the final assault. When she reached the bar she dropped her bum on a stool and studied Simon at the opposite end.

He ignored her presence and his throat convulsed as he swallowed a shot from a bottle he clutched in his other hand. He poured and tossed another. Then he shuddered and stared at the bottle and glass, each gripped in a fist. His eyes slid back and forth. Eventually his left hand – the one that held the glass – lifted, a finger broke ranks and pointed at french doors of proscenium proportions. His eyes never left the bottle.

'They're open,' he said in a desiccated rasp. 'The whole fucking house is open. Path. Other side of the pool. Just follow it. A gate.' He flapped his hand as if trying to dislodge the glass. 'Go … go …'

'I don't think I should leave you alone,' she said. 'Will your wife be home tonight?'

He shook a head attacked by psychic insects. The arm rose higher and the hand flapped like a pandanus in a cyclone. 'No. Clients … business. Charity … thing. Won't be home till,' head shake, 'whenever. But – just – go.'

She began the trek back to her bag, then stopped and turned. 'I'm sorry. The secret love-nest … I thought you had to have something to do with her death.'

The look he fixed on her was bleak, but what shocked her was that it was burning with pity. She imagined for a moment that it was pity for her.

Then suddenly he was pleading.

'Don't you understand?' His voice tightened like a piano wire. 'I loved her. I. Loved. Her. And she loved me!' He rapped the base of the bottle on the bar with each syllable. 'Don't you understand?' His words were beseeching croaks. 'It wasn't … I'm not … I don't hang around schoolyards. Ogle little girls in playgrounds. Don't you understand? Sometimes it happens. It stands to reason it must – I mean … statistically, in the whole wide universe – it must, sooner or later, it must. A young girl, a mature man?

It's not impossible, for Christ's sake? We loved each other. We needed each other. We were both lonely. We tried to find others, but—' Suddenly his eyes were discs focused somewhere over her shoulder. 'Jesus Christ!'

Carol spun around.

A malevolent male Russian Doll was cannoning across the room toward them.

She was slow to exploit the adrenalin spiking her system.

By the time she launched toward her bag he was there and snatched it up with her coat. She checked and dropped into a defensive stance. She was vaguely aware of Simon behind her reeling off the usual litany of 'whos' and 'whats' and 'whys' working his way up to 'if you don't leave immediately I'll call the police'.

The bipedal bludgeon (where had she seen him before?) was striding toward her in a manner that could only be described as earnest. He flashed mild annoyance at Simon and said, 'Shut the fuck up, mate.'

Carol was taken by surprise when he tossed her coat to her and did something with his mouth that might have been a smile. 'Getcha little bum into gear, luv. We gotta get outta here.' He turned toward the french doors. 'C'mon!' He actually expected her to follow.

'Now ... now look, now look!' said Simon, his voice rising in volume and strength, as it must in parliament. 'What the devil is going on here?' The absurdity was penetrating at last.

The bullet dressed like Chance the gardener swivelled with startling speed. 'Your fuckin' wife's home, dickhead!' he spat.

'Hebe ...?' Simon dropped the bottle and glass on the bar and rubbed his palms on his trousers like a boy caught with his fingers in the Vegemite.

The intercontinental ballistic interloper came back, clamped her elbow in a vice and, dangling her bag like a carrot, said, 'C'mon, sweet'eart.' Gently, but urgently.

She resisted: she had put in a lot of extra hours of unarmed combat since being tipped arse over tit by David Edge two years ago. She set herself and could see the missile's guidance system computing force versus persuasion. Their physical and mental struggles were stilled by a new voice.

'Simon! You didn't tell me you were having a party.'

A tall woman stood framed by an archway to a room in darkness behind her. She was wearing a long evening gown and looked like Rosalind Russell in Cruella de Vil's castoffs. Her dress was dark-matter black, but shimmered when she moved. She didn't move much. Her hands were held across her midriff. Her right hand seemed cut off at the wrist. Carol realised it was hidden by a bag of the same material as her dress.

The room was frozen in a parody of domestic tableau: mum, dad, debutante – coat over her arm, beau – hand on her elbow. At some subliminal level Carol was aware of Simon's hushed voice repeating 'Hebe, Hebe' as if coaxing a child.

'Ev'nin', Mizzus Soames,' said the missile insolently. He released Carol's elbow and took a step toward 'Mizzus Soames' as he spoke.

'Castleman,' the woman amended, crisp as June in Ballarat.

'We were just goin'.' He turned and reached out a shepherding arm.

'Oh please,' said Hebe Castleman, coolly, sweetly. 'Do stay and join the fun.'

Carol heard the crack of the explosion, felt the hot backwash of a projectile passing her ear, heard the brittle pop of glass behind her and saw the torpedo's grimace of surprise before she noticed the gun in the woman's hand. Instinctively she ducked, but still witnessed the macabre burlesque of a woman in evening dress missing her first shot and correcting. Hebe assumed the shooting stance: legs spread, bent at the knee, gown tenting, two-handed grip, elbows locked. Save for the evening bag dangling from a wrist: textbook.

It would have been funny if she wasn't dead in her sights.

Then the image was blotted by the bulk of her erstwhile escort.

He appeared to have stepped deliberately into the line of fire. His elbows were high, chicken dancing, as if he was struggling to open his coat. There was another shot. He grunted and spun in profile to her. An impact to her rear and right. A stain bloomed at the left shoulder of his coat. He staggered and Carol back-pedalled. Her eyes frantically sought her bag. Another shot. He was knocked another ninety degrees. Now he faced her, his right sleeve was blooming, his right hand was flapping ineffectually at his coat opening. Two buttons were torn away. 'Fuck!' he said. He staggered and his left hand clutched her shoulder for support, pushing her backwards. 'Gun,' he said. Another shot. He grunted and pitched against her. She lost her footing and fell. He toppled with her and they hit the floor hard. The force of his falling body knocked the breath from hers. Fish-gasping over his shoulder she saw the woman moving to get a better bead on her.

She, Carol Porter, intrepid young police constable, darling of the force, was her target of choice, not the man on top of her. He had simply got in the way.

She saw Simon – cries of 'Hebe' risen to hysterical pitch – dance idiotically before his wife, and then lunge at her weapon. Hebe eluded him easily, a sober Ginger dodging a drunken Fred.

Carol dropped her head back and twisted it to the side, trying to use the body lying on her as a shield.

She saw her bag.

It was half a rainforest away.

She heard the gun again, a splintering sound, and Simon scream: 'Hebe!'

'I'll shoot you too, Simon, if you don't sit down and shut up,' said Hebe's unruffled voice.

Her gun was a semi-automatic of some kind, small in her hand, a Tomcat? What – nine shots? How many rounds had been fired? Not enough. There was no way she could get out from under this body and over to her bag without Simon's help. Could she play dead and hope the bitch needed to get so close for the death-blow that she could grab a leg and throw her?

Gun, he'd said. Did he say gun? He said *gun!*

He had been trying to reach it with his right hand. It had to be under his left arm or in his belt on the left side. Her right hand was outflung, exposed; she couldn't move it and play possum. Her left hand was wedged between their chests. She forced her hand in increments across his body. Her coat, sandwiched by their bodies, impeded and confused her fingers. They squirmed and scrabbled like a spider pinned beneath the complete works of Stephen King. He was a heavy bugger.

She thought she'd managed to get her hand inside his coat when suddenly he moved. He groaned through his teeth and he heaved his torso off hers. Her hand was still inside his coat. Her fingers touched metal.

He grinned down at her like a lover.

'It's okay, darlin',' he rasped. 'I'll take care of ya.'

Then his face exploded and her eyes filled with blood.

60

At what point she realised something was amiss, Maeve was uncertain. It dawned slowly, too slowly: too many late nights.

That woman Ruby, from up the street, had scurried down under an umbrella that should have been sunning on a beach somewhere. Then, about fifteen minutes later, she scurried the three or four doors back home. Nothing odd there: scurry between the two was common.

Maeve lowered the car window to get some of the stale air out. Carbon dioxide build-up made you drowsy on long vigils. She turned her palm up to catch the fresh, feathery tingle of fine drizzle. It was one of the small pleasures of the girl-child that the woman still, almost absently, indulged. Nostalgic frisson denied this time.

Sitting in a stationary car at night, the windows rain-beaded curtains, it was difficult to tell when gentle showers stopped and started.

The light was poor, but her clothing appeared the same: a red, yellow and black Koori trackie. Hard to miss in any light. Too hard to miss.

Was that it? Or the scurry style? Or a fraction less baggage around the derrière? Or was it the redundancy of the umbrella? She had assumed it was still drizzling because of the umbrella. She hadn't seen it. And it wasn't drizzling when she stuck her hand outside a few moments after the woman was swallowed by her shrubbery.

Maeve played a tune on her mobile.

She'd been a bit dubious about Pixie's mate, Beryl, but old Beryl was working out fine. She was learning fast, maintained her enthusiasm, and the boredom didn't seem to be getting to her. Maeve had a feeling that she wasn't quite bright enough for boredom to be a major disincentive. She was a sharp little observer, however – years of experience sticky-beaking over the backyard fence. And she was inspired. Her source of inspiration, as well as technique, being *Stingers* it seemed.

'Maeve?'

'Beryl. Any action?'

'All quiet on the western ... ah ... back bit.'

'A few doors down towards ... uh, Wimmera Street. Anything happening there?'

'That lovely little blackfella lady with the cute kids? The one with the '87 Laser?'

Beryl was determined to not be a bigot. She told Maeve, only the other day, how much she loved lesbians.

'What about the Laser?'

'Just went past. Eastern.'

'What?'

'It's actually the eastern front – back bit – I'm on. Well maybe a bit north ...'

'I'll leave you to ponder that. Over and out,' said Maeve, cutting contact. She was already halfway across the road to Sharon's house.

'Evenin', Ruby,' she said when Ruby answered the door.

61

'My God, Hebe! What have you done?'

'Don't worry, Simon, it will clean up nicely. And we can probably spin it to some political advantage. Confound this gun ... it's stuck.'

'Where did you get that ... thing?'

'Ugh! Ah ... that's better. It's working nicely again.'

'You've killed them!'

'I hope so. They're trespassers, Simon – in our house and in our lives. And you let them in.'

'Hebe …'

'But I don't think the girl is dead.'

'Her face is covered in blood!'

'It could be his. Roll him off her and I'll make sure.'

'What do you mean?' Simon's voice had reached the pitch of the violins in *Psycho*.

'Simon. He's a criminal. And she is obviously his …'

'How do you know he's a criminal?'

'He works … worked for that Barker person. He's a thug – a murderer. I'm sure you'll find he's armed. He was trying to get to his weapon. The fool had his coat buttoned up to the collar. Roll him off. What is the matter with you?'

'You've never mentioned Jack Barker before.'

'He's not the type of person one mentions in our circle. Ah, there, she *is* alive. I saw her move.'

'I'm calling the police and an ambulance.'

'You do that. I'll be fine here.'

Carol heard footsteps receding and approaching. Through slitted eyelids the world was a ruddy shadow play. The woman's dress rustled softly and her voice increased in volume as she lowered to her haunches. 'Head or heart? Head or heart?' she intoned under her breath. 'What will look less … premeditated? I think heart,' she murmured. 'Poor Simon,' she grunted as she shoved at the body on Carol's chest. 'He can't see that all that you little sluts want is our power.'

Since she had hooked her fingers around the gun butt, Carol had been considering some big questions. Did she ease the gun out, slowly, and fire awkwardly from the protection of the body? Did she push the body off, sit up and fire with her left hand and almost certainly miss with her first shot – or shots? She felt sure this woman wouldn't miss. Then again, under fire, perhaps her aim would be spoiled. At this range an exchange of fire would probably end with both of them badly wounded – modest estimate. Did she wait, hoping they thought she was dead, or the woman came close enough for a safe shot? Could she move fast enough for either strategy to work? And – big, big question – was the safety on the gun off or on? Was it off and she'd managed to get it on, or had it been on and now it was off? Was it either? What make of bloody gun was it?

As her ear rode the rollercoaster of their conversation, one ploy jostled frenetically with the other for preference. She wondered if this was the paralysis of fear. Surely fear was redundant now. She was dead – good as – so things could only improve.

The body began to roll. The weight shifted from her arm and it sprung like a mousetrap.

She snapped her eyes wide, but the world was still pink. Trusting the gun pointed at the crimson stain swimming above her, she pulled the trigger.

The stain went away.

Carol sat up, scrubbing at her eyes. The slimy, gritty stuff of human life webbed her fingers. Blinking frantically, she searched to her left. The woman was sprawled on her back, her right arm outflung, her left crooked in an L at her side. The gun was a metre or more from her right hand. The little black bag was on the floor near her jack-knifed left foot.

She heard Simon's voice, but not what it said. One leg of her strange protector lay across hers. She eased from under it, scrambled to her feet.

Simon Castleman was motionless, propped against the bar, with a mobile phone hanging useless in his hand. He stared at the still form of his wife. Her chest was rising and falling like a sleeping child's. There was no blood visible and no obvious sign of a wound.

'Have you called the police?' said Carol.

'What?' said Simon. He stared at her as if a stranger had accosted him on the street. Then he looked down at the phone. 'No, I ... I ... Hebe ...?'

'She's alive. Here, Simon, give me the phone.'

He glanced at the gun in her hand and back to her face. Fear passed behind his eyes like the stutter of light and shade through train windows.

She eased the gun behind her thigh and reached out a hand. 'Here, Simon, I'll do it.'

'I think it's better that Simon do it – but not just yet.'

Carol spun on a heel like Peg-Leg Pete, dropped into the position and pointed the gun at the latest drop-in.

'Very impressive,' said David Edge.

'David!' exclaimed Simon. 'What's going on?'

'Mayhem and murder, it would seem, Simon,' he said and, save for the initial comment, ignored Carol's actions as if they were empty histrionics.

Without breaking stride he crossed the room to the bodies.

Carol followed him all the way over the gunsight. His briskness surprised her and she realised she'd never seen him without a walking stick. Her heart rattled her ribs, due no doubt to the latest influx of adrenalin. She didn't know if it was because she needed a gun in her hand or she was just glad to see him. Maybe it was in anticipation of witnessing another example of crisp professionalism.

Edge gazed down at the supine man on the floor.

Carol noticed that he had approached cautiously, eyes sweeping a grid ahead of each step. His feet now were placed carefully. She could only see his bowed profile but his face seemed deeply sad.

'Digger. Digger, mate,' she heard him say softly. 'Fairer? Yes. Weaker? Never.'

He dropped to his haunches. His gaze ran along the body. He slipped a glove from a hand, reached out and his palm hovered over the bloody face like a blessing, then dropped and his fingers sought the carotid pulse. He stood and moved to the other body – similar approach – squatted and studied it and its immediate surrounds, then stood and turned to face his audience as he replaced his glove.

Simon had maintained a constant litany of shrill questions, but neither Carol nor Edge, it seemed, paid heed.

'I take it Hebe shot Ernie, then you, Ms …'

'Gaylene Kiss,' Simon blurted: the perfect host.

'… Kiss, shot her?' There was a ghost of a smile on his lips. 'You can give that to me now, Ms Kiss.' His open palm asked for the gun.

'She's a policeman!' Simon interjected. Threat and dismay mingled in his voice.

'Then *Constable* Kiss shot her.' Edge's hand was still extended.

Carol lowered the gun, but made no move to give it up.

Simon was saying hastily, 'Yes, yes, David, that's the way it happened. But … but why did Hebe do that?'

Edge looked at him as if he'd asked if the light was on. 'Because she's insane, Simon. She had Soames killed. She had Ariel killed. And she just killed a mate of mine. You were supposed to keep Hebe contained.' An eyebrow arched and his eyes swept to Carol and back. Clearly he thought Simon had failed to keep something contained.

'You couldn't prove she did those things,' Simon said, petulant, defensive.

'No, I couldn't. *That* was the point.' His eyes ran up and down Carol's body. 'But we don't have time to argue. Is that your coat near Ernie?'

She nodded. Christ, Carol, say something.

He went back and scooped it up. 'It's stained,' he said. 'Simon, show C— Gaylene the nearest bathroom and find a garbage bag or its like for her.' He tossed the stained coat to her. 'She'll need something warm to wear. Oh, and a pair of Hebe's gloves.'

Simon's head was bouncing like a ball on singalong lyrics. 'The ambulance, the police?'

'Let me worry about that.'

Simon seemed relieved, eager to relinquish responsibility. He began a hesitant side shuffle across the room. His face was turned expectantly to Carol.

Edge locked his eyes on hers. 'I hope you paid attention in class, Constable Kiss. We want this place left as spotless as you found it. There are important things at stake, such as personal freedom and brilliant careers. Gun?' He smiled. 'I'll wipe your prints.'

She realised she was placing more than the gun in his hands. She removed each shoe and checked the sole – no blood. Glint in eye, he nodded.

'What about Hebe?' she said, at last. And relinquished the weapon.

'Hebe's forfeited a right or two, I'm afraid. Now, be as quick and as thorough as you can.'

She followed Simon from the room, retracing their earlier path. He was in a hurry to leave. He found a bag in the laundry, and a towel, led her to a small bathroom in the grot-lock and left her, mumbling that he wouldn't be long.

She stepped into the shower stall, stripped, bagged her bloody clothes and washed the blood, bone and brain matter from her face and body. She kept the water as cool as she could tolerate. Bathroom walls dripping with condensation would raise awkward questions. And the chill pellets seemed to scour and scourge her body.

The stall was fibreglass, all curves: no corners to trap trace. She washed it clean and dried it with the towel after drying herself. Then bagged the towel with her clothes.

She looked at herself in the mirror over the small basin. Constable Carol Porter, fired upon for the first time, shot back in anger (read: fear) for the first time, acting like a criminal (for the first time). She shuddered. She looked at her hands: not a tremor. Felt her pulse: normal, steady. She shocked herself. She was functioning in some field of dissociation that was almost euphoric, like the boy in a bubble, oxygen rich, free of the pollutants and poisons of the outside world.

Simon rapped on the door. It opened a crack and a hand came through with a bundle. 'I thought some slippers might be useful,' he said.

Poor Simon: trapped in a world beyond his ken. Only the last hour (was it only an hour?) had revealed the abysmal depth of his naivety. How had he stayed with that woman? Was he pathetically dependent? Was it some kind of penance? Was he in a state of denial?

She stepped back into her g-string, not her favourite kind of knickers. The coat was too long but she was beggar not chooser. She shuffled her feet into the slippers. They were a close fit. Twinkle-toes Hebe or flatfoot Carol? As she tugged on the gloves she scanned the room. What had she touched? Nothing she had neglected to clean. She picked up the garbage bag.

She was surprised to find Simon waiting outside the door. They returned to the scene of the crime together. All appeared to be just as they'd left it.

'That was quick,' said Edge, with approval.

In his hand was the gun belonging to the man he called Ernie. As if on cue he pumped a bullet into the chamber, scooped up the discarded shell, dropped it near Ernie's body and turned to the heap of designer labels that was Hebe. He aimed the gun at her head.

'Jesus Christ! David! What are you doing?' Simon cried.

'I believe it's called a coup de grâce.'

'No! No! You can't do that! David, you can't.' He was pleading across Hebe's body now. 'She didn't kill … those girls, it was Poynter. You said so yourself.'

'It's a market economy, Simon,' Edge explained patiently. 'If people don't want to buy death, no one sells it.'

Simon spluttered, tongue-tied with bewilderment.

'Unfortunately, it's a simple matter of self-preservation now, Simon,' said Edge, ever prudent and reasonable. 'If she survives she'll point a Poynter at me. Even you must see that. Stand clear.'

'No, David! Please. I'll do it right this time.' Carol wouldn't have been surprised if he had dropped to his knees.

Edge studied him then said abruptly, 'Okay, Simon. You take care of her. This time.'

He turned and skirted the other body and knelt with care beside it. He folded the fingers of the dead right hand around the butt of the gun and aimed it at a point on the wall, which might have been behind Hebe when she knelt beside Carol.

'Get clear,' he said, waited while they left enough room for an artillery barrage and fired.

He had provided gunshot trace on the corpse's hand.

It was then that Carol noticed that her blood spatter shadow on the floor had gone. He'd rolled the body onto its belly then back again. Now the stains were consistent with an unbroken fall to the floor. From a forensic viewpoint he had erased her presence.

'I drove Simon's car,' she said. 'My prints will be all over it, but trying to clean it will look more suspicious.'

He nodded. 'Simon,' he said. 'You'll tell the story as close to the truth as possible. Did anyone who'd recognise you see you with Gaylene tonight?'

Simon shrugged. 'I'm not sure.'

He looked the question at Carol. She rolled her hands over and showed her palms.

'Alright. Gaylene drove you home, but left immediately in a taxi, which she called for on her mobile. You escorted her to the gate, but didn't wait until the taxi came. Call of nature. You came back through the garage, but paid no attention to what cars were in there. You had a pee, stopped in the kitchen for a glass of water and might have dozed off at the bench. You noticed the light on in this room as you made your way to bed. You called the police as soon as you discovered this.'

Now Carol knew what he'd been doing while she was in the shower.

'You're clearly under the weather,' he added. 'It'll do no harm to be vague about time. Have you seen this man before?'

Simon shook his head morosely.

'Did you know Hebe's connection to him?'

'Hebe told me tonight.'

'But Hebe was shot when you arrived home,' said Edge, gently.

Simon stared, a child in awe of a cheap magician, then slumped against the end of the bar and gazed at the floor. 'I have no idea who he is.'

'Say as little as possible. Just answer questions. Don't volunteer information.' Edge pointed past a heavy shoulder. 'There's a glass of water on the bar.' There was. The shot glass and bottle were gone. 'Make sure you take a drink from it. But, call triple zero first.'

His head snapped up. 'You said you …'

'… would *worry* about it,' Edge completed the sentence.

Carol picked up the phone in a gloved hand and brought it along the bar to Simon.

'I'm sorry I thought it was you, Simon,' she said.

He looked at her with the eyes of a lap dog thrashed by a beloved mistress. 'Who are you?' he said.

Edge took the phone, punched a digit three times, put it back in Simon's hand and patted his shoulder. 'You'll be alright. You're a politician.' Then he turned to Carol. 'Let's go, Constable Kiss, I think we've worn out our welcome.'

62

'Let me know when I need to stop,' he said.

She glared at his profile. Not if – when. Smug bastard.

'Pull over,' said Carol. 'Quick!'

Her seat belt was free and the door was open before the car reached the curb. Her dinner was decorating the nature strip before it came to a halt. A chunder feature: every home should have one.

She was running on empty and the spasms continued. She hunched over the manicured verdure and leaked from every orifice in her face, save her ears. She could feel the prick of night in her sweat. If girls glowed she'd be a weather satellite pin-up by now.

The convulsions eased and she clambered awkwardly back into the car.

'I think there's tissues in the glove box,' he said as the car pulled away from her mess.

She found them and used half the box before her face felt clean.

'There's a small Esky thing behind your seat. I usually keep some water there.'

She found it. There were two sports bottles in it. One contained some water. She took a mouthful, sluiced it around, lowered the window and spat at the city. Then she set about replenishing her precious bodily fluids. Her mouth still tasted like the back alley of a fast-food strip during a garbage strike.

'Feel better?'

She said nothing. She felt like a good sulk.

'I'll get you home soon.'

'You know where that is, of course.'

'Of course.' There was a smile in his voice.

Jesus Christ. Was this just another night out for him: doctoring crime scenes, executing coups de grâce? 'How long have you been watching me?'

'Since I discovered your interest.'

'Was it Keyes?'

'Harry? Who told me?' His reaction seemed genuine. 'That's right, Harry does a bit of teaching at the School. No. That whole business was an itch he couldn't scratch. He's afraid I inherited Jack Barker's ambitions along with his brothels. Harry would probably encourage you.'

'I'm beginning to think he did. In an oblique kind of way.'

'Sounds like Harry.'

'Was it Carol?'

'Harpo? No. Nev – by accident. He thought there was some secret … thing between us.'

'Perhaps there is,' she said, mordantly.

'Perhaps.'

'So secret, even we don't know about it.'

'Can't get more secret than that.' Then: 'Oops!' he added mildly.

He fossicked in his jacket and extracted a mobile phone, thumbed some buttons, looked at the display, sucked air between his teeth and thumbed some more. He was breaking the law, but compared with obstructing just-ice, tampering with evidence and leaving the scene of a crime, it was a minor infringement.

'Maeve. It's Dave.'

Mmm, Dave 'n' Maeve, thought Carol, feeling churlish and petty. Christ, grow up.

'Sorry, I had to turn it off for a while.'

He listened.

'When?'

Frowning.

'How long?' Pause. 'Do you think he's in there?' Pause. 'I was hoping the cops would move quicker. Any sign of surveillance?' Pause. 'With red tape, the Feds might not have got their act together yet – let's hope.' Pause. 'As luck would have it,' his glance at Carol was laced with concern, 'about ten minutes away.'

'I wasn't doing anything else tonight,' she said.

His smile was dour. Then she realised he was registering alarm. He seemed to sharpen like an image through binoculars zoomed abruptly into focus.

'No! Maeve! Don't go in! Stay where … Maeve! Maeve?' He turned off the phone and stuffed it in his jacket. 'Pig-headed old bugger,' he muttered. He looked at Carol, now shivering in her corner. 'Why won't women do as they're told?'

'You have to ask nicely,' she said, through a jaw locked against chattering.

The car turned right at the next intersection. Before the call it might have turned left or gone straight ahead – how the hell would she know? She'd get out and walk if she did.

'I'm sorry,' he said, and it appeared to be a genuine apology. 'I have to make a small detour.'

'Another crime scene to redecorate?'

'I sincerely hope not.' He didn't sound hopeful.

Although he drove with careful cunning, he continued brazenly accumulating minor infringements.

About ten minutes later her shuddering shakes were abating and she said, 'Was Simon a paedophile?'

'Technically, I think so. Only he would know for sure. From the pathological point of view, I doubt it. An old mate on the force kept an eye on him for a while: clean slate.'

'He likes them young.'

'Don't we all. I guess that's why adolescents are paid thirty thousand dollars to pose in as little as possible on the cover of *Vogue*.'

'I guess. But most of us choose the fantasy.'

'I know I do – nowhere near as messy.'

'Where did Hebe spring from?'

'She had an agency watching Simon, reporting directly to her. They thought it was for his protection.'

'They reported following us to the love-nest and it set her off?'

'If you'd gone to a motel she might have managed to keep it stoppered, bide her time, and use a professional, but Ariel's love-nest was a tad too much. I think she came home to get the gun. And stumbled on you there.'

There were a lot more questions she wanted to ask, but the car slowed. He pulled into the curb behind two other parked vehicles. They were on a dark suburban street, well-tended, vintage, middle class as far as she could tell, leafy. They had stopped in the middle of the block but she could make out a lane or easement a few metres away.

Visibility was poor. It had started to drizzle again. He scanned the sky and seemed pleased.

'Constable Porter,' he said turning to her. '*Please* stay in the car. I won't be long.'

He got out, checked the cars in front for occupancy, felt their hoods and disappeared into the easement.

Carol stared at her handbag next to the garbage bag on the rear seat. It held her phone – amongst other things. She could end all this now: one call, nip him in the bud.

But Orpheus had the flute, the music was his; Eurydice could but dance along.

She found herself exiting the car and following him.

And he'd asked so nicely.

63

It seemed too easy.

There could be only one motive for Sharon Kitchen's subterfuge.

Maeve didn't follow her to Lionel Hu's house. She cut a beeline – or the closest thing to one as was possible through an urban grid. Butterfly hopes that by some stroke of luck she'd get there first fluttered in her chest. She didn't.

She parked directly behind Sharon's – Ruby's – car, checked its interior, felt the heat of the hood, from habit, and made another fruitless call to Edge.

She walked the street that Hu's house faced. There was a light on in the house and there were no obvious signs of surveillance. A flat with a vacancy sign, a few doors down and opposite, had shades drawn. If that was being used they had closed shop for the night.

Maeve looped around the block and came up the easement that ran behind Hu's. There was a back gate with a lock and it was off the latch.

Sharon must have a key. Maeve nudged the gate cautiously. It swung without a sound. Well oiled, thank you, Mr Hu. And he liked privacy: there were a lot of tall bushy trees in his backyard. She and the gate shared the black shadow of an overhang.

Easy.

Too easy?

She walked on toward the street where she'd parked the car, thinking. What was playing out in that house? What were the feasible scenarios?

Sharon confronts Hu, calls him for everything she can think of, and storms out. Sharon fronts Hu, blurts out everything she knows, and he bumps her off. Sharon fronts Hu, tells everything she knows, he begs forgiveness, swears true love and they fall into each other's arms. Sharon fronts Hu, he begs forgiveness, swears true love and she puts new buttonholes in his birthday suit.

But would Sharon have a gun? Maeve thought it unlikely. Could she get her hands on a gun? Who would she know that would have one? Who had she been in contact with that might supply one? Certainly not Ruby. Maeve could think of no one likely while she'd been watching – except Hu.

There was always a knife or two lying around, of course.

She had got this far with her speculation when her phone rang. It was Edge. She told him she was going in. She heard a faint, 'Maeve!' as she turned off the phone.

She was nudging the gate again when someone spoke behind her. It *was* too easy. She almost peed her pants – should have gone before she came.

'Whaddayou people do in there?' said the voice.

Jesus, that's all we need: a bloody witness. Playing statues, she raked the shadows of fences and sheds across the easement looking for the human source. Where's Wally? Then she discerned movement and shade upon paler shade. The vague shape of something that resembled a paper hat from a Christmas bonbon perched on a humanoid lump dropped below the fenceline. She heard a dwindling scuff, scuff, then silence. The question had been rhetorical.

Maeve stepped inside the gate and picked her way cautiously through the tall backyard timber. The porch was gained with wet boots and only minor injuries. She rubbed a barked shin and removed a twig from her ear.

The back door was also off the lock and cracked open a hand's breadth. Easy again. Sly Sharon or don't-give-a-flea's-fart Sharon? Maeve felt the insects of apprehension burrow deep into her pores, but pressed gloved fingers against the door and eased it open. For a high-tech bum clencher, Mr Hu was cavalier about early warning systems.

She wiped her boots carefully on the doormat and entered.

This end of the house was in darkness, but Maeve could see light bleeding around a corner or through a fissure ahead. She could hear the cadence of human voices. They didn't seem to be raised in anger.

She felt her way forward, softly softly, slowly slowly. She touched corners and edges, things that moved and things that didn't. She stopped and listened every three or four steps to verify that her presence remained undetected. She groped to a doorway, her eyes slowly adjusting to the darkness. The meagre spill of light was illuminating her path ahead. She was at the entrance of a passage and the way before her appeared to be without obstruction.

Then the door at the other end of the hall snapped open. Sharon was a black brand in the back glow of a room and Maeve was caught in the doorway like a wallaby in a spotlight.

Sharon didn't pause and vanished through a door to her right. A male voice pursued her: 'Sharon? Sharon? Sharon, what are you doing?'

When Maeve managed to swallow her giblets she realised that, in her dark clothes, she hadn't been detected against the darkness of the room behind her. The sound of a hasty search through drawers came from the room Sharon entered. She reapppeared with a large object in her hand and the door at the end of the hall closed to a crack again behind her.

Once bitten, Maeve waited for her eyes to readjust. Although tempted to make swifter progress, the deeper she penetrated the hall the easier it was for them to hear her. She took one small, painstaking step at a time: lift slowly, swing, down lightly. Halfway along someone popped the champagne cork. Maeve's heart did a little jig: the last pickled onion in a shaken bottle.

Her ear heard an explosion like the release of a cork under pressure; her mind knew what it was. She froze. The room ahead divulged nothing. She waited. Silence from the room, the roar of her exhalations and inhalations in the hall. She risked movement. And after an eternity made it to the door.

Eye to the crack she tried to scope the room. Her hands were balled into fists. Any moment now the door would snap open and she'd have to swing first or be swung on. All she could see was wall. Bugger!

She pulled back. She slipped her hand in her pocket. Bugger again! She had one of those weights yuppies in magenta tights clutched in manicured fists when they jogged. Extra clout: left in the bloody car.

What to do?

Advance?

Retreat?

Then she heard the sobbing.

She lowered herself to a racing squat, prepared to run in any direction – both if necessary – placed a palm on the door and pushed. It swung silently and smoothly inward. Thank you again, Mr Hu.

It was a tastefully decorated room. The walls were ceramic-red. The furnishings were Western in style but an Eastern austerity mustered them. The few artworks looked original. Sharon Kitchen stood in the centre with her back to the door, looking at the floor – or something on it – a couple of metres from her feet. From her low angle Maeve couldn't see what it was. A long divan blocked her view.

The wall Sharon was facing was a matrix of shelving. It carried video-tapes, digital recordings, various ornaments and, directly in front of Sharon, slabs of books. Some dark worm-like things seemed to be slithering down their spines. Maeve heard a soft, wet gargling and a drumming on the floor. She pushed upward with her haunches knowing what she would see over the sinking horizon of the divan's top edge.

Lionel Hu lay on the floor like a broken toy soldier. He had been breathing through the hole in his throat, but he had stopped. There was a glistening cherry halo around his head growing bigger as she watched. Maeve wondered what part of his anatomy had beat the tattoo, because she suspected that the bullet had severed his spine.

Sharon held a pillow in one hand and a gun in the other. At her feet was about the amount of down a fox might leave when it takes the duck. She was breathing with rhythmic sobs and tears were falling on her breasts with the constancy of a slow leaking tap.

'Sharon,' Maeve said, softly.

Sharon seemed to not hear, but when Maeve moved toward her she turned slowly and levelled the gun at Maeve's belly.

No need to be a crack shot with that target, thought Maeve. 'Give me the gun, Sharon.'

If anything, she adjusted her aim. 'I didn't think I'd go through with it. But you know what 'e said to me?'

'No.'

'He said 'e did it for me.'

'Where did you get the gun?'

The hand that clutched the pillow moved stiffly out from Sharon's side indicating the body. Hu's – probably kept in the bedroom, maybe under the pillow in her hand.

'Give the gun to me, Sharon.'

'Huh.' A vehement shake of the head. 'He said he had Ben killed for *me!*'

'I understand. But whaddaya need the gun for now, eh?' Maeve – being very reasonable.

'I'm waiting for 'im to die.'

'He's dead, Sharon.'

'Yeah. I thought so. But 'e moved.' The muzzle of the gun didn't waver.

There were too many years, too many kilograms and too much furniture between Maeve and the gun. It was a .38 calibre Smith and Wesson. It would stop her. Well, I can wait, she thought. We also serve who simply stand and … so forth.

Maeve allowed her eyes to stray from Sharon to the body and back. 'A pretty boy,' she said.

'Beautiful,' said Sharon. Her eyes glistened and her nose dripped.

They waited.

'You must be one of 'is cop mates,' Sharon said, dully. 'Too pug ugly f'one of 'is whores. Ever arrested me?'

'Might have. Ben – once or twice.' A lunge back through the doorway would eliminate the furniture as an obstacle.

'Ben. Ben,' breathed Sharon. 'The fuckin' world changed.' A soft snort of barren mirth. 'An' the little bugger keeps changin' it. He left an insurance policy … you know that?'

The words 'and paid a premium' formed in Maeve's mind, and she left them there.

'I did'n know I was goin' to do this. Not really … not till … till I heard the bang.' The gun wiggled in Sharon's hand to underscore what 'this' was. 'But Ben knew.' Arid chuckles issued from deep in her throat and her face was desolate. The muzzle of the gun dropped slowly to point at Maeve's knees as she said this.

'Murder can void insurance policies,' said Maeve. The gun came up again.

They waited.

'He's dead, Sharon. There was no way he'd survive that. What are we waitin' for?'

'You're 'ere,' said Sharon flatly. 'He'll come.'

Now Maeve knew why it had been so easy. 'No he won't. When you bolted I phoned, but his mobile was switched off.' True.

For the first time Sharon showed fear. Panic pushed her pupils around like a hockey puck. Shit, thought Maeve, maybe I *can* leap low couches in a single bound. Maybe that's all I can do. If Dave's her next victim, I'm the one after that, anyhow.

The muzzle went up and down and across and back, just like the opening of a James Bond movie. Maeve could see herself in the centre of its circle: a profile less Roger, more Henry. Oh well, she was thinking of giving up the piss one way or another. Then Sharon's eyes began to leak again. But the muzzle stopped circling.

They were standing like that when David Edge entered the room.

He took in the scene, both women, and an eyebrow hooked in question.

'We've been waitin' for you,' breathed Maeve. She cocked her head at the floor. 'And for Lionel to shuffle off.'

Edge skirted the couch on Maeve's side, removed a glove and held two fingers to Hu's neck. Oddly, Sharon held the gun on Maeve. The old girl's still the expendable one here.

'He's dead, Sharon,' said Edge.

Sharon lowered the weapon.

Edge took a clean white handkerchief from a pocket, wiped his fingers on it, refolded it carefully, put it back in his pocket and replaced his glove. He took two careful steps back from the body and pivoted slowly, the baby-blue-steels taking in the entire room.

'Don't do this, Dave,' said Maeve. 'It's too risky.'

'I've been getting some practice,' said Edge.

'The longer we stay the more trace we leave.'

'You should come with a health warning, Shaz,' he said.

Her gaze rattled nervously at his like stones on a windowpane. 'I wanted to hear it from his lips,' she said with some defiance. 'I was gonna leave. I was gonna ... but he said he did it for me. Killed Ben ... put my kids on a porn site ... for *me*? For me!' She spat the words and her eyes welled and shimmered.

'And you were afraid you'd go back to him.'

It wasn't a question and no denial came from Sharon. Her eyes fluttered and welled and a tremor shook her.

'This was premeditated, Dave,' said Maeve.

Sharon's eyes were glittering slits when they snapped back, and the gun came up.

Maeve was about to take evasive action when Sharon's eyes shifted and full-mooned. The gun swept in the new direction of her startled gaze. Maeve glanced reflexively over her shoulder. And there, in the doorway, was a gorgeous auburn-haired waif, hands stuffed deep in the pockets of an outsized black overcoat. By the time she aimed an enquiring face at Edge he'd loomed over Sharon, her wrist gripped by his right hand and, with his left, was removing the gun from her fingers.

All three women gave each other another once-over and their attention skipped back to him.

Edge sighed histrionically. 'She's here for work experience,' he said. Then: 'Perhaps we should lock the door.'

'Perhaps we should get the hell out of here,' said Maeve.

Edge ignored her suggestion. 'Where'd you get the gun, Shaz?' he said. As he spoke, he took a decorative cotton or linen mat from a matching pair on the coffee table.

'Don't do it, Dave. She's not worth it.'

'It's not for her,' his gaze pinning Sharon, 'is it, Sharon?'

Sharon watched him the way a gambler watches a croupier when the farm is on the baize.

'Where did you get this?' Wiping the gun with the tablemat.

'It's his – Lionel's.' Her voice snagged on the name.

'From the bedside table?' Wrapping the gun in the mat.

'How …?' said Sharon, startled. Then, with a heavy sigh of resignation: 'Fuck.'

'Who else would know it was there?' He slipped the parcelled gun into a pocket.

A shrug. 'Used it as a prop sometimes.'

'Was the bedroom used for photo sessions?'

She dropped her eyes and nodded. Christ, Maeve, look at that, a shame-faced Sharon.

'Good,' said Edge. 'Let's hope he was promiscuous.'

Sharon's eyes flashed up.

He pointed at the pillow. 'Bedroom?'

She nodded.

'Can't do much about that,' said Edge to himself. 'What have you touched?'

'My prints are all over this place,' Sharon said prosaically.

'Tonight?'

Sharon's eye's wandered listlessly around. 'The gun … the pillow … the door – back door … gate …' She flopped a hand at a wooden coffee table. 'The wine glass. Oh … and I … the bedside table. Drawers – and I leaned on it getting to my feet after I got the gun.'

'Where is the liquor kept?'

She pointed at a long, low teak cabinet. Edge went to it and opened a sliding door to an array of bottles. 'What do you hate?' he said.

'What?'

'Is there anything here that your friends would swear would never touch your lips?'

'Rum makes me puke.'

He found a three-quarter full bottle of Bacardi and took two shot glasses from the cabinet. 'Take off your clothes,' he said.

'What?' said Sharon, suddenly the demure matron.

'Find her something to put on, Maeve.'

Maeve grunted disapprovingly, but moved towards the door.

The waif was still blocking it. 'Allow me to fetch a garbage bag,' she said, dry as a beach bunny's bikini, and turned back down the hall.

When both women returned to the room Sharon was standing in her underwear clutching her bundled clothes to her chest. Edge was touching one of the shot glasses to Hu's gaping mouth. He poured liquor into both glasses. He swilled it around the glass that hadn't touched Hu's lips and tipped it back into the bottle. He took the gun from his pocket, removed the tablemat and touched it lightly to Hu's blood spill. He wiped the glass roughly with the stained mat and replaced the glass in the cabinet and closed it. He knelt beside the body and pressed the business end of the gun barrel to Hu's index finger on one side and his thumb on the other. He secured the gun in its tablemat wrapping and slipped it back into his pocket.

Cunning bastard, thought Maeve, he's cleaned the gun but connected it to Hu with DNA, and latents where a hasty cleanup might miss 'em.

The waif held out the garbage bag and Sharon dumped her clothes in it. Edge picked up the wine bottle, stoppered it with the cork and it joined them.

Maeve helped Sharon shrug into the coat she'd found in Hu's wardrobe. 'What about the wine glasses?' she asked.

'I'll wash them and put them in the cabinet.' He held out a palm. 'Key, Sharon.' Sharon's brow creased. 'Just to this place. You won't need it anymore.' When he had the key he said, 'Right – witnesses? Does anyone think they were seen?'

Sharon shrugged and the waif shook her head slowly: maybe. Maeve told him about Wally.

'In the light, he probably thought I was a bloke,' said Maeve. 'It happens,' she admitted sourly. 'But, from what he said, it seems the back gate gets a fair bit of use.'

They looked at Sharon. The eyes dropped, the head drooped and moved in assent.

'That's something in our favour,' he said. 'Okay. Shoe prints. Take her shoes when you get her home. And Maeve ...'

'Ah Jeezus! These are brand new Blundstones. I just broke 'em in.'

'The Salvos'll bless you. Put 'em on my bill,' he said, grinning. 'Shower,' pointing at Sharon, 'and don't forget to clean up her gun hand. Both to be safe. A wire brush, if that's what it takes.'

'My fuckin' pleasure,' snarled Maeve. 'C'mon bright eyes,' to Sharon, 'You lead, I'll follow. Just like old times.'

As they reached the door Edge said, 'Do the kids know you left the house?'

'Of course fuckin' not!' Sharon flared. 'Ruby's watchin' them,' she added, almost apologetically.

'Good for them – not so good for Ruby.' His gaze snarled in Sharon's like strangler vine and he cocked his head in the way of a raven regarding its subterranean lunch. 'See if you can firewall Ruby, Maeve. Check that none of the kids saw her.'

'Ruby's been out drivin' in the rain,' said Maeve sardonically. She nodded at the garbage bag.

Sharon's eyes bucketed, broke loose and sank.

'Nice,' Edge hissed. 'And Sharon?' Green eyes came up to meet blue again, under hooded lids. 'When they come – just the truth. You thought you were being watched and stayed away from him. With two exceptions, the only contact in the last few weeks was by phone. There are phone taps to confirm that. No elaborate alibis. Tonight you were home with the kids. Flat, no frills. If the kids can't account for every minute: bad luck. That's the cops' problem.'

While he spoke she watched him like a sparrowhawk; then the small beak went up and down.

Maeve herded her from the room.

His gaze tracked their exit and rested on the empty doorway. 'Women,' he breathed in droll lament. 'The only less that's truly more.' He faced Carol. 'Well, Constable Porter.' He raised the two wine glasses tweezered between two fingers. 'Now the guests have finally left, shall we do the dishes and call it a night?'

64

She heard his voice as she climbed into fleecy cotton pyjamas, pulled on thick woollen socks and tugged a heavy knit jumper over her damp hair.

The ducted heating was finally negotiating with the thermostat.

Back in the car, the jitters had started again. He'd turned the heater on high, but she felt no warmth. She had been steeped in numbing chill from the moment she stepped into that doorway and watched him contaminate a crime scene for the second time in one night. And her only protest was one sarcastic sentence. She was quaking like a paunch on a jackhammer by the time they reached her digs.

The door opened on a cold void and she charged headlong for a hot shower – another one. It was a cocoon of instant warmth and a private, sanitary cell that – surely – even he couldn't violate. Cold seeped to her core from a cling wrap of death and guilt that was her own skin. The fishmarket smell of a long day's trade pervaded her nostrils.

Hunched under a steaming deluge, her will moribund, she wondered if he'd crossed the threshold or simply closed the door and slunk back into the night. The latter, she prayed. Tonight she'd watched him, thread by thread, unravel two crimes and knit them anew, confounded only by the recalcitrance of death.

He had looped the car through a maze of streets. Then he stopped and tipped over a rubbish bin on a nature strip. If Melbourne garbos were anything like their Perth brothers they wouldn't touch that. The manipulations were not over. He selected one of the wheelie bins outside a strip of industrial-strength townhouses – one of which was a small medical clinic, another a psychiatric consultancy – and tipped it over too. Then dumped the mat-enwrapped murder weapon in clear view in the litter. The theory, she supposed, was the bin owner cleaning up would notice the cuckoo in the nest and check it out. He could make that gun disappear, permanently. He wanted it found: the error of a frantic culprit and the bad luck of drunken yobbos passing by. Was he salting a red herring or loading someone in the vicinity?

The third bin in two blocks upended, he'd slipped back behind the wheel and noted her expression. 'Bookmark,' he'd said. 'Complicated plot – wouldn't want Homicide to lose the thread.'

'Or drop a stitch?' had been her caustic gibe.

'In this case, *suture* is more apt.'

'I overheard enough to know he was a child pornographer, but he's a still a victim,' she'd sniped. 'He didn't deserve to die.'

'Everyone who has the effrontery to be born deserves to die.'

The distant voice persisted. She was warm now, her spirit emerging from hibernation. The assault of abseilers practising on the cavity walls of her chest had taken a smoko. She couldn't hide in her room – could she? No, she couldn't. But a good entrance line was needed – 'get the fuck out of my life' captured her mood but lacked panache.

He wasn't aware of her presence. Facing away by half a turn, he stood in the middle of the striped and barred Serengeti, phone to ear.

'… Christmas in July,' he was saying. 'Thanks for everything, Maeve.' And his voice was warm. He cupped the phone in his palm and stared down at it. He ran fingers through the straw thatch above the blue windows in his cubbyhouse face.

'If you're hanging around because you're afraid I'll finally do my duty and dob us in,' she said, 'don't bother. I'm a selfish, ambitious bitch and it's way too late.' That sounded hard-boiled enough.

His head swivelled wearily. 'Sharon actually said thank you,' he said. 'Muttered, it seems – but uttered,' he added, chirpily, when she maintained a stony gaze.

'Can't be a cop, be a cop-fucker: is that it?'

He slipped the phone in a pocket of his jacket, shifted his weight to one leg, hooked both hands behind his back and let his arms hang.

'My retirement plan was to finish my PhD and find a sleepy sinecure in academia,' he eventually replied. 'But even that's a bloodbath these days.'

'Clean Scene Inc,' she said, ' just your night job?'

'Old debts,' he said. 'Contractual obligations. End of the fiscal year.'

'Do you recommend it? As alternative employment, that is.'

He studied her closely. 'Thinking of a change?'

'I've spent the evening betraying the letter and spirit of the laws I'm sworn to uphold. By commission and omission.' Rage skulked blindly in her vocal chords.

'You're a private citizen in this state.' He began to remove his coat.

'What the shit are you doing?' In sudden alarm.

'Constable Porter,' he said, tossing the coat over a nearby phallic symbol. 'You shot a fellow creature an hour or two ago.'

'I didn't kill her,' she snapped, reflexively. It was inane mitigation, even to her ears.

'I couldn't find an exit wound,' he said gently. 'The gun was a twenty-two, fired at close range into her solar plexus at an upward angle. My guess is that the bullet kicked over a lot of furniture looking for the back door.' He waited as if expecting a rebuttal. 'If it had happened back home in the line of duty, you'd be provided with counsellors, and you'd have the support of family and friends.'

'I'm flying home tomorrow,' she said, almost petulantly.

'And what will you tell them?' he asked softly. 'Your confidantes.'

'I ... I ...'

'Constable Porter ...'

'For fuck's sake call me Carol!' It was nearly a scream.

'That's better,' he said with a smile, as if she had taken her medicine like a good girl.

She glowered at him. 'I'm going to bed. Lock the door as you leave.'

She couldn't resist looking back as the bedroom door closed. He was smiling sadly at a tapping toe.

She didn't sleep. The world was pink when she closed her eyes and red when she opened them. She shivered and shook, sweated and itched. And she rewrote the scene at Simon's again and again. The ending didn't change. She contracted into a ball, clenched every fibre until she vibrated like a tin dunny on a truck route. An impossibly tall, female wraith stood by her bed and aimed a Magnum .357 (the most powerful handgun in the world) at her brainpan and waited for her to open her eyes. She kept them shut; but it's difficult to sleep through your own execution. The future threw its image against her eyelids as a grey steel door that had no handle. That was good, because she knew, if breached, it would gape on a corridor without exits or windows, which penetrated nothing – forever.

Faint light from the window dusted his face. His brow cast his eyes in deep shadow. His chest rose and fell like a child's after a long day in the sandpit. Standing at the foot of the slab signifying 'couch', she was reminded of the cell in Broome – him supine on the narrow bunk – and the suspicion grew that he was awake, observing. From there to here, a two-year journey, and she was back where she started. How much was push and how much was pull? What did she sense in him back then? What was she looking for: some essence of 'copness'? Like a knight who has achieved the Grail and found an old cracked cup, her fascination was morbid, the sight was unbearable, the piquant savour of anticipation sour in her mouth, and she couldn't look away. She had to know … if? – why?

'Who was *your* counsellor?' she asked, softly, but abruptly; it seemed to her without volition. It was loud in her head. She waited. For a while she thought he was indeed asleep.

'Alas,' he said at last. 'I found no sinner bloody-handed enough with whom to plumb the depths of my perfidy. So I'm damned to repeat my mistakes for eternity.'

'Do you make a joke of everything?' she said, tetchily. 'Or … or …' Or do you use a joke to hide the truth in plain sight? She finished the sudden insight in the sudden stillness of her mind. Had he told her why he did things like those he did tonight? *Last* night: it was early morning now.

'The Counsel for the Defence – couldn't cry on her shoulder?' she asked.

His breath stilled.

Then: 'Not without staining her gown.'

'You killed Whitey Poynter,' she stated, another decision after the fact.

'Did I?' He was an effigy carved on a sarcophagus.

'Nothing else fits the … the Gestalt. You knew he did it. You were frustrated, angry. There was no evidence admissible in court. The serial killer tactic was beyond the pale. Even a cool son of a bitch like you loses it sometime.' She held her breath.

He said at last, 'Perhaps he'd just passed his use-by date.'

'What?'

Silence again.

'He'd passed his use-by date,' she said, chafing. 'What's that supposed to mean?'

'Why do you want to know?'

Why? My god! Why? 'I ... I ... This ... tonight ... the ... the ... Everything I've done ... It doesn't ... make sense ... if I don't ...'

'It's your case, Constable Porter, you have the clues. The suspect chooses to remain silent.'

Jesus Aitch Christ! He was a frustrating bastard. She stood over him, her pulse in her ears, stared at darkness and let her mind replay every scenario she – they – had imagined, on fast forward. She strove for Carol Marks's Gestalt. Then:

'Shit.' Flat and dense as billiard table slate. 'We got it right. Keyes said he couldn't understand why Jack Barker trusted you so completely, so quickly. It was a test. Wasn't it?'

Say something, damn you: yes, no, grunt.

'Barker *wanted* to trust you,' she persisted. 'After all – someone with your family connections – that'd be like trashing a case of *Grange* because one bottle might be corked. And Poynter was a liability, drawing too much attention. Barker needed *him* gone and *you* welded on. That was it, wasn't it? He brought you and Poynter together somehow, and got you to kill him. But how ...? You needed him alive to convict Hebe – and you let Hebe live.'

Why was she doing this? Anger reclaiming the night from fear? Saving face? She couldn't stop. Silence hung like a shawl stalactite in a cavernous space. She heard her next words as an echo.

'Barker told you that ... No ... no, not you: you'd need proof. You wouldn't take his word ...' A light penetrated the cave and the shawl glowed like a movie screen. 'Poynter. Poynter himself ... said or did something.' She couldn't suppress her excitement. 'Poynter ... Poynter ... he, he ... *bragged* about it. Maybe the serial killer smoke-screen was part of the contract, maybe it was his idea, but he got off on it. He was out of control. Barker had to switch him off. Barker needed an act that would bind you to him. And you needed something to convince him you were bound. *Synchronicity.*'

She stepped closer, tense, engaged, Sherlock Porter at the cusp of the denouement. She was suddenly sure if he spoke it would be the truth, and if she asked the right questions she'd get the whole truth. It didn't occur to her that if she was right she was within arm's reach of a killer.

'I'm right, aren't I?'

Night slowly dissolved.

'It's an interesting hypothesis,' he said, at last.

'Hypothesis?'

'Physical evidence is the best evidence: isn't that the Detective Training School motto?'

'There is no physical evidence identifying Poynter's killer. Do you have a better one? Hypothesis that is?'

No denial, no derisive laughter, no sound at all.

She counted off heartbeats like a rosary. With Poynter dead there was no way to link Hebe to the murders. So he fastened Simon to Hebe with a collar of guilt and set him as watchdog. What a piece of work was he.

'Covert wanted you welded to Barker, too. Were you ordered – unofficially?'

There was so much pressure, from all sides. She suddenly realised how alone he must have been. 'You had a sackful of motives,' she said ultimately, gently. 'I understand why ... someone might do it.'

'If that's something noble,' he said, softly. 'You don't. Any murderer's motives boil down to a pitiful banality: it seems like a good idea at the time.'

Carol didn't move.

'A simple choice,' he continued. 'Weigh two lives, and sacrifice the one of lesser value – to oneself.'

'Is that what I did?'

'Yup. Take comfort that your blood was hot – and the choice was made back in the primal soup. But now, Constable, own your choice, forgive yourself, go forth and sin no more.'

'Oh, it's that easy?' she scoffed testily. 'That's what you've done, is it?'

'Forgive but *never* forget – soul food.'

'Fall from grace occasionally, eh? Now that I know – hypothetically – I suppose you'll have to kill me too?'

She saw brighter crescents of light form on his cheeks. 'Not imperative – your case is purely circumstantial.'

'Witnesses,' she said.

'Witnesses?'

'There were witnesses,' she insisted. 'Barker would have to know. Somebody made a gangland legend of you.'

'I'm just a rumour, Constable, a day tripper's war story.'

Carol stared into the face of the dark form below her. 'A Chinese whisper,' she said.

'Pardon?'

'If you were innocent, why leave the police force?'

'According to your scenario, if I'd stayed I'd have had to arrest Desmond Poynter's hypothetical killer.'

She lifted the skirt of the jest and glimpsed the 'copness' underneath. 'So, he's still at large?'

'Now and then we meet on the stairs. I'm not sure if he lives in the basement or the belfry.'

She looked at the window and it was an opaque grey rectangle. In the spectral light he looked like a cadaver on a slab. She shivered.

'Are you cold?'

'Frigid.'

'That thing comfortable?'

'A rack.'

'The bed's comfortable,' she said, abruptly, acting once more without conscious decision.

Silence.

'I need someone ... bloody-handed enough to ... share my rack.'

Silence.

'This is an invitation to my *bed*, not my body.'

Slinging his feet off the slab, he said, 'No hanky panky,' in reference to whom was unclear.

She had lain awake for a long time in the spoon of his body, feeling the weight of his arm on her hip and the light pressure of his hand on her belly, just below her ribcage. She wondered if it would drift north or south. She doubted it would drift. She wondered if she wanted it to. She doubted that as well. His heat warmed her back. His breath feathered the fringe of hair on her neck.

'I'd be dead now,' Carol admitted to him – and herself. 'That ... man ... he got caught between Hebe and me. Twice.' Some icy stuff surged in her again as she said it: she could feel the brittleness of her bones. 'How long was he tailing me?'

'Ernie was your minder.' Words borne on a zephyr past her ear.

Carol's breath got lost on the way to her lungs. She thrust up and twisted towards him. 'That's ridiculous,' she rasped. 'You're not suggesting he deliberately ...'

'He watched over you for a long time.' He stopped. She waited for him to continue and wondered what expression was on his face. Then he said: 'He thought you were all three Charlie's Angels in one neat g-string.'

She almost choked on an incredulous hee-haw. 'Now look ... lust I can accept, but ...'

'Oh, Ernie was familiar with that – his love life was nothing if not ... utilitarian. If he spoke of women at all, it was as bits of anatomy. But with you, his vocabulary was ... wanting. He found his words in that fatal choice.'

She didn't want to hear this. She wanted it unsaid. She wanted to push it aside and take her medicine; but she saw a newel post in a suit rise up in harm's way.

'We give up a seat on the bus for strangers every moment,' he added. 'It's nice to know we've kept it warm for a cute little bum.'

Was that it, the reason Desmond Poynter died: murdered and murderer, each just another necessary sacrifice?

He chuckled. 'Look at yourself, Constable Porter. There, but for the grace of a petty crim. Here, in bed with a quarry that can break your neck with a blow of his nose, and still you persist. You're a cop. Get up and get back on the horse. The metaphor covers white ones too.'

'Your horse is white?' She meant it sardonically, an accusation, but it came out a simple question.

'The white ones had bolted, but I found a pale one with a leg on each corner.'

For the first time Carol felt him as kin. Her impulse was to wrap him in her arms, but she embraced her calves and pulled her knees to her chin. On the room's dark wall her mind painted a stark landscape, at its polar extremities a sharp white peak and a deep black rift: right and wrong, good and evil, justice and its absence. The terrain between was grey, torrid and insubstantial, a place of smoke and vapours. He glided through it like a salamander and it wrapped him like a second skin. Perhaps his eyes had the acuity to discern phantom in fog, but she needed a world with hard edges.

'That woman tonight, she's one of your … girls?'

'Rose's. Once.'

'Does *she* deserve to get away with murder?' she said.

She felt the gentle pressure of his hand on her shoulder. 'Go to sleep,' he said.

'Does she?'

'No one does. But, on the other hand, her kids don't deserve a life sentence.'

'What's your get-out-of-gaol-free: two brothelfuls of women?' she murmured in the silence as she lay down in a lazy S that quoted the curve of his body.

'There are things they don't teach at Detective Training School, Constable Porter.'

'Oh, I've learned that, Mr Edge. But if anyone else gets loaded for … '

'Fear not, Constable,' he chuckled. 'I'll get my come-uppance one day.'

The monstrous improbability of the night rose, ballooned in her and burst like a psychic belch. Carol began to giggle. It started as a gurgle and almost got to a belly laugh.

'Constable Porter,' he said. 'Please shut up and go to sleep.'

'I don't think I can.'

'Perhaps a bedtime story will relax you. Once upon a time …'

'Sounds like a fairytale.'

'There's truth in fairytales. Wolves roam the woods and sometimes sleep in grandma's bed.'

'This is meant to relax me?'

'Shhh,' he soothed. 'Once upon a time, long, long ago, there was a maiden-devouring dragon …'

65

Nev was perched on the hood keeping his bum warm with the motor. He had one heel on the bumper. His bum was getting cold. His shoulders shrugged in a shiver to stimulate circulation; he clapped his hands three times and rubbed them together. He'd just made his mind up to leave when the car turned in.

'A bit late for breakfast,' said Edge as he climbed from behind the wheel.

'Brunch'll do. Heavy night?' said Nev.

'That obvious?'

Nev dropped into stride beside him. 'Mate, the bags under your eyes make your face look like a flasher wearin' cargo pants.'

Edge snortled wearily. They began climbing the stairs to his apartment at the rear of the building.

'Where y' been?' asked Nev, even though the question was redundant.

'Identifying Digger's body.'

'Didn't know you were Ernie's next of kin.'

'Separated at birth, like DeVito and Schwarzenegger,' Edge said as he unlocked the security gate on the last landing.

'Never said it, but there is something DeVito-ish about you.'

'In every tall, slim boy there's a small, fat man with short legs on a treadmill.'

They crossed the deck and Edge ushered him through the back door into the kitchen.

'Bacon and eggs or a frittata?' said Edge, as he stripped off his coat.

'Frittata. I'll chop somethin'.' Nev propelled his coat over the bench onto a pudgy armchair.

Edge began transferring stuff from the fridge to the bench top. 'You chop the onion, tomatoes and bacon. I'll peel the potatoes.'

'Do you have a theory why Ernie would be at Castleman's?'

'Is it your case?'

'Nope. I pleaded conflict.' He studied his friend, who had his head lowered as he ransacked a drawer.

Edge found what he was looking for and glanced up. He shrugged.

'Who knows. He never warmed to Hebe. Perhaps he went to tell her so in terms she found unacceptable.'

'Hebe Castleman was thick with Barker?'

Edge hooked his hands in a monkey grip across his chest.

Nev clacked his tongue. 'I'd heard talk about her first hubby – whatsis-name Soames – bein' shonky, but ...'

'Hers were the brains – according to Jack. At least, the ones between the ears,' said Edge, and began to peel a potato. 'You can tell Harpo that Ernie's closed the case at last.'

'Shit,' said Nev, as you might say 'onion'. He began to chop an onion. 'I'da put my money on the Honourable Simon.'

'What case are you on?' said Edge, as he sliced a potato.

'Church. Heard that name?'

'Catholic, Anglican or Uniting?'

'Carroll Christian.' No reaction. 'Deceased. Bit of a loner. Fond of violent computer games. Paid-up member of a pistol club. Habit of disap-pearin' for long periods – mum knew not where – nor cared. Spent most time at home in dad's old shed. Mum knew not what he did there – nor cared. We found a nice collection of guns, most of which shoulda been handed in at the last amnesty. Displayed side by side with his dad's tools of trade – saws 'n' chisels in mint condition. Evidence of 'im making little modifications and accessories – like silencers. Profile sound familiar?'

Edge spread the potato slices in a flat dish.

'We also found a likeness of you. It'd been cut from a larger photo. The Rose Garden address was on the back.'

'That'll be enough tomato,' said Edge.

'Showed 'is photo 'round the Garden. The girl on reception ...'

'Charlotte.' He slid the slices of potato into the microwave, pressed out a pattern on the keypad.

'... Charlotte said you'd – the Garden – had a stalker.'

'I think Boof and Shane were concerned about someone hanging around.' He began breaking eggs into a bowl. 'We call them "tourists".'

Nev pushed a photo across the bench. 'Do you recognise him?'

Edge glanced at the photo. 'They never pointed him out. I don't think he came through the door.'

'You don't think he could be Bernie's hitman?' Nev started on the bacon, thinking about the questions that weren't being answered.

'Sounds like a wannabe. Bernie could pay top dollar for a professional.'

'Well, if he took his wallet to a hit, this bloke was definitely an amateur.'

'Can't see how someone with his background would connect to gang-land.'

'Might take a look at the pistol club.'

'Did Boof or Shane pick him?' He cracked another egg and tossed the shell into a bucket in the sink.

'Nah. Never got close enough to be positive. They said.'

'How did he die?'

'Broken neck. Tongue almost bitten through. Waitin' on th' post-mortem. Appears to be a freakish accident. Milosz says I'm wasting my time.'

Their eyes met. Edge smiled. 'Thorough investigation is never a waste of time,' he said primly, and beat the eggs with a fork.

'My sentiments 'xactly. So checked triple zero and Crimestopper calls around Church's ETD. Day or so before his body was found a bloke reported what he thought was a bullet hole in his car door: needed a police report for insurance. Took a look – it was a bullet hole. Even found the bullet. Hollow point, bit of a mess – useless for ballistic comparison.'

'The ones that hit people tend to watch their figure more.'

'Yeah. Car was parked on a street a coupla blocks from the Garden.' Pause for a reaction – none. 'Some uniforms are canvassin' the neighbourhood.'

'See, thorough investigation is never a waste of time.'

'Yeah.' Dry as a mummy's fart. Nev scooped the chopped bacon into his big hands and dropped it in a small frying pan on the stove. 'Have the Varney business sorted soon,' he said, casually.

'Oh?' Edge ground the peppermill over the eggs and threw in some herbs.

'Yeah. Turoczy finally made a deal. He's produced the security guard's torch, which he claims was the murder weapon. And his brief dug up a tape with a voice claiming to be the fourth man. Corroborates Turoczy's story and puts Varney and the third man right in the shit. Forensics is going over it as we speak. Turoczy swears it's Ben Bovell's voice.' He chuckled to himself as he sliced mushrooms.

'What?' said Edge. He lit the gas under the frying pan and shook it gently over the flame.

'Varney's in the shit in more ways than one.'

'He'd be feeling right at home.' He poked the bacon about with a slide. It hissed and spat.

'He went missin' at lock-down a few days ago. Big search. They found 'im in the equipment store in the gym. He was tied with skipping ropes, wrist and ankles, to one of those big machines the pecs 'n' abs generation copulate with these days. His pubic hair had been shaved and glued to his head with epoxy. He'd been circumcised. Neat job – minimal blood loss. Tats were blotted out with this yellow paint used to mark out the courts an' stuff in the yard. His entire back was painted yellow and some descriptive terms were scratched in the paint. 'Turd tickler' was the most flattering. You know those wooden massage things – cylindrical handle with two balls for wheels – look like Pinocchio's weddin' tackle?'

'I can picture it.'

'One of those stuck up 'is clacker. And a bit of towel he uses to wipe his hands when he's workin' out stuffed in his mouth. It had a list of names written on it in laundry marker. His victims, apparently – the ones *that* side of the bars. Guess who headed the list?'

'Umm.' The chef rolled his eyes to the ceiling and pretended to think. 'Ben Bovell.'

'Good at this aren'cha?' Nev grinned.

The microwave began to complain that no one was paying it attention.

'To top it,' Nev added, 'Don Collison's on the blower to me. Seems he's got a fresh lead on an old partner in crime of Varney's. Can probably put him at the scene of a fatal gay bashin' some years back. Got a picture and a name. We shoot the picture through to Brisbane and Turoczy identifies him as the third man on the warehouse job.'

'Well there you go. Say your prayers, eat your greens and good things will come to you.'

'Lionel Hu. That's 'is name,' said Nev, his gaze resting heavily on his host. 'I'm pickin' Don up in,' consulting his watch, ' 'bout eighty minutes. We're gonna drop by and ask Mr Hu a few questions.'

Edge spread the potato slices in a deep frypan, sprinkled the bacon and mushrooms over it.

Nev watched him pour the egg mixture into the pan. 'Benny Bovell seems to be the common denominator here,' he said. He passed the tomatoes and onion to Edge who spread them over top of the egg. 'Can't link him to Church and Castleman though.'

'It'd be a stretch.'

Edge turned away and put the frypan back on the burner and turned up the flame. Nev waited until he turned back.

'David, my son, what have you been up to?' he said. Father O'Malley couldn't have done it better.

'God's work and the Devil's mischief,' said Edge.

His grin bore no resemblance to a Cheshire Cat's, save that it hung in space while he faded.

Epilogue

Tommy Doherty scampered along a Surfer's Paradise thoroughfare, his toes on the tarmac, his heart in the heights. Long shots and rank outsiders had put a whole new spin on the world. Since that solid tungsten tip a month ago he'd had an unbelievable run of luck. Put a dollar down – didn't seem to matter on what – and the little fucker cloned. And the clones cloned. And the cloned clones cloned. He had the weird feeling he owed it all to Maeve Maguffin. The gods of gambling, who seemed to insist on handicapping a run of good luck with its equal in kilos of bad luck, and vice versa, must view that butch old bitch as a disaster on a cosmic scale, drawing the weight equivalent of a black hole.

Up there in that highrise monstrosity he was approaching – in the bloody penthouse no less, *the bloody penthouse* – awaited the fulfilment of a long cherished fantasy. In his hand was an airline bag and in the airline bag were his winnings. Graz had been more than willing to gratify his whim and give it to him all in cash – lots and lots of crisp, clean notes. Unspoken between them, the knowledge that Tommy would be back eventually and Graz would recoup most, if not all, of it. They were men of the world. In their respective beachside eyries they could see the tide come in and the tide go out. Every bloody day.

But while he had it – more than he'd had before in one lump, more than he'd seen before – in his febrile little hands, he was going to live the dream.

Central to his fantasy was the delectable Ms Manita Stubbs. 'Neet' as he'd dubbed her. Neet: she of the cascade of honey-blonde (dinky di) hair, just like in those computer-enhanced shampoo ads. She of the flawless, strawberry yoghurt skin, of the taut, fruit-in-season fullness of flesh, of the impossible Jacob's Ladder legs that touched dry earth and enfolded moist heavens.

And who rooted like an industrial vacuum cleaner with all the accessories.

By the time he reached the penthouse door it was a matter of highrise in highrise. He flung the door wide and tossed the airline bag into the centre of the plush, flush suite. He'd called her as soon as the nose of the last pony in his trifecta had passed the post. So she knew he was coming – and *what* was coming.

The bag landed, perfectly, at her perfect feet.

There she was, as usual, making clothes look superfluous, in a boob tube that was more boob than tube and a pair of those satin shorts that looked like her arse was swallowing her undies. Her creamy arms were thrust out towards him like Bertram Mackennal's *Circe* at the NGV.

'Tom-Tom,' she said in the milk and honey tones that brought him all unzipped.

He stuck his arms out like Homer Simpson chasing a Duff and barrelled towards her. When she engulfed him in her arms and kissed him he felt like bending one leg at the knee. Shit, he felt like bending two. The third leg was straight enough for both.

'Neet,' he gasped, when his lips were available for verbal communication. 'Did you put the bubbly on ice?'

She was taller than he was and she stooped slightly, kissed the tip of one delicate finger and touched it to the tip of his nose. He loved that, and didn't know why. 'Tom-Tom,' she cooed. 'You're a bit icky and sticky. Why don't you duck under the shower and I'll get everything ready.' The way her lips and tongue caressed 'everything' didn't bend his knees exactly, but they went a little wobbly.

'Why don't you count the shekels?' That should get her juices flowing. 'And then spread it all over the bed.'

'Hmmm.' She gave one of those gurgling, groaning, moaning sighs and kissed him again. 'Why don't I?'

He bolted for the ensuite. 'I'll anoint my body with aromatic oils and unjoonts,' he threw over his shoulder.

'Unguents.'

'What?' He looked back. She was already bent over the bag affording him a view of cleft peach.

'Oong-gwants,' she articulated automatically, without looking up.

'Yeah … them,' said Tommy. She probably knew what it meant too. She said she was an aspiring actress, but he suspected that meant a student at the College of Arts.

Manita had the money stacked in neat piles on the coffee table when the door buzzed.

She sashayed over and opened the door.

The person in the vestibule looked like an ice hockey goalie in a Hawaiian shirt. Her hair was galvanised-iron grey and cut like the chorus in *South Pacific*.

'Tommy in?' she said, entering without invitation.

Manita stepped back to screen the money from view. 'Was he expecting you?' she asked.

'Didn' know he had a wife and kids, didja, sweetbuns?'

'Yes, but …'

At point Tommy emerged from the bedroom, loins betowelled. 'Where's the slash 'n' cash …?' he began exuberantly and ended sibilantly.

'G'day, Tommy luv,' said Maeve.

'She says she's your wife,' said Manita.

'Jesus and Mary! Maeve,' he groaned.

'Maeve Maguffin?' said Manita.

The two women regarded each other with new interest.

'Now look, Maeve ...' Tommy began.

'Come into some money I see, Thomas,' said Maeve.

Tommy's eyes flicked nervously to the stacks on the table, and then he glared at Neet.

'How much would y'say is there, Tommy?' Maeve asked, sweetly.

'Now look, Maeve ...'

'Eleven thousand, eight hundred and thirty-two dollars,' said Manita.

'Neeet!' squealed Tommy. Clutching his sagging towel, he crabbed across the room in a vain attempt to get between Maeve and the money.

Maeve intercepted him and threw a chummy arm around his neck. 'Now, now, Tommy me darlin'. I'll only relieve you of the maintenance Janet's owed. That's an extra month now, mate. Plus' – Tommy groaned – 'plus my fee and expenses. Let's make it a nice round seven thou.'

'Jeez, Maeve,' Tommy whined. With Maeve draped heavily on his shoulders he watched, in horror, as Neet began to count out the amount with the starched and ironed efficiency of a bank teller.

'Oh yeah, I almost forgot,' said Maeve. 'Plus the finder's fee.'

'How the fuck didja find me?' Tommy asked morosely, as he beseeched Neet with bassett-hound eyes. The alacrity with which she was disposing of their shag pile was deeply depressing.

'Did a favour for a friend and 'e did one for me,' said Maeve.

'Didn't think you had any friends, Maeve,' Tommy said, sans fire or fizzle. The sight of Neet separating a small sheaf of notes from his depleted stack, folding it and tucking it in her hotpants, had distracted him. In a back room of his brain a low wattage light came on.

Maeve clamped his neck in brute schoolboy camaraderie and rocked her knuckles on his skull.

'Sometimes, Tommy me old mate,' she said gleefully, 'you only need one.'

THE END

Acknowledgements

Thank you to Linda, Chris and all at Lacuna who toiled to give this book life.

Thanks to my teachers: the authors of all the books I have read.

And to Daina, without whom I would be much less.

About the author

Once upon a time, a boy met Mr Holmes and Mr Marlowe, Mr Templar and Mr Spade, and wanted to grow up to be just like them.

He was born, raised and educated in Ballarat, and encouraged by teachers to become a teacher. He had a knack with pencil and paper, thus became an art teacher and, eventually, a university lecturer in studio practice, visual theory and cinema. Living and working in Warrnambool, Victoria, with his wife Daina and three daughters, he has produced sculpture, ceramics, numerous caricatures and illustrated a number of educational text and extension activity books aimed at primary and secondary students. Two of his short stories have been published and another, 'Just A Line', was runner-up in *The Age* Short Story Award for 2004.

Ross Gray

Photograph by Gemma Gray

The boy's life never grew to resemble that of Sherlock, Philip, Simon or Sam, so finally he was driven to create a fictional hero in their image. *The Dragon's Skin* is the first of the David Edge novels.